Fin Gall
A Novel of Viking Age Ireland

James L. Nelson

ISBN: 13: 978-1481028691
ISBN-10: 1481028693

To Lisa, with Viking Love…

Fin Gall - Gaelic term for Vikings of Norwegian descent. It means White Strangers.

(For other terms see Glossary, page 278)

Prologue

The Saga Of Thorgrim Ulfsson

T here was a man named Thorgrim Ulfsson, who was called Thorgrim Night Wolf. He lived in East Agder, in Vik, in the country of Norway.

When Thorgrim was a young man he became an hirdman for a powerful jarl who had a farm fifty miles away. The jarl, Ornolf Hrafnsson, was known as Ornolf the Restless, and for three summers Ornolf and his men went a-viking in England and Ireland.

Thorgrim was an excellent fighter, and a clever poet as well, two skills much prized by the Vikings. Soon Ornolf raised him from hirdman and made him a chieftain and second in command. Thorgrim was well respected by the men, and loved by Ornolf.

At that time the plundering was very good, and Ornolf greatly increased his wealth, and all the men who sailed with him became rich as well. After three years, Thorgrim left him and returned to his farm in East Agder. With the riches he had won during his time a-viking he purchased more land, as well as cattle and slaves, and soon became one of the most prosperous farmers in the area.

Thorgrim was still much favored by Ornolf the Restless, who did not forget the good service that Thorgrim had done him. When Thorgrim decided that the time had come to marry, Ornolf offered him his second daughter, Hallbera Ornolfsdottir, know as Hallbera the Fair.

Though Ornolf's wife was famous for her wicked temper and sharp tongue, all of his daughters were sweet and mild of temperament. Ornolf loved them and would not force any to marry against their will. His offer to Thorgrim, therefore, was on the condition that Hallbera favored the union. But Thorgrim was a kind and clever man, and also very wealthy, and so Hallbera was eager for the marriage.

At the wedding, Thorgrim presented Ornolf with fifty silver coins as a

1

bride-price, and Ornolf gave Thorgrim a fine farm in the north of the country as a dowry.

Thorgrim and Hallbera were well married, very much in love and pleased with the life they made on their ever-expanding farm in Vik. They had three children. Their eldest son was named Odd, the second son, Harald, and a daughter, Hild. The sons were hard working, and grew strong and became skilled farmers. When Odd grew to be a man, Thorgrim gave him the farm in the north country that had been given to him as a dowry and Odd left home to work his new farm.

Ten years after the birth of Hild, Hallbera was once again with child, but she was no longer a young woman and things did not go well. Despite the best efforts of the midwife, and many sacrifices that Thorgrim made to the gods, Hallbera died giving birth, though the child lived. It was a girl and Thorgrim named her Hallbera after her mother.

Ornolf the Restless had never lost the desire to go a-viking, even though he was now comfortable and wealthy, so he purchased a longship and gathered a crew and asked Thorgrim if he would sail as second in command.

Before that time, Thorgrim was happy on the farm, and did not care to go voyaging any more. But after Hallbera died it was hard for him to be there without her. Also, he did not wish to deny Ornolf, who was his father-in-law, nor was he displeased with the promise of battle, so he agreed. The year was 852 by the Christian calendar, seven years after Thorgils, the Dane who had made himself king of Ireland, was drowned by the Irish people.

Thorgrim's second son, Harald, was then fifteen years old, as strong as most men, and ready to go a-viking, so Thorgrim brought him along.

Here is what happened.

Chapter One

He who has traveled
can tell what spirit
governs the men he meets.
Hávamál
Ancient Norse Poem

The storm was vicious and building in strength. Death-cold spray came blowing sideways, gray-mountain waves rolled down on the laboring longship.

Ornolf the Restless was roaring drunk.

He stood up in the bow of the longship, his longship, which he called Red Dragon. He kept one massive arm wrapped around the slender wooden neck that swept up in an elegant arc and ended fifteen feet above his head with the grinning, teeth-baring head of a dragon. The dragon head was a frightening sight, but not half as frightening as Ornolf the Restless was at that moment.

His hair was red and gray and plastered against his head and back, his beard drenched and matted until it looked like seaweed. The padded tunic that he wore bound with a wide leather belt tight around his thick middle was soaked through. He was engaged in a pissing match with the god Thor.

"God of thunder and lighting, eh?" he bellowed up at the blanket of clouds that hung low and dark over the sea. "This the best you can do!? It will take a damned sight more than this to kill Ornolf!"

The bow of the longship rose on a wave like the hand of Odin lifting Ornolf up into the sky and he whooped with the exhilaration of it. Then the ship slid off the wave, down, down, twisting into the trough. The larboard side ladle-dipped into the sea, scooped half a ton of water that rushed in a wave amidships, crashing against the mast, against the dozens of sea chests lashed to the deck, against the sixty-three or so soaked, miserable warriors who were not enjoying the storm half as much as Ornolf.

"Hah!" Ornolf roared at the heavens. "That it? I can make more water than that!" And to show Thor he was not kidding, Ornolf let go of the dragon's neck and fished himself out of his breeches, urinating half over the side and half on the deck as he tried to maintain his balance on the wildly swinging bow.

Ninety feet aft, Thorgrim Ulfsson braced himself against the steerboard's tiller, guiding the shallow longship through the mounting seas. He turned his head away from the spray and spit the seawater that ran down his face and into his mouth. He could barely hear Ornolf's drunken raving over the shriek of the wind, but he heard enough to make him wish the old man would shut up.

He'll bring bad luck on our heads, just to show Thor he's not afraid of even a god... Thorgrim was personally devoted to the cult of Odin, but he still did not think it was a good idea to taunt Thor in that way.

On the deck amidships, most of the three score warriors who had sailed with Ornolf on this voyage sat huddled under blankets and furs, enduring the cold and the wet. Others were furiously bailing, flinging buckets of seawater to leeward, or shoveling water with leather helmets. The longship was a hundred feet in length, but it was still essentially an open boat. The ranks of round wooden shields mounted on the ship's low sides offered some protection from the wind, but not much.

"Come along, Thor, you sorry creature," Ornolf shouted, "if you have a lighting bolt for me, I'm ready to catch it! Right here!" He held his ass up to the sky, as much as he could. Ornolf had trouble bending in the middle.

The men amidships looked at one another, shook their heads, stared at their jarl with raw anger. Thorgrim was not the only one who wished Ornolf would shut up.

Thorgrim's son, Harald Thorgrimson, took his place among the men. Harald was fifteen, though his size made him appear older, and what he lacked in quick wits he made up for in strength and eagerness. He was shorter than the rest but nearly as broad. He was beardless, of course, but beyond that he was much like the other warriors. He was flinging water overboard, using his iron helmet as a bucket.

The longship's red and white striped sail was lashed tight to the yard, the yard swung fore and aft and hoisted five feet up to give the vessel some steerageway. All around her, the dull, steel gray waves, their tops ripped open white, rose in monotonous succession up around the longship until there was nothing to see but mountains of water on either hand. And then the seas would lift the ship, up and up, and through the blowing spray and the torn clouds they would catch a glimpse of the low green shores of Ireland, a few miles to windward.

Forward, Ornolf raged on, unmoved by the nasty looks flying like spray. One twist of the tiller, Thorgrim thought, and I could drive our bow into the sea and sweep Ornolf away like swatting a fly. But of course he would never do such a thing. He was Ornolf's hirdman. Ornolf was his father-in-law.

"Harald!" Thorgrim shouted to his son, and then louder, to be heard over the wind. "Harald!"

Young Harald looked up, squinting into the spray. His cheeks were bright red and he was smiling, but Thorgrim could see the fear behind the smile. It didn't worry him, that his son was afraid. Harald was young still, and Thorgrim could remember being afraid himself at that age. He could recall the taste of fear, like some food he had eaten once, long ago, and now could just barely recall. There was nothing Thorgrim feared now. Nothing in the physical world, anyway, the world of men and storms.

"Come aft!" Thorgrim shouted and Harald set his helmet down and made his way aft, twisting between the men and leaping the sea chests. He was agile like only a fifteen year old can be.

"Yes, father?"

"Your grandfather has pushed his luck far enough! Grab that rope and lash him to the stem!"

Harald grinned at the thought. He was the only one aboard who might lash Ornolf in place. If any other man tried it, Ornolf would have flung him into the sea, but he would never do anything to harm his beloved grandson.

Harald took up the rope, made of braided walrus hide, and skipped forward as easily as if he were walking down a path on their farm in East Agder and not along the slick, half submerged deck of a violently pitching ship.

Thorgrim watched him, marveled at his grace and recalled a time when he, too, could move like that. Thorgrim was thirty-eight. Two and a half decades of fighting and drinking, hard work and hard seafaring were having their effect. He wondered sometimes how Ornolf, fifteen years his senior, could keep on, but Ornolf's capacity was legendary.

Up in the bow, Harald maneuvered past the swaying jarl and flipped the rope around the stem. Thorgrim could see mouths moving, arms flailing, but he could not hear what was said. Then Harald whipped the rope around Ornolf's mid-section and made it fast, with Ornolf showing no sign of objection.

Harald knew how to handle his grandfather. They were much alike, grandfather and grandson, and Thorgrim did not always think that was a good thing.

Now Harald was coming aft again, moving with purpose, but

Thorgrim could spare him only the occasional glance as he concentrated on keeping the ship bow-on to the seas, keeping her from turning broadside to the wave set and swamping. Over his tunic he wore a bearskin cloak, lashed tight around him, which had kept him warm and dry for a time, but now it was soaked through and heavy as a mail shirt. His arms were beginning to ache from heaving on the tiller, but he had the feel for the ship now and did not dare turn the steering over to anyone else. Nor was there anyone aboard with his skill or experience in such things.

"Father!" Harald came aft, shouting from only a few feet away.

"Yes?"

"Grandfather says he saw a ship. Out there!" Harald pointed over the leeward side, though at the moment there was nothing to see but a wall of water, rolling away down wind.

"Yes?"

"Well, he says we should see what they are about!"

Thorgrim nodded. Plunder. It was foremost in everyone's thoughts, and any inconvenience, such as a storm that threatened to kill them all, was not going to dampen their appetite for it.

They were a month out of Vik, in Norway. In that time they had raided a village on the northeast coast of England, which had yielded little, and then taken a Danish merchant ship after a short fight. The Dane, they found, was crammed with valuable trade goods - furs and iron ax heads, amber, bundles of cloth, walrus ivory and whetstones. Now Ornolf was shaping a course for Dubh-linn, the Norwegian longphort in Ireland, where they planned to sell what they had taken. More was always welcome.

The next in the endless progression of waves moved under the longship and lifted it skyward and Thorgrim swept the southern horizon for the ship that Ornolf had seen, but he could see nothing. The other ship, no doubt, had gone down in a trough as they were lifted up.

"Did you see this ship?" Thorgrim asked.

"No! Perhaps I can now!" Harald slipped around Thorgrim and put one foot on the ship's rail, then flung himself up even as the ship dropped away under him. He grabbed the tall sternpost in a bear hug, squeezed with his feet, worked his way up higher.

A moment later he shouted, "Yes! Yes! There it is, right down wind!" Harald slid back down the slick carved wood and landed on the deck. "No great size," he said, almost apologetically, as if it was his fault, "but right down wind."

Thorgrim nodded as he digested this. It was utterly insane to close with a vessel in those seas, never mind trying to board it, but it never occurred to him not to try, nor would it have occurred to any of the others.

"Go tell the men we are going to turn and run for this boat! Tell them we'll have the yard braced square as we turn!"

Harald grinned as he tumbled off forward. Thorgrim kept his eyes to weather, glanced now and then amidships as Harald spread the news. The Viking host, men who a minute before had been dour and sulking, now cast off their drenched blankets and furs and stood grinning in anticipation. It was as if the heavens had opened and spilled sunshine and mead down on them.

I pray to Odin this is worth it... Thorgrim thought. There was every chance that the vessel was no more than some pathetic fishing boat, not worth the considerable risk of attacking it in those high seas.

Up in the bow Ornolf fumbled for half a minute with the knot Harald had tied in the walrus rope, then pulled his dagger and cut it away, stumbling amidships, shouting orders. Men hunkered down along the sides of the ship, prepared to haul the yard square, and unhitched the braces from the cleats on which they were made off.

"Do you see that, Thorgrim?" Ornolf bellowed as he joined his hirdman aft. "You show Thor you have balls as big as his, and he drops a gift right in your lap!"

"His aim could be a little better!"

"Ah, you young men are soft, like women! You don't know what real fighting is!"

Thorgrim smiled at Ornolf's jibing. He did not feel soft and he did not feel young.

"I'll see my grandson does not become a feeble woman like the rest of you, count on it!"

Thorgrim had only half an ear for Ornolf, his concentration mostly on the set of waves over which they were riding. He renewed his grip on the tiller, waited, waited for the flat spot, the tiny break in the cresting seas where he could turn the longship.

And then it was there, not perfect, but the best he could hope for. He leaned hard on the tiller and watched the tall dragon prow sweep around, falling off the wind, and the men amidships hauled the big yard around.

Another wave came up under the longship and twisted it around and Thorgrim fought back with the steeringboard to keep the ship from turning too far. The wind and seas were behind them now, and the once laboring ship was racing down the waves, rising stern-first and sliding forward down the water hill until the wave passed under and bucked the bow up high. The wind seemed suddenly not as fierce, and with the thought of a victim under their bow, the men seemed absolutely buoyant.

"There! There!" Ornolf had his sword in hand and he used it to point forward. The other ship was cresting a wave, half a mile down-wind.

Irish... Thorgrim thought. It was a curragh, a large one, running down wind with a scrap of sail showing. It could be a fishing boat or a coastal trader. Not likely to have anything of great value aboard.

The Vikings did not care, they were ready for a fight. Amidships men were freeing swords from sheaths and hefting axes and spears. The round shields came off the gunnels. Kotkel the Fierce was swinging his ax in an arc so that others had to duck out of his way. Some thought Kotkel a berserker, and if he was not, he was close enough.

Olaf Yellowbeard and his twin brother, Olvir, were settling their shields on their arms. Vefrod Vesteinsson, known as Vefrod the Quick, pulled off his heavy fur cape and dropped it onto the deck. Harald slid his helmet on his head and adjusted it until it sat right. Thorgrim wondered if the fishing boat would put up enough of a fight to sate all those eager men.

The next rising sea showed that they had halved the distance to their prey - the waddling curragh was no match for the longship in speed. Thorgrim felt the battle-madness creeping over him, and he breathed deep because he did not want to give himself over to those spirits.

Down into the trough of the waves, and up again, closer to the Irish vessel, which now was running for all it was worth, the sail spread nearly full. They had spotted the stalking wolf.

That rig will not last in this wind, Thorgrim thought, and as if his mind controlled such things, the curragh's mast crumpled and fell. The sail smothered the forward end of the boat, and the curragh swung around broadside to the sea and rolled hard.

Now the longship was on them, the Vikings whooping it up, gathering at the gunnel as Thorgrim tried to steer the vessel, like steering a runaway sleigh he could just barely control. There was a better chance they would be killed trying to bring the ships alongside than in any fight with these Irish fisherman.

Thorgrim heaved the tiller, then leaned back, working the longship around. On board the curragh they were hacking at the fallen sail and rigging, trying to make fighting room, swords and axes rising and falling and men clad in mail standing at the gunnel ready to meet the Norsemen.

Thorgrim waited for the right set of the waves, then pulled hard, swinging the longship broadside to the curragh, and for the first time it occurred to him that for a fishing boat she carried a damned lot of well armed men.

Chapter Two

The morning sleeper
Has much undone
The quick will catch the prize.
Hávamál

The two ships slammed together, the longship's larboard side to the curragh's starboard. They hit harder than Thorgrim had intended, but he had little control in those wild seas. If the curragh had been made of sterner stuff it might have sent them both to the bottom, but the leather-sheathed craft made little impression on the longship's oak planks.

Thorgrim left the tiller and rushed forward as the Vikings readied themselves to break over the curragh's side. Vefrod Vesteinsson was foremost. Ax in his hand, foot on the gunnel, he shrieked and launched himself over the narrow gap between the ships and into the twenty or so armed men on board the curragh. Kotkel the Fierce was next, pushing in front of Ornolf who was too wet and fat to move with any speed.

Kotkel flung himself into the air and young Harald was behind him. Thorgrim felt the longship dropping away and he reached out and grabbed Harald's collar and pulled him back just as the longship swooped down into the trough of a wave and the curragh was lifted high over their heads, with Kotkel clinging to the side.

The wave passed under, dropping the curragh down and for a second they were side by side again. There was not much left of Vefrod the Quick. He had been caught alone by the Irish and well dismembered in the few seconds the vessels were apart. They were still hacking at him.

9

"Get the hooks!" Thorgrim roared. "Grapple them!" They could not fight like this - already the next wave was lifting the longship up in the air, so they were looking down on the curragh, the bloody mess that had been Vefrod Vesteinsson, and Kotkel the Fierce, unseen, still hanging from the side.

Then down they went, and a half dozen grappling hooks soared through the air, snagging the leather boat, binding them together.

One of the curragh's defenders lifted his sword, two handed, and slashed at Kotkel, who could do no more than watch. Olaf Yellowbeard cocked his arm, heaved his spear, caught the swordsman square in the chest. The Irishman toppled back and Kotkel pulled himself on board the curragh, ahead of the press of Vikings who poured shrieking over the side.

Thorgrim found a place on the curragh's deck and leapt across, but the curragh was half the length of the longship and there was hardly room to fight. He pulled his sword, which was called Iron-tooth, from its scabbard and held his shield in fighting position, just in time to catch an ax coming down on his head. He had forgotten his helmet.

The ax hit the wood shield and embedded itself, with a force that jarred Thorgrim's whole body. Thorgrim turned the shield aside. The man who wielded the ax foolishly hung on to the handle, exposing himself, and Thorgrim lunged.

His sword caught the man's tunic, rent the fabric, glanced off the mail shirt underneath. *No damned fishermen*, Thorgrim thought. Fishermen did not wear mail. Mail was for men of means.

Thorgrim Night Wolf felt the red madness - that was what he called it - creep in around the edge of his eyes. He tried to hold it back, to remain in the present world. He breath was coming sharp and fast.

The axeman let go of the ax embedded in Thorgrim's shield, fumbled for his sword, too late, as Thorgrim ran his blade through the man's throat, the shower of red blood mixing with the blowing sea spray.

There was shouting and screaming all around now and Thorgrim looked for his next fight, but he could hardly move in that press of bodies. The curragh came back into focus, the colors vivid as the battle spirit passed.

He was nearly all the way aft. He looked to his left. One of the Irishmen was there, but he was not fighting, in fact he was kneeling with his back to the fight. Thorgrim thought he must be praying, or puking - it was madness otherwise to turn his back to the attackers - but then he saw the man was reaching for something in the space beneath the deck boards.

The Irishman stood and turned. He was a young man, perhaps twenty, and there was nothing of the peasant or poor fisherman about him. He wore mail, sword and dagger, and had the bearing of one who was used to command. He held a bundle in his hands, wrapped in canvas, about the size of a bread loaf. His eyes met Thorgrim's and for a second they stared at one another, then the young Irishman turned to toss the bundle over the side.

"No!" Thorgrim shouted and lunged. He did not know what was in the bundle, but if the Irishman would risk his life to keep it from the Norsemen's hands, then Thorgrim was sure he wanted it.

The bundle was over the water when Thorgrim's sword came sweeping up from under, striking the mail-clad arm and twisting the Irishman around so he dropped the canvas-wrapped thing back on the deck of the curragh.

Again they faced one another. The Irishman had no weapon in his hand, but Thorgrim could see no trace of fear on his face. Thorgrim waited for him to go for his sword, knew he could hack the young man down as he struggled to free the long weapon. But the Irishman went for the dagger instead, whipped it out and held it in front of him with the ease and confidence of long use.

Thorgrim paused. Heavy sword and shield against a light, quick dagger in a confined space. An interesting tactical problem, but the Norseman's fighting blood was up and he did not care for subtlety. He took a step forward, pushed with his shield, launched the point of the sword at the Irishman's throat.

He missed. The Irishman ducked quick and Thorgrim's sword found air. The Irishman grabbed the edge of his shield and yanked it hard, throwing Thorgrim off-balance, and now the Norseman's heavy weapons were a liability.

Thorgrim saw the dagger coming up at him, an uppercut that would slice up under his mail. The blade seemed to move slow, the red fog was at the edge of Thorgrim's vision. He saw his own hand drop Iron-tooth and grab the Irishman's knife hand, envelope his hand so the Irishman could not let go of the dagger if he wanted to.

They stood, every muscle straining, the strength of each man holding the other in check, a perfect balance of force and resistance. Their faces were inches apart and through the mist Thorgrim could see the hatred on the young noble's face.

Then the Irishman spoke. Thorgrim could not understand the Gaelic words but the fury was unmistakable.

There was a strength that came with the red madness and Thorgrim felt it surge through him. He felt the sound building in his gut. He opened his mouth and he howled, a terrible sound he would not have thought himself able to make.

And suddenly the Irishman's strength was like that of a child to Thorgrim, and Thorgrim twisted his hand back and plunged the knife into the Irishman's chest, plunged the wicked needle-point right through the mail. Inches away, the Irishman's eyes went wide and he coughed, then coughed again and this time blood came from his mouth and he went limp. Thorgrim let him fall to the deck.

For a moment Thorgrim just stood, until his breathing settled and the madness subsided, like water rushing back after a wave. The world returned to the place it was meant to be, and Thorgrim became aware of the quiet.

He turned. The fight was over. Twenty Celts lay dead. Not a man had surrendered, they had all fought to the end against odds of five to one. Thorgrim had never seen the like, not even when Vikings fought Vikings.

Then he remembered the bundle. He dropped to his knees, shot a furtive look over his shoulder, because he had a feeling that whatever it was, it was not something for all the men to see.

He set his shield down and lifted the thing. It was heavier than he would have imagined, and bound tight with leather cord. Thorgrim pulled the dagger from the dead nobleman's chest and cut the cord, unwrapped the bundle slowly.

He knew it was made of gold before he knew what it was. He caught a glimpse of the yellow metal, luminous even in the muted light of the storm. He unwrapped layers of canvas.

It was a crown. Thorgrim had seen crowns before - there were enough minor kings in Norway - but he had never seen the like of this. A band of solid gold a quarter inch thick and two inches high, with a series of filigrees like little battlements running around the top. On each of the filigrees and around the band there were mounted jewels and bits of polished amber, but lovely, with as little ostentation as was possible in a thing such as a crown. The whole surface was etched with a delicate woven pattern, not unlike the intertwined beasts favored by Norse artisans.

Thorgrim stared at the crown and turned it over in his hand. Its beauty worked on him like magic, enthralled him. He had no sense for how long he squatted there, turning the thing around in his fingers. Then he heard Kotkel shout and he started with a guilty flush. He shoved the crown back in the canvas, grabbed up his shield and held the crown hidden behind it. He stood and turned back to his fellow Norsemen.

Harald was unhurt, save for a scrape on the cheek that left his pale skin smeared with blood. He was smiling, laughing louder than he generally did. Thorgrim recognized the flash of exuberance that comes on the heels of a fight. He himself was too old and too battle-worn to feel that flash any more, but he had experienced it many times in the younger days. Everything was sharper with youth - fighting, feasting, lying with a woman. Things wore dull with age.

Harald was helping Sigurd Sow pull the mail shirt off one of the dead Irishmen.

"Thorgrim!" Ornolf came rolling down the deck of the curragh. "Great lot of work for nothing!"

"Oh?" Thorgrim adjusted his grip on the crown. He could taste guilt in his mouth.

"These bastards..." Ornolf kicked one of the lifeless bodies to further punish the dead man for his disappointment. "They have some silver on them, and some damned fine mail. A few swords worth the having. You wouldn't expect a bunch of fishermen to have such fine weapons. But beyond that, nothing."

"I don't think they were fishermen."

"No? What then, coastal traders?"

"I don't know."

The crown, it seemed, was the only cargo, and twenty well-armed noblemen the crew. There was a tale here, and not a man left alive to tell it.

Chapter Three

Only fools
hope to live forever
by escaping enemies.
Hávamál

The longphort of Dubh-Linn, squalid and ugly, sat huddled on the banks of the River Liffy. It was not much to look at. A small wooden palisade fort, a hundred feet along each wall, stood a quarter mile up the rise from the marshy banks of the river. The palisade wall on the landward side of the fort extended out east and west, slowly curving down to the river, forming a great, half-moon shaped wooden shield that cupped the town and kept the rest of Ireland beyond at bay.

A plank road, largely obscured by the ubiquitous mud, ran from the fortress down to a series of docks that thrust out over the shallows into the deeper water.

Clustered around the plank road were thirty or so buildings, most small, most one story, wattle and daub built with thatched roofs. These did double duty as homes and as woodshops, and blacksmith shops, and goldsmiths and merchants' offices. There were only two buildings that might be called large and substantial, plank built; a temple to Thor to the south, and nearest the docks, a mead hall.

Dubh-Linn was not much to look at on the best of days, but on that day, with the low clouds rendering everything into shades of gray and brown and muted green, and the cold rain blowing in nearly sideways, it was even less lovely.

Orm Ulfsson did not care.

He stood at the gates of the fortress and looked down the slope toward the river, and he knew that the bedraggled appearance belied the town's growing import.

Certainly, Dubh-lin was no rival to such great trading centers as Kaupang in the Vestfold district of Norway, or the Danish Hedeby. Not yet. But Dubh-Linn would rise to take its place among the great ports of the world. Orm was certain of it. That was why, in a bloody purge, he had driven out the Norwegians who had founded the town and claimed the place as his own.

It was happening already, Dubh-Linn's ascendency. Crowds of men stamped along the muddy road, huddled under furs, heads bent into the wind, and they understood, as Orm did, what Dubh-Linn's future would be. They were artisans and merchants and warriors who had come to Dubh-Linn to stay. And they brought their women, Irish women and Norse women who had accompanied their men as wives or slaves.

Now, looking past the crowded road and alleyways, busy even in the face of the storm, past the docks where longships and curraghs, knarrs and merchant ships from the Norse countries and warmer climes were rolling in the incoming swell, Orm might well have been pleased. But he was not.

His eyes were fixed on one longship, mauled by the storm, pulling hard against the current. He could see the yard was snapped a little outboard to the starboard slings, hanging like a broken wing from its halyard. The tall sternpost was also snapped off, and most of the shields which had lined the sides were gone. Part of the upper edge of the gunnels just aft of the starboard bow was smashed in.

Asbjorn Gudrodarson, known properly enough as Asbjorn the Fat, was standing just behind Orm. He let out a low whistle. "Magnus was hard pressed by the storm, so it would seem," he said.

Orm grunted. He was quite indifferent to Magnus's difficulties, he cared only about Magnus's success. If Magnus had met with no success, then Magnus would wish the storm had taken him. Orm would see to that.

The longship crawled toward the dock at a pace too agonizing to watch. Orm turned hard on his heel. "Send Magnus to me, when he lands. If he ever lands," he said to Asbjorn. He pulled his heavy fur cape further up his shoulders and ran a hand through his thick beard to comb the water out. He pushed through the wind and rain back to his quarters.

It was another hour before Orm heard the knock on the door. He was seated then in his imposing wooden chair, one leg over the arm, a cup of warm cider in his hand. The house had a low, square fireplace, more a fire pit, in the center of the room, after the Norse style. The fire was roaring, casting a yellow glow over the dirt floor and the gloomy interior of the small house, built against the north corner of the fort's interior wall. The smoke that was not able to escape through the windows piled up against the thatch ceiling overhead.

Orm's impatience had turned to a smoldering fury, but when the knock came he took a long drink and waited for Magnus to knock a second time.

"Come!"

The door creaked open. Magnus Magnusson stood there. The wind ripped in around him, fluttering the papers on the table beside Orm's chair but it could not move Magnus's drenched fur cape or his long hair, plastered down by rain and spray. Asbjorn hovered behind Magnus and he seemed to be hopping from one foot to the other, though whether from eagerness or a need to urinate, Orm could not tell.

Magnus stepped into the house and Asbjorn followed, closing the door. Magnus gave a shallow bow. He was handsome, clean-shaven, with a reputation that was well earned. He was ambitious. He did not do subservience well.

"Yes?" Orm said.

Magnus shook his head.

"You failed?"

"They failed. Either they did not dare go out, or they were sunk in the storm. In any event, they did not enter the River Boyne."

Orm pressed his lips together and stared off into the dark end of the house. *Damn this impertinent bastard...* he thought. Magnus did not fail often, and when he did, he had a genius for making it appear as if it was not really failure, or that the failure belonged to someone else.

He looked back at Magnus, who stood, stoic and expressionless. Orm had a notion that this was exactly how Magnus would look facing his own execution. *Perhaps we'll find out*, he thought.

"How do you know they did not get into the river? How do you know they are not there now? While you stand here dripping on my floor."

"We kept at the mouth of the river for as long as we could, until my ship could bear no more. We were nearly wrecked half a dozen times. If my longship could barely live, then no ship built by Irishmen could have survived."

Orm grunted. Magnus could well be right. Orm had been a bit surprised to see Magnus's ship come limping in - he had thought it would certainly be lost. If it had been anyone else living through that storm at sea, then he might have won Orm's grudging respect. But Orm reckoned that Magnus had respect enough from every other quarter, and needed no more.

"I suppose," Orm said at last, "we won't know for certain if you've failed until these Celt whoresons are putting our heads on pikes as an offering to their Jesus. Very well. You may go."

Magnus gave another quick bow, turned and left. Asbjorn remained, eager for some intrigue, but Orm had had enough of the corpulent, sycophantic advisor.

"You may go as well," he snapped and Asbjorn wisely said nothing, just gave a hint of a crestfallen look before scurrying out the door.

Damn him... Orm thought, not even certain who he was damning. All of them.

Magnus had done him no good at all. He had discovered nothing, resolved nothing, had left only more doubt behind. He had not even the decency to get himself drowned.

The Celts were a disorganized rabble with nearly as many kings as they had sheep, and as such they were no concern. But if they were able to unite against the Norsemen, that would be a different story.

Orm drained his cup. "Damn!" he said out loud. Morrigan, the Irish thrall he had taken when he took Dubh-linn, looked warily from the next room and Orm flung the cup at her. It was not enough that he should take and hold the town, build it up in a way that the idiot Norwegians could never hope to do. Now he had the Celts at his back and the threat of Norwegian vengeance from the sea. At times he wondered if it was worth the aggravation.

Chapter Four

Wake early
if you want
another man's life or land.
Hávamál

Thorgrim Ulfsson dreamed of wolves.

He dreamed of wolves often. In his dreams he could not see himself, but he saw the other wolves, his eyes level with theirs, and he ran with them, swift and tireless.

He woke exhausted from these dreams. Sometimes there was blood, but he did not know where it came from.

Now he saw himself running with the wolves, and his eyes burned like the red eyes of the other beasts in the pack. They raced though thick forest, trees like giants barely seen in the dark. Thorgrim could smell the pack close by, could hear the snarls from canine throats, the muted padding of their feet on the forest floor.

There was something in his mouth. It was bloody and warm and the sensation of it excited him. Something freshly killed. And he alone had it.

Then suddenly he was no longer running. He was stopped, and there were other wolves around him, not his pack, but wolves he did not know and they were turning on him. He could see teeth flash in moonlight and heard the angry growls. The pack closed in, wary but deliberate, and Thorgrim backed away. He needed his teeth to fight, but he did not want to drop the thing in his mouth. He tried to make a noise but he could not.

Then they were on him, and he had a sensation of hot breath and matted fur, fangs snapping at him, a dozen angry mouths closing on him, and he kicked and shook and tried to fight, but still he would not drop the bloody thing in his mouth.

Then Thorgrim was awake. Sudden, like stepping through a door. One instant he was fighting the wolf pack, and in the next he was lying in his furs on the afterdeck of the longship. The night was cold, the rain falling as a light mist, but Thorgrim was coated in sweat. His breath was coming fast and hard, as if he had been running.

For some time he lay there, eyes wide, body motionless. The wolf dreams left him exhausted, and weak, as if he was coming out of a long illness.

Through the dark and the fog he could barely make out the loom of the mast overhead, the rigging hanging in long sweeping arcs. They had run the longship into a little bay just as the night came down on them, hauling the bow up on a shingle beach and securing the ship with a line ashore. They ate, drank to near insensibility, fell into thick sleep on the deck.

Thorgrim listened to the night. The bow of the ship made a grinding noise on the pebbles as the stern lifted and sank with the incoming waves. The wind was still strong, playing around the rigging and the furled sail. The water slapped at the hull.

He thought of the wolves.

After some time he roused himself and sat up. Harald was asleep beside him, flat on his back, his mouth open. The cut on his cheek made a dark line across his white skin. He was not a pretty boy, but handsome in his way, and broad and strong. Thorgrim loved him deeply. He worried about Harald more than he would ever let Harald know.

For a moment Thorgrim just sat and watched his son sleep, then he tossed the heavy fur off and crawled out from under it. He was wearing only his tunic and leggings and he shivered in the cold, wet air. The snoring and muttering of three score sleeping men sounded like a pack of rooting animals, but Thorgrim hardly heard it, it was so much a part of the night. He moved cautiously around the heaps of fur spread like little burial mounds around the deck, the warriors at sleep. He came at last to the largest mound - fittingly, the jarl, Ornolf the Restless.

Thorgrim shook Ornolf and got only a slight grunt for his effort. He had no illusions about how difficult it would be to stir his father-in-law. As usual, Ornolf had been foremost in the feasting and drinking. Some of the men who had tried to match him, drink for drink, were still sprawled out on the beach. Some might even be dead.

Thorgrim shook him again. "Ornolf..." he said, soft, then shook harder. Five minutes of shaking and whispering finally got Ornolf's eyes open. A minute later he was sitting up.

"Thorgrim...what?"

"Come with me."

With a fair amount of groaning, puffing and cursing, Ornolf extracted himself from his furs and followed Thorgrim aft. On the larboard side, right aft with the steering board, Thorgrim's sea chest was lashed to the deck. He stopped there, kneeled beside it and Ornolf did the same. Thorgrim waited to see that none of the others were awake. He waited for Ornolf to catch his breath.

"There was something on the curragh," Thorgrim said, speaking in just a whisper. "Something I did not think the others should see."

He opened his sea chest slowly, reached under the wool cloaks and tunic until he felt the rough canvas. He pulled the bundle out slowly. He meant to unwrap it, to show it to Ornolf, but Ornolf took it from his hands and unwrapped it himself, which annoyed Thorgrim, though he did not know why.

There was little enough light, with the storm still blotting out the moon and stars, but there was light enough for Ornolf to appreciate what he held. The jarl was silent as he turned the crown over in his hands, ran his fingers over the delicate engraving. "I've never seen its like," he said at last.

"Nor I."

"This alone will give us a profit from our voyage. But what will we do with it? I doubt there is coin enough in all of Ireland to match the value of this crown."

Thorgrim shook his head. "It wouldn't be wise to try to sell it. I don't think it would be wise to bring it into Dubh-Linn at all."

Ornolf looked up from the crown for the first time since taking it in his hands. "Why not?"

"I think this is more than some king's trinket. There is some meaning to it. There were twenty Irish noblemen on board the curragh, and they gave their lives to protect this crown. It was the only thing of value they carried."

"Bah. Irishmen. Who knows why any of them do what they do?"

Thorgrim frowned. He had hoped he would not have to say what he now had to say. "I saw in a dream...that others would want to take this from us. They will kill us for it."

In the dark, Thorgrim could see Ornolf's eyes grow wide. "You saw the crown...in your dream?"

"No. But it was there, I could sense it."

"Wolves?"

Thorgrim nodded.

"Very well," Ornolf said. He needed no more convincing. "What would you have us do?"

"Let's bury it ashore. You and me. Right now. Tell no one else. There it will be safe while we find its secret."

Ornolf nodded his head, considering. "Very well," he said.

Thorgrim went back to his bedding and retrieved his weapons. Like any good Norseman, he had been raised with the adage, "never walk away from home ahead of your ax and sword". He would no more go anywhere without his weapons than he would without his clothes.

In the longship's hold he found a shovel and lifted it slowly, careful to make no noise. This was good, what they were doing. He did not know why, exactly, but he knew it was good.

Chapter Five

By the Prince's Truth fair weather comes in each fitting season...
Testament of Murand
Ancient Irish Morality Tale

Hunched against the cold, his cloak pulled up over his helmet and his mail shirt, Máel Sechnaill mac Ruanaid, of the clan Uí Néill, stood in the dark in the down-pouring rain. Round about him were his bodyguards, that small, elite band of fighting men, the core of the kingdom's professional soldiers. Behind the bodyguard were men of the houseguard. They were, in all, twenty men-at-arms.

Máel Sechnaill was the rí ruirech, the high king of Tara, heart of the Irish kingdom of Brega, and could summon an army of hundreds, perhaps more than a thousand, if he needed them. But twenty was enough for the night's business.

The soldiers shuffled a bit, uncomfortable in the weather, but they made no sound that would carry over the beating rain.

The men of the bodyguard were half Máel Sechnaill's age, and Máel was careful to show no weakness around them. If the others began to flag on a march, Máel Sechnaill increased his pace. If a man was sleepy on watch, Máel Sechnaill stood watch with him. When an Irish king appeared weak, or crippled by age, then the aspirants to his throne, or the rulers of neighboring kingdoms, would be on him like a pack of wolves.

Máel heard movement through the brush ahead. The bodyguard tensed, spears came up to the ready, and the front guardsmen stepped up on either side of their king, as was their proper position. A voice called out, the messenger still unseen in the dark and rain.

22

"Flann mac Conaing, come back, my Lord."

"Come," one of the guardsmen replied. Flann mac Conaing, chief councilor and head of the bodyguard, resolved out of the dark, a black shape carrying sword and shield. He, too, wore mail, a luxury limited to the king and the elite ranks of his people. Two men of the bodyguard followed behind Flann.

"My Lord," Flann said with a quick bow. "They are laying in wait still, but I see signs they are preparing to leave. Ten men in all."

Máel Sechnaill nodded. "How are they armed?"

"Swords, axes, spears and shields. Two have mail."

"Very well." Máel turned to the bodyguard. "They are abandoning their watch, but they may give us answers still. We follow Flann mac Conaing. Be quick. They're better armed than us. Let the ones wearing mail live."

Máel Sechnaill drew his sword - like the mail, it was the province of the elite - and headed after Flann. It had been a year or more since he had carried his sword into combat. It was many years since he had fought in a nameless little skirmish such as this, but this fight was different. The men they were hunting did not belong to some pathetic band of thieves, out stealing cattle. They were a threat to Tara, and the kingdom of Brega itself, and Máel Sechnaill could afford no failure.

The Irishmen moved silent though the dark, the mud sucking at their soft leather shoes. Rain dripped from the edge of Máel's helmet and he blinked and wiped his face. To his left, Máel could see the high ground on which ran the road from the kingdom of Leinster, south of the River Liffey, to Tara. It was along that road that any delegation from Leinster would have to travel.

Flann mac Conaing held up his arm, crouched low, headed off to his right, gesturing for the other guardsmen to go to the left. Máel Sechnaill followed behind the guardsmen, crouching like Flann, his joints protesting the damp and the awkward position. But for all the discomfort, he reveled in the stealth of the attack. This is what they could do, the Irish, move unseen through the dark. Their enemies were bears, powerful and blundering, but they were foxes, swift and cunning.

They slipped over the road, nearly crawling, the mud splattering in their faces, half tumbled down the bank on the other side. A thicket of coarse brush grew along the road, good coverage, which is why the enemy had chosen that spot.

The guardsmen led the way, and a moment later Máel Sechnaill could see them, the watchers crouched by the road forty feet away, their eyes looking south. Máel stepped up. He would take the lead now. With gestures he spread the guardsmen out until they formed a line, spears held at waist height. "Stand ready," he said, softly.

Máel turned and faced the enemy, adjusted the grip on his sword. He could feel his heart pounding, the blood coursing through him. The aches and soreness were gone - he was no longer a fifty-year-old king, but a young prince, vital and strong, fearless, bold.

He raised the sword, took a step forward and another and the bodyguard moved in unison with him. He was slowed by the mud, but not too much. He felt a battle cry build in his throat. He was twenty feet from the enemy before they realized something was amiss. Dark shapes turned to meet them, revealing white faces - in the muted light Máel could see expressions of shock and surprise. The battle cry flew from his mouth, a long, keening wail, and at his side the bodyguard shouted as well.

The Irish rolled into the enemy with a momentum that could not be checked. To his left Máel saw one of the watchers stand, a huge man with ax raised, shouting in his Norse tongue, but before he could even swing the ax he was skewered on the end of an Irish spear.

Another loomed in front of him. Máel Sechnaill had a glimpse of a thick yellow beard, helmet, mail. He parried a sword thrust, lunged, felt the tip of his sword scrape on links of iron.

The Viking knocked Máel's sword aside with his shield, slashed at his attacker and Máel deflected the blow with his own shield. Among all the Irish, Máel was the only one whose weapons were a match for the Vikings, but that did not matter because the Irish had surprise and numbers on their side.

Máel slashed at the Viking and their swords met with a ringing sound, a jarring impact that was painful. Máel saw another of his men charging, spear level at the Viking's throat and he stepped in, pushed his own man aside.

"Alive! I want this one alive!" the Irish king shouted.

Then more of the bodyguard were there, behind the Viking and on either side of him, spears level. The Viking looked around, his face was a mask of rage, and he roared out, but if they were words in his Northern tongue or just noise Máel Sechnaill could not tell.

The Viking swung his sword in a great arc and one of the bodyguard pounced, grabbed the mail-clad arm, pinning it back. Another grabbed the shield, and for all his rage and struggle the Viking was pulled down, shouting and thrashing, the bodyguard barely in control.

Máel Sechnaill stepped up, stood above the struggling men. He reached out with the tip of his sword and scribed a long flesh wound across the Viking's throat, just deep enough to be painful, and that seemed to have a calming effect on the man. He ceased struggling, looked up at Máel Sechnaill, eyes wide, mouth open. He spit out some words, but to the Irish king they were babble.

Flann mac Conaing appeared on the road above, his mail shirt making a metallic rustling as he moved. He climbed and slid down the embankment to Máel Sechnaill's side.

"We had one killed, two wounded, slightly, my lord," Flann reported. "The Norsemen are all killed. Forgive me, the one wearing mail was killed by accident."

"No matter," Máel said. "We have this one." He pointed at the now motionless Viking sprawled at his feet. The men who had brought him down were now standing on either side of him, their feet pinning his arms and legs.

"Remove his helmet," Máel ordered, and they did, but still Máel saw only defiance in the man's eyes. For a moment the Irish king was silent, staring into that foreign face. They were a plague on his land, these fin gall, these white strangers. He turned to Flann. "Did you find anything?"

"No, my lord. Some food, weapons, nothing more."

Máel nodded. "Ask him where he is from."

Flann, who was well-traveled and had spent enough time in the Norse countries to have a decent command of the language, turned and spoke to the man on the ground. For a moment the man just looked at him, his expression pure hatred. Then he spat out a single word.

"He says 'Jelling', my lord, which is in the Danish country."

Máel stepped up and smacked the side of the man's head with the flat of his sword, hard enough to make the man grunt with pain. "Ask him again."

Again the Viking answered with a single word. "Dubh-linn."

"Ask him how he knew that a delegation from Leinster would pass by this way."

Flann translated the words. "He says they knew nothing of any delegation. They were looking for travelers to rob."

That was a lie and not a terribly convincing one. When the Norsemen raided the Irish countryside they did it in large bands, on horseback. They sacked monasteries and kings' halls. They did not lie in wait in the brush by a roadside, where they might be lucky to capture half a dozen cows driven to market.

Máel Sechnaill held his sword straight out, the blunt tip an inch from the Norseman's eye. The prisoner jerked and twisted his head, but he could not move far, and always the tip of the sword was there.

"Tell him he loses his left eye first, then the right."

Flann translated, and the Viking seemed to understand that he had pushed the king's patience to its limits. The words poured out.

"He say that he was ordered by Orm, who is king of Dubh-linn," Flann said when the Viking had stopped at last. "They were to lie in wait until a group of men passed, not peasants, but men from a royal court. They were to kill them all and take what they carried."

"And what was it they carried?" Máel asked.

The Norseman gave a single word.

"A crown," Flann said.

For a long moment Máel Sechnaill stared at the Viking, but his thoughts were elsewhere. The Crown of the Three Kingdoms... How did this foreign whore's son know about it? Does he know what it means?

"Ask him how he knows about the crown. Why he thought it would be passing this way?"

Flann asked, and translated the answer, which was that the man did not know any of that, that he was doing as he had been told by his king.

They worked on him for a bit, with their feet and the flat of Máel's sword, but his answer did not change, and Máel came to believe he was telling the truth. Clearly Orm knew what the crown meant, and he would not be so stupid as to make that information generally known.

So the question was, how did Orm know? And what did it mean that he did?

Máel Sechnaill looked at the Norseman at his feet. His first instinct was to drive the point of his sword through the man's throat. He actually stepped up to do it when he heard in his head the harangue of his irascible old priest, lecturing in his cracked voice about forgiveness and what not.

"Bind him up," Máel said, stepping back. "By the mercy of Christ we will let him live."

Slavery rather than death, the Viking could count himself a lucky man. Perhaps some backbreaking labor in the king's fields would help his memory.

Chapter Six

It is uncertain
where enemies lurk
or crouch in a dark corner.
Hávamál

Donnel the sheep herder opened his eyes and his first thought was, no rain. For the second day in a row the dawn came with clear skies and the promise of sun, and that was enough for a poor man like Donnel to think it was his lucky day.

He sat up. His brother Patrick and he had slept in the meadow where they bedded down the flock. They were five miles from home, twenty miles from Dubh-linn, which lay to the south. Two days herding would get the flock to the town, where the finn gall would pay in silver for fresh meat.

First he counted the sheep. It was as integral a part of waking up as opening his eyes. Fourteen. Very well. Then he looked for his brother.

He didn't see him, and that was odd. Patrick was younger by a few years, but generally reliable. Donnel kicked off the much-worn wool blanket, got to his feet. The morning breeze from the ocean was cool and he pulled the cowl of his cloak over his head and picked up his staff.

Patrick was off beyond the flock, standing at the edge of the great cliff that ran down to the beach and the sea beyond. He was looking out to sea. His back was to the sheep. Donnel could not imagine what he was doing.

He shook his head and trudged off through the dew-wet grass toward his brother. "Patrick, what are you doing, now?" he called when he was close enough to be heard over the breeze.

Patrick turned. "Come here and look at this, Donnel!"

Donnel hurried over. The cliff was high and rugged, and if the wind had been at their backs Donnel would have been nervous about approaching so close.

He stepped up beside Patrick. Below them, the white sands that ringed Barnageeragh Bay stretched away in a semicircle, and beyond that the sea glittered in the early morning sun.

"A boat, is it?" Donnel asked.

"Sure it's a boat. And a fair sized one at that."

For a moment they were silent, looking down at the battered curragh laying half on its side on the beach. It rocked slightly with each incoming wave, as if, in its death throes, it were making one final effort to free itself.

"Should we have a look, then?" Patrick asked.

Donnel glanced back at the sheep. They were grazing and, being sheep, would much prefer to remain where they were rather than be herded off. They weren't going anywhere. And the Lord knew what might be found on board a wrecked ship, particularly one of that size.

"Come on."

The young men worked their way north to where the pasture met the steep path to the beach. They had been this way several times and were quite familiar with the tricky climb. For the moment thoughts of the riches the curragh might hold were set aside as they concentrated on picking their way down the steep trail, still slick with mud and crumbling from the recent rains.

At last they reached the soft sand that lapped like the sea against the cliff and crossed the beach to the wreck. Up close they saw it was much larger than they had thought at first, three perches long at least. It lay at an odd angle, it's deck tilted toward the sea. The mast was broken and the single yard lay across the gunnels, snapped in three places and held together by the remnants of the sail. There seemed to be no real damage to the hull.

Donnel and Patrick slowed their pace as they approached. There was a haunted quality about the wrecked ship, as if the souls who had perished in the storm were not ready to leave, and it made the boys waver in their determination to see what was aboard.

Slowly, as if they were sneaking up on it, they crossed the sand to the curragh's side. Together they reached out and placed hands on the gunnel, stood on tiptoes and peered over.

"Jesus, Mary and Joseph!" Donnel shouted. He and Patrick leapt back, their hands flying from forehead to abdomen to shoulders as they crossed themselves, then turned and fled.

They were twenty feet from the wreck when the panic began to ebb and they stopped and turned back. For a long moment they just stared at the ship. Finally, Donnel spoke.

"They're but dead men. They can't harm us now."

Patrick nodded. The two young men retraced their steps, this time walking around the bow of the ship to the low side. They could see the whole deck from where they stood, the chalk-white, bloated, waterlogged bodies strewn fore and aft. They could see gaping wounds washed clean of blood by the rain and seas.

"Whatever do you think happened?" Patrick whispered, but Donnel did not answer. Instead he climbed over the side of the boat, dropped to the deck, began stepping cautiously around the dead.

"It was the finn gall, I'll wager," Donnel said at last. It was no great mystery who had killed these men. The mystery was who these dead men were.

"Are they fishermen?" Patrick asked. Donnel shook his head. There were too many of them. And though their bodies had been looted and stripped, Donnell could see in the remnants of the clothing that these were wealthy men, king's men, not common folk like him and Patrick.

"I don't know…" Donnel began and then he gasped, tried to scream, but only a choking sound came out. Then Patrick screamed and Donnel found his voice and screamed as well, a shrill sound of unadulterated panic.

He looked down. One of the dead men, his face white, his eyes bulging, had a hold of Donnel's ankle.

Chapter Seven

Who can tell
at the table
if he laughs with angry men?
Hávamál

The sun was setting, brilliant and red, and the wind was gusting hard by the time the longship *Red Dragon* found the mouth of the River Liffey and Ornolf's warriors readied for the hard pull upstream.

For two mostly miserable days they had remained tied up in the cove where Ornolf and Thorgrim had buried the crown. The storm howled around them, dumping rain as they huddled on deck under an awning spread over a frame set up to bear it. They heard sounds from the shore that might well have been trolls, or something worse. The Vikings, to allay their fears, and for want of anything better to do, ate and drank themselves into insensibility.

Finally the storm blew itself out, leaving in its wake blue sky and winds gusting hard. They got underway with a single reef in the sail and Thorgrim taking careful note of the landmarks that would lead them back to the little bay.

They worked their way down the coast with two long tacks before fetching the mouth of the Liffey, but the wind was foul for them to sail up to the longphort of Dubh-linn, so with a fair amount of grousing the Vikings stowed the sail and broke out the long sweeps.

Now Thorgrim stood at his place at the tiller, shielding his eyes from the brilliant orange glow of the setting sun, and guiding the ship between the muddy banks, the low rolling green hills.

Ornolf the Restless was roaring drunk.

He was up in the bow, a cup in his hand, flinging curses at the gods and anyone he could see on shore. His hand rested on the stump of the prow, where the long tapering dragon's neck was generally fastened. The dragon head was always removed when approaching land, in case any land spirits should see it and be frightened, though Thorgrim wondered how a carved head could be any more off-putting than a drunk Ornolf.

He scanned the southern bank of the river. There was a scattering of houses, some sheltered behind circular stonewalls, or wattle fortifications. A church sat back from the water a little ways. *That close to a Norse longphort, it must have nothing of value*, Thorgrim thought. Or, more to the point, it had nothing left of value.

There were a few people as well, a plowman guiding his oxen through the last bits of daylight, some children gleaning a field. A woman was washing clothes in the river and Ornolf shouted to her as they passed. She looked up, watching the longship glide by. Thorgrim wondered if she understood the Norse tongue. He did not think so. If she did, she would have fled in terror to hear what Ornolf was suggesting.

The men, well practiced at the sweeps, pulled with powerful, even strokes. Young Harald pulled an oar with the rest, and Thorgrim watched him when he saw Harald was looking away. Not so long ago, his boy could barely manage that work, though Harald would never admit it. Instead, he would set his teeth and pull and pretend that he was not struggling at the limits of his strength.

But now he pulled with the same ease as the older men - lean forward and sweep the oar blade toward the bow, lean back and pull - over and over, a steady mechanical rhythm that they could keep up for the better part of a day if they needed to.

Thorgrim looked away before Harald saw him watching. Ornolf was shouting. "Ah, you Dubh-linn sons of whores! Lock up your wives, and your daughters, too, if you wouldn't have Ornolf the Restless bugger them all!"

Thorgrim spit in the river. He wished Ornolf would shut up. He felt the black mood coming on.

Nightfall. It often happened around that time of day, became worse as the earth grew dark.

During the day, Thorgrim Ulfsson was pleasant enough. He was, in fact, known for an unusually even temper. The men were happy to come to him for orders, or with problems, rather than deal with the raging Ornolf. But when the sun set, Thorgrim became irritable and prone to fighting. It was the spirit of the wolf, or so he had come to call it, and it made him snappish and mean. It was not something he liked. He'd tried to resist it.

But it was the way he was.

Now the sun was dipping behind the low hills and the longphort was in view up-river, a wooden fortress of sorts and a smattering of ill-conceived houses along a muddy road. Two buildings loomed above the others, and Thorgrim guessed them to be a temple and a mead hall. He knew in which of those the men would be worshiping as soon as the dock lines were secure.

"Ease your stroke!" Thorgrim barked and the men fell into a slower rhythm as the longship made the careful approach to the docks. Thorgrim ran his eyes over the various ships tied up there - ocean-going knarrs and longships, smaller warships and curraghs. Quite a lot of ships. Apparently Dubh-linn was every bit the trading center Ornolf claimed it was.

Around the far end of the up-river dock Thorgrim could see an unoccupied spot. He leaned into the tiller, swung the bow around, angling *Red Dragon* toward the space. "Pull and ship your oars!" he shouted. The men gave one long pull and then ran the sweeps in through the oar holes and laid them out on deck in a neatly choreographed move, while Ornolf bellowed, "Hah! You row like a bunch of old women! It's a good thing Ornolf's here to roger all the girls in Dubh-linn, cause you'd never be able to do it, you bunch of limp peckers!"

Thorgrim scowled and kept his eyes on the dock as *Red Dragon* swept around the corner. Harald was foremost, as ever, standing up in the bow by his raving grandfather, a thick dock line in his hand.

The bow turned in toward the dock and Harald leapt, a long jump over the water, though if he had waited a moment more the ship would have been along side and he could have stepped across. The boy hit the dock, stumbled, ran forward and looped the rope around a cleat, checking the ship's way as it came along side.

"There's my grandson, the only one besides me on this ship with balls or brains, eh?" Ornolf shouted.

One by one the rest of the men tumbled over the side, some attending to the dock lines, some staring around. There were a few men among them who had been to Dubh-linn before, but most had not, and their curiosity was palpable.

Ornolf came rolling aft. "Hey, Thorgrim, we made it, and still alive!" Most men would not approach Thorgrim in his present mood, so late in the day, but Ornolf was either unafraid or completely oblivious. The two men had been together a long time. They had been through too much together for either to take much offense at what the other one did.

Ornolf handed Thorgrim a brimming cup of mead and Thorgrim gladly took it and quaffed it down.

"We'll make a fortune here, our holds full as they are," Ornolf said and Thorgrim nodded his agreement.

"We need to arrange some gift for whatever miserable whoreson is in charge here," Ornolf continued, "to show our respect."

"I'll see what we have, that might do him honor," Thorgrim said.

"Good, good. Now, I am going to bear my grandson away to the mead hall and teach him how to drink and fornicate like a man! Will you join us?"

"No," Thorgrim said. He wondered if he should forbid Harald to go. Thorgrim was not enthusiastic about giving his son over to Ornolf's influence. Hallbera the Fair, Harald's mother, Ornolf's daughter, had once begged Thorgrim to keep the boy away from his grandfather, and Thorgrim wondered if he must honor her memory by doing so now. Thorgrim loved Harald far more than he loved even his own life, but he knew the boy was not the cleverest of creatures, and could easily be led into Ornolf's bad habits.

But Harald was not a child any more. He was trying hard to take his place among men. Forcing him to stay behind would not help.

He felt the anger like tongs squeezing his temples. It was hard to think with the spirit of the wolf sweeping over him.

"I'll stay with the ship. Leave a dozen men behind," Thorgrim said, then turned to lashing the tiller before he said anything else, anything less helpful.

Forward, he heard Ornolf roaring out about the damage he and his men would do to Dubh-linn. Then, once he had the men sufficiently excited about the pleasures that awaited them, he told off a dozen to stay behind, which resulted in the predictable curses and arguments.

"Father?"

Thorgrim looked up. Harald was there. The boy seemed to carry some invisible shield that warded off Thorgrim's anger. If the black mood made Thorgrim hate all the world, still he loved his son.

Thorgrim grunted in reply.

"I'd be happy to stand watch with you, father, or take the watch so you can go with the others."

Thorgrim straightened and looked at his son. A decent, honorable young man, he thought. He gets it from his mother. He sure as hell does not get it from me or Ornolf...

"No. You go. You've earned it," Thorgrim said, the words coming in little bursts.

Harald nodded, tried to disguise his obvious relief, turned and hurried forward. Ornolf the Restless was already leading his men up the plank road to the mead hall.

Thorgrim sat on the after deck, his cloak wrapped around him, staring out at the water. Forward, the disgruntled dozen sat in a huddle and drank and shot ugly looks aft. They blamed Thorgrim for having to stay.

Thorgrim knew it and did not care.

For some time, he did not know how long, Thorgrim stared up river as the Liffey slowly disappeared from sight in the setting sun. With nothing to distract him, his thoughts turned into a disjoined jumble of anger and depression and loathing, an ugly and unfocused surge of emotions. He knew he had to stand, walk, do something - just sitting made the black mood worse - but he could not pull himself to his feet.

There were voices from forward, men talking, but he dismissed the sound as the babble of angry men who would rather be at the mead hall.

The loud bang of a deck board lifted and dropped made him jump and he looked up, annoyed. It was nearly black night, with a smattering of stars gleaming to the east. The men who had been left behind were pulling up the deck planks, revealing the cargo stored below. Someone Thorgrim did not recognize was climbing down to inspect. Olaf Yellowbeard was holding a lantern for him.

With a growl Thorgrim stood and walked forward. His men stood aside as he approached, and watched with nervous expressions, which only irritated him further.

"What's this?" Thorgrim demanded.

Sigurd Sow coughed nervously. "This fellow, he said he had to come aboard."

Thorgrim looked down at the man in the hold. He was dressed like a Norseman. A wealthy Norseman. His fine-made clothes covered a corpulent frame.

"I am Asbjorn," the man said, wiping his hands together. With some effort he struggled out of the hold and on to the deck. "I am the port reeve." His tone was curt and officious. The Vikings shuffled nervously. Some cleared their throats. Thorgrim felt his anger rise.

"Yes?"

"I've come to inspect your cargo. A certain percentage will be claimed by King Orm."

Thorgrim just stared at the man. In younger days, in the wolf-spirit, he might have killed the reeve by now, but age had taught him how to hold the anger at bay. For a while.

Sigurd stepped closer. "Let me talk to this one, Thorgrim, no need to concern yourself."

"No," Thorgrim said and pushed Sigurd aside, not hard, but with feeling. To Asbjorn he said, "Make your inspection and get out. We'll do a reckoning in the morning."

Asbjorn grunted but he clearly saw where discretion was warranted. He struggled down into the hold, continued to poke through the goods there as the *Red Dragon*'s men lifted up the deck planks and Thorgrim, with forced control, watched in silence.

"These are Danish goods," Asbjorn observed, and there was a hint of accusation in his tone.

"Yes," Thorgrim said.

"But you are Norwegian?"

"Yes. Aren't you? Isn't this a Norwegian longphort?"

"No, it is not." Asbjorn struggled out of the hold again, and again made a wiping motion with his hands, as if to rid himself of the *Red Dragon*'s filth, and the motion irritated Thorgrim to the extreme.

"Dubh-Linn is a Danish longphort, and has been for this past year or more. And you," Asbjorn poked an accusing finger into Thorgrim's chest, "have some explaining to do."

Thorgrim looked at the finger like he could not believe what he was seeing. He heard someone gasp. His hand shot out like a snake, grabbed the fat digit before Asbjorn could withdraw it. He twisted, felt the bones on the edge of snapping. Sigurd Sow grabbed his arm, Snorri Half-troll grabbed his shoulders and the others pulled him back as Asbjorn screamed like a pig. Thorgrim felt Asbjorn's finger slip from his grasp.

The *Red Dragon* crew pulled Thorgrim back five feet, a safe distance, and held him tight. "You better get out of here, now," Sigurd Sow said to the port reeve. Asbjorn stared hatred at Thorgrim, and Thorgrim stared it back, but both men were sensible enough to keep their mouths shut.

"I'll be back in the morning," Asbjorn said as he backed off the ship, his tone a threat. Thorgrim struggled against the men who held him but they knew better than to let go, even if it meant a thrashing after the port reeve was gone.

Asbjorn hurried off and when he was lost in the dark Thorgrim shook off the men and stamped aft. *Stupid, stupid...* he thought. The black mood didn't strip him of his senses, at least not after the blind fury had passed. He knew that he had made a grave error, but he had been unable to fight the spirits that possessed him. He could still see that offensive fat finger wagging at him.

He leaned against the sweeping sternpost and looked up the rise at the longphort of Dubh-linn. There were lights burning here and there, and the windows of the mead hall glowed from the fire and lanterns inside. He could hear the sound of the revelry, like a soft land breeze blowing down to the river.

Danish? Dubh-Linn is Danish now? How could that have happened?

Quite easily, Thorgrim realized. Danes and Norwegians often fought side by side, but just as often they fought one another, in the same way that the English and the Irish were generally so busy fighting amongst themselves that they had nothing left to fight off the Norsemen.

He thought of the crown. The dream had told him not to bring it to Dubh-linn and now he saw why. But even without it, they were in a precarious situation.

"Sigurd Sow," Thorgrim called as he walked forward again. Sigurd stood. He looked nervous. "Come with me. And you five." With a sweep of his arm he indicated half the men left on board. "The rest of you keep a bright watch while we're gone."

"Where are we going, Thorgrim?" Sigurd Sow ventured.

"To find Ornolf. We have trouble, and now I've made it worse. It can't wait."

Chapter Eight

*A clear head
is good company
Drink is a dangerous friend.*
Hávamál

Asbjorn the Fat ran up the plank road until his heaving breath would not allow him to run a foot more. He stopped, gasped, cradled his aching finger in his left hand.

Asbjorn envisioned problems as if they were one of those intricate carvings beloved of Norse artists - long, snake-like creatures all tangled around one another. His thoughts followed along each of the paths until he could see where it led; to danger, to opportunity, to nowhere.

He thought of those Norwegians, stupid sons of bitches, sailing right into a Danish longphort with a hold full of plundered Danish goods. Could he derive some benefit from keeping them a secret? His mind followed along that path. He started up the hill again.

No. Orm would find out about them one way or another, and if it was from someone other than Asbjorn, then Orm would think his port reeve either conniving or incompetent. And Asbjorn was not incompetent.

He hurried up to the fortress, passed by the guards at the gate without even acknowledging them, hurried across the inner yard. He paused, let his breath come back, then crossed to Orm's door and knocked. He was about to knock again when Orm called for him to enter.

The main room of Orm's house was lit with a single candle and the glow of embers in the fireplace. Orm was adjusting his tunic as he crossed the room, his bare legs and feet white in the dim light. Asbjorn wondered if he had been rutting with his slave girl. If so, he would not be happy for the interruption. He would not be happy in any event.

"What is it?"

"That longship, it came in at sundown? They are Norwegians."

"Norwegians?" Orm frowned, wrinkled his brow. Asbjorn knew that this news would strike home. Rumors had been floating in for some time of a fleet assembling under Olaf the White. There was not a day since Orm had taken Dubh-linn from the Norwegians that he did not expect them to arrive in force and take it back.

"What do they want?" Orm asked.

"To trade, it would seem. I don't think they realized things have changed here."

"Hmmm. I wonder..."

"I managed to inspect their cargo, before I was attacked. Filled with trade good. Danish trade goods, and no explanation of where they came from."

"You were attacked?"

"Brutally attacked, by half the crew. I just managed to escape."

Orm ran his eyes up and down Asbjorn's person. He did not look like he had just survived a brutal attack, so Asbjorn hurried the conversation along.

"They arrive here with stolen goods, attack the port reeve, act as if they do not know Dubh-linn is a Danish longphort... They are either very dumb, or are playing at some game."

Orm nodded. He turned away, stared into the fire, as he often did when deep in thought. "Where are they now?"

"At the hall."

"Send Magnus. Tell him to keep his mouth shut and listen. Find out what he can."

"Yes, my lord," Asbjorn said.

Of course Magnus would be dragged into this thing. Asbjorn's mind began to follow the trail of the winding beast. He was looking for the path that would end in the defeat of the Norwegians as well as the final humiliation of Magnus Magnusson. Or better still, Magnus's death.

Thorgrim led his small but well-armed band up the plank road toward the mead hall. The night was quiet and the noise from inside grew louder as they approached. It was the raucous noise of half-wild men far from home and beyond even the limited constraints their domestic life imposed upon them. Thorgrim could hear snatches of song, bits of poetry, laughter, shouts and screams, both male and female. He frowned and pressed on.

The door to the hall gaped open and Thorgrim stepped inside, stepped from the dark, still night to the fire-lit, roaring world of the hall. The building was fifty feet long and thirty high, just one big room with an oak table running nearly the full length. A massive fire burned in a fireplace at the far end, and oil lanterns hung from the ceiling at regular intervals, casting an orange light and leaving deep shadows all around.

It was crowded with men. Big men, well armed men. Drunk men. They hoisted cups to their mouths, let mead run down their chins and filter through dense beards as they drank. The plates that littered the table were mostly empty now. The scattering of bones and crumbs and chunks of half-gnawed foodstuff were all that was left of the on-going feast.

Women were few but there were enough of them. They moved through the throng, keeping cups full, bringing more food to the table, enduring the Vikings' indelicate words and hands. Slave girls, some Norse, some Irish, Thorgrim was not so consumed by the black mood that he did not notice how pretty most of them were.

He walked farther into the hall. His arrival, with a gang of armed men at his back, caused not the slightest reaction from the crowd. He could see his own men scattered among the hall, sitting in small knots by themselves or engaging in the general revelry. If they had figured out yet that they were a few Norwegians among Danes, they did not show it, nor did it seem to matter. They were all Vikings, doing what those people did best.

Harald was sitting somewhere near the middle of the hall, looking young in that company with his ruddy, clean-shaved face. His cheeks were flushed and his eyes slightly glassy. He might be able to row like a man, but he still could not drink like one, certainly not one like his grandfather.

As to fornicating, Ornolf had apparently not got to that part of the instruction. There was a girl on Harald's lap, a pretty young thing with dirty blond hair and a slight figure. Harald was laughing like he was enjoying every minute of it, but Thorgrim knew his boy and he could hear the false note, the look of profound embarrassment under the mask of pleasure.

"Harald!" Thorgrim barked.

Harald looked up. His face grew redder still. He said something to the girl, pushed her off his lap so she landed on her rear end on the floor, and hurried over to Thorgrim.

"Father! Is there trouble?" Harald's hand went unbidden to the hilt of his sword.

"Could be." Thorgrim had to talk loud, louder than he wished to, just to be heard. "Where is Ornolf?"

Harald's face flushed again. "Uh...over by the fire, I last saw him..."

Thorgrim nodded. Whatever Ornolf the Restless was up to, Thorgrim did not care. Nor would it embarrass him. He was a long way from fifteen years old.

He headed off toward the back of the hall, threading his way through the crowd, stepping over those sprawled on the floor, the ones who had gone man to man with their cups and lost. How many times, he wondered, had he been in the middle of this exact same scene? It was like Valhalla, the same wild feast repeated night after night. He wondered how, in the afterlife, it did not lose its charm. In his present mood, the atmosphere was not doing much for him.

Ten feet from the fire and he could feel the heat on his face. He wandered off to his right, toward the shadows in the corner. He found Ornolf the Restless there, amid a pile of furs and blankets. His leggings were down around his ankles. He was on top of a slave girl, furiously humping away. The girl's whole body jarred with each powerful thrust. Her eyes were wide and she was gasping for breath, but if that was due to passion or that fact that she could not breath with Ornolf on top of her, Thorgrim could not tell.

"Ornolf!" Thorgrim shouted.

Ornolf looked over at him, annoyed, but his face brightened when he saw who it was. "Thorgrim! Glad to see you've stopped your moping around and come join us!"

"We need to talk," Thorgrim said.

"So, talk…" said Ornolf, never losing a beat. Thorgrim knew Ornolf was perfectly capable of copulating like a bull caribou in rut and holding a conversation at the same time, but with the black mood on him Thorgrim could not do it.

"Talk to me when you're done," he said and walked off. He paused near the fireplace, at the edge of the chaos, like standing at the edge of a thundering surf. The men he brought with him had melted away, joined with their comrades in the bacchanal, but that was fine. Thorgrim had wanted a show of force coming up the road, but he did not need it here. If the Danes turned against them, there was not much his six men were going to do.

"Here, have a drink with me!" a voice roared out, near by, close enough that the man did not need to shout as loud as he did. Thorgrim felt the blast of fetid breath. He turned. The man was huge, six inches taller than Thorgrim and fifty pounds heavier. He held out a cup. Mead sloshed over the sides.

Thorgrim took it and drank, nodded his thanks.

"A polite man would offer a toast," the big man said and there was an edge of anger to his words. Thorgrim felt the rage mounting, despite all his efforts. He raised the cup in a half-hearted gesture.

"Are you too good to toast with me?" the man said, stepping closer. Looking for a fight. Thorgrim had seen this bastard's type often enough. This night he chose the wrong man in the wrong mood.

"Well?"

Thorgrim took another sip then tossed the remainder of the mead in the man's face. The man spluttered, wiped his eyes. Thorgrim wound up and hit him in the side of his head with a force that sent shockwaves of pain through his hand and arm, and the big man went straight down, like the bones in his legs had vanished.

Thorgrim considered the unconscious giant as he flexed his fingers. His hand hurt but his mood was much improved.

"Thorgrim!"

Thorgrim staggered, as if Ornolf's voice had physically struck him, then realized that Ornolf had slapped his back. The jarl was holding his trousers up with one hand, and he tied them as he spoke.

"I do dearly love to go a-viking," Ornolf said. "But these long ocean voyages...no women...it's hard on a man." Copulating always put Ornolf in a thoughtful mood. "There are plenty of women here, get yourself one," he suggested.

"Perhaps," Thorgrim said, and though he loved to be with a woman as much as any man, still when the evening's foul mood came on him he could not stand the thought. "Did you know that Dubh-linn is a Danish longphort?"

Ornolf squinted like he was confused. "It's Norwegian," he said.

"Not any more. Or so the port reeve tells me. The Danes under some bastard named Orm drove the Norwegians out less than a year ago."

Ornolf looked around, wide-eyed. "Well, it seemed a lot of these whore's sons were Danes, but I did not know they had control of the longphort."

"And here we are with a hold full of plundered Danish goods."

Ornolf gave a wave of his hand, dismissing Thorgrim's concern. "No matter. These sons of bitch Danes are as greedy as any men. A good price and they won't care a damn if we took these goods from their mothers, and humped them in the bargain!"

"I broke the port reeve's finger. Or nearly did," Thorgrim said.

"Damn me! And I thought you were having no fun at all tonight!"

Thorgrim looked away, irritated by Ornolf's refusal to see the seriousness of their circumstance.

Or maybe I'm just an old woman... Thorgrim thought.

But now someone else was approaching, a tall and well formed man, clean-shaven with silky hair hanging down his shoulders. He was well dressed, clothes that projected money and power. His blue eyes were mostly steady, but he took in everything.

"Good evening, gentlemen," the stranger bowed, courteous but not overly so. "My name is Magnus Magnusson. You are new to Dubh-linn, I believe. I welcome you."

"And who are you," Thorgrim asked, "to welcome us?"

James L. Nelson

"No one of consequence." Magnus's tone was disarming.

"Pleased to meet you!" Ornolf thrust a meaty hand at Magnus, and Magnus took it and shook.

"You do not look a man of no consequence," Thorgrim observed.

"I am an associate of Orm's who is lord of Dubh-linn, that much is true," Magnus said.

"So you are a Dane, then?" Ornolf asked. "The lot of you here, Danes?"

"Yes," Magnus said. "But it is no matter. Danes, Norwegians, Swedes, we are all here of a purpose. Settle this savage place. Establish trade." He smiled, the kind of smile meant to win converts.

"There, Thorgrim, you see?" Ornolf roared. "I have been telling Thorgrim," Ornolf said to Magnus, "that you Danes are not nearly the treacherous sons of whores most make you out to be."

"Indeed," Magnus smiled. "We are not."

"Well, then," Ornolf said, "I would be proud to drink with you and call you friend."

Be your friend's true friend, to him and his friends, Thorgrim recalled the old saying. *Beware of befriending an enemy's friend.*

Who are the enemies, he wondered, and who the friends?

Chapter Nine

A man should drink
in moderation
be sensible or silent.
Hávamál

For a man of no consequence, Magnus Magnusson commanded a lot of respect, or so it appeared to Thorgrim Night Wolf. With a word Magnus cleared a half dozen men from the table so that he and Ornolf and Thorgrim would have a place to sit in relative private. With a wave of his arm and a nod, mead and wine and food appeared.

"So," he said, after they had all drunk deep and Ornolf had set into the chicken, "you have been lucky in your raiding?"

Thorgrim made a low growling noise, despite himself. He did not care for questioning, could see that this Magnus was too smooth by half. But he understood that it was his own rash actions that had put them in a compromised position, so he held his tongue.

"Lucky?" Ornolf raved, spitting bits of chicken. "Damned unlucky. England was a paradise once, gold everywhere, monasteries and churches bursting with the stuff. You just had to bend over to gather it up. Now? Picked bloody clean. Back when I was your age, when men had balls, we took all there was. Not a damned thing left!"

"Really? I had heard your hold was quite full."

"Heard?" Thorgrim asked. "From who, the fat one who was poking around our longship?"

Magnus smiled. "Asbjorn. A fat one indeed. I heard you nearly broke his finger. I'm sorry you did not cut his throat."

Thorgrim nodded. That was good to hear, anyway, that Asbjorn was not universally loved. "We've had some luck, despite what Ornolf says."

Magnus nodded and his thoughts were moving down some new path. "You were off the coast, in this last storm. Any luck then? Find any of these Irish out at sea?"

Thorgrim shook his head.

"Ha! Irish at sea?" Ornolf raged. He stopped, looked at Thorgrim. His smiled faded. "Oh, no. Not a damned one."

Thorgrim looked at Magnus. The Dane had not missed that, Ornolf's awkward retreat.

"You're certain?"

Thorgrim leaned back and folded his arms. "We had some luck. A trader, loaded to the gunnels. Danish, it turned out. I think you can guess why we are keeping it to ourselves."

"And that was it?"

Thorgim's eyes met Magnus's and held them, and for a long moment they just sat there, unmoving, each staring the other down. Thorgrim thought of the young nobleman he had fought for the crown, the moment when they had gripped one another, each holding the other in check. This was like that, but here it was will and not brute strength.

"That was it."

Magnus looked away and nodded, but the nod seemed to be in answer to his own internal question, and not anything that Thorgrim had said. Then he turned back and smiled, as if any unpleasantness had been whisked away.

"Still, it was a lucky take," Magnus said. "And we Danes are not too worried, when a man has goods to sell, where he got them. It's a dangerous world, you know."

"Ha!" Ornolf roared. "You've said it! Dangerous as long as Norwegians are at sea, and led by Ornolf the Restless! A drink with you, Magnus Magnusson!"

Ornolf held his cup aloft, and so did Magnus and they drank. Magnus raised his hand and the master of the mead hall appeared as if conjured up by the Dane.

"Vali, these men are my guests," Magnus said, gesturing to Thorgrim and Ornolf, "them and all the bold men who sailed with them. Let their cups never be empty tonight, or you will answer to me!"

"Yes, sir," Vali said, backed away and began barking orders to the slave girls, who swept around the crowded hall, filling the Norwegians' cups to overflowing, then filling them again as they were quickly drained.

Thorgrim took a deep drink, felt the warm, sweet mead run down his throat. He looked around. The scene in the hall was reaching its zenith, the roaring, singing, shouting and fighting coming to a crescendo that would soon begin to taper off until all the men there were asleep or dead. He had seen it many, many times. It was like a battle that reached a point of ultimate fury, a madness that could not be sustained for long, and then as more and more men dropped, came to an end.

At the far end of the table, young Harald was already face down, one of the first casualties of the night, his mouth open, his snores lost in the din. He looked almost angelic, an odd contrast to the wild men around him.

Thorgrim Night Wolf smiled, drained his cup, set it down and stood. "Thank you for your kindness, Magnus Magnusson, but I must go."

"Go? Won't you have another cup with me?"

"Forget him!" Ornolf shouted. "He is like an old woman when he gets this way! I will have another cup with you, and then the iron in my trousers will be cooled and ready for another thrust in the fire, eh!"

Thorgrim left them, pushed his way though the men. He recalled that there was no one aboard the *Red Dragon* now, save for the six men he had left behind, and Thorgrim was not happy about that. He was wary by nature, and the strange turns of the evening had only made him more so.

He looked around the mead hall, picking out his own men, considering whether or not to order them back to the ship. They were well mingled with the Danes now, and well in their cups, as drunk as Ornolf had ever been on his best day. There would be no getting them out of the mead hall now. Thorgrim did not even try.

He stopped where Harald was slumped over the table and gave the boy a hard shake, which had no more effect than to make him groan, a feeble sound, and try to brush Thorgrim's hand away.

At least he is still alive, Thorgrim thought. He had not been entirely certain. He pulled Harald to his feet, bent and grabbed him around the waist and hoisted him over his shoulder like a sack of grain. He pushed his way out of the mead hall and into the cool of the night.

The air felt good - moist and clean - after the smoky, hot, reeking hall, and Harald was no great burden as Thorgrim made his way back down the plank road to where *Red Dragon* thumped against the wharf. The six men on board were all as drunk as any up in the mead hall, but that had not made them any happier about being left behind.

Thorgrim climbed aboard under their surly stares and deposited Harald on a pile of furs. He stretched and looked around. The night was quiet, save for the lap of water, the muted noise from the hall, but Thorgrim's nerves were firing, his senses wolf-keen. But he was helpless as well. The pack had run off, he was all but alone.

He made his way forward. "There's some Dane bastard named Magnus, has ordered free drink to all from our ship. You had best get up to the hall before Ornolf has it all."

The surly looks were transformed as if by magic, and the men leapt to their feet and rushed off, fearing no doubt that Thorgrim would come to his senses, revert to his usual miserable self in the nighttime.

Thorgrim watched them hurry up the road. There was nothing those men could do to help if trouble came. Thorgrim alone, in the black mood, was more dangerous than those six drunks, so he let them go.

He wandered aft, wrestled his furs out from where they were stowed, laid down. He feared sleep on nights like this because he knew it would be a night of wolf dreams, but sleep, like death, took him at last.

He was in among the strange wolf pack again, though he no longer held the precious thing in his mouth. The wolves moved around him, watching him, but he could not tell if they would attack, he did not know if they were friends or enemies. He felt taut, like a length of rigging under great strain.

And then the wolves turned on him. At some unseen signal they turned and the pack leapt with teeth flashing white and Thorgrim flew into the fight, snarling and ripping away at the killers bounding at him

He sat up, the sweat coating his body, the cold touch of iron under his chin. First light, the town of Dubh-Linn was lit gray-blue, and a dozen armed men were on board the *Red Dragon*. Thorgrim looked up the length of the spear to the bearded face of the soldier who held the lethal point unwavering against Thorgrim's neck. The soldier expected that the threatening iron would be enough to stop Thorgrim from making any quick move. He was wrong.

Thorgrim took firm hold of the bearskin that covered him, flung the skin aside, flung it over the spear, tangling it in the shaft. He sprung to his feet, Iron-tooth in his hand. The spearman was trying to pull the shaft from the fur when he died, the heavy blade of Thorgrim's sword nearly taking his head off.

The spearman's body had not hit the deck when Thorgrim flung himself at the next man, who came at him with a shriek, battle-ax raised. Thorgrim wore only his tunic and trousers, there was no time to grab up his shield. He caught the swinging ax with Iron-tooth's blade and delivered an awkward punch with his left hand.

The ax-man was a big man, and even a solid punch would not have done much. He kicked upward as Thorgrim swung. Thorgrim just managed to close his legs and ward off the blow that would have ended his fight then and there. The ax-man shoved with his shield and Thorgrim, off balance, stumbled back.

There was someone behind him. Thorgrim had not realized it. He leapt to his right, his eyes on the ax coming at him, saw a spear-thrust miss by inches. He half-turned, drove Iron-tooth into the man's gut, grabbed him by the collar of his tunic and pulled him in front like a shield, just as the wicked ax was coming at his head.

The ax struck the spearman instead of Thorgrim. Thorgrim let go and leapt away, looking for fighting room. There were none of his men there and he had a vision of them waking up thickheaded on the floor of the mead hall, waking as he did with spear points in their beards. Would they fight? Some, but it would not matter.

Harald was forward, kneeling, hands clasped behind his head, four men around him with swords and spears and Thorgrim was glad at least that his son was not fighting. It would be like Harald to follow his father into this suicide attack.

The ax-man was coming at Thorgrim again, and now two more men, and two behind them, circling in as Thorgrim parried here and there. Spears reached in with tentative thrusts, taunting, each looking for a reaction that the other could exploit. The ax-man was circling behind. Thorgrim could just keep him in his peripheral vision, and that was trouble. He had to get his back against something.

"Alive!" A voice shouted out, a voice of command. Magnus Magnusson in his rich red cape, bright sword in hand, gleaming helmet on his head, stepped aft. "I want him alive!"

Thorgrim saw a flutter of activity, some burst of commotion. Harald had leapt to his feet, pushed the closest spear tip aside, jerked the weapon out of another warrior's hands.

"Harald! No!" Thorgrim shouted, even as his own sword turned a spear aside. It was a berserker's death, fighting against that many men. Not for Harald.

Thorgrim's son paid no attention. He whirled the spear, took one of the warriors in the side of the head with the shaft, turned and thrust at another. But he could not fight on all quarters at once. The man behind him buried the wicked point of his spear in Harald's shoulder.

Harald screamed in pain, the most terrible sound that Thorgrim had ever heard, arched his back as he fell. Thorgrim wanted to scream as well, but no sound would come.

And in that instant that Thorgrim's attention was on Harald, the ax-man swung around hard and hit Thorgrim on the back of the head with the flat of the ax. The blow sent Thorgrim sprawling forward, Iron-tooth flying from his hand, clattering on the deck. The spearmen standing behind yanked his weapon out of the way to prevent Thorgrim from impaling himself on it.

He hit the deck on hands and knees, his head whirling, his vision a blur. Strong hands grabbed his shoulders and pulled him back and sat him awkwardly down. He looked up. Through the fog in his head he saw the red-draped Magnus looming over him. Magnus spoke, and his voice sounded distant, and Thorgrim heard, "Now, Thorgrim, we must talk again. Really talk.

Chapter Ten

A guest needs
giving water
fine towels and friendliness.
Hávamál

Máel Sechnaill mac Ruanaid was preparing for war when the stranger arrived. The great hall in Tara, where wattle and daub walls rose up to a rough-hewn beam ceiling so high that the light of the big fire hardly reached among the heavy timbers, the hall that was generally a place of feasts and celebrations was now a staging area for battle.

Two servants bustled around Máel, tightening leather straps on his armor, arranging swords, spear and shields for his inspection. Other servants did the same for the ten other men in various places around the big room. These were the rí túaithe, the tribal kings who owed their allegiances and their military service to Máel Sechnaill. In the quiet before the chaos of leading men into battle they checked that their weapons were in order. They would ride out at dawn.

On the gentle hill on which the great hall stood, nearly three hundred men sat staring into their cook fires or sleeping fitfully in their tents. One hundred or so of them were professional soldiers, the core of Máel Sechnaill's army, and two hundred more were called up from the levy. It was no great host, not enough to drive the hated Norsemen from Dubh-linn, but events had forced Máel to set that goal aside. Tomorrow they would march south. In three days they would fall on the kingdom of Leinster.

"Tighter, tighter," Máel growled and the servant pulled harder on the chest plate's leather belt.

Máel Sechnaill sensed a motion in the big room, a rustle, as if every man's attention was suddenly caught up by a single focus and he knew that his daughter had entered the great hall. He turned, pulling the chest plate belt from the servant's hand.

Brigit came sweeping in from the west entrance. There were tiny flowers woven into her chestnut hair. Her gown was crafted to augment an already flawless figure. The rí túaithe stared with varying degrees of subtlety as she walked past. Those who were unmarried would have loved dearly to have her for wife, but none were important enough for Máel Sechnaill to waste his only daughter on.

Brigit was seventeen and a widow. At fourteen Máel Sechnaill had married her to Donnchad Ua Ruairc, the ruiri, the minor king of Gailenga on the Leinster borderland. It was more beneficial in the long run, Máel Sechnaill knew, to ally with Donnchad than to subjugate him.

But marriage to Brigit had not satisfied Donnchad Ua Ruairc. He and his brother, Cormac, continued to raid north into Sláine and the other túaths, the minor tribal kingdoms which fell under the kingship of Máel Sechnaill mac Ruanaid. Donnchad's raiders stole cattle, sacked churches and monasteries and took slaves. They were more annoying than threatening, but Máel Sechnaill mac Ruanaid did not care to be annoyed.

Máel led his men south where they met Donnchad Ua Ruairc in battle. Máel Sechnaill's army butchered their enemies, killing all but a handful who escaped, led by Donnchad's brother, Cormac Ua Ruairc.

The victory put an end to the Leinstermen's treachery. Máel assumed lordship over Gailenga, taking by force what Donnchad would not yield by treaty. He ordered Donnchad lashed to a pole and personally disemboweled him in front of those Gailenga chieftains who had survived the fight. He hoped the sight of Donnchad shrieking his life away as his guts pooled on the ground in front of him would serve as a dissuasive example.

Brigit was returned to her home at Tara. Máel Sechnaill was ready to marry her again if he could do so to advantage, but she was getting old and had developed something of a reputation for her sharp tongue. Máel Sechnaill could tell by the look on her face that she was about to further that reputation.

"Father, this is a mistake, I know it." She stopped a few feet away, crossed her arms.

Máel Sechnaill sighed, softly. "The abbot of Glendalough decreed that the Crown of the Three Kingdoms should be given to me. If it has not arrived, and the dubh gall did not steal it, then Niall Caille means to keep it for himself."

"Even if he does, the three kingdoms will not rally to him."

"The rí túaithe will obey the man who wears the crown. And Niall Caille must be taught a lesson."

Niall Caille was rí ruirech, the high king of Leinster, the kingdom to the south. He was not a man to be trusted. Máel Sechnaill suspected that he was allied with the Norsemen, was using the dubh gall to help him overrun Brega. It would not be the first time Irishmen had joined with Vikings. The Vikings had become yet another piece in the wildly convoluted puzzle of Irish governance.

It stood to reason that Niall Caille would not want Máel Sechnaill to wear the Crown of the Three Kingdoms.

"You do not know for certain that Niall Caille has kept the Crown," Brigit insisted. "Don't you think a delegation should be sent before a war party?"

Máel Sechnaill shook his head. It was beyond him, how his daughter had come to think she should meddle in men's affairs. Her mother had not, and would not, say a single word concerning Máel's plans for war.

Secretly, Máel Sechnaill hoped that Niall Caille had betrayed him. He welcomed the chance to teach Niall a lesson, to sack his towns, plunder his monasteries, annex his land and sell his people as slaves.

"What you think..." he began when he was interrupted again, this time by Flann mac Conaing, in battle dress, rushing in through the big front door.

"My lord." Flann gave a perfunctory bow. "There is a man here who wishes to see you. He is from Leinster, Lord."

Máel Sechnaill nodded. He did not meet Brigit's eye, though he knew she was looking at him. "Very well. Send him in."

Flann mac Conaing swept out of the hall. A moment later he was back, standing to one side of the door as the man from Leinster entered.

For a royal delegation, if such he was, he did not look too good. His clothes were torn and bloodstained, his hair and beard matted. He was bandaged in several places. In the light of the big peat fire burning in the fireplace Máel Sechnaill could see his skin was pale and drawn. He was supported by two young sheep herds who seemed to be bearing most of his weight.

As painful as it was for the man to walk, Máel Sechnaill did not move toward him, but instead made him cross the length of the great hall.

At last the four men - Flann, the Leinsterman and the sheep herds, stopped in front of Máel Sechnaill. The sheep herds lowered the Leinsterman to his knees, then knelt themselves.

"My Lord Máel Sechnaill mac Ruanaid," the Leinsterman said, and his voice was strong despite his condition. "My name is Cerball mac Gilla, ruiri of Uí Muiredaig. I have come from Leinster, at the behest of King Niall Caille. I am the last man alive of our delegation."

For a moment Máel Sechnaill just looked at the man and no one else dared say a word. Finally Máel spoke. "Did you bring the Crown of the Three Kingdoms?"

"We were charged by King Niall to bring the Crown to you. But we were attacked by the fin gall and it was stolen from us. The others...were butchered. Like sheep."

"You're lying," Máel Sechnaill said. "We caught and killed the fin gall who were waiting for you. And they did not have the Crown."

Cerball mac Gilla met Máel Sechnaill's eyes, defiant and unflinching. "No, Lord. King Niall suspected the fin gall would lie in wait on the road, so he sent us by sea. We were caught in a storm, and truly we thought the storm would be the death of us, when the Northmen attacked. We fought to the last man. The Northmen left me for dead, but God be praised I lived. My curragh came ashore at Barnageeragh Bay where these men found me." He nodded to the sheep herds who glanced up. Sheepishly.

There was silence again, and this time it was Brigit who broke it. She swept forward, took Cerball by the arm and lifted him to his feet. "You've done your duty well, Cerball mac Gilla," she said. She turned to the servants who had been helping Máel Sechnaill with his armor. "Take Lord Cerball to the guest chambers in the Royal house, see that he is fed and his wounds attended to. And see that the sheep herds are fed in the kitchen." To the sheep herds she added, "I'll see you are rewarded for your service."

The servants took their place on either side of Cerball mac Gilla and the little party shuffled out of the great hall. Máel Sechnaill said nothing. When they disappeared through the door, he turned and glared at Flann mac Conaing, who shifted nervously.

"How," Máel Sechnaill said at last, "could the fin gall have the Crown of the Three Kingdoms and I do not know it?" He spoke in a low growl, a sign that he was seriously angry. "Why do the Northmen seem to know more about the Crown than I do?"

"My Lord...I don't know. Morrigan has sent no word. She must have heard nothing, or else something has happened."

"Find out. You, personally. And quickly."

"Yes, Lord Máel," Flann said. He bowed and backed away, and when he was a safe distance from Máel Sechnaill, he turned and practically fled from the great hall.

"You'll not attack Leinster now?" Brigit had a way of making a statement sound half question, half order.

"We will await word from Flann." Máel Sechnaill looked his daughter in the eye, his expression as intimidating as he could make it. "And you will keep your nose out of men's affairs."

"Yes, father." She did not sound intimidated in the least.

Chapter Eleven

The unwise man
is awake all night,
worries over and again.
Hávamál

Ihe spear thrust did not kill Harald Thorgrimsson. He was born
of the stock of Thorgrim Night Wolf and Ornolf the Restless
and it would take more than one battle wound to bring him
down. But soon after, the fever set in, the silent murderer in the night. It
frightened Thorgrim far more than the gaping, bleeding wound to Harald's
shoulder. The wound was a physical rent to the body, it was what it was.
But the fever was brought by spirits he could not see, and did not know
how to fight.

They were held in a big room inside the stockade fort, a room used as
some sort of garrison eating hall, Thorgrim guessed, judging by its size and
by the heavy table that ran most of its length. No sooner had they been
captured on board *Red Dragon* than they were dragged to that place, Harald
shrieking with pain as they hauled him by his arms, Thorgrim, all but
unconscious, his head spinning, trying to fight back, his son's screams
worse than knife thrusts.

Magnus's soldiers had tossed them into the big room. The rest of the
Red Dragon men were already there.

Of the sixty-three men who had sailed with Ornolf the Restless into

Dubh-Linn, fifty-one remained. Two had managed to drink themselves to death on Magnus's free mead. Nine who had woken, as Thorgrim had, with spear points to their throats, had come up fighting. Between them they killed twelve of Magnus's men dead before they were hacked down. Four more had been tossed wounded into the prison.

The eating hall was not an ideal cell, since it had several windows as well as the door, but it was most likely the only single room big enough to hold them all.

For three days they festered in prison. Their circumstances were grim. The food was putrid and scarce. The wounded could do no more than suffer with what little care their fellows were able to provide. Two of them teetered at the gates of Valhalla, with no hope of a proper send off.

Ornolf the Restless spent most of the time raging, but with nothing fermented to drink his raging took on a decidedly morose and self-pitying tone, even if it lost nothing in volume. What their fate would be, they did not know. No one came to the prison, save for the thrall who brought their food.

But for all that, Thorgrim Ulfsson kept the men in good cheer. That was part of his genius, when the sun was up and the spirit of the wolf was not upon him.

On their fourth day as prisoners, Thorgrim climbed up onto the table. It was part of their daily routine now.

"I have a verse," he shouted, "about our great Battle of the Mead Hall." That was what, with grim irony, they had come to call the drunken night on which they had been betrayed.

"Let's hear it, Thorgrim!" shouted Snorri Half-Troll, and the others agreed. Nothing, Thorgrim understood, held the men together so well as a sense of shared history, and nothing gave them that sense better than verse, even ironic verse. It was as much a part of the Norsemen as fighting and farming.

Thorgrim spoke in the loud, clear voice of the skald.

> Bold Ornolf stood,
> more like god than man.
> And any drinking horn
> or woman come to hand
> so he boldly took them on
> until with heavy brow
> and penis limp
> he fell, as ever warrior in battle did.

The men were smiling now, their misery for the moment forgotten. They shouted approval. Thorgrim let them yell. It was a release for them, and it gave him a chance to think of what he would say next. Thorgrim generally made his verse up on the spot.

> And round about him came
> the eaters of the dead
> and feasted they on Ornolf's flesh
> and blood, thick with mead which
> still through his body ran
> until those very Valkyries
> fell drunk...

For ten more minutes Thorgrim extemporized his heroic verse until all the men were smiling and even Ornolf seemed somewhat amused. That would bolster them for a while. Their spirits were like a sinking ship, and Thorgrim held the only bucket. He bailed as much as he could, but he did not know how long he could hold out.

He climbed down from the table. Harald and the other wounded men were arranged in a far corner, made as comfortable as possible on cloaks and tunics offered up by the others. Thorgrim stopped by each man, asked how they were doing, offered some words of encouragement. Giant-Bjorn, a spear wound deep in his stomach, another in his chest, was beyond talking. Thorgrim put a hand on his pale skin, thinking he had finally passed on, but his flesh was warm still. Giant-Bjorn still hung on to life with a stubbornness that had always been his.

Thorgrim came at last to Harald, his face flushed red and beaded with sweat, he breathing raspy. Thorgrim's stomach twisted up and he clenched his teeth to keep his face from showing what his heart felt. His boy, his beloved boy.

Thorgrim tried to show no preference for Harald. He tried to treat all the men, all the wounded, the same. It was how Harald wanted it, nor was it right for a man to show favoritism to his son, when his son was one among many warriors.

There was another reason as well. Thorgrim did not want their captors, Magnus or Orm, to know that Harald was his son and Ornolf's grandson. They would use Harald to get to the leaders. Torture him, kill him in front of Thorgrim and Ornolf, whatever it took. And if they did that, Thorgrim genuinely did not know what would happen. It would not be good, in any event.

He knelt beside Harald, as he had with the others.

"How are you, boy?"

Harald opened his eyes. "I'm fine..." Thorgrim had warned him not to say "father" as long as they were prisoners.

Thorgrim nodded. The boy was not fine. The fever was eating him alive. Thorgrim picked up one of the charms he had arranged around the boy's bed, a small silver hammer of Thor, and rubbed it between his fingers. It was not helping, nor were his prayers to Odin or Thor. He would have made a sacrifice to the gods if there was anything in the prison to sacrifice. Thorgrim had considered offering himself up to the gods, finding something with which to cut his own throat, but the thought of leaving Harald and the others to Ornolf's leadership alone dissuaded him.

I know a hundred ways to kill a man, but nothing of saving one, Thorgrim goaded himself.

Something had to be done or Harald would die. Thorgrim rested his hand gently on Harald's arm. "You rest, boy. Sleep, that's the best medicine." Thorgrim did not know if that was true, but it was the only medicine he knew.

When Harald had closed his eyes and his breathing became more regular, Thorgrim unlaced his goatskin shoe and pulled it off. Hidden in pockets on the inside were six gold coins. He fished one out and pulled his shoe on again.

The eating hall was ringed with guards since the room itself was none too secure. Thorgrim stepped up to one of the windows, looked right and left. What he saw was not encouraging. Hard, pitiless men with swords, spears and shields.

He moved on to the next window and there he saw a likely candidate, a man whose face did not carry that edge of cruelty.

"Hey, there!" Thorgrim said in a loud whisper. "Hey!"

The guard turned and scowled, but there was less malice in the expression than the man had intended. "What?"

"Come here."

The guard glanced around. None of the others seemed to care. It was not the first time the prisoners had spoken to the guards, so the man approached.

"I have wounded men in here who have not been cared for," Thorgrim began. "I'm afraid for their lives."

The guard could not help but smile at that. "You should be afraid for all your lives, all of you Norwegian pirates."

"No doubt. But I still have to do what I can. Is there anyone in the longphort skilled with medicine?"

The guard frowned. Thorgrim held up the gold coin. The guard's eyes went a little wide, though he tried to control himself.

"This is all I have," Thorgrim said. "Bring someone who can help my men, and it's yours."

The guard nodded slowly. "There is someone," he said.

They came for the leaders before anyone came to help Harald. Later that day the door opened and Thorgrim looked up, hoping to see his guard leading an old crone, her basket of healing herbs on her arm. But instead he saw armed men barging in the door, with spears held ready, and they looked as if healing was the last thing they had in mind.

Thorgrim stood as the guards entered. Behind them came a big man, with the presence of command, and Thorgrim guessed this was the Dane, Orm, whom Magnus had mentioned. And behind him stood Magnus himself, and beside Magnus, the fat man whose finger Thorgrim had nearly broken.

"Forgive me," Orm said, arms spread in a magnanimous gesture, "I hope I am not interrupting anything important."

Thorgrim spit on the floor. "More important than talking to the likes of you." He looked past Orm, past the others, hoping to see some avenue of escape. But there were enough armed men beyond the door to make it impossible.

"I imagined you would think so," Orm said. "But still I must insist we talk." He turned to the men behind him. "Is this the man?"

The fat one, with a smug look on his face, nodded. "Yes, this is the man who was in command of the longship. The one who attacked me."

"Very well," Orm began but Magnus cut him off.

"Wait, my Lord." He looked Thorgrim in the eye and Thorgrim met his gaze. "This man is not in command. He is second. That man," Magnus pointed to Ornolf, who was slumped on the bench beside the table, "is the jarl Ornolf, and he is in command."

"And you told me Ornolf is an old fool, and this Thorgrim is the clever one," Orm said.

"Exactly," said Magnus. "And I would rather try to get information from a fool than a clever man."

That seemed to stir Ornolf "Fool?" he roared, getting to his feet. "Give me my sword and we will see who the fool is!"

Orm ignored the request. Instead, he nodded toward Ornolf, and the guards grabbed the jarl up by the arms and half pushed and half dragged him toward the door.

"I'll rip your lungs out, all of you, you bastards!" Ornolf shouted as he was taken from the room.

Orm stepped up to Thorgrim so their faces were just inches apart. For a moment he said nothing, just seemed to study Thorgrim's face, and Thorgrim stared back.

"We'll see what your jarl has to say," Orm said at last, "and then you and I will talk." He turned and stepped out of the room. One of the guards slammed the door and Thorgrim stood looking at the rough wood.

He had not counted on this. He had always imagined they would take him, but they had taken Ornolf instead.

What will Ornolf tell them? Thorgrim wondered. Would he tell Orm everything? And if he did, what reason would there be then to let any of them live?

Chapter Twelve

*Often it's best
for the unwise man
to sit in silence.*
Hávamál

Ornolf the Restless lay in a great fat heap on the floor. After a
moment he managed to push himself up on his arms and
glare with the one eye that would still open at the Danes who
surrounded him. He spit a glob of bloody mucus on the floor.

"You are all a lot of sons of whores... I'll rip your lungs out, you
bastards..." he gasped through split and bleeding lips. And then Orm kicked
him in the side of the head and he went down again.

Magnus was impressed. The old man had taken hours of this abuse,
alternately worked over by himself and Orm and the two guards. And for
all that he had given away practically nothing, and his defiance had not
wavered a bit.

That last kick knocked him out cold, and for a moment Orm stood
panting and looking down at his motionless form.

"Is he dead?" Magnus asked.

Orm nudged him with his foot. Ornolf groaned a bit.

"Water, here," Orm said and one of the guards stepped up with a
bucket, dashed it in Ornolf's face. The jarl opened his eyes. Orm crouched

down and grabbed him by his long gray and red hair.

"Are you part of a Norwegian fleet? Olaf the White's fleet?" Orm asked. He had asked it so often that Magnus had lost count. He was sick of hearing the question. Ornolf, apparently, was sick of denying it.

"Yes, we're part of Olaf's fleet! A thousand longships! We're going to tie you down and take turns buggering you to death, you son of a whore!" He voice was surprisingly strong for someone in as much pain as he must be in.

Orm let go of the hair and Ornolf's head hit the floor. Magnus folded his arms and regarded the old man. He had denied being a part of any fleet and Magnus, for one, believed him. Orm probably did too, but he was too afraid of Norwegian vengeance to let it go at that. Besides, he enjoyed this sort of questioning.

Orm kicked Ornolf in the stomach and elicited another groan. "By Thor, I'll have you disemboweled and burned at the stake for piracy, raiding a Danish ship, if you don't tell me the truth."

It was not an idle threat, Magnus knew. He had seen Orm do it to more than a few men and he would probably do it to Ornolf. But the punishment would have nothing to do with their raiding the Danish trader. No one cared about that. It would be to make Ornolf, or his men, admit to being part of a Norwegian fleet, or, barring that, to make sure that they never would be.

Magnus had his own interest in the interrogation. The Crown of the Three Kingdoms. It had not occurred to Orm that these men might have found the curragh when Magnus could not, but it had occurred to Magnus, and Ornolf's near slip of the tongue had all but confirmed it in Magnus's mind.

Magnus had carried out a systematic search of the longship, in the early hours, while Asbjorn still slept and Orm was busy with other matters. Under the guise of searching for some evidence of treachery, he and his men all but tore the ship apart. Every deck plank was ripped up, every dark corner explored. They found discarded bones, a few coins, a little statue of Thor that had fallen down behind the afterdeck. But they found no crown.

Orm crouched down and looked closely at the bleeding Ornolf. He straightened. "This one is useless. We'll get no more out of him."

"Leave him for me," Magus said. "I'll let him rest a bit, and then try again."

Orm turned his eyes from Ornolf to Magnus. Orm, Magnus knew, saw treachery everywhere. Hardly a surprise. There was treachery everywhere.

"What more do you think you'll get out of him?"

Magnus shrugged. "I'll know when I get it out of him."

Orm wavered, his near complete distrust of Magnus wrestling with his desire to get some genuine information out of the fat jarl.

"Very well," Orm said at last. "Let me know if this pig says anything of interest." And with that he marched quickly out of the room.

Magnus watched him go, then took a seat, relaxing as he waited for Ornolf to regain a little strength. The Crown of the Three Kingdoms represented as great a threat to Orm's rule as any Norwegian fleet. It was why Orm was so desperate to get it. And why, if he discovered its whereabouts, Magnus intended to keep it to himself.

It was past dark, and the spirit of the wolf had Thorgrim in its teeth, when the door opened.

Thorgrim was leaning against the back wall, near where Harald lay tossing and sweating. The rest of the men had moved away, leaving open ground between themselves and their irritable second in command.

At the sound of the creaking door Thorgrim looked up. They had returned Ornolf a few hours before, beaten worse than Thorgrim had ever seen him beaten before, and Thorgrim had seen Ornolf the Restless pretty well thrashed. He imagined they were coming for him now. He was not feeling very cooperative.

A guard came in first, sword in his right hand, a guttering seal-oil lamp in his left. Some of the sleeping men stirred and grunted as the feeble light spread around the room. Thorgrim recognized the man to whom he had offered gold. The guard stepped aside and a woman came in behind him, all but lost under a cloak and hood, and Thorgrim leapt to his feet.

"I've brought a healer," the guard said when Thorgrim approached. He shut the door behind him. He looked nervous. Thorgrim was not sure if he was more afraid of the prisoners inside or his fellow guards out.

Thorgrim took the lamp and despite a near overwhelming urge to drive the sharp end of the lamp's base through the man's heart, handed him the gold coin he had promised, and then a second. "Here is another, which one of my men offered," Thorgrim said with forced control. "You have our thanks."

The guard nodded and he looked pleased despite the concern on his face and Thorgrim was glad, because here was a man he might need again. "This thrall's safety is in your hands," the guard said and with that he was gone through the door.

Thorgrim turned to the healer as she reached up and pulled back the hood of her cape. Thorgrim had expected a stooped and wrinkled old crone - among the Norse such women were generally the healers - but this woman was not. She was young, not much beyond twenty, Thorgrim guessed, and pretty, despite being a bit on the thin side with somewhat overly large eyes.

She looked at him and there was a touch of defiance in her expression, and had she been a man that might have caused trouble with Thorgrim in his present mood. But a woman, and moreover a woman who might heal Harald, was different.

"My name is Morrigan," the woman said. "I am Orm's slave."

"You are not a Dane," Thorgrim observed. She spoke the Norse tongue, but her accent was otherwise.

"No. I am Irish."

"How do you come to speak our language?"

"When my brother and I were young, we lived among you Norsemen in Jelling. And now I am a slave to the Norsemen. First slave to the fin gall, and now to Orm." She did not try to hide the bitterness there. Thorgrim knew that the Irish, generally, made good, docile thralls. But apparently not this one.

"Do you come here by Orm's leave?" Thorgrim asked.

Morrigan smiled. "Certainly not. He'll beat me severely if he finds me out."

Thorgrim felt the spirit of the wolf begin to dissipate like morning fog. There was something about the thrall that affected him, and it gave him hope for her powers as a healer.

"My name is Thorgrim Ulfsson. You'll be rewarded for your risk," Thorgrim assured her. "Now, come."

He led her over to the back wall where the wounded men were lying on their piles of cloaks. Olvir Yellowbeard was the first of them, with a deep gash that ran from his shoulder across his chest and stomach. The wound, undressed, gaped open like an ugly trench dug in white earth.

Morrigan set down her large basket and peered close at the wound, sniffing and probing while Thorgrim held the lamp close. Olvir, asleep, shifted and groaned.

"The rot is setting into this wound, but it may not be too late," Morrigan said soft, and Thorgrim did not know if she was talking to him or herself. He made no reply.

Morrigan pulled a handful of downy material from her basket. "Cobwebs," she said, as if she thought Thorgrim did not trust her. Gently she packed the soft bundle of webs on Olvir's wound. Olvir's eyes opened wide in surprise and he made to sit up, but Thorgrim's hand held him down.

"Don't move, Olvir Yellowbeard," Thorgrim said. "This thrall is a healer."

Olvir groaned and lay still again. With sure hands Morrigan pulled a length of linen cloth from the basket, and a small jar filled with an unctuous paste. She rubbed the paste on the cloth and wrapped it around Olvir's wound.

"That is a yarrow poultice. That's all I can do for now," she said. "We must wait and see how it goes."

Thorgrim nodded. They moved on to the next man and she treated his wounds in a similar manner, and then the next. "You should have sent for me right off," Morrigan scolded. "The medicine is not as powerful when the wounds are old."

Thorgrim nodded, said nothing.

They came next to Giant-Bjorn. Morrigan looked at him close, probing the wounds, looking close in the lantern's light. She pulled out another small jar, and with Thorgrim's help tipped some of the contents into Giant-Bjorn's mouth. "Skullcap will help him sleep. There is nothing I can do for this one," she said and they moved on.

As the minutes passed into the first hour Thorgrim's anxiety rose like the tide. He wanted Morrigan to treat Harald before her presence was discovered. He wanted her to ignore all of them and concentrate her efforts on his son, but he dared not say it, or give any indication that Harald meant anything more to him than any of the others. He did not know what her relationship with Orm was, or what information she might be willing to barter with her master for some consideration.

Ornolf the Restless was next, his face battered, his clothes torn, bruises and cuts visible through the rent cloth. Morrigan looked him over, looked up at Thorgrim. "These injuries are new," she said.

"Orm and Magnus had some questions they asked of him."

Morrigan nodded. "I thought I recognized Orm's hand. Why him?"

"He is the jarl. He is our leader."

Morrigan looked up at Thorgrim. "You are not the leader here?"

"I am Ornolf's hirdman. I am the second."

Morrigan nodded and pulled a small jar from the basket. "This is shepherd's purse, for the bleeding." As she talked she mixed the dried herb with water in a mug. "We must get him to drink it."

Thorgrim helped Morrigan lift Ornolf to a sitting position. They held the mug to his lips, and half conscious, Ornolf drank it down, drinking being a reflexive action for him.

They laid Ornolf down again and Morrigan treated his wounds with cobwebs and yarrow. She gave him a drink from another jar she said was filled with yarrow mead, and Thorgrim had to physically pull it from Ornolf's hands. "The only thing for him is rest, and that will help him sleep," Morrigan said. "He will live, I think, unless Orm has more questions for him. Or burns him alive at the stake."

Thorgrim nodded. "Here, see to this one. I think he is in a bad way," he said, nodding to Harald and trying to sound as disinterested as he could.

Morrigan looked up at Thorgrim, looked him in the eyes, which he realized she had not done before. "Very well," she said and shuffled over to where Harald lay, kneeling beside him.

"He's just a boy," she said, brushing the sweat-drenched hair off his forehead.

"Man enough to go a-viking," Thorgrim said.

Morrigan looked up, and there was a trace of disgust on her face. She picked up the silver hammer of Thor. "What's this?"

"Thor's hammer. A way of asking for the god's help."

"No wonder the fever has hold of him." She pushed the hammer into Thorgrim's hands, collected up the other charms, the little statue of Odin on his eight-legged horse Sleipnir, a tiny silver Valkyrie, and handed them all to Thorgrim. "Keep those away from the boy," she said. She reached up to her neck and pulled a necklace off and put it around Harald's neck. A tiny silver cross with the dying God Christ rested on Harald's chest.

Morrigan made the gesture Thorgrim had seen Christians make, touching her forehead, her stomach and both shoulders. She muttered something over Harald, some incantation, Thorgrim imagined. He was not comfortable with the Christian magic. At another time he might have told her to stop. But he was desperate now, and his own gods had done nothing to help.

When she was done, she began to probe Harald's wounds, muttering to herself, and Thorgrim could not help but notice she treated the young man with more attention and concern than she had the others. She carefully washed and dressed his wounds with cobwebs and yarrow poultice, then mixed up some herbs with water. "False indigo, it will help with the fever," she said as she mixed it. Together, they made Harald drink.

"I'll leave some of this with you. See the guards don't find it. Give it to him thrice a day, morning, afternoon and night."

Thorgrim nodded. In Morrigan's presence he seemed unable to give any other response.

Morrigan stood. "I'm done. I'll try to return tomorrow."

Thorgrim walked with her to the door. He dug in the purse that hung from his belt, extracted one of the gold coins he had earlier removed from his shoe. "Here." He handed her the coin. "You have my thanks."

Morrigan took the coin and looked at it, and her expression was one of faint amusement. "Payment for healing fin gall. Here's something I never thought I would see." She pocketed the coin, took the lamp and blew out the flame and was gone.

Thorgrim stood alone in the dark. The smell of Morrigan persisted, even through the smell of the unwashed men and the burning seal oil.

He felt for the first time since his and Harald's capture some small hint of hope that his son might live. It was a good feeling, a buoyant feeling, and almost the instant he felt it, it was quashed by the reality of their situation.

Harald might live...to what end?

Magnus and Orm would not let them go. It would be more

questioning, and then the stake. Harald would be better off dying delirious with the fever than living to see what punishment Orm and Magnus had in mind.

Chapter Thirteen

"It is the end of the world when peasants like these
rise up against noble families."

Insult made by the king of Tara
to his enemies

Morrigan could feel the straw from the mattress jabbing her in the back like a dozen tiny knives. Orm was on top of her, and his weight made it hard for her to breathe. Her knee banged against the wattle and daub wall with each of Orm's thrusts.

Her eyes were open and she was staring at the ceiling. The rough beams and the texture of the thatch were just visible in the growing light of dawn. Once, in that circumstance, her mind would have been many miles away, off to some fine place where she was not being raped by the man who owned her. But not now.

Now her mind was present, very much in the moment. She considered where Orm's belt lay at the side of the bed, how far the reach to the pommel of his silver-hilt dagger. Her eyes saw the cob webs on the roof overhead but her mind saw her hand softly drawing the dagger from the belt and driving it between Orm's ribs, saw him rear back in surprised agony as she rolled from under him, drawing the knife and plunging it in again.

Then she saw the guards bursting in the door, swords drawn, finding her panting, knife in hand, and soaked in Orm's blood. The vision of Orm, wide-eyed and wool-white in death, made her happy, but it was followed up always with the vision of herself hanged, drawn and quartered, burned at the stake. No crime would be more ruthlessly punished than the murder of a master by a slave. Such things were to be discouraged.

So until the moment was right, until Morrigan could have her vengeance and live to celebrate it, she would suffer the slave's ultimate humiliation.

At last Orm finished with a grunt, lay still for a moment, nearly crushing the air from Morrigan's thin body. Then he stood.

"The mead has gone off. See that there is fresh," he said as he stepped out of the room, fastening his trousers as he went.

Morrigan did not move. She lay on the bed and let her anger settle. She reminded herself of why she was there. At first that thought had been enough to get her through this horror, but it was not enough any more. Like her Lord and Savior, at the moment when her trials were at their worst, she found herself questioning the reason for it all.

At last she climbed off the low bed and straightened her clothes. She could feel Orm's semen running down her thigh and she stepped over to the basin and washed herself. She had long ago decided that if she ever found herself carrying Orm's child, she would kill the dubh gall and herself as well.

The main room of the house was still dark and chill. Morrigan stirred up the coals in the hearth in the center of the room, adding twigs and peat until the fire was burning again. If she let it go out entirely, Orm would beat her. The dubh gall hated the dark.

Outside she could hear the men of the fortress moving around, the guards coming off their night watch, the first work of the day commencing. She heard a knock on the door.

Morrigan straightened and turned and regarded the door for a moment. It was an odd thing, to have someone knocking at such an hour, with Orm already gone. Sometimes, if something important was happening, word was brought to her by one of the many Irish slaves in town, and she wondered if this was such a circumstance. She crossed the room and opened the door.

There was a sheep herd there, a young man and he looked nervous.

"Yes?" Morrigan asked. She spoke her native Celt. The boy was no fin gall.

"Are you Morrigan?" the sheep herd asked. "Slave of Orm?"

"Yes."

The sheep herd shifted nervously. "My master bids me tell you he has fine sheep to sell, for the royal household, if you would look."

"Tell your master no. The fin gall eat pigs."

"My master bids me tell you..." the sheep herd thought for a moment for the words, "that these sheep come from the high hills of Tara and begs you will see them yourself."

Tara... The young man's master was no sheep herd, of that Morrigan was certain. She looked around, suddenly afraid they were being watched, but the men in the stockade, the guards, soldiers and workmen, had not the least interest in what a thrall and a sheep herd might be discussing. Even the dozen men guarding the big room where the Norwegians were held seemed distracted and bored. And even if they were not, there was not a one of them who spoke the Celtic language.

"What is your name, boy?" Morrigan asked.

"Donnel."

"Very well, Donnel. Wait here and I will be right with you."

Morrigan hurried into the house, found her shawl and wrapped it around her shoulders, picked up her basket. The nightmare of the dawn, which generally would have haunted her for hours, was forgotten. She hurried out the door and followed after Donnel, who seemed quite eager to be out of the stockade and beyond the immediate grasp of the fin gall warriors.

They walked down the plank road, Donnel a step ahead, and into the crowded market where other Irish women - some slaves, some wives - and a smattering of Norse women bargained for food and cloth and housewares. A dozen bleating sheep were held inside a wood-fence pen, and by the gate stood two men, two sheep herds. One younger then Donnel, one much older. One a real sheep herd, the other not.

Morrigan stepped up to the pen and looked at the animals as if she had some interest in them. She spoke, soft and in Gaelic.

"Brother, why have you come?"

Flann mac Conaing looked casually around before he spoke. The rough wool hood of his cloak framed his face and his gray and white beard. "The abbot of Glendalough decreed that the Crown of the Three Kingdoms should be given to King Máel Sechnaill mac Ruanaid."

Morrigan gave a little gasp and looked up quick, met her brother's eyes. "At last..." she said.

Flann nodded. "It was put to Niall Caille to see it delivered to Tara, but it never arrived. My Lord Máel was certain Niall Caille meant to keep the Crown for himself. He was readying his army to go south when a messenger arrived. These young men," Flann nodded toward the sheep herds, who were trying to look inconspicuous, "brought him.

"Apparently, Niall thought it safer to send the Crown by ship. He outfitted a curragh, manned it with his most trusted noblemen and sent it north. The messenger was one of the noblemen, the only one left alive. The curragh was taken by Norsemen."

Morrigan shook her head. "Orm does not have it," she said. "It is not in Dubh-Linn."

For a moment Flann said nothing. He prodded the sheep with his staff, trying to look like a sheep herd. "Máel Sechnaill was not pleased that this should happen, and us with no word from you."

Morrigan scowled. She could taste the fury like bitter fruit in her mouth. "I suffer here - suffer like Máel Sechnaill could never know - so that he might have word of what the fin gall are about. If he hasn't heard from me about the Crown of the Three Kingdoms then that is because the Crown is not here."

Flann nodded his head. "It's what I told My Lord Máel. Perhaps it was taken by Norsemen who were not from Dubh-Linn."

"Perhaps..." It was not possible that something so important as the taking of the Crown could have escaped her notice. Very little happened in Dubh-Linn that she did not know about.

"There has been only one longship to leave in the past week, and that was Magnus Magnusson, who must have been sent to find the crown, but he failed. Other than that...." She stopped.

"What?"

"Of course..." Morrigan said, mostly to herself, as the odd events of the week suddenly became clear. "Thorgrim..."

Morrigan did not know where the Crown was, but she was certain now that she knew who did.

It was past midnight when they came for Thorgrim, and that was a bad time to do so. He was hunched in a corner of the big room, far from where Harald lay moaning. He was asleep, and in his dreams he was running with the pack. The taste of blood was in his mouth, the red tints of fury in his eyes.

They grabbed him hard by the arms and yanked him to his feet. Still half lost in his dream world, he swung his elbow around and crashed it into the jaw of one of the men who had come for him. His left fist shot out at another as he groped for a sword that was not there.

But Magnus's men were ready for a fight, and despite such shocking ferocity from a man who was not even entirely awake, they managed to pin his arms behind him and get a braided leather cord around his neck, pulling it taut until his breathing became raspy and desperate. His head was swimming with rage and a lack of air. His wrists were held behind his back and powerful hands passed lashings around them.

Magnus stood in front of him, a few feet beyond arm's reach. He held a lamp. The yellow light of the flame fell on his rich red tunic and left most of his face in deep shadow. Behind him, another four men were tying the wrists of Kotkel the Fierce, who fought like a bear. Another dozen spearmen held the rest of Ornolf's men at bay.

"Bring them," Magnus said when Thorgrim and Kotkel were at last bound and choked until the fight was out of them. He led the way out of the big room. The soldiers shoved Thorgrim and Kotkel after him and behind them the rest of the guards withdrew. And through his rage Thorgrim had presence of mind enough to thank the gods that they had not taken Harald.

Magnus led them to a room somewhere in the fortress, a small room lit with a fire in the hearth that made the place look cheery. The men behind Thorgrim grabbed him by the shoulders and shoved him toward the wall. He stumbled and fell hard, his hands tied tight behind his back.

He rolled over and looked up. The guards made a rope fast to Kotkel's wrists which were bound behind his back, then tossed the other end over the low rafters of the roof. Three men hauled away. Kotkel was lifted screaming and cursing off his feet.

Magnus stood over Thorgrim. "Where is the Crown?" he asked.

Thorgrim looked at him for a long time before he spoke. Kotkel's cries of agony had turned into a stream of curses heaped on the Danes.

"Ask Kotkel," Thorgrim said, nodding toward the man hanging from the rope. "He seems more talkative than me."

"Perhaps. And perhaps you'll be moved to talk. To end the suffering of one of your men."

"Perhaps not," Thorgrim said.

Magnus turned and struck Kotkel in the small of the back with the flat of his sword. Kotkel arched his back and shouted with the pain.

Thorgrim clenched his teeth. He liked Kotkel well enough, but not enough to give in to Magnus for Kotkel's sake. There were few in this world he cared for that much, and when the spirit of the wolf was on him, he would not be moved by pity, only rage.

Nor did Thorgrim believe Magnus would leave them alive, no matter what he told him.

"Unn, get the iron," Magnus said and one of his men drew a glowing hot iron from the fire, held it wavering in front of Kotkel's face.

"The Crown means nothing to you," Magnus said. "A trinket. Save your man's life and yours as well and tell me where it is. I'll even pay you for it."

Thorgrim growled and struggled into a kneeling position. His mind moved in and out of reasoned thought as the rage took hold. "What crown, you whore's son?"

Magnus turned to Kotkel. "Where is the crown?"

"I don't know of any crown, you son of a bitch!" Kotkel gasped. Magnus nodded and Unn applied the hot iron to Kotkel's face. The Viking shrieked, a horrible sound. The room filled with the smell of searing flesh and Thorgrim launched himself off the floor.

From his kneeling stance he pushed off and all but flew across the room, just as iron touched flesh and the sound of Kotkel's agony masked every other sound. Thorgrim slammed into Magnus low on his back and knocking him into Unn, who held the iron. The three of them went down in a heap, but Thorgrim was up in a flash, snarling, lashing out with his feet. He caught Magnus in the jaw as the Dane tried to untangle himself, slammed his foot down on Unn's leg, felt the bones break underfoot as Unn struggled to regain his feet.

Unn shrieked in pain, louder even then Kotkel. Magnus was half on his feet when Thorgrim lashed out again. Magus rolled out of the way of the kick, rolled right over the hot iron, came to his feet with his tunic on fire.

"You bastard!" Magnus shouted as he beat at the cloth. Thorgrim advanced on him again but now one of the other guards came forward, a big fist swinging around in an arc. Thorgrim ducked the blow, but with his hands bound up he could do no more, and the guard caught him with an uppercut from his right hand that lifted him from his feet and tossed him back on the packed dirt floor.

Thorgrim's fight was over, with his hands tied behind his back, and his one shot at surprise spent. He spit a curse at Magnus, braced himself as Magnus delivered a jarring kick to his head. There was nothing more that he could do, beyond enduring the pain and twisting away as best he could from the direct impact of the blows. And soon he was too battered to even do that.

Magnus worked on him and the other guards worked on him, and then they paused and made him watch as they went after Kotkel, and that was the worst. Certainly Kotkel's life wasn't high on Thorgrim's list of importance, still, Kotkel was his man, and to watch him twist in agony as the hot iron was applied, as his legs were broken under him, was worse than the pain of the beating he was enduring.

After a time they left Kotkel and returned to Thorgrim. They worked him until he passed out and then they doused him with water. When he was sufficiently awake they forced him to watch as they disemboweled Kotkel the Fierce, who screamed curses on the heads of the Danes until that last bit of life ran out of him and he hung limp over a pile of his own entrails. Then they turned on Thorgrim again.

Thorgrim had little doubt that he would be sharing Kotkel's fate, and it was not long before he found himself wishing they would just get on with it. Consciousness was becoming more and more elusive - Thorgrim was not sure if he was among men or wolves now, if the blood he tasted in his mouth was his or that of something he had taken down. And just before he moved at last from the world of the fortress and the Danes to that of the woods and the pack, he heard Magnus say, "Enough. I don't want him dead. Let him recover and we'll talk to him again."

Chapter Fourteen

Beware
of befriending
an enemy's friend.
Hávamál

I t was nearly a full day before Thorgrim was conscious again, and
two more days before he was able to stand, and even that seemed
incredible to Morrigan.

As Orm's slave, and the only healer in the Viking longphort of Dubh-
Linn, she had seen any number of men who had endured severe beatings.
Few had been beaten like Thorgrim and lived. None had recovered as
quickly.

She came three times each day to treat the prisoners and she no longer
had to be secretive about it. Magnus did not want Thorgrim dead, and he
convinced Orm that the Norwegian should be kept alive. Orm in turn
ordered Morrigan to care for the men. It was an irony that Morrigan could
appreciate.

She went to the market to buy the herbs she needed to restore the
men's health, to make the captives strong enough to endure further
beatings. The sheep-herds, Donnel and Patrick and Flann mac Conaing,
had sold nearly all of their sheep, but they remained in hopes of selling the
last few. Anyone watching might have wondered why Morrigan had such an

insatiable interest in sheep which she did not intend to buy. But no one was watching.

"Magnus has said nothing about the Crown, but I'm sure he thinks Thorgrim knows where it is," she said in her soft Gaelic. She and Flann were leaning on the pen, looking at the sheep. Donnel and Patrick lurked about, keeping their eyes open for anyone taking an interest in Morrigan, but no one was.

"Do you think this Thorgrim has the Crown?"

"I don't. If he had it, Magnus would have found it, and if he had he would certainly have killed Thorgrim by now. But I do think Thorgrim knows where it is."

"Magnus has said nothing to Orm?"

"No. He's playing some game. Perhaps he intends to keep the Crown himself. Or ransom it."

"These fin gall are bastards. They won't keep faith even with one another."

The Irish, of course, were no better, raiding one another's lands, enslaving fellow Irishmen, sacking the churches and monasteries of their own Christian faith. But Morrigan did not bother pointing out the hypocrisy of her brother's outrage. There were more immediate concerns.

"Thorgrim is a strong one, as strong as any man I have seen. I reckon he'll be ready soon."

"We have little time. The danger grows with every minute. If Magnus or Orm beat us to the Crown, we are lost."

"Tonight, then," Morrigan said.

"Will he be ready?"

"Tonight."

It was well past dark when Morrigan filled her basket and pulled her cloak over her shoulders. She moved to the door, trying to be quiet. She did not know if Orm was asleep. She did not want to wake him if he was, and did not want to speak to him if he was not.

She had her hand on the latch when the door to the sleeping room opened. "Where are you going?" Orm demanded.

Morrigan turned to him, but kept her head down, her eyes averted.

"I am going to tend to the prisoners, my lord."

Orm grunted and crossed the room until he loomed over her. She thought that perhaps he was going to take her, right then, and she braced herself, but the Dane had other things on his mind.

"Why do you think Magnus is so concerned with the lives of a few Norwegians?"

"I'm sure I don't know, my lord. Except that he thinks they may have knowledge that would be useful to you."

Orm grunted again. It was a sound that was hard to interpret. "If you hear anything, you let me know."

"Yes, my lord."

"And don't be all night with the prisoners. A waste of time, healing dead men."

"Yes, my lord."

Orm gave one last grunt, then turned and walked back to the sleeping room. Morrigan stared at his back, envisioned the dagger plunging in, then opened the door and stepped out into the dark. The little fortress was quiet. The guards at the gate and around the Norwegians' cell stood lethargic and bored. A few windows glowed with lamp light. Even the usual din from the mead hall farther down the plank road was less impressive than usual.

The night was quiet and subdued, and that was good. It meant the dubh gall were not as alert as they might be. Morrigan brushed the cowl off her head, turned her face up to the sky. She felt the first drops of rain from the clouds that had been building all morning. That was even better.

She crossed the compound to the dining hall where the prisoners were kept. She was a familiar sight to the guards, even more so since she no longer had to be clandestine about her visits.

One of the guards leaned against the doorjamb, his spear propped up against the wall. He straightened as she approached and stepped over to her.

"Good evening, Morrigan."

"Good evening."

The guard held out his hand and Morrigan handed him the basket, a ritual they repeated three times a day. The guard peered into the basket, shuffled the linens and cobwebs and bottles around, feeling for any weapons hidden among the strange potions. He handed the basket back to Morrigan, nodded for her to enter.

She opened the door and stepped inside. As usual, the room was black save for the light of a single oil lantern that burned on the table. Morrigan looked around at the fifty or so men within.

Thorgrim was hunched against a wall in the far corner and Morrigan wondered why he was always sequestered away from the other men whenever she came after dark. He looked over as the door opened. Their eyes met and he stood. Moving was painful for him, she could see that, but still his motion was smooth and strong.

Ornolf was up as well, sitting at the table, having mostly recovered from his beating. Morrigan could only marvel at the strength and endurance of the Northmen.

Thorgrim took up the lamp and accompanied Morrigan over to her first patient. It was their routine now. She had tried to look after Thorgrim first, right after his encounter with Magnus, but he would not stand for it.

Olvir Yellowbeard's wound was mending nicely, and the yarrow had killed the rot before the rot killed Olvir Yellowbeard. The one called Giant-Bjorn was still alive, how, Morrigan did not know. In fact, she was starting to think he might live, and she was happy to think her healing arts might have had something to do with it, but she knew in truth it was mostly the Viking's inhuman strength.

There were fewer patients now. Ornolf needed no further care, though she gave him herbal wine and yarrow mead out of kindness. Two others were also healed enough to require no treatment.

"And this one?" Thorgrim nodded to the boy near the corner. They knelt beside him. He was still wet with sweat and restless, his face flushed.

"The fever still has him."

"I see," Thorgrim said. There was a feigned disinterest in his voice, and it did not fool Morrigan. As she treated the boy, she could not help but see how much his looks favored Thorgrim. They were not built the same - the boy was more broad and stout - but around the eyes and the mouth there was a great similarity. And the nose.

"What is his name?"

"Harald." Thorgrim was straining to keep any feeling from his words. Morrigan could hear it in his voice.

"Harald is still in danger. But he is strong, like all you fin gall, and he is young, which is in his favor." She pulled a bottle of yarrow mead from her basket. "Help me."

Thorgrim shuffled closer and held Harald's head up as Morrigan tipped the bottle to his lips. She had never said a word to young Harald, he had been delirious or unconscious every moment she had known him, but still she had taken a liking to the young man. There was something honest about his face, a lack of cunning that she found refreshing. It would take young men like this, fin gall who might accept the love of Christ, to bring the Viking slaughter to an end.

"Good." They eased Harald's head back onto the blankets. Morrigan looked around the room. Everything ten feet or more beyond the flame of the lamp was lost in darkness. There were no guards. They did not like to be in among so many of their enemies.

"Come here, let me look at you," she said to Thorgrim and Thorgrim came over to her, kneeling beside her. Morrigan held the lamp close as she examined Thorgrim's various bruises and wounds. She poked at a wicked laceration along his arm. "Mending nicely," she said.

She emptied the contents of her basket and made up a yarrow poultice and wrapped it around his arm. She opened the basket's false bottom and with a nod told Thorgrim to look. The dozen daggers hidden there gleamed in the flame of the lamp.

Thorgrim looked down at them, then up at Morrigan. He said nothing.

"Orm will kill you all if you don't escape," Morrigan said, breathing the words. "I can do no more for you than this."

"We need no more than that," Thorgrim said, nodding to the weapons. "But why are you doing this? There is nothing you Irish love more than to see us Norsemen kill each other."

"I have healed your men. I don't want to see them killed. Besides, I'm a Christian. I can't stand by as innocent men are butchered."

Thorgrim smiled, a thing Morrigan had rarely seen, and she knew her words would not fool this one.

"You must think I'm a child, like Harald," Thorgrim said. "Since when do you look on any of us Vikings as 'innocent men'?"

They heard a grunt, like an animal waking up, and the sound of goatskin shoes on the hard-packed floor. Ornolf the Restless came lumbering over, and with some effort knelt beside Morrigan.

"What's all this talk?" he asked. "Is it about Harald?"

Morrigan studied his face. Ornolf had expressed no concern over any of the others. Why is the jarl Ornolf concerned about young Harald?

"Morrigan has brought us these," Thorgrim said, nodding toward the basket. Ornolf leaned over and looked down and his face brightened like the sun breaking through clouds.

"Sweet Odin!" he said, though he had sense enough to speak no louder than a whisper. "We'll butcher them all!"

"I would know why she brings us this gift," Thorgrim said. Morrigan could see his mood darkening.

"Why?" Ornolf said, louder than Morrigan thought was prudent. "Who gives a damn why?"

"Because it might be a trap."

"Trap? Ha!" Ornolf said. "That bastard Orm is going to string us up and pull our guts out with a hook! Who cares if it's a trap?"

Thorgrim scowled. Morrigan said nothing. But they both knew that Ornolf had hit on the truth of the thing. The Norwegians were dead men, and they faced the worst kind or death, bound up like swine and horribly butchered for the amusement of the Danes. She offered them a chance to escape, or barring that, the chance to die with weapons in their hands. There was no need for debate.

"You must go tonight," Morrigan said.

"We go tonight," Ornolf assured her.

Chapter Fifteen

One may know your secret
never a second.
If three, a thousand will know.
Hávamál

Thorgrim Night Wolf pressed one hand against the thatch of the ceiling to steady himself and worked the blade of the dagger into the dried reeds. He was standing on the back of Skeggi Kalfsson, who was on hands and knees on the table. Skeggi's back was so broad and solid that Thorgrim might as well have been standing on the table itself.

Thorgrim slashed sideways. The thatch gave way before the razor edge of the knife, falling like soft rain on the table and Skeggi below.

"Another," Thorgrim said softly and Snorri Half-troll handed him a new knife as the edge on the old one grew dull. Thorgrim worked at the thatch as quiet as he could, though even he could barely hear the sound of the blade over the beating of the rain that had begun to fall.

More thatch fell and Thorgrim could feel rainwater seeping thought the remaining layers. "Put the lamp out," he whispered and someone snuffed out the flame. Thorgrim sliced away at the remaining reeds and they fell away and he smelled the fresh night air and felt the cool rain on his face.

He tapped on Skeggi's back with his toe. Slowly Skeggi raised himself to his knees as Thorgrim stepped onto his shoulders, then Skeggi pushed himself to his feet, easing Thorgrim up and out the hole he had just cut in the roof.

It was raining hard and the thatch was slick. Thorgrim thrust his knife in among the reeds and used it as a hand-hold to keep from sliding off, and when he knew he was secure he looked around.

There were always half a dozen guards encircling the dining hall, but he could seen none of them now. They were huddled under the eaves of the roof, he guessed, seeking what shelter they could find. The fortress gate was barely visible through the night and the rain. There were guards there as well, Thorgrim was certain of it, but he could not see them either.

He rolled on his stomach, his hand still gripping his knife, the rain beating hard on his tunic and head, running in rivulets through his beard. He put his head down into the hole he had cut. "Come on," whispered.

Snorri Half-troll's head appeared through the hole and he was lifted up on Skeggi's strong back. He climbed swiftly onto the roof, scampering away, driving his knife into the thatch as he moved, as if trying to murder the prison itself. One after another the men came through the hole until there were six in all, half a dozen gleaming daggers, the other six held in ready in the room below.

The men spread themselves along the roof and then the little burst of movement was over and it was still again, the rain driving down hard on the longphort of Dubh-Linn, as if holding the town under its palm.

Thorgrim looked around. He clenched the hilt of the dagger in his hand, felt every muscle taut and ready. The lingering pain from his beating was gone, those places on his body that had been tender and sore were burning hot and pulsing with energy. He was the predator now, and his pack was on the hunt.

He looked left and right. The men were watching him, waiting. He nodded his head and pulled the dagger from the thatch, felt himself begin to slide down the pitched roof. Left and right his men did the same, pushing themselves ever so slightly as they slid down the slick thatch.

The edge of the roof was a black line with even deeper blackness beyond, the edge of the void, and on the other side was a fight to the death. Thorgrim could feel the wildness building. His feet came off the thatch and he pushed off and jumped for the ground he could not see, hit it and went down into a crouch, felt the mud and water splash up against his face.

He whirled around, still crouched low, the dagger in front of him, heard five more splashes as his men dropped to the ground. He had come down just to the right of the door where he knew a guard would be posted.

"Here!" a voice called out. Not a challenge, more an expression of fear and surprise. Thorgrim could hear the edge of terror in the man's voice, to see dark creatures dropping from the sky on such a night.

Thorgrim took two steps forward. In the dark and rain, against the wall of the prison he could see the shape of a man drawing a sword but it was too late for him. Thorgrim was on him, his left hand reached up and grabbed a fist-full of wet hair and jerked it back. The man made a strangling sound and a whimpering cry and Thorgrim slashed his throat. The man's blood, warmer than the rain, splattered against Thorgrim's face as he let him drop.

Snorri was beside him, lifting the bar from the door, pushing the door in. Thorgrim bent over and pulled the sword from the dead man's scabbard. It felt good to have a weapon in his hand. He felt whole again, and he knew he would not put it down until he was safely away from Dubh-Linn, or he was dead.

The men inside slipped out through the open door, led by Ornolf, whose girth did not allow him to get through the hole Thorgrim had cut in the roof. Thorgrim gestured for them to spread out, to lose themselves in the dark by the house. He and Ornolf walked down the length of their former prison as fifty men splashed out into night and moved into the darker places along the walls. Six guards lay dead and stripped of weapons.

"Svein!" Thorgrim said in a whisper. "Give that sword to Ornolf."

Svein the Short, who had come down the roof with Thorgrim, stepped up and reluctantly handed his new-won sword to the jarl.

"Keep your dagger," Thorgrim said, but Svein did not seem happy with the trade.

"We'll work around the edge of the palisade," Ornolf said, "keep in the shadows, fall on the guards when we get to the gate."

Thorgrim nodded. Sobriety was good for Ornolf's leadership, if not his mood. "I'll get the men with weapons in the fore."

No alarm had been raised, but that good fortune would not last long. The hard fighting, Thorgrim knew, was yet to start. Still, they were out. The pack was loose.

Morrigan crouched by the window and peeked through shutters that were open no more than a crack. Directly across the fortress yard was the dining hall in which the Norwegians were held. She had prayed for rain to hide the escape and her prayers were answered and she thanked God for it. But now the rain came in sheets and kept her from seeing or hearing what was taking place.

She squinted and leaned forward, certain she saw some movement in the dark. Her ears picked out a muffled thud from the steady noise of falling water. Midnight was an hour or two past. It was time for Thorgrim to act.

There was more sound now, splashing, feet running on wet ground, so soft you would never hear it if you were not listening for it. But Morrigan heard it, she was certain. Thorgrim was on the move. Her turn now.

She shifted the knife to her left hand and wiped her sweating palm on her dress, then resettled her grip. She was done with Dubh-linn and the torture of slavery. One way or the other.

She stood and listened. Orm was snoring in the sleeping chamber. Lying by the hearth, pretending to sleep, back to the door, she had heard him return from the mead hall, had listened to the noise of him rustling and groaning his way to sleep as the rain drummed on the thatch above. Then, no sound but the loud, steady breath. It had been that way for an hour or more.

The room was lit only by the orange glow of banked coals in the fireplace, a feeble light, but Morrigan knew every inch of the house and she crossed the floor, quick and silent. The door to the sleeping chamber was half open and she slipped in and stood there, silent. The room was windowless and all but black, the tiny light from the hearth barely creeping in through the door. She could see nothing, so she stood still, waiting for some sound that might indicate Orm was awake. But there was only snoring.

She pulled the knife from under her cloak and stepped across the room to Orm's low bed. The blankets were over him and all she could see was a dark hump in the dark room, but it was enough.

She wanted to stop, to listen, to be certain, but in her mind the voice shouted *No, no! Do it!* For all the time she had fantasied about this moment, the actual doing of the thing was harder than she thought. She had never killed a human being, and though she did not think it a sin to kill a pagan and a pig like Orm Ulfsson, still she flinched at the thought of actually driving a knife into a man's back.

And then Orm moved, shuffled a bit, made a low noise and Morrigan flushed with panic. The hesitancy fled, the fear fled, all conscious thought gone as she stepped up, lifted the knife high and plunged it down into the blankets and the man underneath.

The knife went in smooth then hit something - bone, Morrigan supposed but she did not think about it, just pulled it free and plunged it in again and again, and at last she sunk the blade in to the hilt.

Orm was thrashing, screaming, loud and high, screaming like a woman, but Morrigan barely registered the sound. She backed away from the thrashing hump of blanket, the great furor of sound that filled the room. She backed away until she found the sleeping chamber door and ran through it, ran across the room and out the front door. She gasped as the driving rain hit her in the face. But it was good, clean and purging, like the murder she had just committed. Orm's blood meant no more to her than the rainwater that ran down her skin.

Orm was still screaming that weird, high-pitched shriek. Through the rain she thought she saw some movement by the gate. She raced for the dining hall, for Thorgrim and her passage out of Dubh-linn.

Thorgrim was back inside the prison, seeing to the wounded men, when he heard the horrible sound.

"Use the blankets, use the blankets, a man on each corner!" he said to the men he had brought with him to carry their comrades, when suddenly a scream cut through the night, a terrible, high-pitched scream.

"Almighty Thor!" Olaf Yellowbeard gasped. "A ghost? Or a troll, do you think?"

"Shut your mouth, Olaf, and lift your brother," Thorgrim snapped, but he was not certain that Olaf was wrong. It was a black night of rain and death, the kind of night a man might expect evil spirits about.

Whatever was making that sound, it was going to attract the guard's notice. Thorgrim looked out the door. Men were running through the rain, running for the small house up against the palisade wall.

"Ornolf! Let's go!" Thorgrim shouted. Here was opportunity. The screams were a distraction.

Ornolf held his sword aloft, gestured forward, led the men along the wall where their movements would be more hidden.

Thorgrim stepped back into the dining hall. "Go, you men! With the others!"

The wounded men were lifted in blankets and carried out the door, Harald last of all. Thorgrim heard Harald give a low moan, saw a glimpse of his yellow hair and white skin through the folds of the blanket as he passed. This would not be easy on the boy. Thorgrim wondered if, in saving his own life, he was sacrificing his son's.

The fighting and the screaming and the rain were starting to work on his head. He felt the rage coming on, and the night seemed to swim in front of his eyes and he heard the sound of his own breath as he panted.

A figure was moving through the rain, coming toward him, running right across the open ground. Thorgrim stepped forward, his sword held ready. With his left hand he wiped the water and hair from his eyes. He growled. Whoever this was, if they were not one of his men, they were dead.

"Thorgrim!"

The voice seemed to come out of the rain, a feminine voice. Thorgrim looked around.

"Thorgrim!" It was the figure running toward him. He lowered his sword.

"Morrigan?" The young healer ran up to him, and when she was only a few feet away he could see it was her, her long hair plastered back on her head, her rough wool cloak soaked through and clinging to her. He felt the blinding rage lift like smoke swirling away.

"Where are your men?" Morrigan asked.

"They are circling to the gate. What is that screaming?" Even as he said it he realized the sound was dying away.

"Orm. I put a knife in his back. We have to go, the guards will come for us."

"We?"

"I'm coming, too. They'll kill me now, after what I did."

Thorgrim nodded. He could not see Ornolf and the others, lost in the rain, but suddenly his appetite for sneaking around was gone.

"Come." He walked off, stepped off fast for the front gate. His tunic was heavy with the rain and he wiped his eyes as he moved. Morrigan followed behind. He could hear shouting now, coming from Orm's house. Not much longer.

"Who's there?" The challenge came from someone Thorgrim could not see, someone huddled near the gate.

"Thorgrim Night Wolf of Vik!" he shouted and he did not break his stride. The guard stepped out of the shadows, sword drawn, shield on his arm. He was a much bigger man than Thorgrim. He wore a mail shirt.

This one will be hard to kill, Thorgrim thought. He could sense the man's confusion. The guard did not know what was happening, who was who. The screaming must have unnerved him.

"Who are you?" the man demanded and Thorgrim swung his sword at the man's neck; the move so fast and unexpected that the Dane just had time to raise his shield and stagger back under the blow.

Thorgrim had expected to hit the shield. He let his sword bounce off, spun around, wielding his weapon like a scythe, slashing at the man's waist. But the man had a fast arm and his sword was ready to take the blow. Iron hit iron and the blades rang out with their familiar music. Thorgrim whipped his sword over his head, brought it down hard on the man's arm. The man grunted, the blade slid off chain mail, and Thorgrim leapt clear of a counter-attack.

Thorgrim circled around and the man circled as well, face to face, both ready, both looking for the opening. But the guard had the luxury of time and Thorgrim did not. Thorgrim lunged, made the man move. The man beat Thorgrim's sword away with his shield and lunged with his own.

Thorgrim swung his foot up, kicked the sword to one side, thrust his blade into the opening, the point right at the man's face. The man flinched and Thorgrim's sword caught his beard and Thorgrim could feel the blade drag over skin.

The big man roared and swung his blade up, knocking Thorgrim's away before any real damage could be done. But Thorgrim had first blood, and he knew how that would work on a man's mind.

He was right. The big man was angry now. He slashed wildly but Thorgrim dodged, wolf-quick, took another stab at the vulnerable exposed neck. Thorgrim's world was closed down to that fight. There was nothing else. So when he heard Morrigan screaming his name it seemed to drift in from someplace he did not know.

"Thorgrim! Behind you!"

The big man hit Thorgrim hard with his shield, made him stagger under the blow and suddenly Morrigan's words and the sense of movement behind came together in a warning too fast to find voice in his head. He leapt to his right, hit the mud with his shoulder and rolled, sprang to his feet as the man behind him was swinging his sword at air.

He did not get a chance at a second stroke. Thorgrim leapt off the balls of his feet, sword out, drove the point right through the man's tunic, right under his arm.

Thorgrim swung the shrieking man around and used his body as a shield against the first man's sword, but now there was the problem of pulling his own sword free before the other man cut him down.

He swung the dying man in front of himself again, was thinking on the problem when Skeggi Kalfsson and Snorri Half-troll came charging out of the night, swords in hand. The Dane was still turning to meet the new threat when Snorri drove the point of his sword through the man's neck.

Beyond Snorri's panting form, Thorgrim could see the big stockade door swinging open, the Red Dragons clustered by the walls.

He could hear shouts across the compound. The alarm sounding. There were many more men than had been on guard duty, and now they were turning out.

"Come along, Thorgrim!" Snorri shouted. "We've no time for you to play your games!"

They turned and jogged for the open door. Thorgrim remembered to turn around and look for Morrigan. She was ten yards back. Her hood was off and the rain was running down her face and her long hair. He waved her on, and turned and ran as well.

Chapter Sixteen

It is uncertain
where enemies lurk,
or crouch in a dark corner.
Hávamál

The thrall stopped screaming at last and Orm imagined she was dead. He gave her body a push and she rolled over on her back, her arm flung out to the side. He had taken her home from the mead hall, tired of humping his scrawny Irish housekeeper. He had expected a number of things from her. Taking the point of an assassin's knife had not been one of them.

He did not know how many of the murdering swine there were, or if they were still in the house. He had waited and tried to listen as the thrall screamed her life away, but when she finally stopped, and the night was quiet, Orm still did not know how things lay.

He kicked off the blanket and climbed slowly out of the bed. His bare feet hit the dirt floor, his hand wrapped around the hilt of his sword and he pulled the weapon from the sheath. He cursed the drumming rain that muffled all other sound.

Now he could hear shouting, off in the night. He cocked his head and tried to get a sense for what was happening. The Norwegian fleet? Magus leading a mutiny? He had no idea.

He was naked and he suddenly felt very vulnerable so he set his sword down on the body of the dead thrall and grabbed up his tunic from the floor. He was just pulling it over his head when he heard the outer door to his house burst open.

"Bastards!" Orm shouted, jerked the tunic down and snatched up his sword. If they were coming for him in force then he would go out like a man and commend his spirit to the Valkyries.

He flung the bedchamber door open and burst into the main room, his sword ready. There were four or five of them, dark shapes in the muted glow of the hearth. He went for the closest.

"Murder me will you, you whore's son!" he roared as he swept the room with his sword. The man in front of him had time to do no more than grunt and fend off the blow with his sword, and Orm lunged again.

One of the others, by the hearth, thrust the oil soaked end of a torch in the embers. The torch sputtered and caught and the light spilled across the room. Orm saw that he was facing the half-dressed Magnus Magnusson and four of his most trusted men.

"You son of a bitch," Orm growled, but the brunt of the anger was directed at himself. *Why didn't I kill this bastard when I had the chance? Now he has killed me.*

Orm lunged again and Magnus parried the blow and his expression was more shock and confusion than anything else.

"My lord, no!" Magnus shouted as he jumped back, clear of another attack. "We heard screaming...we came..."

Orm paused and in the light of the torch he looked at the men's faces and he had to admit they did not have the grim look of men set on doing murder. He lowered his sword.

"Are you all right?" Magnus asked. "What was that screaming?"

"Someone tried to murder me but they killed a thrall by mistake."

"A thrall? Morrigan?"

"No." Orm glanced at the pallet by the hearth. "Where is that little bitch?"

"She wasn't here when we came in, my lord," said Kjartan Swiftsword, Magnus's chief man, standing just behind Magnus. Orm scowled. Realization spread like the light from the torch.

"That treacherous little Irish whore..." Orm muttered and he pushed past Magnus and out the door, into the rain and the chaos.

He could see men running in the dark, fighting by the gate. He could hear the clang of iron on iron, and he saw the front door of the palisade swing open. He gasped, looked to his right. There were no guards at the dining hall. A dark place in the wall showed where the door was gaping open.

"That bitch!" Orm screamed into the night. "The damned Norwegians are out! Magnus, rouse the men, to arms, we have to stop them before they get to their ship!"

"Yes, Lord." Magnus turned to go.

"See the men are organized. Don't let them run out in a mob. If the

Norwegians are laying a trap, our men will be butchered.

Magnus stopped. "The Norwegians have no weapons, Lord."

"No, but they're clever, and that's more dangerous. Be careful."

Magnus raced out the door and Orm followed, charging out into the night with only his tunic and sword. The mud sucked at his bare feet as he ran. *Never again,* he vowed, *never again will I let any such traitorous bastards live...*

Ornolf led the men out the palisade gate. Thorgrim stood with the rear guard, a half dozen men, among the few with weapons, as they backed through the gate, watching for attack. None came, but it would not be long.

"They know we're out!" Snorri Half-troll shouted to Thorgrim. "Look at them run!"

There were indeed men running, men tumbling out of the small buildings that lined the wall, men waving arms. The Danes knew what was acting, and they knew better than to attack in ones and twos. They were gathering, and when they did, they would form a swine array and fall on the Red Dragons in force.

"We have to get to the ship," Thorgrim said. He stepped back faster and the others followed and then they were through the main entrance and onto the plank road.

"Shut the doors! Shut the doors!" Thorgrim shouted and Snorri and Sigurd Sow heaved on the heavy timber doors and swung them closed. They would not slow the Danes up long, the doors could not be barred from the outside, but at least it would make the Danes hesitate and gather to face a threat that might be waiting. It was something.

Thorgrim turned and hurried down the plank road and here was Morrigan, waving to him, and beside her three sheep herds, one armed with a sword, two with spears, as if the night was not weird enough.

"Hold up!" Thorgrim shouted to his men and they stopped.

"Thorgrim, these are my friends," Morrigan said, and her voice conveyed the desperation of their circumstance. "They are here to help!"

Thorgrim looked with suspicion on the sheep herds. They did not look like fighting men. The two younger ones, in fact, looked terrified.

"Your ship's ready, they've seen to that. We must go! Quickly, they will be on us!" Morrigan said and Thorgrim nodded.

Then Ornolf was there. "Thorgrim! We need weapons! Pointless to escape without weapons, they'll hunt us down like dogs!"

Ornolf was right. Morrigan was right. The battle fever was up in Thorgrim and he did not want to think, he just wanted to fight. His eyes fell on the mead hall. The windows glowed with the weak light of dying fires. Thorgrim could picture the heaps of drunken men passed out on the floor like the dead after a grand battle.

"There!" he pointed with his sword "There are weapons to be had there! We'll sack the mead hall and be gone!"

"Thorgrim, let me take the wounded to the ship!" Morrigan said. "They will only hold you up!"

"Yes, yes, take them to the ship," Thorgrim said. Whatever she suggested, he would agree to. She seemed to affect his thoughts in some strange way, and he wondered if she was working some sort of magic on him.

This was not the time to think on that. "You men bearing the wounded, follow Morrigan! The rest, with me and Ornolf! Go!"

Morrigan waved on the men who carried the wounded in their blankets and they followed, hurrying down the plank road. Thorgrim and Ornolf led the armed men forward toward the mead hall that loomed like a cliff in the dark night.

Thorgrim held the men up outside the door. There was no sound from within, which had to mean most of the men there were passed out drunk. Even the rain would not have muffled the sound of Vikings in full revelry.

"You men," Thorgrim pointed to a cluster of twenty, "go around the back, come in the back door, catch anyone trying to flee. The rest come with Ornolf and me."

"Should we kill them?" Snorri asked.

Thorgrim frowned. It made sense to kill as many of the enemy as possible, in any circumstance. But even when the fighting madness was on him, Thorgrim did not care to butcher unconscious men. He did not think the gods looked favorably on such things.

"Only if they fight," Thorgrim said. "Lets go."

The others raced off for the back door as Ornolf pushed in the front. The fire in the big fireplace was dying, the few torches on the wall sputtering their last. There were forty men at least in the hall, slumped over the tables, sprawled on the floor, mouths open as they snored. They were all well armed.

Ornolf's men spread out. They pulled swords from the scabbards of sleeping men and eased shields out from under prone bodies. They slipped daggers out of scabbards and used them to liberate purses hanging from belts. Snorri Half-troll tried to peel the mail shirt off a man roughly his size, but Thorgrim told him to stop.

Thorgrim turned to Hall Gudmundarson and Egil Lamb. "Find some sacks, collect up all the food you can find. Skeggi, watch at the door. Keep out of sight."

It seemed to Thorgrim a long time that the silent looting went on, with no sound beyond snoring and the drumming of rain on the roof. Once he heard behind him a mutter of protest as one of the sleeping men stirred, but a swift blow to the head with the flat of his sword ended that.

"Thorgrim!" Skeggi, crouched by the door, called in a harsh whisper and Thorgrim moved fast across the hall, crouched beside him.

The door was opened just the slightest crack and through it they could just see the plank road. The rain came cascading from the roof and splashed up in their faces. The Danes were on the move.

There were a hundred men at least. They were in a swine array, moving cautiously down the road. Thorgrim could make out shields and swords, spears, helmets. They were well armed.

Slave-sons...

Thorgrim watched them as they passed the mead hall and moved further down the road.

They don't know we're here...

But why would they? They would assume the Norwegians had made for their longship as quickly as they could.

"Wait here," Thorgrim whispered. "Tell Ornolf I am gone, and to stay put. I'll be back."

Before Skeggi could reply, Thorgrim slipped through the door on silent goatskin shoes, moving low into the shadows of the mead hall. The rain fell blinding in his face but he did not notice. His body felt taut and ready, his senses wolf-sharp. He could smell the Danes even through the rain, could hear the tiny clink of mail shirts, the shuffle of shoes on the plank road.

He moved along the edge of the building, half-crouched, sword held low and ahead of him. He felt the earth through his shoes, felt the night on his skin. He moved through the dark, a part of the darkness, silent as a spirit.

Thorgrim Night Wolf slipped over a low fence at the edge of the mead hall, moved down the edge of the plank road, working his way in and out of the shadows of the buildings that lined the walk. He could hear snatches of talk from the swine array. Grousing. Concern. It was a frightening night and it might have frightened Thorgrim as well if he was not a part of it.

They were getting close to the river now and suddenly Thorgrim thought of Harald, carried off to the longship, lying helpless and burning with fever on the deck. The Danes would not hesitate to kill him. He moved faster, slipped around behind an ironworker's shop, leapt over a fence, skirted down along the road. Someone peered out of a window, looked right at Thorgrim but did not see him as he slipped past.

Thorgrim arrived at the river's edge fifty feet ahead of the cautious swine array. There were men hiding there, he could sense them as much as see them, crouching in the brush by the water. Thorgrim circled wide, moved up behind the one furthest from the water. He slipped his sword in his belt and pulled the more nimble dagger.

He was ten feet behind the man, stalking him, the taste of blood in his mouth, when he realized it was Olaf Yellowbeard, sword drawn, watching the road.

"Olaf..." Thorgrim whispered and he shuffled close.

Olaf turned. Thorgrim could see his eyes open wide. Olaf did not expect to hear his name whispered from behind.

"Thorgrim! By Thor's hammer I thought you were some night spirit."

"I am. Where is Harald? And the other wounded men?"

"That Irish healer-woman has taken them off, where it's safe, she said. I had men posted on the road, they warned us the Danes were coming. We spread out. Hid."

Thorgrim nodded. "Good."

They fell silent as the Danes closed the distance down the plank road to the longship. They were moving faster now, realizing that they were alone. They reached the dock and their formation fell apart as the clambered on board the *Red Dragon*, looking for the escaped prisoners, looking for some sign of where they might be.

"Damn!" Thorgrim heard a voice shout out and he was certain it was Orm's. "Where in all hell have they gone?"

No one answered. No one knew.

"They must be in the longphort still." That voice was Magnus.

"Find them, damn you! Leave twenty men here, the rest, search the town!"

Thorgrim leaned close to Olaf Yellowbeard. "Stay here. Remain hidden. Pass the word to the others. I'll lead the rest back here."

Olaf nodded and then Thorgrim was gone, whipping back into the dark night. He kept away from the plank road, moved past the clustered houses, racing through kitchen gardens, hopping over low wattle fences. He crouched low, panting with the effort, but he moved fast and silent as if padding down a forest trail.

He came at last to the mead hall, approached from the back and slipped in the back door which, he was not pleased to see, was unguarded.

"Ornolf!" The jarl had found a barrel of mead and was making up for a week of deprivation in the Danish prison. "Ornolf, the Danes are down by the ship. They've left a small guard but the rest are searching the town. Here's our chance."

"Ah, damn the Danes!" Ornolf roared, causing the half-dozen unconscious men around him to stir. "Let the Danes come, I'll bugger them all! Good strong drink has gotten me randy again!"

Good strong drink had also taken the hard edge off Ornolf's leadership, Thorgrim was sorry to see. "You men," he pointed to three men who were rifling through one of the drunk men's clothes, "take up this barrel of mead and carry it down to the ship." He knew there was no chance of Ornolf following if the mead did not come as well. "The rest of you, gather around."

Ornolf was not the only one who had gotten into the mead, but that was all right, since any Viking worthy of the name would fight better with a belly full of drink.

Thorgrim pulled one of the smoldering torches down from the wall, crossed to the fireplace and used it to stir up the coals. Soon the torch was blazing again.

"Egil Lamb," Thorgrim called.

Egil, lithe and sinewy, unlike most of his brethren, with a long thin neck and a sparse and sorry bit of hair on his cheeks that he called a beard, hurried over.

"Take this torch," Thorgrim instructed, "and climb up there, set the roof on fire."

Egil Lamb looked up at the roof, high overhead, ran his eyes over the various handholds and footholds on the wall. He nodded, took the torch, began to climb.

Thorgrim led the rest out the back door, out into the night. The rain had eased off some, still steady but not coming in torrents. The men huddled in the dark by a clump of brush. They could hear tiny thunderclaps of shouting in the longphort as the Danes spread out in search of them. They kept their eyes on the mead hall.

The flame was like a candle at first, no bigger than that. It peeked out through the thatch of the mead hall roof, dancing and wavering in the rain. And just as it looked as if it would go out, another appeared, and another, and then the entire roof burst into flame as the fire ate away at the still-dry thatch underneath. The timbers supporting the roof were dry and tarred and the beams were still covered with bark. The hall would burn well.

The back door opened. Egil Lamb stood framed against the now bright light of the interior.

"Let us go," Thorgrim said.

They worked their way down to the water, following the route Thorgrim had found earlier. They were slowed by the bundles of food and the barrel of mead, but it did not matter because the Danes had other things to worry about now.

They were still two hundred yard from the river when Orm's men discovered the fire. The occasional shouts that they had heard before multiplied and multiplied again as the Danes became aware of the magnitude of the disaster. The mead hall was burning.

Men pounded up the plank road. Men tumbled out of houses and shops, pulling tunics over their heads as they ran. They shouted for water, for axes, for more men to join them.

The mead hall was burning.

Thorgrim Night Wolf led his men down the hill, past the shops, across the tangled ground to where Olaf Yellowbeard still crouched and watched. "Not a man who was guarding the longship has gone off," Olaf said.

Thorgrim nodded. These were disciplined men who would not be distracted from their duty. They would be skilled warriors as well.

The more rational part of Thorgrim's mind told him it was a time for tactics - circle around, attack from two places, work men in from behind. But he was in no mood for that nonsense.

"You men carrying loads, get aboard the *Red Dragon* as soon as you can, get all the lines cast off, save one. The rest of you, come with me. Kill as many as you can. Remember, we don't have to win, we just have to escape."

He turned and leapt through the brush. He did not wait to see if anyone was following.

The men on the dock were alert and they would not be taken by surprise. Thorgrim saw heads turn, weapons come up ready as he leapt over the small briars and through the tall rushes, down the slope of the hill toward the river.

"Who's there?" someone demanded. Thorgrim felt a howl build in his throat and he let it go as he rushed in with sword over his head. He howled and shrieked and bared his teeth and came in with sword swinging.

The first of the Danes to step up never had a chance. There was no checking the momentum Thorgrim had built up in his rush into battle. Thorgrim swept the man's sword aside and literally ran over him, leaping in the air, stepping onto the man's shield, bowling him over. They came down together, the man on his back, Thorgrim still on his feet, standing on top of the man. He drove his sword straight down into the man's chest even as he flung himself shoulder first into the next man behind.

The Red Dragons broke like a wave on the Danes, howling out of the night, but the Danes met them, howl for howl, blade for blade. The conquerors of Dubh-linn were too skilled and too experienced to be thrown off by a surprise attack. Shield hit shield, swords clashed in the rain, spears sought out their targets.

Thorgrim was snarling as he wielded his sword, slashing and probing, but the man he fought now was good, very good, and he countered Thorgrim's blade and sought advantage for his own. And he had a shield, and mail as well.

Thorgrim lunged. The Dane knocked the sword away with his shield, lunged himself, and Thorgrim twisted out of the way of the blade. Ten feet away, fighting Olaf Yellowbeard and Svein the Short at the same time, was Magnus Magnusson.

"Swine!" Thorgrim shouted. He swung his sword in a great sideways arc, slamming into his adversary's shield, making him stagger and then Thorgrim was done with him. As if he had forgotten the men completely he shoved his way through the mob, pushed Svein aside, leapt into the fight.

His eyes met Magnus's even as Magnus was fending off a blow from Olaf Yellowbeard and the mutual hatred came though as clear as if they had shouted it. Thorgrim lunged, straight arm, right at Magnus's throat and Magnus knocked the sword away, an inch before it killed him.

Thorgrim's eyes followed the sword in Magnus's hand. *Iron-tooth!* Magnus was carrying the sword he had stolen from Thorgrim. Iron-tooth in the hands of his enemy!

Thorgrim screamed. He lashed out at Magnus, missed, lashed again in the kind of wild attack that generally left two dead on the field. The night was turning red in his eyes and he felt himself slipping away, as if the human part of his soul was fleeing, to be replaced by something more primal.

"Thorgrim!"

His blade met Magnus's sword - his sword - and swept it aside and he lunged but Magnus was quick and side-stepped the blade.

"Thorgrim!"

Someone was calling him. It came though like a light in the fog, someone was shouting his name.

"Thorgrim! To the ship!"

Hands were pulling him now, and others were jabbing at Magnus with spears, holding him off and Thorgrim was dragged back, still howling, still flailing with his sword.

Then suddenly his legs banged against something and he stumbled back and he landed hard on a rough, wet surface. He was looking up at the black sky and the rain was lashing him in the face and his whole world was moving, the earth no longer stable under him, and he had no idea what was happening.

The ship! We're on board the ship! Thorgrim realized now. They had pulled him on board, cast off. The ship was rocking in the stream. He had told the men they only had to escape, not win, and then he had ignored his own orders.

The fighting madness dissolved away and Thorgrim pulled himself to his feet. They were twenty feet from the dock already. A spear came whistling through the rain and passed a foot from Thorgrim's face, another thumped into the planking by his feet. Some of the Danes had bows, and now arrows were whipping through the air. One found a mark in the arm of Thorgerd Brak and he shouted and tumbled to the bottom of the ship.

The Danes on shore were raging but there was nothing they could do beyond flinging spears and shooting arrows. There were too few of them to come after the *Red Dragon* in another longship. They would have to wait for the others, but the others were fighting the fire at the mead hall.

Ornolf was on the bow, shouting insults at the Danes. A spear embedded itself in the neck of the prow inches from his belly but Ornolf seemed not to notice. Most of the men, more pragmatic than their leader, were swinging the long oars into place.

Thorgrim stepped aft to the steerboard. Morrigan was there, and Thorgrim was surprised to see her.

"How did you get here?"

"I snuck aboard during the fighting."

"Good." Thorgrim took up the steer board's tiller and pushed it away, turning the longship away from the dock. The first few oars were in place and the men pulling them. The *Red Dragon* built speed through the water.

And then Thorgrim remembered. He looked frantically around the longship. Nothing. He turned to Morrigan. "Where is Harald?" he asked.

Chapter Seventeen

Cold are women's councils...
Norse Proverb

O rm Ulfsson wanted to kill someone. More than anything else he wanted to drive his sword into someone's guts, and if he could have found one person alive whom he felt reasonably certain was to blame he would have killed them.

He would have killed the men guarding the prisoners but Thorgrim and his men had done the job for him. He would have killed that traitorous Morrigan but she was gone, off with the Norwegians, he guessed.

Orm wanted to kill Magnus Magnusson, because he suspected somehow Magnus had something to do with this. But there was no proof. Magnus had always sworn undying loyalty to Orm. Magnus had come to his home to protect him when he thought Orm was being murdered. And besides, Magnus was not without his followers, men loyal to him and not necessarily to Orm. Killing Magnus might cause more problems than it would solve.

He wanted to kill Asbjorn the Fat for no reason at all. Just because he wanted to kill him.

But he stayed his sword. He had been around long enough to know that just killing men because you felt like killing them was counter-productive in the end.

The first light of day was turning the skies gray to the east before Orm had a chance to think on any of that. His first priority, even over catching the Norwegians, was saving the mead hall. The mead hall was the social and spiritual center of Dubh-linn. Without it he would be hard pressed to keep his small community of surly, rough men placated.

The roof was fully involved by the time he got there, and there was nothing anyone could do about it, but they could prevent the fire from consuming the walls as well. Orm led a clutch of men into the burning building and together they dragged bundles of flaming thatch out the door. They beat the thatch with rugs, doused it with water hustled up from the river. They dragged dead and half-dead men out of the flames. The rain did the rest.

It took hours of brutal effort, but in the end the fire was out and the walls of the mead hall still stood. It would be no great task to replace the thatch roof. Dubh-linn, for now, was safe.

Orm returned to his house, leaving instructions for his men to finish cleaning the charred debris away. Magnus followed. Asbjorn the Fat, who had slept through it all, was summoned.

Orm collapsed in his wooden chair. "Bring me some ale, damn you!" he shouted before he recalled that there was no one left to shout at. His thrall was gone.

"Allow me, my lord," Magnus said, snatching up two cups and filling them. Magnus was being unusually solicitous. Orm wondered if he thought his life was in jeopardy for the Norwegians' escape. If he thought that, he was not entirely wrong.

Asbjorn the Fat appeared at the door, breathless. Magnus sat. He did not offer Asbjorn a cup.

"My Lord Orm," Asbjorn managed. "By Odin, what has happened here?"

For a long moment Orm just stared at Asbjorn and wondered how the pig could have slept through all that chaos. Asbjorn was clever, but that was all he had to recommend him. "The Norwegians have escaped," Orm said at last. He felt suddenly very weary.

"Damn them," Asbjorn said.

"They won't be far," Magnus said. "I took the sail out of their ship."

"I'll get a longship fitted out," Asbjorn said. "One hundred warriors. The wind is getting up from the southeast, we'll overhaul them by noontime."

Orm nodded. Asbjorn was obviously trying to get back in his good graces, but that was all right. Decisive activity was welcome for whatever reason.

"Hold a moment, my lord..." Magnus said. He leaned forward in his chair and Orm thought, *Now we shall hear what this smooth character has in mind...*

"There is something I have come to suspect, my lord," Magnus continued. "From something Thorgrim said when I was questioning him. I think the Norwegians have the Crown of the Three Kingdoms."

Orm sat more upright, despite wishing to appear unflappable. *The Crown of the Three Kingdoms?* It was the one thing he feared even more than the Norwegian fleet.

"What did he say?" The generosity Orm had been feeling toward Magnus was melting away fast.

"It was a slip of the tongue, no more. As if he started to say something about it and caught himself. I could not beat the information out of him after that. He's a tough one. I didn't get the chance to question Ornolf on this."

The three men were silent for a moment, digesting the words. Asbjorn turned to Magnus. "You searched their ship," he said, more an accusation than a statement. "And you did so without informing my lord Orm or myself. If they had the crown, then now you must have the crown."

Orm could see the anger in Magnus's eyes but his voice was controlled. "The crown was not aboard. If it was, then my lord Orm would have it now and we would have no further concern. They must have hidden it before sailing into Dubh-linn."

Orm pounded his hand on the arm of his chair. "Then why in Odin's name are we not chasing after them with our swiftest ship?"

Asbjorn jumped in, even as Magnus had opened his mouth to speak. "Because they will not try to retrieve it if they know we're right behind. If they see a well-armed longship in their wake, they will not go to where the crown is hidden."

"So..." Orm began but Magnus cut him off, unwilling to be upstaged.

"We follow on land, my lord. The Norwegians have only their oars to propel them. Horsemen on shore could keep up. If they are going to fetch the crown, under oars, they won't go too far off shore."

Orm nodded and considered the two men in front of him. He didn't really trust either of them. In truth, he didn't really trust anyone. It was for that very reason that he did not dare leave Dubh-linn himself to pursue the crown.

"Very well." Orm leaned forward in his seat. "You will go after them. You will both go after them."

Asbjorn was the first to break the stunned silence. "My lord?"

"You will both go after them. Magnus, pick twenty of your best men. Asbjorn, you do the same. That should be enough, those Norwegians are wanting for arms. Follow them. When they make landfall for the crown, attack and kill them."

For a moment neither man spoke or moved. Then, as if both realizing at the same instant that the first to obey would gain advantage, they both leapt to their feet and hurried for the door.

Orm watched with amusement as they rushed into the street. *They are all traitorous bastards,* he thought, but he hoped two traitors together, each out for his own good, would act as checks on each other's ambitions. Or they would kill one another. Either way.

The elation that the Red Dragons felt at escaping certain and painful death soon turned to grousing and complaining when they discovered that their sail was gone and they had to row themselves to safety.

"Shut your mouths!" Thorgrim shouted forward when he could no longer stand the sound of the men's muttered griping. If Harald had been there, and in health, he would have pulled an oar and been grateful for the chance.

They made their way down the Liffey in the dark, with Skeggi in the bow probing with an oar for mud banks. They touched once but were able to back off before grounding out hard. It was their good luck to have the tide flooding as they made their escape, which made the rowing harder but kept them from being swept down river and pinned against a shallow place, or going up on a bar on a falling tide.

They made the mouth of the river just as the light was breaking in the east. The rain tapered off to a drizzle and then stopped completely, and the rising sun brought a new surge of optimism to Thorgrim, something he could not feel in the dark hours. The open sea was under their bow and no longship was coming in pursuit.

Ornolf came ambling aft, a cup of mead in his hand. "Pull, boys, pull!" he shouted to the rowers, by way of encouragement. "We'll pull clear to Norway if we must, but these Dane bastards won't draw our guts from our bellies, eh?" The jarl's efforts to raise morale were not having much effect.

Ornolf stepped up onto the afterdeck. "Where's Harald?" he asked.

Morrigan was huddled at Thorgrim's feet, leaning against the side of the ship with her cloak pulled over her for warmth, but she looked up at Ornolf's question and Ornolf in turn looked surprised to see her.

"Who's this?" he asked Thorgrim.

"Morrigan. The Irish healer woman," Thorgrim said.

Ornolf looked closer at Morrigan. "So she is. What's she doing here?"

"She brought us the daggers, remember? She stuck a knife in Orm. She reckoned it would be better if she did not remain in Dubh-linn."

"Reckon not," Ornolf roared. "Good for you," he said to Morrigan. "Always good to have some pretty little thing on board. Now where's Harald?"

"Ask Morrigan," Thorgrim said.

Ornolf looked at Morrigan. Morrigan said, "You seem very concerned about Harald."

"Of course I'm concerned! He's my grandson, and the only man worth a damn on this whole boat, besides myself!"

"I see," Morrigan said. She wiped a stray strand of hair from her face. "Harald was too ill to travel by ship. So were the other wounded men. Those sheep herders, one was my brother, Flann mac Conaing. He has seen the wounded men taken to a safe place. I can lead you there to get them back."

Flann mac Conaing? Thorgrim thought. *That does not sound like the name a poor sheep herd might carry.*

"Well, I suppose we owe you another debt of gratitude," Ornolf said, "but I have to say, I'm not so happy about having my men split up thus."

Thorgrim was not happy about it either. And he suspected there was more to this than Morrigan was letting on.

The *Red Dragon* was well past the mouth of the Liffey now, and her bow was meeting the ocean swells, lifting up high and swooping down in that way that told Thorgrim they were in open water. It was time for a decision.

"We're free of the land now, Ornolf," Thorgrim said. "Where do we go?"

"We get Harald, that's where we go. This thrall will lead us to Harald." He looked down at Morrigan. "Where away?"

Morrigan did not answer. She stood, and her motion was quick and agile. She stretched her arms and pulled the hood off her head. Thorgrim realized he had never seen her before in the light of day, outside their dark prison. She was even younger than he had thought, her skin smooth, a pretty face with prominent cheekbones. But there was also a hardness in her eyes he had not seen before, the kind of look he associated with men who led warriors into battle, not thralls with the healing arts.

Morrigan spoke at last, and the hardness of her voice matched the look in her eyes. "There is something we must speak of, first."

Thorgrim tensed and frowned. He had no notion of what was coming, but he knew it would not be to their advantage. Suddenly everything Morrigan had done - the healing, the daggers, the murder of Orm, the offer to carry the wounded away - all took on a different look as if, like her face, Thorgrim was seeing her actions in daylight for the first time.

"Speak," he said.

"There is a crown, an ancient crown, that is held in the keeping of the abbot of Glendalough. It's called the Crown of the Three Kingdoms. The abbot decreed that the crown should be given to the king of Tara, Máel Sechnaill mac Ruanaid. It was sent by boat, in the care of twenty noblemen. It never arrived at Tara."

Thorgrim was silent. He resisted meeting Ornolf's eyes. Finally he prompted Morrigan. "Yes?"

"I think you have the crown."

"You may search the ship if you wish. Magnus did, and he found nothing."

"I know it's not on board. You were too clever to bring it to Dubh-linn. I think you hid it somewhere first."

"What is the meaning of this Crown of Three Kingdoms?" Thorgrim asked. "Why is it so important?"

"That's not your business. It's a matter for Irishmen, not fin gall. The crown is important, that's all you need to know."

"Damn your impertinence, woman!" Ornolf roared. "And damn this crown, and damn whoever has it, I say!"

Morrigan was unmoved. "The future of Ireland rests with the crown. So does the life of Harald and your men."

"Harald?" Thorgrim said and then he caught her meaning and he felt his fury rise like a storm, fury at Morrigan's treachery, fury at himself for being taken in like a silly child.

"You black-hearted..." Thorgrim growled. "Where is my son?"

"He's safe. He's unhurt. He will be well cared for. And when the crown is brought to my lord Máel Sechnaill, who should rightfully posses it, then he and your other men will be returned to you."

This time Thorgrim looked up at Ornolf, and he could see the jarl, Harald's grandfather, was feeling as furious as he was, and just as trapped.

Without a word, Thorgrim pushed the tiller to starboard and swung the *Red Dragon*'s bow north, making his head for the little bay where the Crown of the Three Kingdoms slept under the sand.

Chapter Eighteen

By the Prince's Truth the great armies
are driven off into the enemies' country.
Testament of Murand
Ancient Irish Morality Tale

Brigit wiped the young man's brow with a damp cloth. *These fin gall are a well-made race,* she though to herself. This one - Harald, they called him - was genuinely handsome. Blonde-haired, square-jawed. A few years younger than herself. Not tall but well set up, solid, even after the wasting effects of the fever. The sunlight coming in through the one window illuminated his skin and hair so he seemed to glow, like an angel might.

He stirred a bit and moaned and Brigit took the cloth from his forehead and watched close, wondering if he would say anything. Every once in a while he uttered some strange word in his Norse tongue which she did not understand. There was no one at Tara who could speak the fin gall language save for Flann mac Conaing, though Brigit had insisted he teach her a few words.

Flann had arrived the day before, with the two sheep herders and the dozen men who had gone to Dubh-linn with him, the men who had waited with horses and carts beyond the palisade walls of the city to get Flann and the hostages back to Tara. The wounded Norsemen were given rooms in the king's great house, with healers to care for them and guards on the doors, as befitted men who were hostages, not prisoners.

Brigit put the cloth down and picked up a bowl of broth that sat on a table by the bed. She took a spoon-full and touched it to his lips and reflexively he took a sip. She did it again.

She heard footsteps in the hall. She expected them to pass by but they did not. The door opened. Brigit turned as her father walked in. He was dressed for court and not for war, with a red cloak that hung nearly to the floor and a green tunic, elaborately embroidered.

"This is the one?" he asked.

"Yes."

Máel Sechnaill crossed the room and frowned down on Harald as if looking on some unknown and generally disagreeable creature. "Will he live?"

"He's strong. Gormlaith has been in to see him, and she says Morrigan did a good job with her healing. His fever should break soon. I can already see improvement."

"Humph," Máel said, the life of the fin gall apparently a matter of complete indifference to him. "Why God does not strike all these heathen dead is a mystery to me."

"Ask Father Gilbert."

"I have. It's a mystery to him as well."

Máel Sechnaill watched as Brigit fed Harald broth. "Has he said anything?"

"He's made sounds. Whether they are words or not, I cannot tell."

"Perhaps we should get Flann to listen. Try and divine what these vicious animals are about."

Brigit looked up at her father. She could hear that familiar tone in his voice. "Father, this one is a boy."

"Boy... And a wolf cub looks the dear puppy, but still it will grow to be a wolf. So it must be killed first."

"But you can't kill Harald. Or the others. They are hostages. When the crown is brought to you, they must be released."

Máel Sechnaill did not answer, but rather stared down on Harald, his look an odd mix of curiosity, revulsion, hate and indifference. "Of course," he said, then turned and left.

Magnus Magnusson watched as the last of fifty horses was coaxed aboard the longship and tethered in place. Fore and aft the crew lifted the long oars from the V-shaped racks on the gunnels and passed them along to the men at each of the fifty rowing stations. In the bow, mail-clad and well armed, were the twenty men he had picked to go with him on his hunt for the Norwegians. In the stern, similarly equipped, stood Asbjorn's men.

The shipboard part of their journey would not be long. Three hundred yards to the north shore of the Liffey, and then by horse along the rugged Irish coast.

Asbjorn the Fat came huffing up from the dock where he was supervising the loading of a cart onto a knarr that he himself owned. He, too, was dressed in a mail tunic, black from the oil that had been applied to it to keep it from rusting. The armor showed little sign of wear. His waist was bound around by a belt. A sword with an elaborately engraved silver hilt hung at his side.

How many cows died to make a belt big enough for that fat pig, Magnus wondered.

"I hope you are right, Magnus, that the Norwegians went north," Asbjorn said when he had recovered his breath. "After all this, we'll never find them if they went south."

"They went north," Magnus said. "I had men follow."

"An impressive degree of foresight. One wonders how much of this you knew beforehand."

"Wonder if you wish. Foresight is something a man develops when he fights battles. It is hard for women and children and men who stay at home as...advisors...to understand. What is in the cart?"

"Food. Bedding. I provide for my men."

"My men provide for themselves. That cart will slow us down. Leave it."

"I'll leave it if I decide to leave it. I take no orders from you."

Indeed... Magnus thought. Two leaders, each with his own hird, sent on the same mission. It could not be better organized for disaster. Magnus was certain that Orm knew it and planned it that way. Not that it mattered, really.

Kjartan Swiftsword waved from the steerboard of the longship. The horses were all aboard, the rowers had settled in place, oars held up. "Lets go," Magnus said and he headed down to the dock. He did not wait to see if Asbjorn was following.

It took less than twenty minutes for the longship to cross from the south shore of the Liffey to the north. The first of the horses was untethered and led to the gangplank even as Magnus's feet stepped onto the lush Irish grass. Asbjorn, who had elected to cross the river in his knarr, was fussing with the crew to see his cart safely offloaded.

The cart was still swinging from ropes made off to the yard when the last of the horses was led ashore. Magnus stepped down to the edge of the muddy riverbank.

"I told you that cart would hold us up, damn it."

"Haul away!" Asbjorn called to the men at the fall of the tackle. They pulled and the cart lifted slowly off the deck and was guided onto a long gangplank run up over the muddy bank to the shore.

"We'll waste more time raiding for food than it will take to get this cart ashore," Asbjorn snapped. "Ease away, there!"

The cart was lowered onto the gangplank where a half-dozen men grabbed onto to keep it from rolling away. The tackle was cast off, the cart eased down the wooden boards, which bowed dangerously under the load.

"I admire your concern for your men's bellies, but I suspect...," Magnus began when the gangplank gave a great cracking sound and then buckled, snapped right in two, dropping the cart and the six men into the mud below.

"Catch up to us when you get this straightened out," Magnus said. He turned and walked away before Asbjorn could make any reply. Twenty paces from the river, his men and Asbjorn's men were saddling their horses.

"Mount up," he shouted to the collected men, though he knew only his own men would follow his orders. Kjartan Swiftsword handed him the reins of his horse. He put his foot in the stirrup and swung himself up. He adjusted the shield that was slung on his back and saw that his sword was hanging right and his score of men did the same.

Asbjorn struggled ashore, climbing along the broken gangplank to avoid waddling though the thick mud. He would not tolerate Magnus riding off on his own.

"Go!" Magnus shouted. He reined his horse over and gave it a kick in the flanks, trotting off across the rolling countryside, with the pounding of twenty horses behind him.

They were in open country now, the green fields like long ocean rollers stretching away on either hand, broken here and there with clumps of trees and ragged stone walls that snaked between fields. Off to the east, visible when they crested the low hills, the straight horizon of the sea blinked in the muted sunlight. They rode on.

The Liffey and the longships were far behind them when Magnus finally twisted in his saddle to see who was following. His men were still riding in a tight group, grim-faced with bright colored shields slung over their backs. Half of Asbjorn's men were there too, and though their loyalty was given to Asbjorn, Magnus knew them to be good men, hard fighters, reliable warriors. And they would be his men, before too long.

Behind them all rode Asbjorn, awkward and clearly uncomfortable. His heavy face was red and he was sweating quite a bit, but Magnus's sympathy was with the horse, bearing its fleshy burden. Asbjorn might hate this hard riding, but he would think it preferable to letting Magnus ride off on his own.

They came at last to the high cliffs that looked down on the ocean below. Magnus reined his horse to a stop, swung his leg over and dropped to the ground. Behind him, thirty men did the same. He could hear Asbjorn grunting as he dismounted.

The longship was less than a mile off shore. It was exactly where Magnus had known it would be, crawling north along the coast, no sail set despite the fair wind from the south west. They were too far away to see any detail, but they could make out the steady rise and fall of the oars. Magnus smiled. He could almost hear the grousing of the men at the rowing stations.

"Well done, Magnus," Asbjorn came huffing up behind him. "There they are."

"There they are," Magnus repeated. "Leading us at a comfortable pace to the Crown of the Three Kingdoms."

"Comfortable, indeed," Asbjorn grunted. "Plenty of time to off-load my cart. But now I've had to leave it behind, with half my men to bring it along. And us with no food."

Magnus turned to Asbjorn. It was time to drive a verbal sword into his fat belly. The real one would come later. "My men supply themselves like Vikings, not like women who bring their provender with them." He turned and looked north, and when he spoke again his voice was louder, his words for everyone to hear. "Five miles north along the coast there's a monastery at a place called Baldoyle. It has not been put to the sword for years. We'll sack it, take what we need, take what we want, and follow the longship. What say you, Asbjorn?"

He turned and looked at Asbjorn again, and the fat man was not happy. Agreeing to the plan would make it look as if Magnus was in command, and he, Asbjorn, just tagging along. On the other hand, his own men would certainly turn on him if he tried to prevent them from sacking a rich monastery.

"My lord Orm would not be happy with our ignoring his orders and rushing off on our own," Asbjorn tried, but it was weak.

"Those of us who have been a-viking know these things can be done fast. If we ride hard, we'll have everything the monastery has that is worth taking before the longship has even drawn up with us."

He looked around. The expressions on the men's faces, the eager wolf-looks, the smiles, told him all he needed to know. They were with him, now. Leading men, raiding, fighting, this was his territory, not Asbjorn's, and Asbjorn had made a fatal mistake following him there.

Chapter Nineteen

*...[T]he pagans desecrated the sanctuaries of God,
and poured out the blood of the saints about the altar..."*

Alcuin
from his letter to the
community of Lindisfarne

The steady rhythm of rowing, and the effort it took, soon quieted the Red Dragons' grumbling. Also, the wind was fair for their heading, and while that only helped a bit with the ship under bare poles, at least they did not have to row against it, and that was good.

Thorgrim held the tiller, steering the longship due east before angling off north around the big headland that sat like an island at the north end of the bay of Dubh-linn. He looked aloft. Egil Lamb was sitting on the hoisted yard, an arm flung around the mast like it was a serving girl in a mead hall. He was keeping a bright look-out. Thorgrim had charged him with looking astern for any ship following, ahead for any danger there, and to seaward for any ship from which they might acquire a sail. For all that long morning the seas had remained empty.

Morrigan was sitting on a sea chest pushed up against the larboard side of the afterdeck, eating a hunk of bread and pork, part of the stores they had plundered from the mead hall. It was not much, perhaps two day's food for the fifty or more men aboard the ship. They would need more.

Morrigan was staring off toward the horizon and she did not see Thorgrim looking down at her. She had shed her cloak and wore just her thin dress and apron. Her head was uncovered and her hair had dried out to its true light brown color. Whatever she was thinking, it did not show on her face.

"So where is Harald?" Thorgrim asked. His anger had faded some with the coming of day and he was able to speak to her in a controlled manner.

"He's safe, if the dubh gall...if your people, did not kill him."

"Orm and his fellows are Danes, they're not my people."

Morrigan shrugged, as if to say Norsemen were all one to her. "Harald and your other men are at the great house at Tara."

"Tara?"

"The seat of the Irish kings of Brega. When we have the crown, I'll lead you there."

Thorgrim ran his eyes around the horizon, as was his habit. Morrigan was growing freer in her speech, but it was of no use to him. He had no notion of where this Tara was, or Brega either. So far, the best option seemed to be doing as Morrigan instructed.

"What is this 'Crown of the Three Kingdoms?'" he asked.

Morrigan looked up at him and their eyes met and Thorgrim felt something jump between them. Morrigan was silent as she decided what to say.

"That is not your concern," she said.

"It is my concern. It could not be any more my concern than it is."

Morrigan nodded, understanding the truth of that statement. She was about to speak when Egil Lamb called out from aloft. "Smoke, smoke there! Ashore, off the larboard bow!"

Every head aboard turned in that direction, though the rhythm of the oars did not alter in the slightest. A column of dark smoke was rising up from some place just over the headland, it's top torn apart in the breeze. More smoke than would be produced by any purposeful activity, cooking or smithing or the like. Something had either caught fire by accident, or had been put to the torch.

Morrigan was on her feet, staring at the smoke. Her face was set in a frown, her hand clenching the top of the bulwark.

"On the oars, double time, now!" Thorgrim shouted and the men picked up the pace, pulling with a will as Thorgrim swung the bow around to close with the shore. Where Morrigan saw something troubling, Thorgrim saw opportunity.

Ornolf came aft. "What, ho, Thorgrim what have we here?" he roared.

"I don't know. Ask the healer-woman. She seems to have some idea."

Ornolf looked at Morrigan. "Well?"

"I do not know."

They closed fast with the beach, the shallow draft longship skimming the gentle rollers under the thrust of her oars. They were abeam of the smoke and half a mile off when Thorgrim called for the men to ship oars.

All of the longship's noise, the creak and thump of oars in the oar-ports, the shuffle of men pulling the oars, it all fell away and the only sound left was the gentle slap of water on the hull.

They stared at the smoke and they listened. And soon they heard, barely audible over the distance, the crackle of flames, the screams of victims, the clash of iron on iron. The sounds of a raid, as familiar to the Vikings as a lover's voice.

"It is the monastery at Baldoyle," Morrigan said, softly.

"Egil Lamb!" Thorgrim called aloft. "Are there longships on the beach, there?"

Egil did not answer at first. Finally he called down. "None that I can see."

"Hah!" Ornolf cried. "Not the work of Norsemen, here?"

Morrigan was scowling even deeper now. "It seems not," she said, biting off the words.

"You Irish are as hard on each other as we Northmen are on you," Thorgrim said. If this was not a Viking raid, then it had to be Irish sacking Irish, a thing Thorgrim knew happened often enough.

For some time they were silent, watching the rising smoke and listening to the dim sounds of the fight, as the *Red Dragon* rose and fell on the long ocean swells.

"This is what the crown is about," Morrigan said at last, and Thorgrim at first did not know if she was talking to him or to herself.

"What?"

"The Crown of the Three Kingdoms. This is what it is about. To stop this shameful...this plundering, one Irish kingdom against another."

Thorgrim and Ornolf were listening now, their full attention on the Irish woman.

"The crown is an ancient thing," Morrigan continued. "It was forged even before the true faith came to Ireland by some long forgotten druids. It has always been held in the kingdom of Leinster, to the south of Brega."

"Where is Brega?" Thorgrim asked.

"This is Brega." Morrigan nodded toward the shore. "All this land, north of the Liffey."

Thorgrim nodded. This knowledge brought him closer to knowing where Harald was held. Closer, but not by much.

"The Irish kings have always fought one another. We have many kings, the rí túaithe, who rule the small kingdoms, the ruiri, who rule over them, and the kings of overkings, the rí ruirech. They are constantly at war.

"Even after Ireland came out of the darkness and embraced the true faith, it did not change. Only the crown can stop it, and only for a while. Whenever the rí ruirech of one of the kingdoms is given the Crown of the Three Kingdoms, he is for that time the undisputed king of Brega, of

Leinster, and of Mide to the west. He can summon armies from the three kingdoms, and their allegiance must be to him."

Ornolf made a grunting sound. Thorgrim pictured the crown as he had first seen it, peeking out of its canvas wrapping on the deck of the vanquished curragh.

"Sounds like a lot of nonsense to me," Ornolf declared. "If three kingdoms want to form an alliance, they can form an alliance. Why do you need some gaudy crown?"

Morrigan shook her head. "The kings of Ireland are too independent - too stubborn - to form any alliance. Even if the rí ruirech formed an alliance, the rí túaithe would not be much moved to serve under another king. But the crown is a powerful thing. It carries the magic of the druids, and even though we no longer believe in the old ways, still, it is a powerful thing.

"The crown is rarely given out, and when it is, it is not given for life, but only for the time it is needed, and then it is given back. The people will obey the king who wears the Crown of the Three Kingdoms, obey without question."

"A lot of horse shit," Ornolf announced. "You mean to say some local king is granted that much power and then gives it up voluntarily?"

"I mean that exactly. The crown's power is too great to trifle with. No king would dare hold it against the will of those who control it."

"I understand," Thorgrim said, and he did. He understood the power of this crown now. With the kings of Ireland all at one another's throats, anyone who could command the loyalty of three kingdoms could rule the entire country. He understood that, but much of it was still a mystery.

"Who holds the crown? Who decides who should wear it?"

"The druids in Leinster, in the old days, created the crown and the legend of the crown and made it the powerful thing it is. They decided when the threat to Ireland was so great that a worthy rí ruirech should be given the crown, and when he should abdicate it. After the true faith came to Ireland, the crown came to be held by the abbot of Glendalough, in the monastery there. The abbot, in his wisdom, now decides who should wear the crown. It is not a decision made lightly. The crown has never been given out in my lifetime, nor my parents'."

"Why now?"

Morrigan hesitated before she spoke. Her eyes were still on the distant smoke. "Ireland is in grave danger. We are invaded."

"Invaded?" Ornolf said. "By who?"

Thorgrim smiled. He knew what Morrigan meant.

Morrigan turned to them and looked Ornolf in the eye and Thorgrim saw that look he had seen before, a look of defiance, as if there was nothing that anyone could do to her to keep her from speaking the truth.

"We are invaded by the dubh-gall and the fin-gall. The Northmen."

"Invaded?" Ornolf roared. "One longphort, some raiding on the coast? That is an invasion?"

"That's a start. And it must be ended as soon as it starts." Morrigan's face was set hard as she spoke, the words coming sharp and fast. "The abbot of Glendalough understands that. That is why he decreed the crown should go to my lord Máel Sechnaill mac Ruanaid, who of all the kings can best drive this plague from our home. And I understand it."

"And Orm knows of the crown as well," Thorgrim said. The Danes were safe in Dubh-linn as long as the Irish were fighting one another, but an alliance of the three kingdoms could easily drive the Norsemen into the sea.

"So," Thorgrim said, "you have kidnaped my son in order that me and Ornolf should help you rid Ireland of our own people?"

"Your people? They are Danes, I thought they were not your people."

Thorgrim smiled. She is quick, he thought.

"What think you, Thorgrim?" Ornolf asked, pointing toward the column of smoke to the west. "Should we land, see what there is for the taking?"

Thorgrim saw the anger flash in Morrigan's eyes. "Pray do not lose sight of the mission we are on," she said.

"She's right," Thorgrim said. "Our only concern now is to help the Irish drive us from their land. Besides," he added, looking at thick smoke, like a black finger of God pointing toward the desecration of His temple, "I reckon there isn't much left there worth taking."

Chapter Twenty

Vikings will come across the Sea,
They will mingle among the men of Ireland.
                                    Berchán, Irish Prophet

The monastery at Baldoyle was well sacked and Magnus's men were happy. He counted among them the men who had come with Asbjorn the Fat as well. After this raid, he did not think they would put much stock in what Asbjorn had to say.

The Vikings had come up over a low rise a half a mile from the dirt and wattle wall that circled Baldoyle - not the largest monastery in Ireland, but respectable. Like all Irish monasteries, Baldoyle was in essence a self-sufficient little village. Unlike most villages, however, it could be counted on to have silver, gold, jewels.

At the foot of the wall was a ditch, and thorn bushes grew along the top, and it represented not the least impediment to the Norsemen.

Magnus stood in the saddle. "Danes, follow me!" he shouted, sword held over his head. He pounded off toward the monastery, riding over the tilled fields that surrounded the enclosure. Behind him came thirty-five Vikings, the full host, less those left to deal with Asbjorn's cart.

Asbjorn himself was at his side, riding hard, trying for all he was worth to keep up. But he was no horseman, and his horse was carrying far more weight than the other animals, and soon Asbjorn fell behind and Magnus alone led the men to the gates.

The monastery was in panic. They could see it from a few hundred yards away. Farmers, the bóaire, cowmen, as the Irish called them, rushed for the shelter of the walls, families in tow. Brown-robed monks urged them on as they shoved the wooden gates closed.

Idiots, Magnus thought. Everything the raiders wanted was within the walls of the monastery - the bóaire were in more danger inside than out. But that was not his concern, not at all.

The tilled ground gave way to a plank road and the horses sounded louder still as they raced for the palisade gate. There were men on the walls now, archers, perhaps half a dozen of them, but Magnus was caught up in the frenzy of the charge and they did not worry him. Twenty feet from the wall and he felt an arrow pass close by his head. Another glanced off his mail shirt at the shoulder, ripping his tunic and hanging up in the cloth, beating against his legs as he rode.

But the Danes had archers as well, and they reined to a stop, whipping arrows at the heads that appeared over the wall. Magnus charged for the gate, pulled his horse to a stop beside it. It was eight feet high, no more. Magnus kicked his feet out of the stirrups and stood on the saddle. He swung his shield around on his arm and took hold of the top of the gate.

A spear flew at him from an oblique angle, missed, struck the man beside him square in the chest, sent him screaming to the ground, but another man was there even before the first was down. Magnus pushed off his horse's back, vaulted the fence, came down hard on the packed earth inside the monastery.

He was still recovering from the drop when the first of the monastery's defenders was on him, a monk in long robes, sword over his head, shouting in his Gaelic tongue, and he died at the end of Magnus's sword before he even began to swing his own.

Christ-men, Magnus thought with disdain. They were not bred to the sword like Norsemen were.

There were more men from the monastery coming at him, monks and the bóaire armed with clubs and a few spears, but no real fighting men that Magnus could see. He shouted, stepped into the attack, the sword singing in his hand. The Norwegian's sword. Thorgrim. A fine blade, made finer for being a trophy of war.

The defenders of Baldoyle fell as they came. Magnus and Kjartan Swiftsword and a few others, standing shoulder to shoulder, formed a shield wall that would not be broken. Behind them, others who had come over the wall knocked the bar from the gate and swung it open. Horses pounded through, into the former sanctuary. The fight was over.

"The church! The church!" Magnus shouted up to the mounted men, pointing to the largest of the dozen or so buildings within the circular walls, a formidable plank-built structure with a high thatched roof and a big wooden cross mounted on that. If there was anything to be had here it would be in the church, and it had to be secured before the monks carried it off.

The horsemen kicked their mounts on, pounding off for the church. What little defense there was of the monastery had collapsed entirely, and now the monks and the bóaire were fleeing in every direction. Families were racing for the smaller gate at the far end of the compound. There were men and children who would make valuable slaves, women for the pleasure of the Viking hirdmen. At another time Magnus would have had them rounded up, the valuable bounty of a successful raid. But he did not have enough men to deal with captives. He had brought no chains. And he had far bigger things planned. He needed smoke.

Smid Snorrason was on his knees going through the purse of one of the dead farmers, an exercise not likely to yield much. "Smid, leave that," Magnus said. He looked around. To his right stood one of the larger buildings in the monastery, a round building with thatched roof that he guessed to be the monks' residence.

"There." He pointed to the building. "I want that burned. I want it burning in five minutes. There'll be nothing worth having in there."

Smid stood, nodded, and hurried off.

Asbjorn the Fat, last of all, came riding through the gate, red-faced and puffing. "Humph," he said, looking around the monastery, the fleeing defenders, the Vikings racing for the church. "Orm will not be pleased," he said. "Orm will not be pleased."

"Shouldn't you be attending to your precious cart?" Magnus asked, pulling the dangling arrow from his tunic.

"This is a distraction," Asbjorn said, ignoring the dig. "We are after the crown."

"Oh, see here," Magnus said. "A cart, of all things! And food in the barns and store houses, I'll warrant. And gold and silver in the church."

Asbjorn said nothing. There was nothing for him to say. With the longship still in sight off shore and the men reveling in plunder he was not going to convince anyone that the raid was a bad idea.

Magnus left him and walked toward the church, the energy from the fight draining from him. There was still fighting going on, shouting and the clash of steel, little pockets of violence where those who could not escape from Baldoyle fought their last, but it was nothing of any real concern. He looked around. There was a small orchard within the monastery, kitchen gardens and workshops, and a scattering of round wattle-and-daub built houses. Magnus had sacked a dozen like it.

The big church was near the center of the compound, secluded by a wood fence with a cemetery to one side which Magnus guessed would be put to use again that very day. One of the Danes was scaling the thatch roof, sent up by Kjartan Swiftsword, Magnus was certain, to see that they were not taken by surprise. Some monasteries had lookout towers for that purpose, but Baldoyle did not. Magnus wondered if building one would become a new priority.

The church was cool and dark inside and Magnus found it hard to see until his eyes adjusted to the gloom. Two men in monk's robes lay dead by the alter, sprawled out in pools of their own fresh-spilled blood. They had tried to keep the trappings of their faith from the heathen's hands and had died in the effort.

"Not the richest monastery," Kjartan Swiftsword complained. At his feet was a pile of silver and gold - chalices and incensers and candlesticks and a gold box like a little treasure chest. Magnus picked up the gold box and opened the lid. Inside, resting on a bed of rich red cloth, was a small bone, a human finger bone by the looks of it. Magnus frowned and wondered what sort of religion led men to enshrine small bones in gold boxes.

Behind him, one of Asbjorn's men tore the jewel-studded cover off a thick book, tossing the useless pages aside. Three more men worked at prying the gold inlay off of the high alter. They were not gentle in their business.

"No matter. There'll be more in the workshops," Magnus said.

There was a shout from outside, a reply from somewhere. Magnus turned as one of his men came in through the big front door. There was some urgency in his step.

"Lord Magnus, Vifil Ketilsson is on the church roof. He says he sees riders, coming from the north."

Magnus nodded. "I'll come."

He walked down the center aisle of the church, between the rough benches, and stepped blinking into the sunlight. The building he had sent Smid to burn was fully involved, the flaming thatch sending great plumes of black smoke up into the blue sky. He looked up at Vifil Ketilsson who stood with one foot on either side of the high peak of the church roof.

"Vifil, what do you see?"

"Riders, Lord Magnus. Fifty or more, coming from the north. Riding fast."

Asbjorn was there and he made a disgusted sound. "That's marvelous! Thanks to you we are now trapped in this stupid place!"

Magnus did not bother to reply. "Kjartan," he said to his man who had stepped from the dark of the church, "place archers on the walls, near the gate, and form up the men inside in a shieldwall. But not all of them. I want five men left to finish gathering up anything here worth having."

"Yes, Lord Magnus."

Asbjorn was in full fluster. "Are you going to ask my opinion on the distribution of men? Do I have some say over how my own men are used?" Asbjorn considered it a rhetorical question. Magnus did not.

"No. You have no say," Magnus said, and strode off for the gate.

The riders were easily visible by the time Magnus mounted the ladder leaning against the earth wall and found his footing among the thorn bushes on the top. Vifil was wrong about the numbers. Perhaps it had been wishful thinking. There were closer to a hundred men. Sun glinted on armor and spear points. Two bright banners floated aloft above the riders. Far behind them, two wagons bounced along, drawn by a dozen horses. It was an Irish war party, fully outfitted, and bound for Baldoyle.

Magnus looked around. A dozen archers were fanned out along the wall, and behind the gate most of the remaining men stood in a line, round shields overlapping, swords in hand, ready to counter an enemy who came though the gate as they themselves had done less than an hour before.

Magnus looked north again. The riders were lost from sight behind the column of black smoke roiling up from the monks' home, but soon they were visible again. Their pace had not slackened.

It took another fifteen tense minutes for the riders to approach the gate. At their head was a young man, his beard dark brown and cropped short, his helmet glinting bright. He wore a white tunic over his mail shirt and a red cape. He looked like a king, and such he was. He reined his band to a stop twenty feet from the gate.

Along the wall, bows were raised to the ready. "Archers! Lower your bows!" Magnus called and the bows came down again.

The Irishman in the white tunic approached, and behind him came another, not so well fitted out, and one of the standard bearers as well. The lead man raised his hand and spoke. His accent was Gaelic, but his speech was Norse.

"Lord Magnus!" he called.

"Lord Cormac Ua Ruairc," Magnus called back. He looked down at Kjartan Swiftsword, standing on the right end of the shieldwall. "Kjartan, it's all right. Open the gate."

"Open the gate?" Asbjorn, standing well behind the shieldwall, shouted his impotent protest. "I forbid you to..."

Asbjorn's forbidding came too late. Kjartan tossed off the bar and pulled the gate open. The shieldwall melted away, the Vikings standing to either side as the Irish war party rode slowly in, Irish and Norse eyeing one another warily, like two packs of wolves that come upon one another in the woods.

Cormac Ua Ruairc slid down from his horse. He extended a hand to Magnus. Magnus took it, shook, clapped Cormac on the shoulder. It was only the second time they had met, though their couriers had gone from one to the other for a month or more. The Irishman looked as Magnus remembered - strong, smart and able. A king and worthy of the title.

"I demand to know what this is about!" Asbjorn said as he came puffing up, but Magnus could hear the edge of panic in his voice.

You would do well to panic, Magnus thought. He addressed Cormac. "My Lord Cormac, this is Asbjorn Gudrodarson, known as Asbjorn the Fat."

"Well named," Cormac agreed. His men were fanning out on their mounts, making a presence there inside the Baldoyle monastery. There was nothing overtly threatening in their actions, but there was also no question as to where the military strength rested.

"Asbjorn," Magnus continued, "this is Lord Cormac Ua Ruairc, king of Gailenga."

Asbjorn glared at Cormac. Cormac looked with amusement on Asbjorn, then turned to Magnus. "Who is he? What is he doing here?"

"Orm foisted him on me. He is of no concern."

"Of no..." Asbjorn sputtered and Magnus turned, swinging his fist, and hit Asbjorn hard in the face. Asbjorn staggered back, blood flowing from his open mouth, then tripped on his feet and fell hard. Magnus was over him in a flash. He yanked the sword from Asbjorn's scabbard and tossed it aside. No one, not even Asbjorn's men, made a move to interfere.

"Where is the crown?" Cormac asked.

"We are being led to it now. No more than a day or so."

Cormac frowned. "I thought you would have it."

"So did I," Magnus said. "But I do not."

"Pray don't forget what that bitch's whelp Máel Sechnaill is capable of. After he stole his whore daughter from my brother Donnchad, he tied my brother to a stake and personally ripped the guts out of him. They told me you could hear the screaming half a mile away. He will do the same to us. We cannot stop him, and take Brega, if I do not wear the Crown of the Three Kingdoms."

"A day or so. No more."

Cormac looked into Magnus's eyes, looked hard. "You had better be right, Lord Magnus," he said, and for the first time since this great chance had presented itself, Magnus Magnusson wondered if he might have made a mistake.

Chapter Twenty-One

...[H]eathens shall come to you from me...
a race of pagans who will carry you into bondage...

The Epistle of Jesus
9th Century Irish Text

Two days after arriving at Tara, Harald Thorgrimsson's fever broke. It was like stepping from a dream world into daylight, like stepping from a sweltering smith's shop into the night air. One moment he was burning up, tossing in a nightmare sea, and the next he was cool, comfortable, aware.

His eyes were closed and he kept them closed as he tried to organize his thoughts. He did not know where he was. He listened. The few sounds he could hear were distant and muted and nothing that he recognized. The air had no familiar smell.

He opened his eyes. He was looking up at the underside of a wood-plank ceiling with carved beams. The room was bright and sunlit. He could see the tops of stone-built walls covered with whitewashed plaster.

He wanted to sit up but understood that he did not have the strength. He rolled his head to the right. There was a tapestry on the wall, a polished table with a silver bowl and pitcher. It was a fine room, finer than he was used to, finer even than his grandfather's home in East Agder, which was the finest home he had ever seen.

He heard a little gasp on his left side and rolled his head that way, alarmed now. It was a girl, but he did not recognize her. He looked at her face and she looked at him and his first thought was that she was beautiful, a beautiful girl. Green eyes. Dark brown hair that reminded him of the luxurious mane of a horse his father had once owned.

She leaned closer to him and put her hand on his forehead. Her skin was smooth and soft and cool and felt delicious. She said something in a sweet and lilting voice but the words made no sense. Harald was suddenly afraid that this was a Valkyrie, come to take him away, or that he was being welcome into Valhalla. But Valkyries, the eaters of the dead, he had always understood, were not gentle and kind like this one.

The girl turned and spoke toward the door and her tone was loud and commanding. A voice on the other side of the door responded and Harald heard footsteps going away.

The girl turned back to him and she smiled and he tried to smile as well. His lips were dry and they hurt when he moved them. The girl took a damp cloth and wiped his face and Harald no longer cared where he was.

It was not long after that the door open and a man came in, an important man, Harald gathered, judging by his clothing and manner. He looked down at Harald but his face did not have the same tenderness as the girl's and it made Harald, who had thought himself among friends, a bit apprehensive.

"You're awake," the man observed.

Harald nodded.

"What is your name?"

"Harald." The word came out like a croak. His voice sounded odd to him. And it was only then that Harald realized the man could speak his own language. A thousand questions floated in his head.

"What is this girl's name?" he asked.

The man frowned and looked at first as if he would not answer. "Brigit," he said at last. "And I am Flann mac Conaing, chief councilor to my Lord Máel Sechnaill mac Ruanaid, King of Tara, rí ruirech of Brega."

Harald nodded. It seemed as if those words were meant to impress, but in truth he had no idea what this man was saying. Save that the girl's name was Brigit.

"Where am I?" More practical questions began it insinuate themselves. "Where is my father? And Ornolf, and the others?"

"Who is your father?"

"Thorgrim Night Wolf."

"He is the jarl in command of your ship?"

"No. Ornolf is. Where are they?"

The man frowned. "They are coming for you. The crown that you took, it belongs to my Lord Máel Sechnaill. They are returning it. Until then you will stay here."

Harald squinted at the man. There seemed to be some implied threat there, though he could not be certain.

Crown? he thought. He did not recall any crown, but again there seemed to be a great deal he did not recall.

"What crown is this?" Harald asked and he saw something pass over the man's face and had the idea that he should not have asked that question.

"The crown you fin gall...you Norsemen, captured from the curragh."

Harald nodded. He remembered the curragh, the fight on the heaving seas. Vefrod Vesteinsson hacked to bits by the Irish crew. He did not remember any crown, but he thought it was best if he did not say as much.

Despite Harald's nodding agreement, that uncertain look was still on the man's face. He said something to Brigit and she said something back, and then he turned and left.

Harald looked up at the girl. *Beautiful. She is beautiful,* he thought and he was sure he would think that even if he were not as weak as he was, if she had not been there to care for him.

"Brigit..." he tried her name.

She smiled at him. "Harald," she said. Her expression, her tone, was that of a mother speaking to a gravely sick child, one unlikely to live, and it made Harald uneasy.

Máel Sechnaill was not happy to suffer any fin gall to live. He was most certainly not happy having them under his roof, eating his food, tended to by his men.

The taking of hostages was a common enough practice, and there was protocol that dictated how they were to be treated. But hostages in the past had always meant Christian hostages, not heathen Norse swine.

Máel Sechnaill was not happy.

And he was even less happy listening to what Flann mac Conaing had to say.

"He knows where the crown is. He's lying if he says otherwise," Máel said, but it was more of a question. "All these gall lie. They don't know how to tell the truth."

"I don't think so, Lord Máel," Flann said. "He's young, and he lacks any subtle art. I think he genuinely knows nothing of the crown."

"You think these swine don't have it after all?"

"I don't know."

"Your sister said they have it. She is with them still."

"Yes. And Morrigan is generally not wrong about these things. But now there's some doubt. As your chief counselor I thought I should warn you."

Máel nodded and ran his fingers through his short-cropped white beard. This whole hostage thing had been Flann's idea, Flann and his sister

Morrigan, and it took substantial courage for Flann to come before his king and admit it might be going wrong. But Flann was courageous that way, and rarely wrong, and that was why Máel Sechnaill kept him.

"That one, Harald, is just a boy. He might not be privy to everything. How many other of these fin gall do we have?"

"Two, my lord."

"Bring them here."

Ten minutes later the other Northmen were kneeling on the stone floor in front of Máel Sechnaill's low wooden throne. One was called Olvir Yellowbeard and the other Giant-Bjorn, or so Flann had informed Máel. The names went out of Máel's head as quickly as they came in. He was no more concerned with names for the fin gall then he was for names for the boars or harts that he hunted.

He turned to the one called Giant-Bjorn, who seemed the bigger and dumber of the two. Even on his knees his head was even with Máel Sechnaill's chest. His hair was wild, his beard was like an unkept hedge. His hands were bound behind his back.

"What did you do with the crown?" he asked. Flann translated.

"I don't know of any crown," Giant-Bjorn said.

"The crown you took from the curragh," Máel said, his voice growing softer, a danger sign for those who knew him.

"There was nothing on the curragh. A few weapons, some mail shirts, we took those. There was nothing else."

Máel Sechnaill kicked Giant-Bjorn hard in the stomach and the big man fell over, gasping for breath. Máel waited. Giant-Bjorn shouted something, spitting in fury as he did. Flann did not bother to translate. Máel Sechnaill could guess at the Viking's general meaning. He nodded to the guards and they lifted the fin gall and put him back on his knees.

"There was a crown on the curragh and you took it. What did you do with it?"

Flann translated the words. Giant-Bjorn glared. Máel did not intend to waste much more time on this. Giant-Bjorn did not know it, of course, but this questioning was for Olvir Yellowbeard's benefit, not his.

"What did you do with the crown?"

"There was no crown."

"Are you a Christian?"

The last question, when translated, took Giant-Bjorn by surprise. When he did not answer, Máel Sechnaill tried again. "Do you believe in Jesus Christ? Would you take him as your God?"

Now Giant-Bjorn looked more confused than anything. "Jesus Christ, as my God? My gods are more powerful than yours. I wouldn't crawl to your Jesus like you do!" He spit on the floor for emphasis.

Máel Sechnaill pulled the double-edged dagger from his sheath. He had done his duty, as far as he or Father Gilbert were concerned, had offered the heathen a chance at salvation. With that, he slashed the man's throat, the razor-sharp blade opening his neck wide. Giant-Bjorn fell on his side, feet kicking, writhing, making a gurgling sound as the blood ran over the stone floor and the life drained fast away.

Máel Sechnaill turned to Olvir Yellowbeard, who watched with wide eyes the results of being uncooperative. It was his turn now, and if Olvir Yellowbeard knew nothing, then it would be the turn of the one they called Harald. The fact that Harald might be the son the jarl, and thus a hostage worth bargaining for, would only keep him alive for so long.

"Where is the crown you took from the curragh?" Máel Sechnaill asked Olvir Yellowbeard. Flann translated.

Chapter Twenty-Two

You can't feel a battle
in your bones
or foresee a fight
Hávamál

Thorgrim Night Wolf was caught in a river, deep and cold and fast moving. He swam hard but it did him no good. The water had him in its grip and swirled him away, and as much as he fought he could do nothing to save himself.

He felt his body hit against rocks and drag along the bottom but there seemed to be nothing he could do free himself from the nightmare because the water was in charge and he was not. He felt his fury mounting at his own helplessness.

And then he realized he was not helpless, that he did not have to be swept down the river. He felt the spreading fire of strength inside him, and he found he was not in the river anymore, but on the bank now, powerful and ready.

He slipped out from under the blanket of furs, moved soft and silent among the men sleeping around the deck. There was a lookout in the bow, but he did not hear Thorgrim and he did not turn.

Thorgrim slipped over the side of the longship and dropped to the shingle beach on which the *Red Dragon* was hauled up for the night. They were still a day or two's rowing from the cove where he and Ornolf had buried the Crown of the Three Kingdoms. The last embers of the fire they had built on the shore glowed like dragon eyes in the dark.

Thorgrim moved along the surf line, low and swift, alert, and disappeared into the brush that ran down to the beach. There were enemies out there, he could feel them in his bones. Dangerous men. A lot of them. He moved through the low brush, instinct guiding him, his footfalls lost in the sounds of lapping waves and the cry of nightjars.

His eyes felt like they were glowing as they pierced the dark. His mouth was partway open. His breath came in soft pants as he moved. There was someone nearby, Thorgrim could smell him, and though he could see only dark shapes under the sprinkling of stars, his nose told him infallibly where the man crouched.

Thorgrim circled around wide, stepped from the brush into an open place and moved at a silent loping trot over the wet grass. The smell of the man came powerfully to his nose - dry sweat and wood-smoke and mead and the sharp smell of iron. And then he saw him, crouched down against the dark brush, looking toward the beach where the longship was grounded out. Watching. He did not see Thorgrim Night Wolf coming up behind.

Thorgrim was twenty feet back when he stopped. It was entirely his decision whether the watcher lived or died, and the watcher did not even know it. But this was not the watcher's night to die, at least not by Thorgrim's hand. The gods or the spirits of the land or the trolls in the woods might have different plans, but Thorgrim did not care about the watcher, only about who had sent the watcher there. He turned, loped off up the hill, inland, away from the sea.

The camp was a mile or so from the beach, well inland, where it would not be detected easily. Thorgrim moved at an easy pace, and once he had gained the high ground of the hill that sloped up from the water his nose told him exactly where it was. He passed three more watchers spread out along the way, placed so they would see any man who tried to slip by.

The camp was well guarded, too, huddled in a clearing surrounded by a stand of oaks, with men posted on all quarters. If it had been on open ground, Thorgrim would not have dared approach. But the men who had picked the spot had looked to the stand of trees to shield them, which it did, and it shielded Thorgrim as well.

He moved through the trunks, his feet falling on a carpet of leaves and sharp acorns. The smells were everywhere now, overwhelming his senses - smoldering coals and cooked food and unwashed men. Horses. Many horses. He could hear them shifting nervously and making little snorting sounds.

He came to the edge of the trees and peered out through the bracken. There was a guard there, tense and alert, looking out into the night. At one point he looked directly at Thorgrim, as if he was looking him in the eyes, but he did not see the Night Wolf.

Thorgrim circled the camp. There had to be nearly two hundred men there. Most were huddled on the ground, but there were also tents, two of them, big, circular tents, like a nobleman might carry on campaign. They glowed from the inside, lanterns still burning, even at that hour.

Around the back side of the camp he came on an odd sight, a fat man, stripped nearly naked and covered in filth, with a chain around his neck, staked down to the ground. A guard sat on a rock nearby, bored, while the fat man quietly sobbed. There was something familiar about the fat man, like he was part of some dream Thorgrim had had, but Thorgrim could not place him.

He circled the camp twice, took in all he could. These men were his enemies. In younger days he might have begun to kill them right then, one at a time, killing silently and methodically. But he was older now, and he knew that thinking had to come first, planning, and then the killing if the killing was the thing to do. He slipped off into the dark.

Thorgrim awoke in the pre-dawn. He was tired, as if he had been running all night. The strength was gone from his arms and legs. He was not sure he could move. He could feel dirt on his hands.

Morrigan was sleeping beside him, her back pressed against his chest and his arm was around her but he did not recall how they had come to be that way.

With a groan he pushed himself up on his elbow and looked around. There was no hint of the morning sun. Overhead the stars had wheeled around in the sky, the only sign that time had passed at all. The *Red Dragon* was moving gently in the lapping waves, creaking and grinding on the shingle.

The night began to resolve in his mind, like a fog clearing away to reveal an unfamiliar landfall behind. He remembered the watchers. He remembered the camp.

Thorgrim sat up and ran his fingers through his hair. Morrigan stirred, rolled on her back, propped herself up on her elbows.

"What is it?" she asked in a whisper.

Thorgrim shook his head. He was not sure yet. It was all coming into focus. Morrigan waited, silent. She was a patient woman, Thorgrim had noticed it before. He liked that.

"There are men out there," he said at last. "More than a hundred. They're watching us."

Morrigan looked with wide eyes toward the beach as if she might see this army gathered in the dark. "Who are they?"

"I don't know."

For a long moment they were silent. Morrigan pressed closer to Thorgrim, pressed herself against him, which surprised Thorgrim but did not displease him.

"Magnus," Morrigan said at last. "Magnus or Asbjorn."

"Who?"

"They were the foremost of Orm's men, the dubh gall who lorded over Dubh-linn," Morrigan said. "Before I killed him. Now his men will be looking for us."

"Yes." Thorgrim remembered now. It seemed a long, long time ago. Of course it would be Orm's men. It had not made sense to Thorgrim that no longships had come in pursuit. In that wind it would have been easy enough to catch the *Red Dragon*, easy enough to overwhelm her poorly armed crew. But with the *Red Dragon* stripped of her sail, men on horseback could easily keep up with her, and never be seen.

They heard a grumbling, shuffling, banging forward and they tensed. Thorgrim's hand fell on the hilt of his sword. In the starlight they saw Ornolf, like an old bear stumbling off to hibernate, clambering up over the side of the longship. He held his trousers up with his right hand and only after he had gained the deck did he pause the tie them.

"Ornolf!" Thorgrim called in a harsh whisper and the jarl made his way over. What little mead they had pillaged on their way out of Dubh-linn had been divided up among the men, and Ornolf's share amounted to far less than he would generally have consumed, so Thorgrim had reason to think the jarl would be somewhat clear-headed.

Ornolf knelt on the deck. He looked at Thorgrim and Morrigan and gave them a lascivious grin which Thorgrim ignored.

"There are men out there," Thorgrim nodded toward the beach. "One hundred and more. Maybe two hundred. They're camped a mile inland but they have watchers in the brush."

Ornolf turned and looked toward the beach, just as Morrigan had, and like Morrigan he could see nothing.

"How do you know?" Ornolf asked.

"I saw them," Thorgrim said.

Ornolf studied Thorgrim's face. "Was it a wolf-dream?"

Thorgrim hesitated. "Yes," he said at last. He really was not sure.

Ornolf nodded. Thorgrim knew that for his father-in-law, a wolf-dream was the strongest possible proof of a thing. And indeed they were rarely wrong.

"They are Orm's men. They must be," Morrigan said. "They must have guessed we would retrieve the crown. They'll attack once we have it."

"Damn the crown, then!" Ornolf said, loud enough that several men shifted and made grunting noises.

"Without the crown, my lord Máel Sechnaill will never release Harald," Morrigan said. "I wish it was not so, but it is." There was a note of sincerity in her voice, and it surprised Thorgrim.

The three of them were silent, the night filled with the lap of water, the rustle of leaves in the morning breeze, somewhere on shore.

"Very well," Ornolf finally said. "We'll get the crown, we'll bring it to this whore's son, Máel Sechnaill."

Yes, Thorgrim thought. But it is different now.

Before, they were the hunted. They were the dumb goose that does not see the stalker creeping up behind. But now they were the wolf, who allows pursuit until the time is right for him to turn and attack.

"Let us mount the dragon's head on the prow again," Thorgrim said. "If there are any spirits in this land, let them know that in us they have something to fear."

Chapter Twenty-Three

Men with black, keen spears
will blight the fruits of noble rule.

Irish Poem of Prophecies

It was not Brigit's duty to care for the hostages. It annoyed her father that she did so, her, the daughter of the rí ruirech of Tara. But it was her nature to want to help those who were weak, who could not help themselves.

It is no more than the Christian thing to do, she thought to herself, seated on the stool by Harald's bed. Máel Sechnaill would have preferred the fin gall in the stone-built prison, eating the scraps that the hogs left behind, and not in the royal house, eating the king's food, but that was not how hostages were to be treated. Not as long as Brigit was part of the royal household.

The king did not like it, but they were cut from the same cloth, Brigit and Máel Sechnaill, and the rí ruirech would rather remain silent than argue with his daughter.

Harald was asleep now, the remnants of the first real meal he had eaten since he arrived at Tara sitting on a trencher on the table and scattered across the floor.

She had tried feeding him broth, after the fever broke. She spooned it into his mouth, thinking that in his weakened state his stomach would not tolerate solid food. Harald, the Norseman, felt differently.

He used gestures, it was all they had to communicate. He gently pushed the broth away and with his other hand made eating gestures. Brigit shook her head, pointed to the broth, thinking that he did not understand that this was food. Harald shook his head, made more emphatic eating gestures, along with exaggerated chewing. Brigit smiled and nodded. Real food. Harald was a strong young man and he was ready to eat.

The minor kings, the rí túaithe who had gathered at Tara for Máel Sechnaill's attack on Leinster had not left. They still hoped for some action, or to attract the king's favor, or even better, Brigit's favor. They enjoyed feasting, slaughtering calves at a prodigious rate, and as a result there was an unusually ample supply of hearty fare to be had, at any hour. Brigit sent word for one of the slave girls and gave her instructions. Ten minutes later the girl returned, the trencher piled with beef and kale cooked in drippings, coarse bread and butter as well as a bowl of porridge and a horn full of mead.

Harald's eyes went wide when he saw the food, and his face had that look of desire that Brigit generally found directed at herself. He sat up, swung his feet over the edge of the bed. He swayed a bit, then steadied himself. He paused to regain his balance then reached for the trencher and attacked it like a Viking.

Brigit tried to gesture for him to go slow, tried to communicate that it might be dangerous for him to wolf down the heavy food, but his hunger eclipsed his reason. He tore in, and all Brigit could think of was the way her father's hunting dogs went after a chunk of meat tossed into the middle of their pack.

Brigit sat back and watched with a mixture of delight and not a little revulsion as Harald went at the food with his knife and fingers. The rí túaithe were not the most decorous of men, but they seemed absolutely delicate in comparison to the way the young Norseman ate.

It took Harald about ten minutes of chewing, ripping, swallowing and wiping his mouth on the sleeve of his none too clean tunic before he set the trencher down and laid back with a contented sigh. He looked over at Brigit for the first time since the food had arrived and smiled at her, a smile so warm and full of genuine affection that the memory of his eating habits fled from her mind. He said something, she had no idea what, but the tone sounded very much like "Thank you." He paused, and then added, "Brigit."

"You're welcome, Harald," she said and he smiled and nodded.

They sat like that for some time, and then Harald fell asleep again, his mouth slightly open, his breathing soft and steady, with none of the labored rasping of his fevered sleep. Harald, she decided, must have an extraordinary constitution. She would have expected him to be far more wasted by the fever than he was. He seemed as if he had just woken up from a nap.

Youth... she thought. She reminded herself that he was only a few years younger than herself.

Brigit remained where she was, watching him as he slept, the strong jaw, the yellow hair swept back behind his broad shoulders.

Is this the face of a heathen murderer? she wondered. She thought of the great atrocities that had been done to her people by the Vikings, the sacking of the monastery at Iona where dozens were butchered, the destruction of Rathlin and Skye, the rape of Inishmurray off Sligo and Roscam in Galway Bay.

Were those Harald's people?

Then she recalled watching from her window at the royal house of Gailenga as her father ripped the living guts from her husband, Donnchad Ua Ruairc. The fact that he deserved every second of the agony he suffered, and she knew it, did little to lessen the horror of the memory.

Brigit gave a sigh that encompassed all the weakness of men, then stood and stepped quietly from the room.

With Harald asleep, she walked down the hall to the room where the one called Giant-Bjorn was held. While Brigit considered it her Christian duty to care for all the hostages, in truth she gave only perfunctory attention to the other two, and devoted nearly all of her time to Harald, but she did not dwell on why that was.

It was two days since Brigit had looked in on Giant-Bjorn. At the last he had been mending well, and now, but for a slight limp, was as good as if he had never been wounded. Flann had ordered two guards to stand outside his room, since, unlike Harald, he was once again strong enough to pose a genuine threat.

But there was no one in the hall outside his room now, and Brigit could not understand why that might be.

She paused by the door. It was made of two-inch thick oak and iron-bound, intended to slow down anyone trying to get in quick. She listened, but could hear nothing from within. She knocked, tentatively. It was an odd thing - she did not often knock on doors. She heard no answer, no sound.

Slowly she lifted the latch and swung the door open, just enough to peek inside. The room was a wreck, the bed tossed on its side, the table smashed to pieces, the cross that had hung on the wall broken in two and thrown in a corner. It looked as if they had locked a wild bear in the place. But it was empty.

Brigit closed the door and stared off into the twilight of the hall. She wondered if Giant-Bjorn had been moved, if her father had finally become sick of having the fin gall under his roof and had moved them to the prison. He might have spared Harald, might have sensed his daughter's special affection for the young man.

If he sensed that, he would slit Harald's throat, Brigit thought. She walked down the hall to where it opened into the great hall, where a dozen servants and slaves made ready for the evening feast. At the table a handful of the rí túaithe were already into the mead, and they greeted her with looks and words that expressed their appreciation of her royal bearing, but she ignored them. Brigit crossed the hall to the south wing of the house. The other one, Olvir Yellowbeard, was kept there.

There were guards at his door, two men, well armed, so she knew he was within. She stopped at the door, waited for the guards to open it, but they hesitated. She saw glances exchanged between them.

"Open the door," Brigit said, but still they did not move.

Footsteps in the hall, and the guards looked over gratefully to Brian Finnliath, master of the guards at Tara, as he approached with his usual active step.

"Master Finnliath," Brigit said, stepping over to meet him. Brian Finnliath had been master of the guards for most of Brigit's life, and while it was his sworn duty to protect all of the royal household, he had always cared more for Brigit than any of them. He used to carve her little wooden swords, when she was a girl, and teach her to fight. When one of the rí túaithe had once, in his cups, made a lewd comment, Brian had beat him half to death, and then saved his life by not reporting the comment to Máel Sechnaill.

"Brigit, my dear, what is it?"

"I wish to check on the well being of the fin gall, but these men will not let me pass."

Brian Finnliath looked nervously around, just as the other guards had. "Mistress, I don't think..."

He got no further. Brigit turned and before any of the three men could act, lifted the latch and swung the door in.

Olvir Yellowbeard was there, as she had surmised. Not on the bed, but on the floor, leaning against the bed. His arm lay by his side at an odd angle. His hair and beard were stiff with dried blood. His tunic was wet where he had urinated on himself. He looked up at her with his one eye that would open, the other swollen shut under humps of bruised and bloody flesh.

Brigit gasped. She put her hands to her mouth and backed away. She felt one of Brian Finnliath's hands on her shoulder but she shook him off. She swallowed hard, then turned and ran.

Chapter Twenty-Four

We fought; I paid no heed
that my violent deeds might be repaid.
My lightning sword I daubed with blood.

Egil's Saga

Harald was in a deep sleep, a profound sleep. His body felt heavy and he was completely comfortable, as if there was a mattress on top of him as well as below, and it was pressing him down, encompassing him with warmth and softness.

He dreamed of the sea. In his dreams he was on board the *Red Dragon*, except it was much longer than the real ship, and the mast, as big around as a tree and with no sail or rigging at all, rose up and up to the sky. All his fellows were there, and his father and grandfather. Brigit was there, too.

The ship was pitching with short and jerky movements, as if she was cutting though the in-shore chop, her bow headed for some rocky beach.

And then he was awake. Or so he thought. He could see the room, dimly. It was dark but there was light, yellow, dull and wavering, and it gave Harald a sense of relief because he hated the dark. There was a hand on his shoulder.

He turned his head. Brigit was beside him, shaking him.

Brigit... he thought. He had thought of little else, since his fever broke. *Lovely Brigit, come for me...*

It was like paradise. He was warm and rested and here was the beautiful Irish girl come to share his bed with him. But there was a dream-like quality to it all, and suddenly he was not so sure that any of it was real.

131

He looked around, trying to remember where he was. He recalled Brigit, but what else? Where was he?

He tried to think because if he could remember where he was then he would know if this was a dream or not, if the lovely Brigit was a real woman or just a soft vision in his sleep world.

But here she was, pulling on his arm. She wanted him to get out of bed, apparently, which he did not want to do. Rather, he wanted her to get into bed with him. Despite his grandfather's urging, Harald had never been with a woman before - the idea made him a bit nervous - but somehow he felt it would be different with Brigit. He and Brigit would just melt together, they would commingle like warm porridge and honey and it would be fine and lovely.

But she was definitely pulling on his arm so he swung his legs over the edge of the bed and sat up, as much as it grieved him to leave that warm, soft place.

Once he was sitting up, Brigit turned away, hunting for something. Harald looked around the room, lit by a small oil lamp which Brigit must have brought with her, and he began to recall his situation. They were holding him in this fine room, though he was not sure who they were. They were treating him well, but still they would not let him leave the room, and he was not sure why. He recalled the jarl who had spoken to him - Harald assumed he was a jarl - the one named Flann. It was only after he left that Harald realized Flann had answered none of his questions, save to say that his father was coming for him.

Father... Harald had not really thought of his father, or Ornolf, or the others. There had been so much to consider, and he was so weak, and Brigit was so much on his mind. But now, sitting on the edge of the bed, he was taken by a profound sense of loneliness, such as he had never felt before. Not the loneliness he felt working the high meadows in the springtime back in East Agder, but something much deeper than that. Like treading water in the open sea. Everything he knew was gone.

Then Brigit was in front of him again, with her lovely heart-shaped face and her dark hair tumbling around. She held out his shoes and he looked at them, unsure what she wanted, and nodded his head.

Brigit thrust them at him with an exasperated expression and Harald took them and put them on, and that seemed to be what she wanted. He kept his eyes on her as he wrapped the laces around his ankles and tied them. There was something different about her. She was wearing a heavy wool cloak, like one would wear out of doors. He had never seen her wear such a thing before.

There was a sewing basket at her feet, from which she pulled a large piece of dark cloth. She beckoned for Harald to stand and he did as he was directed.

The cloth turned out to be a cloak or a coat of some sort, woven from course wool, a rough garment. Brigit held it up bottom first for Harald to slip over his head. The night was warm and he felt no need for more clothing, but he was getting the sense that Brigit did not stand for argument so he pulled it over his head and found the sleeves with his arms.

He looked down at the loose fitting robe as Brigit tied a rope belt around the waist. It looked very like the robes Harald had seen the Christ priests wearing in the monasteries he and his fellows had sacked. He wondered if they were going somewhere, he and Brigit.

Brigit reached up and flipped the cowl of the garment over Harald's face. It was big and obscured his view, but again he made no argument. Brigit stepped back and examined him, then nodded, apparently pleased, and that made Harald happy.

Brigit picked up the oil lamp and the basket and moved soundlessly to the window on the far wall of the room. It was covered by a thick wooden shutter that was barred from the outside at night - Harald had tried it several times. But tonight apparently it was not, as Brigit blew out the lamp's flame and slowly pushed the shutter open to peer outside.

The night air spilled into the room, cool and moist and fresh, and with it, muted and distant sounds. Harald crossed over to Brigit, eager to look out the window and smell the fresh air and perhaps touch the girl, but he was still not certain what she was about.

His legs felt unsteady as he crossed the room, and his head seemed to swim. He had not been on his feet for more than a few minutes at a time for as long as he could recall. He thought back. Since the fight on the longship.

He stepped close to Brigit and she put her hand to his chest to stop him and he stopped. She looked out the window again, looked left and right, and then with a quick motion that surprised Harald, she dropped the basket through the window, then hoisted herself up on the sill and eased herself down to the ground outside. She looked around again, then turned and beckoned.

A few things were coming clear. Brigit wanted him to leave with her. He was not sure why. Was he in danger in that house? He had thought he was among friends.

Brigit beckoned him again with an emphatic wave of the hand and he too climbed up onto the windowsill and dropped to the ground. He felt awkward, his arms and legs not moving the way they once had.

There was movement in the dark, the sound of running feet, and suddenly three big dogs were on them, panting and growling. Harald stiffened and felt a surge of panic - he did not like dogs - but Brigit held out her hand, down low, and the dogs sniffed and rubbed against her, eager for her sharp nails to scratch their necks.

The past few days had been sunny and warm, but now a light mist was falling, cool and wet on Harald's face and hands. It felt good. Brigit picked up the basket and walked off and Harald and the dogs followed.

He looked around as they walked, curious about this place he had been for...he did not know how long. The moon behind the thick clouds illuminated the area with a dull light. There were a dozen or so buildings, from small, round, thatched places to a big wooden structure that towered over the others and that Harald guessed was a mead hall or a temple of some sort. Well-beaten roads edged with rail fences crisscrossed the huge compound. There were orchards and gardens as well. He could smell horses and the remains of fires, dying away.

The entire area was surrounded by a circular wall, perhaps twenty feet high and easily a mile in diameter. In the dark he could not tell what it was made of, but if it was like the other walls he had encountered in his raiding in Ireland it was built up of earth and wood.

It was a lovely night, despite the light rain, and Harald was enjoying the stroll after his long confinement. As he moved he felt the strength and coordination come back to his legs and arms, and that was good.

Then Brigit stopped short and he all but ran into her. She turned and looked at him. They were nearly the same height. Her face was creased with concern, which surprised him since he himself was having such a nice time.

She reached up and adjusted his hood so it covered more of his face, making it even harder for him to see, but he did not object. He wondered why she was doing this, what was going on.

And then with a lightning flash he understood. She had decided they must run off together! She was in love with him, but her father would not have them marry for some reason, perhaps because Harald was a Norseman, or too young, so she had decided they would just run away. It was the only thing that made sense.

Harald felt a warmth spread over him, like slipping into a bath. He smiled at Brigit and she smiled back, a tentative smile. It was only natural that she would not be as light-hearted as he was, Harald understood that. It could not be an easy decision for her to give her life to a man with whom she had never actually spoken.

There was a new vigor to Harald's step as he continued to follow behind his soon-to-be lover. He could see now they were headed for a gate in the wall, though from the size of it he judged it was not the main gate. He wondered at the hour. It seemed well into the dark, dead time of the night.

They were twenty feet from the gate when Harald saw a man move out of the shadows, and he started a bit. He was not expecting to see anyone. And then another, on the other side of the gate. Guards. Brigit did not break her stride and Harald followed behind.

One of the guards spoke. The words were meaningless to Harald but the tone seemed part deferential, part challenge. Brigit said something in reply, pointed to Harald. Harald tried to retreat deeper into his cowl.

Now the other guard was there, and he was studying Harald while Harald studied him. He wore a helmet, no mail. There was a big knife on his belt and he carried a spear but no sword. The other guard, the one who was still talking with Brigit, was armed the same.

They're all but naked, by our custom, Harald thought. A Viking wouldn't go to the mead hall so lightly armed, to say nothing of standing guard duty.

Harald turned back to Brigit, who was still in conversation with the first guard. Their voices were louder, their tones more strident - it sounded very much like an argument. Suddenly the second guard stepped up to Harald and with a quick movement pulled the cowl back. The conversation stopped. The guards wore a self-satisfied look. Brigit looked near panic.

This is ridiculous, Harald thought. *Why were they bothering with all this talk? Two guards, armed only with knives and those awkward spears, and not in the least prepared for a fight?* Harald had been bred to combat since he was a child, had already been in more fights than most professional soldiers, and he knew when a thing could be easily done.

Am I strong enough? he wondered. He could feel the wasting effect of his sickness in his arms and legs.

Yes. The walk and the food earlier had done him good. He might not be in shape to charge a shieldwall, but he could certainly best these two ill-prepared guards.

With that he flung out his arm and yanked the spear from the hands of the guard closest to him. The guard, surprised by the lighting move, made no effort to resist. He was just starting to make some noise, utter some protest, when Harald drove the butt of the spear into his stomach. He doubled over with the sound of air being driven from him and Harald caught the man's head with his knee and snapped him back, flinging him to the dirt.

He whirled around just as the other guard was lunging with his spear, but Harald knew he would do that so he sidestepped the thrust and using his spear like a staff in those close quarters hit the man on the side of the head. The wooden shaft made a dull clanging sound on the guard's helmet. The guard staggered sideways and Harald swung the spear the other way and slammed it into the other side of his head.

The guard went down on his knees. Harald drew the spear back and directed the wicked iron point at the place in the man's chest where it would kill him quick and silent. He tensed for the thrust, then felt a hand on his arm, holding him back, and he heard Brigit say in a sharp whisper, "No!"

He turned his head to look at her. Brigit's eyes were wide and she was shaking her head. For some reason she did not want him to kill the guard. In the intensity of the moment he had forgotten she was there. The dogs were bouncing around, panting and growling, but did not interfere.

He is one of her people, Harald realized. She was Irish, just like the guard. She was not a Norseman. He would have to remember that, if they were going to spend their lives together.

Harald nodded and was rewarded with the look of relief on Brigit's face. The guard was still on his knees, still partly stunned. With the tip of the spear, Harald flipped the man's helmet off and then swung the shaft like a club, catching the guard on the side of the head and knocking him out cold. He would live, but he would raise no alarms for a while.

Harald dropped the spear and grabbed the guard's legs and dragged him into the shadows of the gate, then did the same with the other. He pulled the knives from their sheaths and stuck them in his rope belt, then gathered up the spears. He was breathing hard and his legs felt wobbly.

Brigit hefted the heavy bar that held the gate shut and pushed it open, just enough for a person to squeeze through.

"Come along," Harald said in a whisper, gesturing for Brigit to follow him through the gate, but Brigit hesitated, shaking her head. Harald gestured again and again Brigit shook her head, pointing at him and then pointing through the open gate, as if she wanted him to go on by himself.

Harald frowned in frustration. With the love that they shared, words had not been necessary, until now. How could he assure her that it would be all right, that he would protect her? He shook his head, beckoned, but still she would not follow.

"You...go...alone," she said. Harald could make no sense of the words, but he guessed she was saying she was too frightened to carry out her plan of running off with him. But he was a man now, not a boy, and Thorgrim had taught him that being a man meant, among other things, being decisive, taking charge.

He shifted the spears to his left hand and took a quick step toward Brigit. Before she could react, before she could even move, he bent over, wrapped his right arm around her thighs and straightened, with Brigit draped over his shoulder.

"Oh!" she said, a little exclamation of surprise, with just a hint of outrage. In three steps Harald was out the gate, bearing his true love off to their new life together.

Chapter Twenty-Five

The morning sleeper
has much undone.
The quick will catch the prize.
Hávamál

The weather had been remarkable - five days of sunshine on the Irish coast. But with the coming of dawn came the end of that good fortune.

During the dark hours, a light mist had begun that coated everything with wet. Then, soon after first light, the storm clouds rolled in low and the rain began to fall in earnest.

Magnus Magnusson, sitting his horse on the top of the rise and looking out over the ocean, felt the first rivulets of rain working their way through his cloak and between the links of his mail, making cold wet spots on his wool tunic beneath. He wiped the water from his eyes, ran his fingers through his beard, and stared at the place where the longship had disappeared into the rain and the mist.

"This was a mistake," said Cormac Ua Ruairc, also mounted and standing beside Magnus. "We were fools to have not taken them when we had the chance. Now, who knows if we will ever see them again?"

Cormac was not talking to Magnus, but rather to the man mounted on his other side, Niall Cuarán, who was second in command of the Irish troops. Niall was what the Irish called a rí túaithe which, as Magnus understood it, meant he fancied himself king of some insignificant little shit-hole.

"It was not a mistake," Magnus said. It was supremely irritating to him when Cormac spoke as if he was not there, which he found Cormac did quite often.

"If this rain does not lift," Niall said to Cormac, "We'll never know where they might come ashore."

You would, Magnus thought, *if you knew the first thing about ships, you ignorant, self-satisfied, sheep-buggering Irish fool.*

"They have only their oars to move them. I saw to that," Magnus said. "They can move no faster than a man on horse back, riding at a moderate pace. Nor can they come ashore just anywhere. There are only certain places one can beach a longship. If we follow on shore, with riders spaced a mile or so apart, and watch the beaches within a day's ride, then, by the Hammer of Thor, we'll find them."

Cormac and Niall exchanged glances. Magnus was certain he saw a trace of a smirk on Niall's face. "By the Hammer of Thor, indeed," Cormac said, and he and Niall together made the Christian gesture, touching forehead, stomach and shoulders.

Magnus did not know what that charm was supposed to accomplish. He did know he had had a belly-full of their condescension.

Magnus wheeled his horse in front of Cormac, so he and the exiled ruiri of Gailenga were face to face. "Do not forget it, Cormac..."

"Lord Cormac," Cormac corrected.

"Do not forget it, Cormac, that you cannot find the crown without me, and without the crown you will never be more than what you are right now, which is a minor king who does not even rule the pathetic little cow pasture he calls a kingdom. Crawl to your god if you will, and I will bargain with mine, but do not presume to mock me again, or by my gods we will cross swords."

He dug his heels into his horse's flanks, pounded off toward the soggy field where the servants were just starting to break camp. Even with the cold rain running down his face he could feel his skin burning with anger.

Magnus and Cormac, the leaders of the Danish and Irish alliance, already a shaky coalition, were not the only ones watching as the *Red Dragon* disappeared into the rain and fog. Huddled in the brush, his fur wrapped around his shoulders, Thorgrim Night Wolf watched as his ship was seemingly swallowed in the mist. An uneasy feeling - Thorgrim did not like to be separated from his ship - and the way the vessel slowly faded from view looked so much as if it was moving from this world into another that it made Thorgrim nervous.

Judging from the murmuring and shifting of the dozen men behind him, he was not the only one who felt that way.

He reached under his fur cape and fingered the two silver pieces hanging from a cord around his neck - a Hammer of Thor given to him by his father many years before, and a cross, give to him by Morrigan in the prison in Dubh-linn. Between the two he felt he was pretty well covered.

"Stop that muttering, you cowardly, superstitious old women," Thorgrim scolded as he twisted around, still in his crouching stance. The rain was running though his hair and beard and down his face. He wiped the water away. Normally his helmet would have provided some protection, but that was long gone, taken by the Danes, and the few helmets they had plundered from the mead hall had gone to his men.

Morrigan was next to him, the cowl of her cape soaked through and plastered to her head. She had made it clear that she did not wish to stay aboard the longship without Thorgrim, particularly as Ornolf's comments were growing more lewd and direct. Thorgrim agreed she should come ashore. Someone who knew the land and the language would be helpful.

There was a rustling in the brush and then Egil Lamb appeared through the bracken. "They left one man behind to watch the beach," he reported. "Now they have one man less, and Egil Lamb has a shield."

He swung the shield off his back. Round, with a protruding, pointed boss, the shield was covered in thick leather. It was unpainted.

"That's no Danish shield," Thorgrim said.

"No. This fellow was Irish, by the looks of him," Egil Lamb agreed.

Thorgrim frowned. He met Morrigan's eyes and she looked uncertain as well. If these were not Orm's men following them, then who were they?

"Let us go," Thorgrim said. He moved cautiously out of the brush and looked along the rolling fields in every direction. They were alone. He stood and stepped into the open, feeling very exposed, and his men followed.

They moved up the hill, walking in a loose swine array. The country was open, which would allow them to see an attack from a ways off, which was good, because they still had a dearth of weapons. Each man had a sword or a spear, at least, but there were only six shields, including Egil Lamb's, and four helmets between the dozen of them. If they did not have surprise, they had practically nothing.

They crossed a half a mile of wet grass, skirting behind stands of brush and trees to keep out of sight. The country looked quite different to Thorgrim in the dim daylight than it had at night in his wolf dream, but still he recognized the land and knew without doubt where he was going.

"We'll keep below the crest of this hill, work over to that stand of brush," Thorgrim said, pointing toward the unruly thicket that stood near the high point of the hill they were climbing. Hunched over, moving fast, the fin gall worked their way along the ridge and shuffled into the brush. Thorgrim heard low curses, stifled shouts of pain as his men took twigs in the eyes and stumbled over twisted vines.

They came at last to a place where they could look out across the fields. Half a mile away, the enemy was breaking camp. The big tents came down in balloons of fabric as the center poles were removed. A dozen or so men swarmed around the camp. Two horse carts stood ready to accept their loads.

A dozen men, Thorgrim thought, *and the rest are off hunting for us.* If he were looking out for a longship in this weather, Thorgrim imagined, he would have riders spread out along the coast, and racing ahead to find the beaches where the longship might land. He would leave just a handful of men, servants mostly, with a minimal guard to protect against bandits and to break camp.

He imagined that that was exactly what Orm's man had done.

It took the Danes another hour to pack the tents and poles on the wagons and stow away the casks, crates, iron pots, spits, all the accouterments of a field campaign. Thorgrim wondered how these people, moving at that glacial pace, had ever made it out of Denmark, never mind taking Dubh-linn from the Norwegians.

Still, he was grateful for the lack of enthusiasm for their job, as it made his easier. He led his men further north along the muddy track - it could hardly be called a road - that ran across the fields, along which the baggage train would have to travel. They came to a place where the path split an oak grove before climbing up to higher ground. Thorgrim spread his men out on either side of the road, nestled deep into the undergrowth, and there they waited.

Thorgrim was just starting to think he had made a mistake, that the baggage train was heading off in some other direction, when he heard the first squeak of wooden axles and the muted thumps of horses' hooves over the sound of rain on leaves. He glanced to his left. Skeggi Kalfsson and Svein the Short were crouched there with weapons drawn and faces intent on the path beyond. To his right, Thorgerd Brak, recovered from the wound he received escaping Dubh-linn, was ready as well, and two others that Thorgrim could not see through the brush. On the other side of the road, well hidden, waited Egil Lamb and the five men with him.

Thorgrim's breathing became quick and shallow as he tensed for the fight. He felt his mind sharpen until nothing else existed save for the world of battle. And then the enemy was there.

A rider came first. He wore a mail shirt and cone-shaped helmet and carried a bright colored shield and there was no doubt that this fellow was a Dane. Thorgrim wished to Thor and Odin he had archers who could take these men down first, but that was not to be. Their bows and arrows had been taken in Dubh-linn, and there were none to be had in the mead hall.

And then the thought of archers and tactics and such went right out of Thorgrim's head, like ripples in a pond that spread out and disappear. He felt the war cry in his throat and before he could even think about it he was on his feet, shouting like a madman, howling and charging out of the brush and right for the mounted Dane.

The surprise could not have been more complete, and it was clear from the look on the Dane's face, in those last seconds before he died on Thorgrim's sword, that he was not sure these creatures charging from the brush were men at all. Ireland was a haunted place. It was a fact well known to all Northmen.

The Dane was still slumped over in the saddle when Thorgrim pulled his sword free and whirled around to take on the next comer. Half the party with the baggage train were unarmed slaves, and they were running as hard as they could back down the road, and Thorgrim's men let them go.

Skeggi Kalfsson and Hall Gudmundarson were locked in a fight with the man at the lead wagon, a huge man with thick beard and a great swath of hair that even in the rain refused to lie down on his head. He was lunging and parrying with his spear while the two Norsemen tried to get past the lethal point to put their swords to work. They looked like nothing so much as dogs baiting a furious bear.

Thorgrim rushed to the fight, but before he could join in, the men on the other side of the baggage train, recovered from the shock of the ambush, came leaping over the traces and around the wagons, swords and spears in hand, slinging bright painted shields and leather covered shields off their backs and onto their arms. Thorgrim stopped himself short, twisted aside as a sword was thrust at his neck, a shield battered his own sword aside.

And just as the new men plunged into the fight, just as Thorgrim's men might have been overwhelmed, just as the guards saw themselves gaining the upper hand, Egil Lamb and his men, their timing perfect, came charging out of the brush with war cries bursting from their throats.

The men guarding the baggage train hesitated, confused by this fresh attack. And in that instant the fight was over.

The man facing Thorgrim turned to look for this second attack and Thorgrim drove his sword right through the man's chest. The big man with the wild hair was down, felled by three swords, but not before he had driven his spear into Hall Gudmundarson's throat.

Thorgrim stood panting, sword in hand, looking at the dead and wounded around him. Of his men, only Hall was dead and a few others wounded, but just slightly.

"Egil, hurry up the road and see that the others are not returning," Thorgrim said.

Morrigan stepped out of the woods. If she felt any horror at what she had just seen, she did not show it. She walked over to the big man, who lay by the wagon, eyes wide, bleeding his life away, the blood mixing with the rain and running in rivulets down the muddy path.

She spoke to him, in Irish. He glared up at her. She spoke again. He spit the words at her, three words, then closed his eyes and did not move.

Thorgrim stepped up to her side. "What did you say?"

"He's an Irishman. I asked him who is master is."

Thorgrim looked down at the man. By the clothes, by the weapons, it was clear he was no Norseman. But the man who had led the procession was a Dane, there was no mistaking it.

"What did he say?"

Morrigan was frowning. "He said 'Cormac Ua Ruairc'".

"Who is that?"

"He is the brother of Donnchad Ua Ruairc, who was ruiri, the king of Gailenga. Donnchad was husband to Brigit, the daughter of my lord Máel Sechnaill. Until my lord killed him."

Thorgrim grunted. These Irish seemed to kill one another faster then the Vikings could, but he had no time to sort out the complicated relationships that Morrigan described.

"Skeggi, get these wagons turned around," Thorgrim said. "You men, go catch those horses that bolted. Snorri, go tell Egil Lamb we are moving now."

With some difficulty and not a little cursing the wagons were wheeled around and the baggage train, led by its new owners, headed back from whence it had come. Thorgrim spit rainwater from his mouth and shivered in the cold. His only comfort came from the thought that his enemy, whoever he was, now deprived of his food and shelter, would be more miserable still.

Asbjorn the Fat watched the fight from the relative safety of the oak grove. Wearing only torn trousers, shivering in the cold, filthy, starving, an iron collar around his neck, Asbjorn for the first time since he had come to that low place was able to forget his misery as he watched the ambush, and the slaughter of his tormentors.

He had expected the traitor Magnus to kill him back at the monastery of Baldoyle, but their enmity ran far too deep for that. Magnus would have his fun. He would torture Asbjorn first, make him suffer crushing humiliation.

He had stripped Asbjorn all but naked, had put an iron collar around his neck, had his man Hallkel Half-wit lead the prisoner like a cow, stumbling along bare-foot behind the wagons. Asbjorn could barely comprehend how quickly his fortunes had changed.

He spent the night staked out like an animal at the edge of the camp. Morning had brought no relief, just greater misery, with the cold rain falling on his corpulent, naked body, the iron collar digging into the soft flesh of his neck, as Hallkel led him along.

The baggage train was approaching the oak grove when Asbjorn stumbled, fell in the mud, and was too miserable to get up, even with Hallkel pulling on the chain and kicking him. The wagons were a hundred yards ahead of them when they rolled into the ambush in the trees.

Hallkel Half-wit, as his name implied, was not the brightest of Magnus's men, but he was loyal and he followed orders. And his orders had been to look after Asbjorn the Fat. So rather than abandon Asbjorn and charge into the fight, Hallkel led Asbjorn into the woods, where they hunkered down in the bracken and watched the quick, bloody, one-sided battle.

"Keep quiet," Hallkel whispered to Asbjorn as the wagon train was turned around, the ambushers heading back toward the place they were hiding.

Asbjorn shook his head. *Idiot,* he thought. As if he was going to call out to men who had just slaughtered the entire guard of the wagon train. But as he sat there, completely silent, completely still, save for the involuntary shivering, clenching his teeth to keep them from chattering, Asbjorn Gudrodarson recognized an opportunity.

He did not speak as the baggage train rolled by, the raiders' feet making sucking noises in the mud as they walked. He remained silent even as he looked into the face of the man leading them and recognized Thorgrim Night Wolf, the very man they were hunting, now hunting them. He did not speak until the entire train had rolled out of sight, back the way it had come.

"Do you know who that was, that attacked the wagons?" Asbjorn asked, speaking softly.

"No," Hallkel said. He was still looking down the road, toward where the wagons had gone. Asbjorn could hear the confusion in his voice. Hallkel was not sure what had happened, or if he had done the right thing, or what he should do now.

"Those were Irish raiders," Asbjorn said. "We Danes are no match for them."

"Hah!" Hallkel made an indignant sound. "There are no Irish that are a match for us."

"You think we Danes, Orm and his men, could best an Irish army?"

"Of course! We are as good fighting men as any in the world! Better."

"Hmmm," Asbjorn said. He waited.

"What? What are you saying?"

"Well, it doesn't look well for you then, does it? You've joined with the Irish against Orm, and now you say that the Irish will lose."

Hallkel was silent as he chewed on that. "I haven't joined with the

Irish...," he protested, but there was more confusion than conviction in his voice.

"You follow Magnus. Is Magnus riding beside Danes, right now? No, he is riding with an Irish king, who wants only to drive us into the sea. What will happen to those who follow Magnus, when Orm defeats the Irish, as you say he will?

"Look at me," Asbjorn continued. "I could have joined Magnus. But I would rather suffer this great humiliation now, than suffer what Orm will do to those who turn on him."

That speech left Hallkel silent for some time. When he finally spoke again, he sounded more confused, more frightened then ever. "What can I do?" he asked.

"I will tell you what to do," said Asbjorn.

Chapter Twenty-Six

The traveler must
train his wits.
All is easy at home.
Hávamál

Magnus Magnusson was riding the cliff edge. To his left the wet fields rolled away inland, their usual startling green color muted in the rain and fog. To his right, the steep, rocky ledges fell to the breaking surf below.

He looked out over the water, to the place where the sea and fog melded into one another. He hoped very much to see the Norwegian longship come dipping out of the mist, hoped the Norwegians would decide the safest bet was to keep an eye on the shoreline, so that he could keep an eye on them. Magnus was worried.

The deal was simple enough. The Crown of the Three Kingdoms, and Cormac Ua Ruairc's rule over Brega, Leinster, and Mide, in exchange for the combined Irish army deposing Orm and setting Magnus in his place. An alliance of Irish and Danes. Once they stopped fighting one another, all of Ireland would be at their mercy.

The alliance with Cormac had taken months of terribly dangerous negotiations. One misplaced word, one betrayal by any of the several men involved, and Orm Ulfsson would have put Magnus to death, just as he wanted to. Through it all, Magnus had steered his course true, had managed to pull together all these elements, fire and water. But now things seemed to be coming apart, and Magnus was starting to wonder if the time had come for him to cut and run.

He reined his horse to a stop and stared off north along the coast. Cormac and that bastard Niall Cuarán had ridden off by themselves. *What are they plotting?* Magnus wondered. Once they had the crown, they would have no further need of him. The truth of that had occurred to Cormac and Niall Cuarán, Magnus could see as much, and they were intending to take advantage of the fact.

He looked over his shoulder. *Maybe I should just run now,* he thought. There was no other way to extract himself, that he could see. His men were outnumbered by the Irish, and though they were better armed and better able to fight, they might well be butchered if they tried to leave.

I could ride back to Dubh-linn, tell Orm we were attacked by an Irish war party. Everyone was killed. Chances were if he did that, Cormac would kill all his men, so there would be no one left to speak against him. It would be most important of all, of course, that Asbjorn be killed.

Perhaps I should kill Asbjorn now, Magnus thought. *Yes.* Regardless of what he decided to do, Asbjorn was too much of a liability to be left alive. He had had his fun with the fat whore's son. Time to end it.

He wheeled his horse around and headed back toward the place where they had made camp. The baggage train would be coming from that direction, with Asbjorn on his leash following behind. He heard hoof beats, twisted in the saddle, saw the familiar shape of Kjartan Swiftsword riding toward him.

"The riders are well spaced, and I sent Vifil Ketilsson, he has the fastest mount, sent him on ahead to see what beach those Norwegians might come to tonight," Kjartan said, reigning up beside Magnus.

"Good," Magnus said, though he wondered how the Norwegians would find the beach in that weather, or if they would even dare close with the shore. Or if they had decided to just piss on the crown and row back to Norway. He scowled as his mind wrapped around those thoughts.

"Where away, Lord Magnus?" Kjartan asked after they had rode some distance in the wrong direction.

"Back to the baggage train. I've had my fun with Asbjorn. Time for him to die."

Kjartan did not say anything. He had favored killing Asbjorn straight off.

Magnus pulled his cloak further over his shoulders. His clothing was soaked clean through to his skin and the best he could hope for was that the cloak would block the wind a bit. As an experienced raider and campaigner, he was well used to such misery, but that did not make it any less miserable. He thought of the big, comfortable tents that Cormac and Niall Cuarán carried with them and he found himself longing for one, and bitterly resentful that he did not have one, and would not be invited into theirs.

"Those men left with the baggage train are taking their own time," Kjartan observed and his voice pulled Magnus from his funk.

"What?"

"The baggage train. I would have thought it would be here by now, but I can't even see it."

Magnus looked down the worn, muddy strip that passed for a road. The baggage train was nowhere in sight. Sure, they could not see far, thanks to the rain, but far enough that they should have been able to see it by now.

"Let's go give those lazy dogs a kick in the ass," Magnus said, digging his spurs into his horse's side, pushing the animal to a canter. Hard riding helped dispel his own irritation, doubt and suddenly gnawing worry.

The path ran over a low hill then dipped down into a stand of oaks. They crested the hill and still could not see the wagons. They had left an even number of Danes and Irish to guard it, along with the dozen slaves Cormac and Niall Cuarán brought for their own comfort. Magnus would have expected the Danes, at least, to show a little more initiative in getting things moving along.

They rode down into the arms of the oak grove, slowing their horses to a walk as the trees rose up on either side of them. The path twisted off to the right. They were just rounding the turn when they saw the first body. Vestein Osvifsson, who had been left in charge of the baggage train. They recognized him by his bright colored tunic, though when they had seen him that morning there had been a mail shirt over it. He was face down in the mud.

"By the hammer of Thor!" Kjartan shouted but Magnus's stomach was twisting and he did not trust himself to speak. As they rounded the curve in the path more and more of the scene of the disaster opened up to them. Dead men strewn around the grass, hacked down with swords, run through with spears. Irish and Danes. If the men who had done this had lost any in the fight, they had taken the bodies with them.

Magnus looked on the scene in silence while behind him Kjartan cursed enough for the both of them. The bodies had been stripped of anything worthwhile - mail, purses, helmets, shields. There was not one weapon left that Magnus could see. He searched the ground, rode past the death scene, hoping desperately to see Asbjorn's fat corpse staring blankly at the sky, but Asbjorn was nowhere to be seen.

"Damn!" Magnus said. He wheeled his horse around and rode back into the trees. Kjartan was on the ground, looking at the tracks.

"Bandits, do you think?" he asked.

"No," Magnus said. Half these man had been killed with swords. Bandits did not carry swords.

"You can see here where they turned the wagons around," Kjartan said, pointing to the torn-up, muddy patch on the ground. He straightened and followed the path with his eyes. "Headed back from whence they came."

Magnus nodded. His mind was racing through the implications. How long ago did this happen? Judging from the state of the bodies, they had been lying there for an hour at least. The blood had been washed clean by the rain, leaving the horrible jagged wounds gaping open, and faces white as fine linen.

"Let me ride back and get a party together," Kjarden suggested. "We may be able to run these whores' sons down yet."

"No," Magnus said. "Let us go, you and me, and see where these tracks lead."

Kjartan mounted and they rode off. The tracks were easy enough to follow, the horses and wheels of the wagons leaving deep cuts in the sodden grass. Magnus kept a sharp eye out for Asbjorn, or for Hallkel Half-wit, dead or alive, something to tell him how things lay. But he saw nothing.

The wagon tracks left the path once it emerged from the trees and ran down hill toward the water, and Magnus's certainty and horror grew with every perch they rode. They crossed fields, winding around clumps of brush, following the wagons' tracks down hill toward the sea.

They found the wagons on the beach. Abandoned, broken up, parts taken for firewood, most likely. Everything was stripped out of them - food, mead, utensils, weapons, everything. The horses were gone.

"Thor, strike those sons of bitches down!" Magnus shouted in pure rage. That fat loud-mouth Ornolf had utterly outfoxed him, standing off shore and then returning to the same beach to come up behind them. How had he known that they were following on shore?

Damn them all, he thought.

Asbjorn was gone, and there was no doubt he was heading back for Dubh-linn, with tales for Orm of Magnus's treachery. There could be no abandoning Cormac now and returning to Dubh-linn himself. But any status he still enjoyed with Cormac would be gone once this was discovered. He had nothing left.

Magnus slid down off his horse and walked around the shattered wagons. They had really taken everything there was to take, including the big tents. That at least gave Magnus reason to smile. Cormac Ua Ruairc and Niall Cuarán would be sleeping in the rain like the rest of the dogs.

Why would they take the tents? Magnus wondered. Tents would not do them much good on board a longship. What they needed was a sail.

Magnus stopped short as he realized what they were about. "Oh, damn them!" he shouted into the rain and the fog.

Chapter Twenty-Seven

When passing
a door-post
watch as you walk on,
inspect as you enter.
It is uncertain
where enemies lurk
or crouch in a dark corner.
Hávamál

Brigit struggled for all she was worth. She kicked her legs, beat at Harald's back with her fists, but it seemed to have no effect. It was maddening. She could not believe the strength of the young fin gall's arms, even after a week of wasting fever. Her only real experience with a man's embrace had been with her husband, Donnchad Ua Ruairc. Donnchad was a warrior, and no weakling, but his strength was nothing beside Harald's.

She did not scream. She considered it, felt fairly sure that it would bring the guard running in pursuit, but still she held her tongue. If they caught Harald carrying her off they would kill him in some brutal way. Angry as she was, she could not bring herself to condemn him to being publicly and horribly put to death.

"Harald! No! Put me down!" she said in a harsh whisper, but he did not respond to the words any more than he responded to the kicks and punches.

Oh, God help me, I am such an idiot! Brigit thought as she watched the road pass by beneath her, Harald's goatskin shoes moving back and forth in a steady, unbroken rhythm. Stolen by a Viking whom she herself had set free. It was the last word in humiliation and it made her furious, and in her fury she began pounding on Harald again.

Brigit punched and kicked for as long as she could, and then she slumped over in exhaustion. Harald's pace did not slacken at all.

*Dear God, this is humiliating...*she thought. They were too far now from Tara for her screams to be heard, even if she wanted to scream, which she didn't. For all the stories about Vikings raping their victims and carrying women off to be sold in the slave markets of the Moorish countries, she did not think that that was Harald's intention. He was stealing her away, to be sure, but she did not think he meant her any harm.

I wonder if he wants to make me his wife? she thought. The idea was only a little less worrisome than the slave market.

Brigit was spent, hanging limp over Harald's shoulder like a sack of barley, when he finally slowed and set her down. She stumbled, dizzy, finding herself suddenly upright again. Harald's big hand shot out and grabbed her by the arm to steady her. She saw the look of concern on his face. Whatever stupid thing he had in his dull Norse mind, he had no intention of hurting her.

"Well..." she said as the spinning faded. Harald was breathing hard and even in the dim light she could see his face was pale. He had used much of his diminished strength in carrying her off.

Maybe he'll faint, she thought. Then she could escape.

She looked around. They were on a road, surrounded by dark fields and darker patches of trees in the distance. Dawn was still some hours away. It was raining harder now, and Brigit felt the water seeping through the front of her clothing, which had remained dry while she was draped over Harald's shoulder.

She had no notion of where she was. She did not often venture away from Tara, and when she did, it was with a company of guards in attendance. The Irish countryside was far too dangerous for a princess to travel alone. Even if Harald fell over dead she could not find her way back.

Harald crouched down, resting on his heels. He was still grinning his stupid grin and suddenly Brigit wanted to slap him, but she resisted. That would not help things. She tried to think of what *would* help things.

For several minutes they remained there, Harald smiling, Brigit trying to guess where she was and what she could do, the rain falling on them with increasing force. Finally Harald stood again, nodded to Brigit, then turned and marched off down the road.

Brigit watched him go. Harald was two perches away before he realized she was not following. He stopped, turned back and gestured for her. She hesitated.

She could not get back to Tara on her own. She did not know the way, and even if she did she would likely be robbed and killed or worse if she tried. Harald could not bring her back because he would be killed if he returned. She could not stay where she was. She was stuck.

"Ahhh!" she shouted, a sound of pure exasperation, then marched off after Harald.

They walked for hours, side by side. The dark sky lightened until it was wolf-gray and the rain continued to fall, sometimes just a mist, sometimes a torrent. The road they followed was soon no more than a long, winding patch of mud that grabbed at their shoes and splattered their legs. Brigit wondered if Harald knew where he was going. She did not see how he could, though he walked with the bold confidence of one quite familiar with his path.

If they had met with anyone, a sheep herder, a band of traveling monks, a theater troupe even, then Brigit would have asked the direction back to Tara, and would have promised a substantial reward for returning her to her father's court. But no one was abroad in that driving rain.

It was around noon, by Brigit's estimate, when her hunger and exhaustion finally became more than she could bear. She had by then fallen several paces behind Harald, and when she saw a large rock which presented an irresistible seat she stepped off the road and sat. She closed her eyes and savored the delicious sensation of taking the weight off her feet. After a moment she opened her eyes again. Harald was marching off, unaware that she was no longer behind him. She toyed with the idea of just letting him go.

"Harald!" she called at last, and he turned and looked back. "I need a rest."

Dutifully he came back to where she was sitting and she had a sudden urge to scratch him behind his ears and see if his tongue would wag when she did. He sat beside her and smiled and she ignored him. She picked up the sewing basket she had set on the ground and dug around under the linen cloth. The biscuits she had packed for Harald were sodden, but with care she was able to pick them up complete. She handed one to Harald and he took it gratefully. It fell apart as he tried to eat it, but he caught the bits in his hands and put them one by one into his mouth. Brigit did the same.

The dried meat fared better, and was even somewhat improved for its soaking, which made it less leathery. They ate that as well, and Brigit felt a bit better, though she was soaked through and starting to shiver.

These miserable damned Norsemen may be used to this sort of thing, but I am not, she thought. Then Harald reached a big arm around her and pressed her close to him. She could feel his warmth, even though various layers of wool, and her misery dissipated a bit, along with the cold.

After some time of that, Harald stood and helped Brigit to stand. Her feet ached and her muscles protested and she felt as if she could not straighten up. But Harald seemed not to be feeling any ill effects from the cold and the hardship of walking, despite his prolonged sickness. Brigit did not want to appear weak, so she forced herself to stand straight and to match Harald's pace.

They had gone half a mile from their resting place when they saw the smoke. Brigit thought at first it was a darker, wispy cloud, low down on the horizon, but as they drew closer she realized it was smoke, from a hearth most likely, whipped away in the wind as it rose.

"Harald, look!" She tugged at the sleeve of his monk's robe, which she had thought would be such a clever disguise, and pointed toward the smoke. Harald looked in the direction she was pointing. Finally he saw the smoke too. He nodded gravely and turned to walk in the opposite direction.

"Harald, no!" Brigit said. She pointed toward the smoke again, more emphatically this time. The sight of the smoke, and its promise of a warm, dry hearth, blankets and food, were suddenly irresistible to her. And where there was smoke there was someone who could take her back to Tara.

Harald shook his head and pointed in the opposite direction. *He thinks there's danger there,* Brigit thought. *Or perhaps he really is stealing me.*

It did not matter. The thought of a warm house, even some rude sheep herd's cottage, now quashed any other consideration. She turned and marched off in the direction of the smoke.

She covered maybe ten paces before she felt Harald's hand on her arm, but she was not going to be carried off again. She whirled around, breaking his grip, and smashed the sewing basket into the side of Harald's head. The thin reed basket was too insubstantial to make any real impression, but from surprise alone she managed to knock Harald clean off his feet. She wound up to kick him hard but he was faster than that, sweeping his leg in an arc and knocking her feet out from under her. She fell with a grunt, right on her rear end, scrambling back to her feet before Harald could pounce.

She turned to face him, furious, the basket held ready to hit him again, but to her surprise Harald was laughing. He got to his feet, slowly, smiling, keeping his eyes on hers as he did. He picked up the two spears he had dropped with her surprise attack. He nodded and pointed toward the smoke.

Brigit lowered the basket. She nodded, and walked off. She felt in charge, in control, for the first time since the fight with the guards that morning. It was a good feeling. Brigit was used to being in control, and she liked it.

The source of the smoke was a mile away, at least, hidden behind a low hill. Brigit and Harald crossed the open ground that ran up the hill, and then suddenly, as they neared the crest, they saw spread out below them a river, gray under the thick clouds and fog.

They both stopped, surprised by this unexpected sight. It was not a stream, but a substantial stretch of water, half a mile wide, and rolling along to the eastward, its surface broken and confused in the rain.

"Boyne," Brigit said, pointing, for this had to be the River Boyne. There were no others this substantial within a day's walk of Tara.

"Boyne," Harald said, nodding and smiling. The sight of water seemed to have cheered him greatly. Brigit wondered if he understood that Boyne was the river's name, and not the Irish word for river.

Not that it mattered in the least. Nor did the sight of the river distract her long from her goal of reaching the house beyond.

"Come along," she said to Harald and walked off with her young Viking following behind.

The hill rolled down to the water, and the house stood in a clearing near the bank. It was low and stone-built, round with a high-peaked thatch roof, like a hundred poor homes in Ireland. The land around the house was trampled into mud. A big hide-covered boat was pulled up on shore. Nets were hung out on stakes, presumably to dry, though there was little chance of that.

Fishermen... Brigit thought. She could smell fish and wood smoke and animals. She tried to picture in her mind the humble, honest fishing family that lived there, good Christian people eager to help strangers at their door. Or so she desperately hoped.

A thin and mangy dog was laying by the doorway and it stood and growled as Brigit and Harald stepped into the trampled yard. The growl turned to a full-throated bark as they approached and he bounded away from the house, racing for them. Brigit saw Harald tense, saw him bring one of the spears up to a fighting grip, when the dog reached the end of its tether and jerked back violently into the mud.

Brigit swallowed hard. *No matter what sort of people these are, they will take Harald for a monk and won't dare harm us for that,* she thought.

They moved closer, ten feet from where the dog strained at the end of his rope, barking like mad.

"Is anyone there?" Brigit called, trying to make her voice heard over the ferocious barking. "Anyone there?"

It was a full minute before the wooden door creaked open and a man stepped out, a big man, so tall that he had to stoop to make his head clear the lintel. He stepped out into the yard and looked at them. He wore a filthy, mud-caked tunic. His beard and hair were wild. He looked more a bandit than a humble fisherman.

"I'm Brigit..." Brigit called out, but the man did not seem to hear. Then a second man stepped out for the house and he looked to be a twin of the first, just as big and filthy. They looked at her with a mix of surprise, curiosity, and something else she did not care for.

Brigit felt her stomach knot up and she sensed Harald tense as well.

Perhaps we should just leave, Brigit thought. She took a step back then turned. There was a third man, older than the first two but just as big. He was standing a perch behind them. There was a long club in his hand. Brigit had no notion of how he got there.

"I am Brigit, and my father is your king, Máel Sechnaill mac Ruanaid!" she shouted, and that garnered some reaction at least, a faint smile on the lips of one of the twins. He stepped off, circling around to the right. He reached behind him and from an unseen sheath drew a long, heavy bladed knife.

Harald drove the point of one of the spears down into the mud so it stood upright, quivering, and he held the other in his right hand. Brigit spared him a glance. His blue eyes were everywhere, moving from one man to the next, and he half turned so he could keep an eye on the man behind. If he felt any of the panic that she did, she could not see it on his face. He looked...intent. He did not look frightened.

Then the man by the door leaned over and with a jerk of the bitter end released the rope that held the dog back. The animal nearly fell head over heels as it bounded away, free, trailing the rope, eyes wide, it's lips pulled back to reveal its vicious teeth, spittle trailing as it ran, charging right at Brigit.

Brigit screamed, hands over her face, twisting away as the dog became airborne, leaping at her throat. And then the barking changed in an instant to a howl of pain, a pathetic whimper, and Brigit opened her eyes to see the animal twisting on the ground, impaled on Harald's spear.

The twin with the knife howled in rage and charged, blind and senseless. Brigit felt Harald's arm push her aside as he stepped up, arm cocked, and launched the remaining spear at the man's chest. Man and spear met ten feet from where Brigit stood and the impact of the missile made him stagger, but did not halt his charge. Brigit screamed again but Harald just stood in front of her, shielding her, as the man stumbled and fell dead at their feet.

Harald leapt over his body, grabbed the shaft of the spear that had killed the dog and pulled it free, whirling around with the iron point level. The other two were advancing from opposite directions, but carefully, unwilling to make the same stupid, fatal mistake the first had made.

Harald backed away, keeping himself between Brigit and the two men moving toward them. The older one had his club held high, and the remaining twin now held a knife like his brother had.

"Did you hear what I said?" Brigit shouted in frustration. "I am the daughter of Máel Sechnaill! He will reward you if you help me!"

Why do they not even speak?

The one with the club moved in, stepping quick, while the other circled around, so that Harald could not watch them both.

"Harald!" Brigit warned. "Watch behind!" There was a branch, four feet long and thick around as Brigit's arm, on the ground where someone had been cutting wood. She picked it up and held it like a club.

She turned to look back at Harald. The man with the club was no more than ten paces away. Harald shouted, the first sound from his throat, a wild battle cry. He cocked his arm and then hurled the spear forward. The older man twisted sideways and then back, a look of triumph on his face that he had avoided the weapon.

And then the look was gone as he and Brigit, in the same instant, realized that Harald had not actually thrown the spear at all, had only pretended to, and in that fleeting second of the man's confusion Harald threw the weapon for real. The iron point found it's mark in the man's chest, knocking him back so he fell flat in the mud, twisting in agony, screaming and clawing at the spear shaft.

Harald whirled around, in his hands the knives taken from the guards at Tara, just as the third man charged. The Irishman was a good foot taller than Harald and a hundred pounds heavier, and he came on like an enraged animal, eyes on Harald. He did not see Brigit swing the branch in her hand, seemed unaware of her until the branch slammed into his shins and he stumbled, eyes wide, and Harald slashed his throat open as he fell.

He went face down in the mud. His hands clawed at the brown ooze but he made no sound. Harald and Brigit stood over him, gasping for breath. And then his hands stopped and he did not move again.

Harald looked up at Brigit, and as his breath returned he nodded his head and smiled. Brigit smiled back, a weak effort, then turned around, bent double, and vomited.

Chapter Twenty-Eight

Spying and prying
the predator eagle
approaches the ocean.
Hávamál

This fog is a good thing, Thorgrim thought. *We are lucky to have it...* He looked warily over the *Red Dragon*'s gunnels, half a cable length over the water to where everything was lost in the thick, white mist.

We just need to keep a sharp eye out for rocks and such, he thought. There were navigational hazards in the fog. And there were evil spirits as well that hid in the mist, and Thorgrim knew that it was those that were truly worrisome.

He was not the only one glancing nervously out into the fog. He could see men all along the deck look up now and then and stare outboard. Once they heard something splash in the water nearby and every head jerked up at once. Some of the men gasped. Thorgrim thought Svein the Short might even have wet his trousers.

The Norsemen did not like fog.

Happily, most of the men on board the *Red Dragon* had something to occupy themselves. Ever since the longship had put to sea for the second time that morning, now loaded with all the plunder of the baggage train, the men had been working at tearing the tents apart and reassembling the fabric into a sail.

They went at the seams with knives, cutting them up into their individual panels, and then Thorgrim assembled the panels on the deck, trying them first one way and then another until at last he had come up with the best arrangement. Then the men took up awls, needles and sinew thread and began to furiously stitch as the longship wallowed in the milky netherworld.

Thorgrim fingered a corner of the sail and tried to distract himself. It was waxed linen, and not as heavy as he would have liked. Nor did they have extra cordage to sew diagonal reinforcements onto the sail, as they would if they were building a new one. It was not ideal, but it would hold up to a moderate breeze and drive the longship much faster than anyone following on horseback could travel.

He wanted to order the men to sew faster. Every moment that Harald was out there, someplace where Thorgrim could not protect him, was agony, a slow, burning agony. It was torment enough to have his progress toward his son slowed to the pace of the longship under oar. To be wallowing motionless in the spirit-bound fog was nearly unendurable.

But the men were stitching as fast as they could, and there was nothing for Thorgrim to do there, so he dropped the fabric and walked back to the afterdeck. The driving rain had tapered off to a drizzle. Ornolf was sitting on a sea chest, drinking the mead liberated from the Irish.

"The men will not be pleased if you drink that all," Thorgrim said.

"Ha! Even Ornolf could not drink this all!" he said. "Well, perhaps I could."

Thorgrim leaned on the impotent tiller and tried not to look out into the fog. Morrigan threaded her way through the men and came aft.

"Come, have a drink with Ornolf, my darling!" Ornolf roared but Morrigan pretended he was not there.

"I perceive the men are worried," Morrigan said to Thorgrim in a low voice. "Is there something wrong?"

"It's the fog."

"What of the fog?"

"It makes the navigation hard when you can't see the shore. There could be rocks, or such."

Morrigan nodded. Thorgrim didn't tell her about the evil spirits. He wasn't sure she would believe him. He fingered the cross and the hammer of Thor around his neck.

"Will you be able to find the place where the crown was hidden?"

"Yes. And then what?"

"We bring the crown to the man whom God has deemed should wear it. Máel Sechnaill mac Ruanaid."

"How? Over land? There is an army ashore, waiting for us."

"Somewhere north of here, not far, there's a river that runs into the heart of Ireland. The River Boyne. It will take us to within a day's walk of Tara."

Thorgrim nodded. The longships were shallow draft, in part so that they could work their way up rivers and allow the Vikings to raid far inland. If they could get to Harald by water, that would be a good thing. The Vikings were always more comfortable on water.

Forward, Sigurd Sow and Snorri Half-troll, working opposite ends of the head of the sail, stood and pulled the fabric taut. Thorgrim straightened. The stitching was done. The sail was an ugly, misshapen thing, an embarrassment for a lovely longship like the *Red Dragon*, but it was a sail, a functional sail, and it was much, much better than nothing.

"Come, let us bend that on!" Thorgrim shouted, stepping forward, desperately glad to have some seamanlike challenge to occupy his thoughts.

In short order the head of the sail was lashed to the yard, the sheets and bowlines rigged. Thorgrim thanked Thor and Odin for tricking the Danes into leaving the rigging when they stripped *Red Dragon* of her sail. The best sail in the world would have been useless without it.

Thorgrim looked fore and aft. All was ready. He nodded his head and the men at the mast hauled away on the halyard, and foot by foot the yard jerked up the mast, and the sail spread to the soft, wet breeze.

"Sheet home! Haul away, your lee brace!" Thorgrim cried. The long tapered yard swung around. The sail fluttered, collapsed, then filled to the wind. The *Red Dragon* heeled over, just a bit, heeled and stayed heeled under the pressure of the sail. The men were silent. Then up from below, from the place where hull met water, came a soft gurgling sound, a murmur, the gentle noise of water rushing past. The *Red Dragon* was alive once more.

Thorgrim looked with delight at the curve of the sail, and while the ugly thing would have horrified him in the past, now it was the most beautiful thing he had seen. His eyes moved down the mast and then outboard. Around the edge of the old tents he could see the longship's dragon head, returned to its rightful place on the bow.

And beyond that, only whiteness, and Thorgrim felt the old anxiety return. They were underway, to be sure, plowing a wake though the gray sea. But they were sailing blind, and into what, only the gods could tell.

Cormac Ua Ruairc was in an absolute fury. Even Niall Cuarán, whom Magnus had decided Cormac was buggering, seemed to shy away from the ruiri of Gailenga.

They were standing among the wet and bloated dead at the site of the ambush. Cormac was kicking the corpse of Vestein Osvifsson, still face down in the mud. He was shrieking in a weird, high-pitched voice. He was shrieking in his native Gaelic, and by the look on Niall's face, Magnus was glad he did not understand the words.

At last Cormac left off kicking the dead man and rounded on Magnus. "Bandits? You think bandits did this?"

Magnus shrugged. "Who else?"

"Who else? You stupid... Damned peasant bandits with sticks and clubs could not have done this! Armed men! Trained men! That's who did this!"

"Perhaps it is Máel Sechnaill," Magnus suggested. "Perhaps he knows you are loose in his kingdom, and he is hunting you down."

Magnus did not really believe it, but he knew the idea would shake Cormac up and he was right. The Irishman paused, his eyes went wide with the thought, and then he shook his head, as if trying to fling the idea away with the water that whipped from his hair.

"That whore's son Máel Sechnaill did not do this! If he was here we would be fighting him right now, and your filthy guts would be in a pile at your feet!"

Cormac swung himself up on his horse again, walked the animal down the road to where the wagon tracks rolled out of the mud and onto the green field. "Did you follow these tracks, see where they led?"

Magnus shook his head. "No. I have bigger concerns than wondering who stole your precious tent. So do you."

"Do not tell me my business, you sheep-biting dubh gall." With his eyes on the sodden ground, Cormac began to ride along the tracks made by the wagons' wheels, the track Magnus had followed just a few hours before.

Magnus had done everything he could to discourage Cormac from examining the sight of the ambush. As it was, their "partnership" was not working out at all as Magnus had envisioned. If Cormac discovered, as Magnus had, that it was Ornolf who had staged the ambush, then it would destroy what tiny bit of reputation Magnus still enjoyed with the Irish king.

But he had not succeeded in keeping Cormac away. Cormac insisted on seeing where the fight had taken place. Niall Cuarán, as ever, tagged along like a faithful dog.

"These tracks run down to the sea," Cormac said, still walking along the path through the grass.

Magnus looked up, out to sea. The fog had lifted somewhat, visibility was two miles or better to the place where the horizon was lost in the light rain. The *Red Dragon* was nowhere to be seen.

"Why would anyone take the wagons toward the sea?" Niall Cuarán asked. "I should think they would take them inland."

Stupid troll, Magnus thought. If they had not smoked it yet, perhaps they were too stupid to figure it out at all.

From north up the road they heard a horse's hooves, a rider coming fast, and they wheeled their horses around. It was one of Cormac's men. He reigned to a stop. He was breathing hard.

"My Lord Cormac! The fog has thinned! We've sight of the fin gall ship!"

Cormac looked out to sea, looked down at the tracks in the grass, looked at the messenger, unsure which way to go.

"Very well," he said and spurred his horse back toward the scene of the ambush. He met Magnus's eyes as he rode past. "We will leave it for some other time to discover who engineered this colossal failure of yours."

Of mine? Magnus spurred his horse to follow Cormac. *So any blunder is my fault, that's how it's to be?* Still, for all his outrage, Magnus felt a tremendous sense of relief that the *Red Dragon* was under their eyes once more, as well as a profound dread of what might Cormac might find when he saw her.

They threaded their way through the bodies once more and then spurred their horses on to a gallop, riding hard over the wet shore road, north up the coast in pursuit of the fin gall. Cormac's horse kicked mud back at Magnus until Magnus had to wipe his eyes and face and move his mount off to one side to be clear of the spray.

They rode along the cliffs that dropped down to the sea below, rode past their own men, Irish and Danes, who were spread as watchers along the shore. "Move up, move up, the fin gall are spotted!" Cormac shouted as they rode, spurring his men to join in the chase.

They rode hard for several miles, until at last they had left all their men behind, and it was only Cormac and Magnus, Niall Cuarán and the messenger who were on the road, riding north. They came to a high point on the shore, a grassy rise that stood a couple of perches above the rolling fields. The messenger rode up to that high place and reined his horse to a stop and the others did the same.

"There!" The man pointed out to sea.

The rest looked where he was pointing, and at first they did not see anything, save for the gray water rolling away toward the misty horizon.

"Where?"

"Off there, my lord, to the northward."

They looked again, and that time they saw it. At first they had been looking for a ship near shore, but this was a mile or more away.

For a minute they stared at the ship, growing more indistinct in the fog. Finally, Cormac Ua Ruairc turned to Magnus. He turned slowly in the saddle, deliberately, and Magnus saw in his eyes something that went well beyond his former anger.

"You told me," Cormac said, speaking slowly, "that they had no sail. And yet..."

The four heads looked back at the distant ship. There was no mistaking the shape. A longship under sail. If the crew of the *Red Dragon* had not had to spend hours in the fog sewing the thing together, or so Magnus imagined, then they would have been well over the horizon by then.

"They have a sail now, I perceive," Magnus said. "Thanks to you."

"Me?" Cormac nearly choked on the word.

"What do you think they made a sail from, you stupid Irish half-wit? They sewed it together out of your tent! Yours and this...this...buggering lap dog of yours! If you had it in you to campaign like a man and not some silly woman with your tents and your wagons and your damned slaves this wouldn't have happened!" Cormac was not the only one there who could be pushed too far.

"Are you...you mean to tell me, they are the ones that ambushed the wagons? The fin gall?"

"Of course, you fool! Any idiot could see that, straight off."

Cormac looked to Niall Cuarán, looked out to sea, looked at the messenger. He clearly was not accustomed to men speaking to him in that manner and it had thrown him.

"Now," Magnus broke the silence, hoping to swing the momentum his way, "Let us get the men and ride hard to the north. That sail will not drive them fast, and if the wind gets up any it will blow to ribbons. They are still ours."

Cormac still did not speak. But Niall Cuarán did.

"My Lord Cormac," he said, and his tone was calm, almost bored. "This pathetic dubh gall came to you with assurance that he alone could find the Crown of the Three Kingdoms, which clearly God wishes for you to wear. We took him at his word. Now we find that all he can do is tag along the shoreline, following this ship. We can do that. As it turns out, we have no need of him."

"No need of me?" Magnus roared. "Without my help, Ornolf will gather up the crown and sail off and you will never see it again, you miserable worm."

"Oh, indeed?" Niall Cuarán said. "And what do you plan to do? What indispensable knowledge do you bring, besides suggesting we follow along on shore? If we had attacked them last night, as my Lord Cormac suggested, they would have told us by now where the crown is hidden. Instead, they have plundered our wagons and now are sailing off."

"You could not have made them talk. They may be from Vik, not Danes, but they are still Norsemen and tougher than any Irish sodomite."

"You miserable bastard!" Cormac shouted and his hand went for his sword but Magnus was faster than that. Any hope of an alliance against Orm was over now. Now there was nothing for Magnus to do but save his own life.

Thorgrim's sword flew from the scabbard. Cormac's messenger had the look of an experienced soldier, clearly the most dangerous there, but beyond the reach of Magnus's blade. Magnus lunged, drove the tip of his sword into the flank of the messenger's horse. The horse shrieked, reared, bounded away, the rider struggling to hang on.

Magnus turned to Cormac, who had his sword clear of the scabbard. Cormac swung his sword; Magnus caught the blade with his own, turned it aside and lunged. Cormac screamed in surprise, threw himself back to avoid the reach of Magnus's blade. Behind him, Niall Cuarán acted as if he was trying to get into the fight.

Cormac was half out of his saddle and Magnus saw his chance. His men would have to fend for themselves, it was his life in the balance now. He pulled his sword back, backhand, and smacked the butt of Cormac's horse hard with the blade. The horse reared, Cormac clinging to the saddle. Magnus reined his horse over hard and put the spurs to its flank.

The horse bolted away, racing inland. Magnus did not care where he was going, he needed only to put distance between himself and Cormac's men.

Behind him, he heard the scream of the horses, the shouts of outrage, but he did not look back. He just rode. Time to think later. Now was the time for escape.

Chapter Twenty-Nine

I have wielded a blood-stained sword
and howling spear; the bird
of carrion followed me
when the Vikings pressed forth.
Egil's Saga

I t was just before daybreak when the half-dead guards were
discovered. Brian Finnliath, master of the guards at Tara, found
them on his morning rounds. They were crumpled in a heap by
the south gate and he thought they were drunk. Very drunk, lying in the
mud, oblivious to the cold, driving rain.

He gave one a swift kick, then the other, but got no response, not
even a moan. He looked closer. They had been stripped of their weapons.
One had a vicious bruise on the side of his head.

Flann mac Conaing was alerted. Huddled under a wool cloak and cowl
to protect against the downpour, Flann followed Brian across the
compound. The guards had been left where they lay, so that Flann might
see them undisturbed. The light was gathering by then, and Flann could
clearly see the bruises, the fact that their weapons were gone, the south gate
ajar.

"Was there no disturbance last night?" Flann asked. "No thieves,
intruders of some sort?"

"No, sir."

Flann stared at the gate. If someone had knocked at it, and the guards
had gone against their orders and opened it, then the strangers might have

killed the guards and gained entry. But wouldn't the intruders have closed and barred the gate? The open gate would raise an alarm. But if it was someone escaping Tara, then they would not be able to bar the door from outside the wall.

Why would someone have to do this? If they wanted to leave, they could just leave.

Flann regarded the motionless bodies of the guards. "It would have taken more than one man to kill them," he said.

"Yes, sir," Brian Finnliath agreed. "You're sure they're dead, sir?"

Flann looked at the man, annoyed. "I assumed they were dead. Did you not check?"

"Ah, no sir."

"Well, check, damn you!"

They were not dead. Incredibly, their hearts still beat, their mouths still drew breath. Flann had them carried to the guards' quarters, stripped and set in beds with wool blankets. He paced. He wondered if he should report this to Máel Sechnaill. He decided to wait until there was something to report.

One of the guards groaned, rolled his head. Flann stepped over, hopeful, but the man was still far from awake. Flann resumed his pacing.

Who was there who would need to escape from Tara?

He stopped pacing. "Brian Finnliath, quick, send men to check on the fin gall prisoners."

Oh, damnation, this is not good…

The one guard was coming to, muttering a few words, when Brian's men returned. "The fin gall that was questioned by Máel Sechnaill, sir, he's still in his room. He's not in good health, sir. The other one, the young one, he's not to be found."

Flann mac Conaing sunk his head in his hands as he contemplated this disaster. He looked up. "Turn out the guard. Get dogs. We have to hunt that little villian down."

Brian Finnliath began issuing orders.

My lord Máel Sechnaill must be told, Flann thought to himself, but every bit of him resisted doing so. This whole notion of taking the fin gall hostage had been his idea, his and Morrigan's, and Harald's escape would be seen as a colossal failure on their part.

He wondered at the effect that Morrigan had on him, her ability to talk him into whatever notion she had in mind. She was a strong woman, too strong for her own good, at times.

The guard on the bed moaned and his eyes fluttered open and Flann knelt beside him.

"Are you awake?" Flann asked. The guard's eyes roamed around the room then fixed on Flann's face. He looked confused.

"Who did this to you?" Flann asked.

For a long time the guard did not respond, just looked into Flann's eyes, as if trying to recall all of his life up until that point. "Water," he said at last.

Impatiently, Flann ordered water for the man and he drank and that seemed to revive him more.

"Who did this?" Flann asked again.

"The fin gall," the guard said at last. "The yellow-haired fin gall. Dressed...like a monk."

Flann nodded. "But not alone," he said. "He's a boy, he did not overpower two guards by himself."

"No," the guard agreed.

"Who, then? Who helped him?"

"Brigit." The guard closed his eyes again. "Brigit Sechnaill mac Ruanaid."

They left the three dead men and their dog where they fell in the mud and approached the house, moving cautiously, as if they were sneaking up on it. The horror she had just witnessed, the terror of the moment, the squalor of the cottage had not dissuaded Brigit from her desire to get near a fire.

They came up with the door and Harald held up his hand for Brigit to stop and she did, pulling her cloak further around her shoulders. She was ready to let Harald take the lead once more, aware that her own leadership had nearly gotten them killed.

Harald stepped up to the door and peered inside, looking left and right. He held one of the big knives in each hand, and with the handle of one pushed the door further open and took a step inside.

Brigit followed, standing just outside the door as Harald moved slowly into the one room building. The smell of the place wafted out of the door - cabbage and fish and peat fire and musty wool.

Then Harald was back at the door, an odd look on his face. Troubled. Disturbed by something inside. Brigit frowned and stepped forward, but Harald blocked her way, and he looked as if he was not sure he should let her enter. But the rain was falling hard and the cottage held the promise of a fire and it was going to take more than one young Viking to keep her out.

She pushed past Harald, who yielded to her, and stepped gratefully inside. It was dark, the only light coming from the low peat fire burning in the fireplace in the center of the single room, over which hung an iron pot from a crane. In various corners of the room there were pallets of straw, blankets and furs, benches, all the trappings of a peasant's cottage on the banks of the Boyne. The warmth was delicious. Brigit's eyes moved beyond the fire. She gasped, put her hands to her mouth.

Two people lay dead. A man and a woman. The man was face down, a staff clenched in his hands, the only weapon a poor fisherman could manage. The woman beside him must have been his wife. She lay with one leg over the man's back, eyes open and staring at the ceiling, a great red blossom of blood on her dress.

She must have fought hard, Brigit thought. Those men, dead in the yard, would not have killed her quick if she had not.

Harald said something that had the tone of an apology and stepped around her. He grabbed up a blanket from a pallet by the wall and draped it over the woman, then picked her body up and carried it outside. He did the same with the man, then came back inside. Death swarmed around the cottage, but the fire was warm.

The peat had burned down to little more than embers. Harald picked up a stick and poked at it, but not with any confidence in what he was doing. Peat fires were unknown to Norsemen. Brigit gathered bricks of peat from where they were stacked against the wall and deftly added them to the fireplace. Soon the embers flared and the fire caught the newly added fuel and the flames leapt high, illuminating the room and the sundry detritus stored there.

Harald stepped over to the door, positioned himself just inside and looked out to the yard beyond. There was no way to know if the three bandits they had killed were the only ones in that raiding party. The young Norseman stood silent and still, the knives ready in his hands, his eyes sweeping the cottage yard. He put Brigit in mind of an animal, a hunter, keen and alert for prey, or for danger.

Brigit understood the need for vigilance, but the fire was too seductive. She stared into the flames, leaping and wavering. She undid her cloak and tossed it aside, let the warmth sweep in waves over her soaked dress.

She was shivering, despite the fire, and the weight of the wet fabric seemed to pull her down. She stole a look at Harald - he was still staring out at the approaches to the cottage as if nothing else existed.

Brigit stepped away from the fire and snatched up a blanket from a pallet against the wall. It was course wool and smelled of wood smoke and sweat but it was dry. Quick as she could, with her eyes on Harald's back, she stripped off her dress and let it fall in a heap at her feet. She wrapped the blanket around her shoulders. It was long enough that it swept the floor around her feet. She stepped back to the fire. The shivering stopped as she stood, dry and wool-wrapped, by the blazing peat.

Brigit stared into the fire, the lovely fire, and her mind wandered off into some other place. Her thoughts were vague and disjointed, lost in the wild twisting of events over the past twelve hours. Tara... It seemed so far away. The warmth on her skin was wonderful. There was something wicked about standing there, naked, save for the wool blanket, the handsome young Norseman mere feet away. It gave her a little thrill. Pulled from her life at the court of Tara, she felt as if she had been pulled from everything that regulated her life.

After some time - Brigit had no idea how long - Harald turned away from the door. He said something in a soft voice as he stepped toward her. His tone was reassuring, even if the words were meaningless. He set the knives down and pulled the monk's robe over his head, struggling to free himself from the wet garment. He tossed it aside, and seemed to just then realize that Brigit was naked, save for the blanket.

His eyes went wide and he stepped closer to her, then hesitated, unsure of what to do, and Brigit found that charming. *So much for wanton raping and pillaging*, she thought.

Harald took another tentative step. Brigit smiled at him and he smiled back and closed the distance with her. He put his arms around her in a rough hug, pressed his lips against hers, kissing her hard. She pulled away. There was longing in his eyes, confusion at her resisting.

Brigit let the blanket hang on her shoulders as she undid the belt around Harald's waist and let it fall to the floor. Harald reached through the folds of the blanket, ran his hand lightly over her breast. His hand was rough and calloused, but his touch was light, and it sent a chill through Brigit. She tugged up on the hem of his tunic and Harald pulled it over his head and tossed it away.

His chest was broad and strong, as smooth and hairless as his face, and the muscles on his arms stood out bold in the light of the fire. Brigit ran her hands over his chest and his arms. Once again, Harald, in his eagerness, grabbed her and pulled her roughly toward him. Once again Brigit pushed him back. "Slowly, slowly," she cooed and he seemed to understand.

Brigit's late husband, Donnchad Ua Ruairc, was the only man she had ever been with. She had been fourteen, Donnchad was twenty-eight. Brigit had been terrified.

But Donnchad, perhaps not as considerate as he might have been, still was not cruel, had not just used her for his own pleasure with no thought for hers.

Her wedding night was a blur of terror and uncertainty. It was terribly painful, despite what Donnchad did to make it better.

And Donnchad was a passionate man. He came to her nearly every night after that. And soon the pain passed, and soon after that it became a genuine pleasure, and soon Brigit was looking forward to the night as much as Donnchad.

She missed that, since her father killed her husband, missed the strong embrace of a man, the wonderful sensation of helplessness as she was taken by one whose strength was so much greater than her own. She had looked with longing at some of the rí túaithe who courted her at Tara, strong and handsome young men. But they looked on her first as a way to gain political power, second as a way to sate their lust, and third, if at all, as a woman with whom to share themselves. Brigit could not stomach them.

That feeling, that desire she had felt for Donnchad had come again as she sat by Harald's bed, watching the young Norseman as he convalesced. At Tara she would never have acted on such a thing. But now, it seemed as if there were no rules anymore.

She pushed Harald back, just a step, and kneeled in front of him. She looked up at him. His blue eyes were wide with surprise. Before, she had wondered if Harald had ever been with a woman, but now she knew for certain he had not. She would not have thought of a Viking as an innocent, but here he was.

Brigit untied Harald's shoes and he kicked them off. She untied the leather thong that held Harald's trousers in place and pulled them down his muscular legs and he kicked those off as well. She stayed on her knees and she introduced him to things he probably had never thought of, learning about sex by watching the animals on some farm in Norway. His breathing came hard and fast. Twice he almost fell over.

Finally Brigit stood and let the blanket fall to the floor. Harald looked her up and down and ran his hands over her skin, over her neck and her back and her breasts, but he moved slow now, the roughness was gone. In its place was a sort of worshipfulness.

Brigit took his hand and led him over to the straw pallet. She lay down and pulled him down after her, and he followed, eager. He pushed her down on the straw and gently pushed her legs apart, but she shook her head and pulled him down beside her. She wanted to make the pleasure of the touch go on and on. She did not think that the final act would last very long.

For some time they lay on the straw pallet, caressing one another, until finally she could stand it no more and it was clear that Harald felt the same. She rolled back and pulled him toward her and he pressed himself down on top of her. She gave a gasp at the little jab of pain she felt as he entered her - it had been some time since her husband's death - but soon it felt simply wonderful and they moved together, the straw crunching underneath them.

As Brigit imagined, it was over soon, and it was not as entirely satisfying as it had been with Donnchad, but still it was wonderful, the sensation of being with a man, even a young man, such as Harald. They lay together, her cheek against his smooth chest. There was no awkwardness. They could not speak even if they had wanted to.

Not very much time passed before Harald was ready to go again, which surprised Brigit, as it took Donnchad much longer than that to regain his strength. But that was fine with Brigit, and the second time was better than the first. Harald was a quick learner, and she was happy to instruct.

After that they fell asleep, warm, spent, dry and content, and Brigit thought that the whole amalgam of sensations was as wonderful as a thing could be.

They slept for hours, undisturbed. When Brigit finally came awake, it was slowly. She felt Harald beside her and reached out her arm. He was sitting up. She propped herself up on her arm and looked at him. He was staring off into the dark room, his face lit by the last embers of the fire. He was listening, focused on the sounds from beyond the stone walls.

Then suddenly, to Brigit's utter surprise, he leapt out of bed and snatched up the trousers he had left crumpled on the floor. He pointed at his ear, and at the wall.

Brigit listened. That was when she heard, far off, the frantic barking of the dogs.

Chapter Thirty

It is better to live
than lie dead.
A dead man gathers no goods.
                                    Hávamál

It was a long and ugly morning, but by the time the sun was heading for the western horizon, Cormac Ua Ruairc was starting to feel better about his circumstance.

Magnus had escaped, rode clean away to the north. He had run off while Cormac was trying to get his horse under control. Niall Cuarán, rather than pursue Magnus, had leapt off his own horse and grabbed up the reins of Cormac's, steadied the animal, and helped Cormac dismount. Niall showed admirable concern for his Lord's wellbeing. And Cormac, though he would have rather Niall Cuarán had gone after Magnus, was touched by the sentiment and said nothing.

By the time they had straightened themselves out, there was no hope of catching Magnus. They did not even try. Instead, they rounded up their Irish warriors and fell on the dubh gall, cutting them down like deer driven into a pen. No more than half a dozen escaped, fleeing off south, no doubt making for Dubh Linn.

Cormac let them go. They would be put to the sword eventually, after he had the Crown of the Three Kingdoms, after he had avenged his brother by ripping Máel Sechnaill's heart out, after he had taken Tara for himself and led the combined armies to clear all the filthy Norsemen out of Ireland.

170

And then around noon they experienced some luck, or what one might think was luck, if one did not recognize the hand of God. First, the rain slacked off to a light drizzle and the fog cleared away, leaving several miles or more of visibility. Enough, anyway, that they could keep the fin gall ship in sight as they hurried along the hilly shore.

Their second bit of good fortune came when the fin gall, for some reason, took down their sail.

Magnus had mentioned a few reasons why the sail might not work, though Cormac could not recall what they were. He was too furious at the double insult of losing his tent on a rainy day, and having that same tent used by his enemy to escape, to listen to what that incompetent had to say. But Magnus must have been right, because for some reason the sail came down and the oars came out and the longship slowed to a crawl. Soon Cormac's small army was even with the ship, easily matching its pace across the water.

And that put them in just the right place when the longship swung its bow around to the west and started closing with the shore.

Cormac stood, with Niall Cuarán at his side, at the edge of a cliff. His horse was a few paces away, nibbling at the grass. Cormac never liked sitting on top of his horse near a cliff. He always had this vague worry that the animal would decide to fling itself over the edge.

At the bottom of the steep, rocky drop was a small, shingle beach, nearly lost in the gloom of the gathering dark. Two miles or so out to sea, the longship was pointing like a weathervane at that beach.

"Here is where the crown is buried," Cormac said with finality.

"No doubt, my lord," Niall said, then, after a respectful pause, added, "Or it may be where the fin gall intend to spend the night."

"No. The crown is here," Cormac said. "In any event, we won't let them escape again." If the crown was not there, then Cormac would most certainly make the fin gall tell him where it was. The coward Magnus might not have the stomach to do what needed to be done to make these men talk, but he, Cormac Ua Ruairc, deposed ruiri of Gailenga, certainly did.

A rider approached, swinging off his horse as he reined to a stop. "Lord Cormac, there's a path to the south that will lead down to the beach. Treacherous, to be sure, but not impossible."

"Very good," Cormac said, his eyes still on the longship. "Let's get the men down now, get them in place."

It took the better part of an hour for the hundred men in Cormac's army to file down the narrow trail to the beach. Cormac went fifth, behind the color bearers and a couple of pages. In that way he was ostensibly leading, while the four in front of him would find any weak places in the trail before he got there.

The shingle beach was a hundred perches wide and half as deep, with rocky ledges and sparse brush pushed up against the cliff side, just enough to hide his men. They kept to the cliff wall as they spread out, though Cormac did not think that in the evening dark, and with the longship still a mile off, they were any in danger of being seen.

They were soon positioned, couched down in the various hiding places the beach offered, waiting. The men had their instructions. Anyone who moved before Cormac, who gave away their position or spooked the Norsemen in any way would be impaled, then and there.

The longship seemed to melt into the dark sea as it approached with the setting sun, until finally Cormac could not see it at all, and a spark of fear began to glow inside. *Did they see us, from out there? Is it not too dark for them to beach their damned ship?*

And then from over the water, and close by, he heard a voice call out, the guttural tongue of the fin gall, announcing the depth of the water, and Cormac felt a surge of relief.

Soon the Crown of the Three Kingdoms would be his.

After all this time, after all the careful planning. All the work convincing his brother Donnchad to spit on his marriage alliance, so that Máel Sechnaill would kill him and clear the way for Cormac's succession. After the humiliating truce with the dubh gall Magnus, soon it would be his. The only road by which the brother of a ruiri of a minor kingdom might become the rí ruirech of three kingdoms, and by extension the most powerful man in Ireland.

Just a matter of minutes.

Cormac startled at the loud grinding sound of the longship running up on the shingle, breathed deep and shallow as his heart settled down again. There were voices now coming out of the dark, the fin gall calling back and forth. They were making no attempt to be silent. They did not know the enemy was in hiding, and ready to fall on them.

A dim light came from the dark place by the water where the longship was grounded. It grew brighter, revealing the outline of the ship, the mast, the horrible dragon's head on the bow. Someone stood on the ship's deck, a torch flaming in his hand. He touched the fire to another torch, and another, and soon the longship and the Norsemen were clearly visible in the light of the flames.

Fools, Cormac thought. They gave their own position away and blinded themselves to any threat from the dark. They were making his task all the easier.

The torch bearers led the way down the gangplank and onto the beach and two dozen men followed, armed with swords and shields, and behind them, to Cormac's giddy delight, three men bearing shovels. There was only one reason he could think of to carry shovels onto that beach at night.

Every bit of him wanted to shout and to lead the attack now, but he forced himself to wait. *Let the fin gall do your work for you, let them show you where the crown is...*

The party of Vikings marched up the beach, moving slow, spreading out, the lead torchbearer searching the ground as he moved. Someone in the band of men behind shouted, "Thorgrim! It is more to the north!" The lead man with the torch shouted back, "No, it is this way! You men, spread out, keep your eyes open!"

Cormac shook his head at their stupidity. *"Keep your eyes open!" And yet he blinds his own men with torches!*

"Here!" the one called Thorgrim shouted. A few others gathered around to look. They stared down at the beach where the first man pointed. "There is the mark I left. The crown is here."

The torchbearers stepped aside and the men with the shovels stepped up and Cormac felt a surge of panic as the first shovel ground into the rocky sand. If the Norsemen grabbed the crown right then, they could get back to the longship and get away before he could stop them.

Cormac leapt to his feet, driven by the cold terror that he had waited too long in hiding. "At them! At them!" he shouted as he drew his sword.

With wild yells and the sound of running feet and metal drawn against metal the Irish warriors burst from the brush and from behind the rocks that hid them and raced for the fin gall, ten perches away. Cormac ran as well, once the first wave was sufficiently advanced, shouting his war cry and brandishing his sword.

The surprise was complete. Over the war cries of the Irish, Cormac heard the panicked shouts of the fin gall. The torchbearers flung their torches at the charging enemy, turned and fled down the beach. Only the lead man stood his ground, torch in one hand, sword in the other, shouting, "Come back! Stand and fight, you worthless cowards!"

But it was no use. He was alone, and he could not fight off Cormac's army by himself. A spear flew through the air and into the circle of light surrounding his torch, missing him by inches, and that was the end of his defiance. He, too, flung his torch, turned and ran for the shore.

"After them! After them!" Cormac shouted as his men continued down the beach, toward the edge of the water and the fleeing fin gall.

Cormac himself had no intention of following the Norsemen. He ran up to the place where the shovel still stood upright in the gravely beach, where the fin gall had begun to dig, and there he stood. He would not lose that place, after all he had done to get there.

In the light of the guttering torches Cormac looked down at the beach, trying to find the mark that the fin gall leader had mentioned, but one rock looked like another to him. No matter. This is where they were digging. This was where he would find the crown.

There was shouting and splashing and the sounds of a fight down by the water. Cormac strained to see what was happening, but now it was he who was blinded by the torches and he could see nothing. Soon after he heard the crunch of men walking on the shingle and then Niall Cuarán stepped into the light.

"We could not stop the fin gall," he said. "They got aboard and shoved off before we could stop them."

"No matter," Cormac said. They had not come for the fin gall, he did not care about the fin gall. He was, at that moment, physically closer to the Crown of the Three Kingdoms than all but a few had ever been in the history of Ireland. He was desperate to have the thing in his hands, on his head.

"Pick up those torches, don't let them go out," Cormac snapped. He wanted to pick up a shovel and go after the crown himself, but such eagerness was unbecoming for the soon-to-be rí ruirech of the Three Kingdoms.

"You there," he pointed to one of his men, "take up that shovel. Dig, right there."

The man nodded and grabbed the shovel, jamming the blade into the gravel.

"Careful, you idiot!" Cormac shouted. The crown was probably not buried deep. He did not care to have that ancient symbol of Celtic power sliced in two by some fool with a shovel.

The soldier curbed his enthusiasm, digging carefully, scraping layer after layer of pebbles and sand away. The men holding the torches crowded close, to let the light fall on the hole, and the rest crowded up to them, eager to catch the first glimpse of the near-mythical Crown of the Three Kingdoms.

As the hole grew wider and deeper, Cormac grew more annoyed. "You men with the torches, step back. The rest of you fools, stand away. Niall, set a guard around the beach. We are just asking to be attacked here, with every eye staring into a hole in the ground!"

Niall Cuarán shuffled the men away, gave out orders for watchers to be stationed at all the approaches to the beach. Cormac stared with irritation at the growing hole in the beach, shuffled with irritation as Niall Cuarán, rather than remaining with the men, came back to watch the digging.

"This is absurd," Cormac said after twenty minutes of careful excavation. He pointed to the other discarded shovels. "Get some more men digging here."

Minutes later there were five men with shovels, tearing at the beach, and Cormac's mood was not improved by realizing that the shovels the fin gall had left were his, taken from his baggage wagon that morning.

The hole grew deeper and deeper, and when finally they dug so deep that the bottom of the hole was continually filling with seawater, they began to dig outward, expanding the area of the search.

As the men with the shovels began to flag, more men were brought in to replace them, and eventually men to replace those. All though the dark hours they dug. When the torches began to sputter out, men were sent to collect brush and wood and a fire was built at the edge of the hole so that the diggers could see, so the firelight would illuminate that first glimpse of gold, glinting out from the mud. All night long men fed the fire, while others flung dirt from the hole.

Dawn came grudgingly through the thick overcast. Cormac stirred, realized that he had fallen asleep, though he could not even recall sitting. He stood quickly.

The men were still digging, but with little enthusiasm. The hole was twenty feet wide in any direction, and six feet deep, down to where the seawater flooded in. The horizon was empty, the fin gall were long gone. There was no crown.

Chapter Thirty-One

The warrior's revenge
is repaid to the king,
wolf and eagle stalk
over the king's sons.

Egil's Saga

Flann mac Conaing made his weary way from the guards' barracks to the main house. His wet cloak weighed him down, but not half as much as the anticipation of the coming interview.

Máel Sechnaill was at breakfast in the outer room of his sleeping chamber. The guard outside the door announced Flann, and Máel beckoned him in.

"It's the fin gall, Lord Máel, the young one," Flann made his halting start.

"Humph," Máel Sechnaill said, stuffing a hunk of coarse bread into his mouth. He chewed, swallowed. Flann waited. Máel Sechnaill would surely choke to death if he was given the news with his mouth full.

"What of him?" Máel asked. "Did he die from the questioning?"

"No, Lord. Not that one. The young one, the one called Harald." Flann did not remind Máel Sechnaill that Harald was the important one, the grandson of Ornolf who had the crown. He thought it best if Máel did not remember this.

"Yes, yes," Máel said with a wave of his hand. "My daughter's little pet. What of him?"

"Ah...well...it seems he has escaped..."

Máel looked up sharp at that. "Escaped? How?"

"We're trying to learn that, my Lord."

"No matter. We'll hunt him down." Máel Sechnaill stood, and now he had an eager look on his face. "Have some sport out of him."

"There is one other thing, my Lord..." Flann felt his guts turning into some viscous substance. "It seems he stole your daughter, Lord. He stole Brigit."

Máel Sechnaill froze. He stood absolutely still. His eyes burned into Flann's. Even after decades of combat, including three near fatal wounds, it was the longest, most frightening thirty seconds of Flann's life.

"He...stole her?"

"Yes, Lord." It was a lie, of course, a calculated lie. The guard was clear on the point - the fin gall was not stealing Brigit, Brigit was helping him escape. But Flann could not tell Máel Sechnaill that. It was too much. "Sir, he...", Flann continued and he was cut short.

"Why are you standing here, you God forsaken idiot? Why are you not hunting him down?"

"My Lord, I have turned out the guards, with dogs. They are on the trail now, and I..."

"Damn the guards! Damn them, you pathetic fool! Rouse the rí túaithe, have them get their men to arms! Immediately! I want every man-of-war riding out of Tara in twenty minutes. We will come down on this fin gall son of a bitch like the wrath of God!"

"Yes, Lord!" Flann said, turned to rush off and get the army camped at Tara started. Máel stopped him.

"Flann mac Conaing," he said, and Flann stopped and turned back. He did not like the tone in his king's voice.

"Yes, Lord?"

"You brought this wolf into my house. You and your sister, and your damned clever notions. I have not forgotten."

Flann waited for Máel Sechnaill to say more, but he did not. He did not have to.

"Yes, my Lord." Flann hurried out the door, past the other sleeping chambers to the great hall where the rí túaithe who were not too drunk or too hung over would be having their breakfast. He burst through the door, knocking a slave girl and her tankards of ale to the floor.

"To arms! To arms! The fin gall has escaped and stolen the princess Brigit!"

For a moment no one moved or spoke. They looked at Flann, stunned into silence as Máel Sechnaill had been. Flann could practically hear the reckonings going on in their thick heads. The man who rescued Brigit from the fin gall would certainly win her esteem, and Máel Sechnaill's as well.

The rí túaithe broke like surf on the rocks, leaping from their seats, vaulting over benches, calling for pages, armor, horses, for their men to turn to, to take up arms. Flann had never seen them move so fast, not even when the dinner bell was rung.

It was not quite the twenty minutes that Máel Sechnaill had ordered, but near enough, when all of the men-at-arms at Tara were mounted up - those who had horses - or turned out armed for the march. Of the three hundred who had gathered for the attack on Leinster, nearly two hundred were left. Most of the levy had drifted away, back to their farms, but the professional soldiers and the rí túaithe had little reason to leave, when life was so bountiful and free at Tara.

And now they were moving out. And the seriousness of their mission did not quell their excitement, pleasure, and their hope that it would end in great personal advancement and gain.

Máel Sechnaill led the army. He wore the armor that had been put away when the attack on Niall Caille, rí ruirech of Leinster, had been postponed. Flann rode beside him, wearing helmet, mail and tunic, a cloak pulled over those. He was soaked through and miserable, though to be sure he would have been miserable in any weather.

Brian Finnliath came pounding up on his horse, reined to a stop. Over his mail shirt was his trademark tunic, a green garment with a bold white and red cross on the front. "I have men with dogs off in every direction, Lord," he reported. He was breathing hard and he had a desperate look on his face. Brian Finnliath loved Brigit like she was his own daughter. Indeed, he was often more a father to her than Máel Sechnaill. "But forgive me, Lord, it is hard going, tracking in this rain, that washes signs away."

Máel Sechnaill said nothing, and no one dared say anything more to him. He scanned the horizon. From his mount, on the high hill of Tara, he could see for miles, until the green countryside was lost in the rain and mist. Water dripped from the edge of his helmet like rain running off the eaves of a roof, but he seemed not to notice. He squinted into the rain, his pale blue eyes all but lost in folds of skin.

Flann shifted in his saddle. He was starting to think he should say something when Máel Sechnaill finally spoke. "He will go to the water," Máel said. "He is a Norseman and the Norsemen are drawn to the water. Master of the Guards!"

"Sir!" Brian Finnliath tried to steady his horse.

"Get your men and dogs, get them on the north road. Fan them out, cover as much land as you can. We will split up, follow behind. But as sure as my hope of heaven, they are making for the River Boyne."

At first, Harald did not hear the dogs. He came to in that warm, soft place where he and Brigit had so enjoyed each other. Still half asleep, he was aware of being wrapped in a wonderful sensuous feeling before he had any real idea of where he was.

He felt the girl beside him, and that was the first memory to come back, and he found himself instantly aroused and ready to have her again. Indeed, that idea seemed to wipe out everything else, the desire so strong that no other rational thought could penetrate.

He rolled over and gently pushed on Brigit's shoulder and moved his body over hers. She had shown him a lot of fancy things before, things he had known nothing about, and while it was all undeniably good, now he just wished to get right to the central business.

Brigit was still asleep but she made a little cooing sound that drove Harald wild and he thought he might explode right then. But for all that, as he became more awake, he became more aware of some ill-defined warning vying for attention with his lust.

He ran his lips along the lovely line of her neck, moved his hand over her breast, and at that instant the voice in the back of his head broke through, loud enough to be heard.

Dogs!

Harald whirled around and sat up and stared into the dark. He felt Brigit stir, put her arm around his waist, and then push herself up on her elbow. He felt her eyes on him, but his focus now was beyond the wattle walls of their cottage.

Dogs...

Not a great hunting pack, but more than one, that was certain. A mile away? Perhaps. Maybe closer.

Harald flung the blankets off and leapt to his feet, searching out his clothes in the dim light. He found his trousers lying in a heap where he had kicked them off. He snatched them up and danced around the room, pulling them over his legs.

Brigit was looking at him now, wide-eyed. He pointed to his ears and pointed to the wall and nodded and she nodded as well. He picked up her dress and tossed it to her and made a gesture of hurry, which he hoped she understood.

He grabbed his tunic and slipped it over his head. It was damp and cold and uncomfortable. He had lost the chance to dry it over the peat fire, but he had been in no position to think of such things when he had flung it to the floor.

He moved across the cottage, snatched up a spear, and opened the door, just a crack. The yard was lit in a dim, blueish light and a heavy mist was falling. Harald was disoriented, there was a dream quality to everything. What time of day was it? Morning? No. It had been morning when they arrived at the cottage. They had slept through the afternoon. Evening, then.

He felt better now that he knew what time it was, but the dogs were getting closer, much closer. He turned to Brigit. "Hurry!" he urged, and was rewarded with a glance at her naked body as she pulled the dress down over her head.

Harald picked up the monk's robe, the two knives and the second spear. Brigit was flinging her cape around her shoulders. There was a loaf of bread and some meat on the table by the fire. He pointed to those and Brigit nodded and picked them up.

Harald headed for the door, gesturing to Brigit as he walked, and she followed, a hunted and wary look on her face. They stepped out into the cool, wet evening. The dogs were just over the far rise, judging from the sound. At least Harald did not have to think about how they would escape. He already knew that, knew it the second he had laid eyes on the cottage.

Half running, Harald led the way around the cottage, past the white, bloated bodies of the three bandits. He tossed the monk's robe and the spears into the boat pulled up on the shore. It was a curious looking thing, a twenty-foot long wooden frame covered in sewn hide, unlike anything seen in the Norse countries. But still it was a boat, and as such it gave Harald a measure of optimism and hope.

Brigit was there with him. He could see the fear in her face. "It's all right, it will be all right," he said, hoping the tone at least would covey some comfort, but as far as he could see it did not.

He took the bread and meat from her, placed it on one of the thwarts. The dogs were louder, and clearly headed for the cottage. They were hunting dogs, and Harald had no doubt the dogs were hunting for them.

Harald scooped Brigit up in his arms. She gave a little gasp of surprise and he lifted her over the gunnel and set her down beside the bread and the meat. He grabbed the gunnel and shoved. The boat began to slide toward the water, but it was harder going than he had anticipated. He realized he should not have put Brigit in first, but it was too late, and he did not want to appear foolish, taking her out again.

He pushed. The boat slid half a perch. And then the dogs broke over the low hill to the south and came tearing down at them, at Harald and the boat.

Harald looked at the dogs, looked at the river, looked back at the dogs. He could not take Brigit out of the boat now, not with the dogs there, and he could not get the boat in the water before the dogs were on him.

Kill the dogs first, Harald decided. He snatched the spears out of the boat. He hated dogs. Why did these damned Irish have so many dogs?

The first of the pack was two perches away and racing for him with open mouth and lolling tongue. The light was fast fading and it was difficult for Harald to see. He wiped the water from his face and eyes, dropped to one knee and held the spear in front, the butt end of the shaft against his foot. It was a boar hunting technique, but it worked on the over-eager dog, as the animal charged right onto the point, impaling itself and dying with never a sound.

Harald released the spear, grabbed up the second one, swung the butt end like a club at the next dog. He hit the animal, made him cry in pain and surprise, but that dog and his fellows were not as eager as the first. They kept their distance, barking and snapping, as Harald thrust and swung with the spear.

He was backing away toward the boat when he heard the sound of hooves. He was not surprised. Packs of dogs of course would be followed by riders, men who were determined to run him and Brigit to ground. They were the hunted, now.

"Odin, All-father, I could surely use your help!" Harald shouted out into the mist. He backed away, took a last swing at the pack, and then swung himself up into the protection of the boat, the sides too high for the dogs to clear.

Brigit looked more frightened than ever. She looked at him with a question on her face and he wished to all the gods in Asgard he could speak her tongue, but he could not. He grabbed her by the cloak and pulled her down onto the bottom of the boat, hidden from view, and half laid on top of her, pulling the monk's robe over them both. He lifted himself up, just slightly, and peering over the gunnel.

It was only one rider, and Harald gave a thanks to Odin, as this was certainly the best he could have hoped for. The horse followed the path the dogs had taken, the rider reining to a stop in the muddy yard. One man, wearing a green tunic with a big red and white cross on it, the symbol of the Irish Christ God.

Harald ducked low again, out of sight. It was not a question of hiding - the dogs were baying all around the boat - it was just a matter of gaining a tiny bit of surprise.

Harald could see nothing. His nose was full of the smell of the wet wool. He heard the horse moving closer, cautious steps toward the boat. He readjusted his grip on the spear, shifted his foot to get a better purchase on the bottom of the boat.

The horse made a snorting sound, very close by, and Harald judged the moment. He threw off the monk's robe, leapt to his feet with a shout. The rider was there, just half a perch away, and he wheeled his horse in surprise. Harald cocked his throwing arm. Brigit pushed herself up from the bottom of the boat. She shouted, "Master Finnliath!" and Harald threw the spear.

It was a good throw, straight and strong, but the horseman was ready for an attack. His shield was up and the sharp spear point embedded itself in the wood. The horseman was knocked off balance with the impact and Harald leapt from the boat and landed in the soft mud.

The dogs were nipping at his legs and he kicked at them as he raced for the man on the horse. The spear, still embedded in the shield, was swinging wildly around. Harald grabbed hold of the shaft and pulled, yanking the rider clean off the horse.

One of the big knives was in Harald's hand and he stabbed down at the man's throat but the man caught his wrist and held it. Harald tried to force the knife down, but the man on the ground was very strong, stronger than he was, Harald could tell. He reached around for the other knife, and suddenly he was knocked sideways, knocked right into the mud, the knife flying from his hand.

Dog... was all he could think, one of the dogs had leapt at him. He grabbed the second knife from his belt, scrambled to his feet, crouched low and ready for an attack. Brigit was standing over the man on the ground, and it appeared that it was she who had knocked him down, but that made no sense.

"No!" Brigit cried. She shook her head. "No!"

Then Harald remembered. He remembered the guards at the gate, how Brigit did not want them killed. She could not bear to see her fellow Irish killed. Fair enough.

The man on the ground was half up, struggling to his feet, still off balance from his fall from the horse. Harald stepped up and kicked him hard in the stomach. Through his soft shoes he could feel the mail shirt under the tunic and he knew his blow would not be very effective, but it was good enough, tossing the man back to the ground. It would gain them seconds.

"Come along!" Harald shouted, waving and running for the boat, but Brigit did not move. "Come along!" he said again, with more authority to the order.

"No!" Brigit said. She used that word a lot, and Harald was beginning to wonder what it meant. Perhaps that she was afraid. It was the gate all over again.

He advanced on her and this time she hit him, hit him hard, right on the jaw. It surprised him, and it hurt, and without thinking he started to hit her back, swinging his fist around in a reflex reaction, stopping just inches from her face as he realized what he was doing.

Brigit had her face in her hands, shying from the blow, and she did not see it coming when Harald scooped her up again and tossed her over his shoulder.

The horseman was on his knees, sword drawn, and he swung the blade in a wide arch, but Harald sidestepped him, raced for the boat with Brigit over his shoulder, screaming, pounding his back and kicking her legs. The dogs were leaping and barking and snapping but they did not bite.

With his left arm and shoulder Harald heaved on the boat, pushing it toward the water, and now, free of Brigit's weight, it began to move faster. Brigit twisted around and began hitting Harald on the back of the head.

"Odin and Thor, what a burden these women are!" Harald shouted in frustration as the stern of the boat hit the water and it began to float free. He tossed Brigit over the gunnel, into the bottom of the boat, aware that he was not being as gentle as he had been before.

The horseman was on his feet and charging for the boat. He shouted something that sounded very much like "Brigit!" and swung his sword at Harald's head.

Harald ducked and felt the blade swish past. Hands on the gunnel he leapt, both feet off the ground, and kicked the man hard in the chest, sending him sprawling. There were more riders now, Harald could hear the hooves pounding as they rode hard, but he did not have time to look. He shoved the boat farther out into the river. Brigit had picked herself up and was looking over the side of the boat, down into the water. Harald gave one last shove and swung himself over the gunnel as the boat floated free.

The man on shore was shouting something and now Harald could see the other riders charging up, he could see their armor gleaming dull in the fading light. But it was too late for them.

The boat drifted further from the shore and then the current caught it and swirled it away down river. Harald felt a great sense of relief. He was afloat. He never had any doubt, ever, during his captivity, that his father would come for him. Thorgrim Night-wolf would hunt for his son and bring him home. And he would come by water. It was the Viking way. And now he, Harald was on water too, and could go to a place where he and his father would meet.

Harald caught his breath, then looked over at Brigit, who was sitting on a thwart. He smiled at her, and she flung the piece of meat at his head.

Chapter Thirty-Two

You have not often fed
wolves with warm flesh.
Egil's Saga

The *Red Dragon* put out to sea, driven by her long oars and then the makeshift sail, after Ornolf's men yielded the beach to the Irish. Soon the ship was engulfed by the dark and the rain. The land was lost entirely in the gloom, save for the three torches on shore, and soon those too were swallowed up.

Morrigan stood aft, where she generally stood, because that was where Thorgrim stood and so it was the only place on the longship she felt at all safe. She stared out into the dark. It was an odd sensation, this sailing through the night. Morrigan had little enough experience with ships. She had never been at sea in the dark before. There was something frightening and wonderful about it, all at the same time.

She looked forward. She could just make out the Norsemen sitting on their sea chests or leaning on the side of the ship. They did not look particularly happy, and she imagined that they were worried about the trolls and the sea monsters and whatever other nonsense they conjured up in their thick pagan skulls.

Morrigan made the sign of the cross and knelt down. In a soft but strong voice she began the Lord's Prayer, which she knew would do more to protect them than all the spitting and sacrificing and appealing to false gods that the fin gall could muster.

She was about to move on to one of the Psalms when she became aware of a certain restiveness. She looked up. Most of the men were shooting angry looks back at her. She crossed herself again, quickly, and stood.

Stupid heathen fin gall... she thought. She found a place on the deck near where Thorgrim stood at the steering board and went to sleep.

She woke to a morning of heavy overcast and gray, marching waves, capped with curling white water, but the rain was mostly gone. She pulled herself to her feet and stood, gripping hard to the ship's rail. The motion was unlike anything she had ever felt, a swooping and rolling and pitching and her stomach heaved with every twist of the ship.

She looked around the edge of the sail but there was nothing to see but water, inhospitable gray ocean sweeping clear away to the edge of the world. She looked to the right, peering at the horizon, but still there was nothing but water and Morrigan began to panic.

What are they about? Are they leaving Ireland, and me with them?

Morrigan whirled around. There, on the larboard side, several miles off, was the shoreline, dark gray and green and low down in the sea.

Most of the crew were awake already, moving around the deck, engaged in various shipboard tasks. They looked more relaxed now, even cheerful, despite the fact that they were so far from shore and the waves, to Morrigan's mind, seemed alarmingly big.

Thorgrim, who had been sleeping on the deck beside her, stirred and sat up. Morrigan glared down at him and there must have been something about her appearance that he found amusing, because he smiled, which made her want to slap him.

"Good morrow," he said.

"Is that Ireland?" Morrigan snapped, pointing toward the shoreline.

Thorgrim stood slowly and looked out over the rail. "Ireland?" he said.

"Don't mock me," Morrigan said.

"Yes, that is Ireland. Even the *Red Dragon* does not sail so fast that we might leave Ireland behind in one night."

"Why are we so far from land?"

Thorgrim grinned and Morrigan was certain she would have hit him at that moment if she was not suddenly afraid she would vomit, so she clenched her teeth and glared.

"We stood off shore all night. There are rocks, close to land. A great danger in the dark."

"And trolls too, I suppose? And evil spirits?"

"Those too." Thorgrim's hand went to the cross and the hammer around his neck, a gesture Morrigan had noticed he did more and more frequently.

"How are we to find the crown now?"

Thorgrim looked out toward the land again. He seemed to be really studying it. "That headland, there," he said, pointing. "Just around there, there lies the beach where I buried the crown."

"How do you know?"

"I recognize it."

Morrigan was mollified at first by Thorgrim's confidence, but as the *Red Dragon* continued her rolling and swooping motion she soon found her concern for the crown, or Máel Sechnaill, or Ireland itself, waning until she cared not a whit about any of it. She curled up on the deck, hugging her cloak close to her, wishing it would all stop. She fell in and out of sleep.

Some time later the men forward built a fire in a portable stove and cooked pork they had taken from the baggage train. A quirk of wind brought the smell to Morrigan's nose, and she leapt to her feet and leaned over the side of the ship. She retched, miserably, and tried to vomit, but there was nothing in her stomach.

Thorgrim came to her side. He had a cup in his hand. "Here is water with a little mead mixed in. Drink this, it will help." There was genuine concern in his voice, actual tenderness. Morrigan would not have thought the fin gall capable of such a thing. She took the cup and drank and relished the liquid in her parched mouth. It helped.

Thorgrim set a couple of thick furs on the deck. "Lay down," he said, easing her onto the bed. "We will be closer into land soon, and the seas will not be so rough."

Morrigan looked at him with more gratitude than she had felt for anyone in a long, long time. "Thank you," she said.

Thorgrim shrugged. "You cared for me when I was wounded," he said. "And for Harald, which is far more important. And you, with plenty of reason to hate us. Us dubh gall." He smiled when he said that.

Morrigan shook her head. "The Danes are dubh gall. You are fin gall."

"Ah, I see."

Morrigan closed her eyes. When she opened them, Thorgrim was still there, looking at her. She did not want him to leave, not then. She wanted to hear his voice.

"Why does Ornolf carry such a beautiful sword, with silver inlaid, and you such a plain one?" she asked.

Thorgrim looked down at his sword, which lay in its sheath on the deck beside her. He picked it up as if he was discovering it for the first time. "This is not my sword," he said. "This is one I took at the mead hall when we escaped. My sword is a Frankish blade, far better than Ornolf's. His name is Iron-tooth."

Fin gall, like children, Morrigan thought. *Naming their swords...I imagine they give their penises such fearsome names as well.* "Why don't you have him... it...now?"

"Iron-tooth was stolen. In Dubh-linn, by some whore's son named

Magnus Magnusson. Do you know him?"

"Yes." Arrogant, vicious, plotting Magnus Magnusson. He had caught her alone once, at the mead hall, where she had been sent for a breaker of ale. He raped her. Not because he wanted her, but because she was Orm's.

"Yes, I know Magnus. And he *is* a whore's son."

"I pray to the gods that I will meet this Magnus again, so I may kill him and get my sword back. It's a great dishonor, to lose one's sword. Worse, to have your enemy carry it."

Morrigan's eyes moved from the sword to Thorgrim's face. He had a far-away look, a despondent look, and Morrigan's heart went out to him, even though it was just a stupid piece of iron, an instrument for killing. Though perhaps he was thinking about more than the sword. "Don't you hate me," she asked, "for my part in stealing Harald?"

Thorgrim did not answer right off. He looked out to sea for a moment, then back at her. "If there is one thing we Norsemen understand, it is vengeance. It is as much a part of who we are as longships and farming. We do not love our enemies, like you Christ followers say you do. We take our vengeance on them. So I know why you did what you did, and I don't hate you for it. The same way I don't hate the wolf that kills my cattle, though I will kill him for it."

"Will you kill me, for what I did?" The thought of dying right then did not seem so unwelcome.

"Not unless I have to. I'm grateful that you made sure Harald was safe. A Viking would have cut his throat."

Morrigan smiled and her stomach turned and she was not sure it was the motion of the ship in that instance. She had assured Thorgrim that Harald was safe. But Máel Sechnaill mac Ruanaid was a hard man. You had to be, if you wished to survive a week as a king in Ireland. She did not, in all honesty, know that Máel Sechnaill would be scrupulous in preserving the hostages' lives. She closed her eyes and prayed for Harald's safety, and as she did she fell asleep.

It was some time later - she did not know how long - that Morrigan opened her eyes. She lay still on her bed of fur. Things had changed. The light was different now, and she realized she must have slept through the bulk of the afternoon. The motion of the ship was different as well, the swooping and rolling was gone and the ship was very steady.

"Thank you, dear Jesus," she said out loud, but soft, as she understood that the heathens did not care to have the name of the true God spoken on board their ship.

She sat up. They were not far out to sea any longer. The point of land that Thorgrim had mentioned was now close by on the larboard side and the men were at the oars, pulling to get the ship around the far end.

Morrigan lay down again, and when she woke the next time, the longship was pulled partway up on a beach, with lines running ashore and a gangplank over the side. Armed Vikings were at various places along the shore. The sun was making a dull spot of light through the thick clouds as it headed toward the west. The smell of grass and dirt was strong on the offshore breeze.

"Good morrow, my beauty!"

Morrigan turned. Ornolf was seated on a sea chest on the other side of the afterdeck. He had a cup in his hand. He took a long drink and wiped his ample beard with his sleeve.

"Where is Thorgrim?"

Ornolf nodded toward the shore. "Gone off to have a look around. Make sure there are none watching us."

Morrigan nodded. She was not happy to be left alone here, with Thorgrim off. But Ornolf seemed to be in one of his rare, subdued humors, judging from the fact that he had not yet suggested fornication, despite Morrigan's having been awake for a full minute.

"Is this the beach? The beach where the crown is buried?"

Ornolf nodded. "We rounded the headland under oar, with the wind on our prow. Thorgrim insisted we keep the dragon's head mounted." He nodded toward the bow and the long tapered figurehead lashed to the stem. "Not everyone was happy with that. Most figure it's only good spirits will be frightened off by such a thing. The evil ones don't care."

Morrigan did not care either, about such nonsense. "Have you dug it up yet?" she asked eagerly.

"No. No hurry, we are here for the night in any case. Better to make sure none of those sheep-biting Irish are ready to fall on us again, before we reveal its whereabouts."

That made sense, so Morrigan did not argue, despite her great eagerness to get at the Crown of the Three Kingdoms, to hold that ancient and powerful thing in her hands. "When will Thorgrim be back?" she asked, but Ornolf only shrugged.

"Hard to say, with Thorgrim," Ornolf said after another drink. "In any event, you don't want to talk to him now, not with the sun going down."

Morrigan looked out toward the beach. She had noticed that before - Thorgrim could be more kind than she would have thought a fin gall could be, but when the darkness came on, he seemed to change, his mood growing black along with the sky.

"Thorgrim is a singular man," Morrigan said. "Why does the anger seem to come on him with the dark?"

"Huh!" Ornolf made a chuckling sound. "You don't know?"

"No."

"Thorgrim is a shape-shifter. That is why he is called Kveldulf. Night-Wolf. Do you know what a shape-shifter is?"

"No."

"Of course not. You Christ followers don't know anything. On some nights, when the darkness comes, Thorgrim changes. From what he is." Ornolf seemed to falter in his explanation. "He turns to a wolf."

"Jesus, Mary and Joseph," Morrigan said, the words no more than a whisper, and she made the sign of the cross.

"Sure, you would be right to use what charms you have. Thorgrim can be a dangerous man. After the change."

Morrigan was silent for a long moment. She of course did not believe in such things as men turning into wolves. At least she had grave doubts. "I think that is nonsense," she said at last, with as much conviction as she could muster.

"You do, do you? Well, how do you think he knew those Irish were there, following us? Or how he knew to bury the crown in the first place. This magic allows him to see things you and I can't see."

Morrigan thought on that for a bit. "Aren't the men afraid of him?" she asked.

"They keep clear of him, when the night comes on. But shape-shifters like him don't turn on their own. And they know things, as I said. See things. They can be a great benefit."

Again Morrigan was silent, trying to understand all this. Finally she asked, "You have seen him? Yourself? Turn into a wolf?"

"Well," Ornolf began but he was interrupted by the sound of feet padding up the gangplank. It had grown much darker, and they could just make out the shape of Thorgrim as he came up over the side of the ship. Morrigan made the sign of the cross again, though she could not help but notice that Thorgrim was not, in fact, a wolf.

He came aft, with the dark, scowling night-look on his face, and sat down heavily. There was mud on his shoes and a tear in his trousers. He looked at Ornolf and then at Morrigan, then looked at Morrigan again and squinted, as if trying to look into her mind, and Morrigan realized she was staring, as if she was staring at some freakish creature she had never seen before. She quickly looked down at the deck, then out at the beach, which was nearly lost in shadow.

"Well?" Ornolf asked.

"The Irish soldiers are not here. They are probably still digging up the other beach. There are some sheep herds a mile or so to the north. Nothing else."

Ornolf grunted. "Good. Let us get this damned thing that's given us so much trouble."

He stood and Thorgrim stood as well. Thorgrim held out a hand for Morrigan, almost grudgingly, and she took it and he helped her to her feet. They grabbed up shovels and headed for the gangway. Amidships, Svein the Short lit a torch and followed behind.

They marched down the springing gangway and crunched across the gravely beach. Thorgrim led the way and he moved with none of the uncertainty he had displayed on the other beach while pretending to look for the Crown of the Three Kingdoms. The Vikings spread out on the beach or sitting around the small fire they had blazing began to fall in behind.

Ornolf had explained to them all what the crown was, after Morrigan had explained it to him and Thorgrim. Ornolf told the men how it had happened to be buried on the beach, and why they now had to retrieve it and bear it up to Tara.

It had surprised Morrigan to realize that Ornolf and Thorgrim were the only ones of the Northmen who knew of the crown's existence. But none of the others had raised the least objection to a task that was unlikely to gain them any spoils. They were loyal to their leaders, these fin gall.

Thorgrim stopped two perches from the water's edge and looked down. There was a flat rock at his feet, and scratched on it, faintly seen in the torchlight, was a single rune, a straight line with two shorter lines coming off at an angle to the right. No one would have seen it who was not looking for it.

"The rune means wealth," Ornolf told Morrigan. "Very lucky. See, the stone is undisturbed."

Thorgrim lifted the stone and tossed it away, revealing the recently turned earth underneath. He took his shovel and stuck the blade gently in the ground and began to toss the dirt aside.

Morrigan realized she was holding her breath. All her life she had heard of the Crown of the Three Kingdoms. Most people thought it was no more than a myth, but she knew differently. And since it had first come to light that the crown was ordered given to Máel Sechnaill mac Ruanaid, and had gone missing, there was little else she had thought about. And now it would be in her hands.

The Vikings stepped closer, peering down into the hole. Thorgrim wielded his shovel gently, digging deeper, and then he stopped. He handed the shovel to Snorri Half-troll and got down on his knees. He scooped some earth away with his hands and then pulled a canvas bundle from the hole, brown and dirt-covered.

Thorgrim stood and the Vikings took a step forward. Gently, Thorgrim unwrapped the canvas. Morrigan pressed her hands to her mouth. She felt a tingling down her back.

The canvas fell away from the crown and Thorgrim held it high for all to see. The light of the torch fell on the gold and the jewels and Morrigan sucked in her breath. It was magnificent. Like nothing she had ever seen, and she had been raised in the seat of the high king of Tara.

The gold was thick and substantial and glowed a deep, rich yellow. On each of the filigrees that ran around the upper edge of the crown there was mounted a precious jewel - a diamond, a ruby, a sapphire - and Morrigan could just see in that light the elaborate and delicate etchings that arched and swirled over the surface of the crown. It was unearthly. She had never seen its like. She had to have it in her hands.

But instead, Thorgrim handed the crown to Ornolf, who frowned and turned it over in his hands. "Not a bad piece of work, for your Irishman," he pronounced and handed the crown to Snorri Half-troll, who also examined it and then passed it on. For the next minute or so the crown was passed from one heathen hand to the next, defiled by the touch of the barbarians, until Morrigan could stand it no more.

"Give me that!" she snapped as Egil Lamb passed it in front of her to Sigurd Sow. She snatched it from Egil's hands, held it tight, ready to fight anyone who tried to take it back. The fin gall looked at her, surprised, but no one made any attempt to take it back.

"Very well," Morrigan announced, emboldened by the fact that she was not challenged. "I will keep a care of this, until we reach Tara."

"Why you?" someone asked from the crowd.

"Because I am the only one here who is not a damned thief and a murderer!" she snapped.

The Norsemen were silent for a moment, then Ornolf broke the silence with his great bear laugh. "She's right, you know! By the hammer of Thor, the little vixen is right!"

And with that the others laughed as well and headed off, back to their fire, leaving Morrigan clutching the Crown of the Three Kingdoms. And now that it was in her hands, she did not think she could ever let it go.

Chapter Thirty-Three

A bad friend
is far away
though his cottage is close.
Hávamál

It took Asbjorn the Fat four days to make his way back to Dubh-linn, and the only easy part was convincing Hallkel Half-wit to assist him. Indeed, it took only a fraction of Asbjorn's persuasive powers before Hallkel was for all practical purposes Asbjorn's thrall.

Hallkel used the butt of his knife to knock the collar off Asbjorn's neck. He gave up his cloak and his shoes so that Asbjorn, stripped nearly naked, would have some cover. He went ahead, scouting the way back toward Dubh-Linn, in case there were more ambushes, with Asbjorn following a dozen perches behind.

Asbjorn used Hallkel the way he would have used any thrall. He sent him for wood to build fires at night, and off to the small ringforts they passed to beg or steal food. Hallkel, terrified of being caught up it the retribution Magnus would suffer, as described by Asbjorn, made every effort to bring comfort to his master. But for all his efforts, there was little comfort to be had, running from their enemies, exposed to the rain and the cold night air, walking for miles every day. Asbjorn's feet bled and his stomach was in a constant agony of hunger.

The two men assumed at first that Magnus and his Celtic allies would try and hunt them down. They hurried across open ground, moving from one hiding spot to the next, pausing to see if there was anyone on their trail before moving on. But as the first day passed, and then the second, with no pursuit, they gave that up. They walked boldly down the road, across open fields, their only goal to reach Dubh-Linn and the safety of the longphort.

By the evening of the third day, even Asbjorn, who had no head for directions, knew where he was, and where away sat Dubh-linn. It gave him an immense sense of relief. Anyone they might now encounter would be one of Orm's men. He, Asbjorn Gudrodarson, would live.

Sometime in the black hours of the morning, with Hallkel Half-wit snoring loud and sleeping the dead sleep of the stupid, Asbjorn slipped the knife from his belt and slashed Hallkel's throat. He did not need anyone at Dubh-linn who might contradict the story he would tell Orm. He did not need tales of his humiliation tossed around the mead hall for the amusement of the mob.

He was moving at first light, and by late afternoon he was stumbling across the ford north of the longphort and making his way up the plank road toward the palisade fort and Orm's house. There at last was the familiar smell of smiths' fires and rough cooking and drying fish. A gang of workmen were half-way through thatching the roof of the mead hall.

Orm's new thrall opened the door, an old and nearly toothless woman, stooped and gray. Orm, apparently, had had his fill of pretty young Irish slaves.

"Asbjorn, by the gods, what has happened?" Orm asked, sounding more annoyed than alarmed or concerned as he looked Asbjorn up and down. Asbjorn was a sight and he knew it, clothed only in Hallkel's cloak and shoes, his hair wet and sticking out in various ways, his legs and cloak muddy. He was splattered with Hallkel's blood but he had not bothered to wash it off as it gave him the appearance of hard fighting.

"Lord Orm, you are betrayed!" Asbjorn announced, staggering dramatically and grabbing at a table for support.

"Woman, a chair and some mead for Asbjorn!" Orm ordered, though his tone was still that of one more inconvenienced than concerned. Asbjorn sat, took the mead and drank. He was ready to eat, eat copiously, but he knew that would have to wait.

"Very well," Orm said with a sigh, "I take it it's Magnus who has betrayed me?"

"His treachery, Lord, is worse than I could have imagined," Asbjorn said, and launched into his tale of Magnus's alliance with the Irish king Cormac Ua Ruairc and their mutual search for the Crown of the Three Kingdoms. He told Orm of Magnus's plan to use his alliance with the Irish to take Dubh-linn for himself. That was not something that Asbjorn knew with any certainly, only what he guessed at, but he related it to Orm as known fact.

He went on to describe his heroic escape, killing his guard with his bare hands, stealing his weapons and fighting the sentries to flee into the night. But by that point he could see he was losing Orm's interest, and straining his credulity, so he wrapped it up quickly.

Orm sat silent for a moment, and then with a lighting move flung his mead cup against the wall, shattering it and making a wet spot on the daub. "May Thor rip his lungs out!" Orm shouted. "And if he does not, I swear I will!"

Orm stood and paced, back and forth, saying nothing, and Asbjorn had the sense to keep his mouth shut. Finally Orm stopped. "I have it on good word now," Orm said, "that the Norwegian whore's son Olaf the White is assembling a fleet to take Dubh-linn back. For all I know they have sailed already. As if that is not bother enough, now I have this to contend with!"

"My Lord, let me take care of this trouble for you. A swift longship, a hundred men or so, is all it will take. The Norwegians are under oar, we can overhaul them, and where they are, the Irish and Magnus will be."

"You said this Cormac Ua Ruairc had a hundred men, and another forty Vikings with him."

"My men will not fight against Danes," Asbjorn assured him, "and the Irish have only Irish weapons and cannot stand up against us for long. One hundred Danes and we can finish this, and I'll bring Magnus back in chains."

Actually, he would bring Magnus back dead, so that Magnus would never again have Orm's ear, but that was an issue for later.

For a long moment Orm sat there, staring into the fire burning in the hearth in the middle of the room. Asbjorn could see he was wavering.

"Lord, this is not the time for you to leave Dubh-linn, not with so great a threat on the horizon."

Orm looked up sharp. "What do you know of it?" he snapped.

"Nothing, Lord! Nothing beyond what you have told me!" Asbjorn protested, but he knew at that moment he had ruined his chance to take Magnus alone. Orm was too paranoid now for that.

"I will go," Orm said and he stood at last. "I will get a crew together for my longship and I will hunt that traitor down, and the Norwegian Ornolf as well, and by the gods I will make them all curse their mothers for bearing them."

"Yes, Lord Orm, it is what they deserve, no more. And would it please you if I was to remain in Dubh-linn, and see to your affairs here?"

"No, it would not please me!" Orm snapped, so quick and loud it made Asbjorn cringe. He kept his mouth shut. Orm was seeing traitors everywhere now, and Asbjorn knew he had to take care that Orm did not see one in him.

* * *

194

Through all the dark hours of the night they made their way down the River Boyne, and Brigit, for all the time she remained awake, stared into the dark water and cursed herself for an idiot.

What could I have been thinking? She lashed herself for her stupidity. *I help this animal, and he repays my kindness by raping me!*

She stared at the water bubbling and tumbling around the boat.

Very well, he didn't rape me...

Angry as she was, she could not lie to herself that way, to that degree. And she felt all the more foolish for having given herself to him willingly.

They could hear pursuit at first along the bank. The riders were shouting to one another. Brigit could make out the voice of Brian Finnliath, which pleased her, because she thought Harald had killed him. Another voice she thought might have been Flann mac Conaing, but it was hard to hear over the yapping dogs.

The men from Tara followed as well as they could, trying to keep up with the boat. But the boat was light, like a leaf on a stream, and the current was fast and it swept them away down stream, faster than riders or dogs could hope to follow in the failing light.

There was a single sweep lying across the thwarts. Harald lifted it up and fitted it into the thole pins on the transom and began to scull the boat down river, moving the sweep back and forth with an expert hand. The barking of the dogs faded and soon it was lost in the sound of the river and the light falling rain.

Brigit would have thrown herself over the side to escape, but that was as much as suicide because she could not swim. She wondered if it would be a mortal sin, since her intention would not be to kill herself, even if that was the likely outcome. Surely not a mortal sin, for then would it not be a mortal sin to go into combat against great odds?

She dismissed the whole line of reasoning. She was not ready to give up her life yet, not when she still had the strength and will to escape the fin gall.

Her thoughts wandered to the piece of meat lying back toward the stern where she had flung it at Harald's head. She was very hungry, but did not want to get any closer to Harald, lest she reinforce whatever insane notion he had concocted. She tore a piece of bread from the loaf and stuck it in her mouth. It took quite a bit of chewing to get it down, and by the second piece her jaw ached so she gave it up.

For some time she just stared out into the dark and down at the water and cursed herself and tried to think how she might avoid being carried back to Norway as the unwitting bride of some lunatic young Viking. She thought about hitting Harald over the head with something, but there was nothing sufficiently big and heavy in the boat that she might use. Nor did she think she was strong enough to deliver a blow that would do any damage to his thick head.

She fell asleep at some point in the night, sleeping fitfully across her thwart.

When she woke it seemed oddly dark - not nighttime dark, but something different. She looked up. Harald had lashed the monk's robe to the gunnels to form a shelter over her and keep the steady drizzle off her as she slept. She found that very annoying.

She sat up, ducked under the makeshift shelter. It was full daylight, a milky white dawn with a steady drizzle that gave a gray cast to the bright green country along the riverbanks. Harald was still at his place in the stern, slowly and steadily sculling the boat down stream. Brigit wondered if he had been at it all night. He seemed as fresh as if he had just hopped out of a feather bed. She found that even more annoying.

Harald looked at her and smiled his toothy smile and that was the most annoying of all. She looked around the boat for something to heave at his big, dumb head. There were nets and ropes of various size and some smaller tools, but nothing that would be really satisfying to throw.

As she searched for a weapon, it occurred to her that escape would be easier if the fin gall did not know she wanted to escape. She closed her eyes, summoned her resolve, then met Harald's eyes and rewarded him with a big smile. The look of pleasure on his face made her even more eager to throw something at him, but she held fast to her subterfuge.

What now, what now? She desperately had to urinate and it was making it hard to think. *How am I supposed to do that, in this idiot boat?*

And then the plan came to her, seemed to spring full born into her head. She took a step aft, smiling at Harald. She pointed to the bank, a clump of brush and trees near a bend in the river.

Harald frowned and shook his head. Brigit pointed again and again Harald shook his head.

How on earth am I supposed to make this fool understand?

Brigit sighed, made a squatting motion, pointed to the bottom of the boat. Harald's white skin flushed red and he suddenly looked very uncomfortable. He nodded his head in agreement, then fixed his eyes on the river bank by the trees, as if it would be lost forever if it left his sight for a second.

The boat ran silently into the mud and came to a stop. Harald pulled the sweep in and made ready to climb out, but Brigit swung herself over the gunnel and dropped into the stream below. The water was up to her ankles and the mud grabbed at her shoes but she did not mind, as she was already all but soaked.

She looked Harald in the eye and as emphatically as she could pointed to his seat in the boat, trying to convey the idea that he was to remain there. Harald was still blushing and he wore a very uncomfortable look. He nodded his head and patted the seat beside him, indicating his unwillingness to interfere with any female issues.

"Good," Brigit said out loud. She rewarded Harald with a smile and then slogged through the mud and clambered up the river bank and into the thick brush growing there.

The branches grabbed at her cloak and tangled her hair as she fought her way though the undergrowth. She looked back to see if Harald seemed at all suspicious, but the river and the boat were already lost from sight. She pulled up her skirts and squatted and relieved herself, a great relief indeed, and when she stood again she felt vastly more able to take action. She fought on through the bracken and came at last to the far end of the copse, where the thick brush yielded to open fields, rolling away to the distance.

That was easy, she thought, but she was not free yet, she had to remember that. Still, she was sure her father's men would be following the Boyne east, hoping to intercept them before they reached the sea. All she had to do was follow the Boyne west to meet up with them. But first she had to get well away from Harald.

Across the open ground there was another clump of brush and trees, no more than a quarter mile away. She stepped out into the open ground and moved fast toward the next hiding place. Again and again she looked over her shoulder, making certain that she kept the trees on the riverbank between herself and the boat. She wondered how long Harald's discomfort would keep him from coming in search of her. Long enough to get to the next hiding place, or the one after that, she hoped.

She ran, lifting her skirts and cloak out of the way, splashing through the wet grass. She felt her breath coming harder but she did not slow, save to turn and check that the trees still blocked Harald's view of her, and that he was not chasing after her.

She was heaving for breath when she reached the next hiding place, crashing into the brush and dropping to her knees. She looked back the way she had come as she tried to regain her breath. Harald was not following, which was good, but her feet had left a clear path through the wet grass and she would be easy enough to follow when he finally decided he should go looking for her.

I have to keep going... she thought. She forced herself to her feet and pushed on through the tall growth, toward the far side of that stand of trees. She had to find the next hiding place, but not get so far from the river that she lost her way. She thought of the bandits Harald had killed back at the fisherman's cottage. There were plenty of dangers for a woman on her own in that wild country.

She came at last to the far end of that patch, where once again the open fields stretched away. There was a rider, half a mile distant and coming toward her. She felt a great surge of hope. Bandits and peasants did not ride horses. This one had to be a noble, or at least a man of wealth, and if he was either of those, then he was most likely one of her father's men, out searching for her.

She kept to her hiding place, watching the man as he came closer. He had a red cape around his shoulders, a tunic over what she guessed was a mail shirt. A man of wealth, to be certain. She wondered why he was riding alone. Not that it mattered. Any man of means in Brega owed his allegiance, his fortune, even his life to Máel Sechnaill mac Ruanaid.

Brigit made to step from the undergrowth, but then hesitated, some warning sounding in the back of her head. *This is ridiculous,* she thought, but still she paused.

And then she thought of her wet track through the grass, the easy trail for Harald to follow. The Norseman had beaten down every attack against him. But this fellow on the horse, he looked as if he would be a match for Harald.

"You there!" Brigit stepped boldly out of the wood. Two perches away the man on the horse reined back in surprise, the horse spinning a tight circle before the rider had it under control.

"I am in need of help!" Brigit called, walking confidently toward the man. "I am Brigit mac Ruanaid, daughter of Máel Sechnaill mac Ruanaid. Princess of Tara."

The rider had his mount under control now, and he rode the few paces to where Brigit stood. A handsome man, light hair, with a few days' growth of beard on his square jaw. He looked down at her. He did not speak. It made Brigit nervous.

"My father will reward you, handsomely, if you bring me safe to Tara."

The man on the horse smiled. He spoke. Brigit heard the word "Magnus" which she thought might be the man's name. But she understood nothing else, because, to her horror, he did not speak in her lovely, lilting Gaelic, but rather in the coarse, rough tongue of the Vikings.

198

Chapter Thirty-Four

The good dream-woman
led me, the poet, to sleep
there, where soft beds lay.
                    Gisli Sursson's Saga

Morrigan felt her whole world rocking, as surely as the *Red Dragon* rocked in the swells rolling in toward the mouth of the Boyne.

They spent the night on the beach where the crown had been recovered, a restless night with watchers stationed at intervals inland, looking for any sign of the Irish army that had been following behind.

Morrigan did not let the Crown of the Three Kingdoms out of her sight. In truth, she did not let it out of her grip. She loved the feel of it, the weight of it. She held it in her lap and put her hands under the coarse cloth and ran her fingertips along the cool metal, feeling the intricate designs etched in the surface, the smooth, hard stones embedded in the gold. When no one was watching she unwrapped the canvas and stared at the dull yellow band and buffed it with her sleeve to make it shine. She had never, in her life, seen its like, and it took hold of her like nothing ever had.

Well into the dark hours she sat up on the afterdeck, the crown pressed tight in her lap, until Thorgrim Night-Wolf came back from his rounds of the watchers. She looked at him close, though she could see little beyond shadows in the dark. But she could see with certainty that he was a man, fully a man. If he was a shape-shifter, he was not shifting tonight.

"You are awake, still?" Thorgrim asked, standing over her. "How are you?"

She clutched the crown tighter. "I am well," she said. As much as getting possession of the Crown of the Three Kingdoms had worked oddly on her mind, so too had Ornolf's revelation about Thorgrim. The old people, the ones who still half clung to the old religions, talked of such things as men who became wolves. Morrigan dismissed it all as nonsense.

But she could not deny that Thorgrim seemed to know things that other men did not, and she had never seen a man who could fight like him. Ireland was a land infused with magic, and it was hard to dismiss such a thing as this. She found herself frightened and fascinated, all at once.

Thorgrim took his leave of her and made his way forward. She watched as he moved among his men - Ornolf's men, really, but it was clear to her who was really in command - talking to them in low tones. He was a good leader. Strong, unyielding, and yet he cared about his men. She had seen that even back at Dubh-linn, when she first came to tend to their wounds.

Morrigan leaned back on the rail and hugged the crown to her chest. Her mind wandered off to thoughts of the incredible wealth that the crown represented. The gold and jewels alone were worth more than she or Flann would see in several lifetimes, and they with their close ties to the very king of Tara.

Such a thing as this, hidden away, given out by rich abbots to wealthy kings.

Finally Thorgrim stepped aft. "I'm worried," he said.

"Worried?" Morrigan came out of her reverie with a guilty start.

Thorgrim sat on the chest beside her. "I am worried about Harald. I am getting a sense for trouble with him. Something is wrong."

Morrigan wanted very much to ask him if this was a wolf dream, but she did not dare, and part of that was because she was afraid to hear the answer. "Do you...get these feelings?"

"Oh, yes," Thorgrim said. "It is sometimes as if Harald and I have one mind. I know when he is in trouble, or if he is in a good way. It has always been thus."

Morrigan thought about that. "Does Harald also get such feelings?"

"Sometimes. Sometimes he does, sometimes he knows how I am, or what I will do. But he does not see as clearly as me."

"The king will not harm him," Morrigan said. She was trying to sound reassuring, but she did not have enough conviction herself to make her words sound genuine. Máel Sechnaill could be a cruel, thoughtless bastard. Morrigan, in all honesty, did not know what he might do with a Viking who fell under his authority, even one who was a hostage.

When she thought about it, she had to admit that Máel Sechnaill had probably killed Harald already. She had no notion of what she would do when they all arrived at Tara, so she tried not to think about it.

Thorgrim looked over at her, and she could see her words did nothing to mollify him. Indeed, he looked more concerned for her attempt at reassurance. There was a vulnerability she had not seen before, a fear that his son had come to harm. Morrigan guessed it was the only thing on earth that Thorgrim Night-Wolf feared.

Finally he made a grunting noise. "Soon we will know," he said. Then after a moment of silence, as he stared out into the night, he said, "Will you sleep?"

"Yes."

Thorgrim stood and then lay down on the deck, on the pile of furs set out there. Morrigan lay beside him as had become her habit. She felt vulnerable, sleeping among the Norsemen, but pressing close to Thorgrim made her feel safe. Even now, unsure about who or what Thorgrim really was, she felt safer with the feel of him against her.

Thorgrim pulled a heavy fur over the two of them, a bearskin so big it covered them both completely, even up over their heads. It was warm underneath, and the fur kept them from the soft rain that was still falling. She hugged the crown tight. Her head felt as if it was spinning. And soon she was asleep.

Morrigan woke in the dark hours of morning. She pulled the crown tighter to her and listened to the night sounds. An owl somewhere ashore was speaking in its eery voice and it made her shiver. The ship, where it was grounded, made a soft crunching sound as the small surf charged and retreated, charged and retreated along the beach.

The crown was still in her arms and she hugged it tight. Forward she could hear the sounds of the men snoring where they lay, thick animal sounds, just what she might expect for animals such as them.

Thorgrim was asleep, his arm flung over her, and she could feel his chest press against her back as he breathed. Automatically now her hand reached under the crown's canvas cover and she ran her fingers along the slick gold surface. She shuffled closer to Thorgrim and Thorgrim made a soft murmuring sound but did not wake.

Morrigan unwrapped the canvas and stared at the dark metal of the Crown of the Three Kingdoms. Her Crown. Somehow, it changed everything.

She rolled over so her face was inches from Thorgrim's. He was frowning in his sleep, his brow creased, and she wondered if he was running with wolves in his dreams. He made a soft growling noise.

The crown was between them now, so Morrigan carefully set it down on the deck above her head, the first time since she had snatched it from Egil Lamb's hand that she was not physically touching it. She reached her face up to Thorgrim's and pressed her lips against his. His bristly beard pricked at her skin, tickled her, but she did not mind. She felt a sudden and desperate need for closeness. It was a thing she had not felt in some time.

Thorgrim did not wake up as Morrigan kissed him, so she pressed tighter and kissed him again, kissed him with some force. With a start he woke, eyes wide. He half sat up and his hand shot out for the sword that always slept at his side.

"Shhhh, shhhh," Morrigan said, soft and soothing like the surf on the beach. She saw Thorgrim visibly relax as he understood what it was that had disturbed his sleep. He eased himself down again, down on his side, and pulled the fur back over them. Their faces were almost touching, and for some time they just savored the closeness.

Finally Thorgrim leaned toward Morrigan and kissed her and she kissed him back. His strong arms reached out and wrapped around her and she felt completely enveloped, completely safe in that powerful embrace. She pressed her lips into his, lost herself in the smell and taste and feel of him.

Thorgrim's calloused hands moved over her back, though her hair, his touch amazingly light for such a man. During her time as Orm's thrall, he had taken her, brutally and whenever he wanted, and she had come to think she would never be able to endure a man's embrace again. But here she was, shivering with the pleasure of Thorgrim's hands on her, warm and languid in their bearskin cocoon.

Morrigan pushed away from Thorgrim, just a bit. She grabbed on to the damp wool of her dress and pulled it up over her head, squirming out of the garment, still covered over by the thick bearskin. She felt Thorgrim's hand exploring her, running over her back and her bottom. She felt the gooseflesh stand up on her arms and neck.

She grabbed the bottom of his tunic and pulled, more as a way of signaling her desire than in any hope of getting the tunic off. But Thorgrim understood and he pulled the tunic up over his head, disrobing somewhat less gracefully than she had.

Morrigan ducked down under the bearskin, like withdrawing into a cave, and felt around for the ties that held Thorgrim's trousers around his waist. With one pull of the bitter end the ties came loose and she helped him ease the trousers off his legs. He kicked the trousers off his feet as she caressed him and stroked him and took pleasure in the way he writhed and tried to stifle his enthusiastic moans.

She ran her lips over his hard stomach, ran her fingers through the thick hair on his chest, over the hard, raised lines of sundry scars. *He is half wolf now, shape shifter or no,* she thought, but the memory of that wicked secret made her even more excited.

She pushed Thorgrim on his back and squirmed up on top of him, the dried flesh of the bear skin rough on her naked back. They came together easily, and she worked her hips back and forth, closed her eyes and made a soft moaning noise, deep down. The feel of Thorgrim inside her was more wonderful than anything she had felt in a long time.

They moved together like that, utterly lost in their own world under the bearskin, and all the horror Morrigan had known or would know was forgotten in the moment. Thorgrim ran his hands over her as they moved together, ran his hands over her back and her breasts and held onto her waist. Then after some time of that he gently pushed her over and rolled over on top of her. She lay with her back now on the soft, warm fur spread on the deck and Thorgrim, up on his elbows, was on top of her. She wrapped her legs around his waist, dug her heels into the small of his back and he moved faster, and with more need.

Morrigan could feel the tension building in her, she was ready to shatter like glass. She bit down on her lip to keep from shouting out loud, felt a coppery taste of blood in her mouth. She reached her arms up over her head and her hands fell on the Crown of the Three Kingdoms. She grabbed it, squeezed it hard, so hard it dug painfully into the flesh of her palms. Thorgrim was moving fast, she could see the white of his clenched teeth, and her whole body shuddered with every thrust.

They both cried out, despite themselves, and then it was quiet as they lay wrapped in one another's arms. As their breathing subsided, Morrigan could hear the snoring of the men, the grinding of the bow on the shingle, the night birds in the brush. She pulled the crown under the bearskin and soon she and Thorgrim were asleep.

For all the long night they slept, and in that time there was no threat to the men or the crown.

It was still dark when Thorgrim shuffled out from under the bearskin. Morrigan, half awake, was aware of the movement, wondered why Thorgrim had to leave their warm place.

And then the thought came to her that perhaps he had shifted, perhaps he was off to prowl the night in his wolf form. She felt a sudden panic, and a horror at the thought. Her eyes shot open and she rolled over.

Thorgrim was standing beside the bearskin, pulling on his trousers, very much a man. He looked down at her in surprise. "I didn't wish to wake you," he whispered.

Morrigan just looked at him. He was not a pretty man, but good looking in a different way. In a way that made a woman feel safe and that was the best way.

"Where are you going?"

"I have to check on the watchers," he said. He knelt down, kissed her, grabbed up his tunic and sword and was gone.

At daybreak the longship put out to sea, the big men hauling at the oars and then spreading the sail to the early morning breeze. They tacked north, making several long boards, until the gaping green jaws of the River

Boyne opened up for them, a watery version of the great Roman roads, leading them into the heart of Ireland.

Morrigan stood at her familiar place by the rail, watching the shoreline close around the ship, glad to be on a river and not the wide ocean. The ocean frightened her with its vastness, and the constant worry that the Vikings would just sail off with her on board. For years now her life had been carried along by the whims of various men. She had killed Orm, escaped thralldom, and would not easily yield her freedom again.

They worked their way up the river with the sail still drawing in the southeasterly wind. The ocean swells gave way to the smooth water of the River Boyne, and soon the ocean was lost from view altogether, and Morrigan was happy for that.

They carried the sail for another hour before the wind failed them entirely. Then the yard was lowered and the long oars broken out and the Norsemen set into their slow, rhythmic stroke, a stroke Morrigan knew they could keep up for hours. It was no mystery to her now how these men became so strong of arm.

By midday they were well up the Boyne, and there was little to see from the *Red Dragon*'s deck, save for the odd sheep herd who fled with his flock at the first sight of the longship, and the occasional ringfort along the shore. And though there was low talk among the men about stopping and raiding one or the other, nothing was done, and the steady stroke continued uninterrupted.

They came around a wide, sweeping bend in the river, where it ran though open country with occasional stands of trees here and there. Tied to the south bank was a boat, a small leather boat of around twenty feet in length. It looked abandoned.

"Look there," Thorgrim said to Ornolf, nodding toward the boat.

"Humph," Ornolf said. He sounded unimpressed.

"What do you think, Morrigan?" Thorgrim asked.

"A fishing boat. I have seen a hundred of its like."

"Such a boat could be of use to us," Thorgrim said.

"Damn the thing," Ornolf announced. "Stupid Irish, building boats from cowhides!"

Morrigan said nothing. She knew how to keep her tongue still. Being a thrall taught a person that, if nothing else.

"Still, I would like to have a look," Thorgrim said, and there was a tone in his voice that did not admit of questions. Ornolf made his grunting sound again. Thorgrim turned the steering board to starboard.

They crossed the river to the far bank and Thorgrim called for the men to toss oars. The long sweeps came up together, a great bird folding its wings, and the *Red Dragon* glided silent over the distance between her and the leather boat. Men along the larboard side leaned over the rail and grabbed onto the boat, checking the longship's way.

Thorgrim stepped off forward. He did not invite Morrigan to follow, or Ornolf either, but Morrigan's curiosity was up now, wondering what it was about that humble boat that attracted Thorgrim's interest, and she followed behind.

Thorgrim stopped in the longship's waist and looked down at the leather boat. Nets, buckets, fishing gear were strewn around the bottom. A dark robe was lashed from gunnel to gunnel over the forward thwart, making a rude shelter underneath. Thorgrim stepped over the side of the longship and onto the fishing boat. For a moment he did not move, just cast his eyes around. Then with a quick movement, he snatched up the long oar that lay across the thwarts. He stared at the blade of the oar, squinting and frowning.

He climbed back aboard the longship, bringing the oar with him. "Ornolf!" he called and Ornolf stepped forward. Thorgrim held out the blade of the oar, and now Morrigan could see that it was covered with a series of cuts and slashes. She looked closer. She recognized the runes of the Norsemen.

"See here," Thorgrim said as he held out the blade and Ornolf in turn squinted at it. His lips moved before he spoke.

"They look like Harald's runes, to be sure," Ornolf said. "There are few men educated enough to write who still do it as poorly as my grandson. Can you make the words out?"

Thorgrim studied the oar blade. "'Harald Thorgrimsson... made...these runes... He has gone...in search...of his...'"

Thorgrim looked up, made an odd face. "'In search of his bride,'" he said. He shook his head.

"Hah!" Ornolf shouted. "Either Harald mistakes his runes, or he has gone off and married some Irish bitch!"

Thorgrim looked ashore, his eyes moving far off across the countryside. "One way or the other, we go after him."

Chapter Thirty-Five

Men in ships, warriors with spears,
without any faith, great will be the plague,
they will inhabit half the surface of the island...
　　　The Voyage of Snédgusa ocus Maic Riagla
　　　9th Century Irish Poem

Magnus knew the girl would be valuable, damned valuable, though he was not sure how.

She was no dumpy farm girl or fisherman's wife, that was clear from the first glance. She was too lovely by far, a genuine beauty. Not the rustic prettiness of the peasant girls, her skin was smooth and white. Her clothes, wet and rumpled though they were, were clearly cut of expensive cloth and well made.

He listened as she spoke, trying to make out the words. He had picked up some of the barbaric Irish tongue during his time in Dubh-linn, and in his association with Cormac. He had the impression that she was telling him who she was, and how important she was. He heard "Máel Sechnaill mac Ruanaid" and perhaps that she was Brigit mac Ruanaid, and if he heard right, then that was the best fortune he could have hoped for.

Magnus Magnusson had been riding west from the coast for two days. Asbjorn was gone, and Magnus had to assume he had returned to Dubh-linn and alerted Orm to his betrayal. Cormac Ua Ruairc, once an ally, was now a sworn enemy. As far as powerful men with whom to align himself, that left only Máel Sechnaill of Tara.

Magnus had followed the River Boyne west in the general direction of

Tara. He intended to go to Máel Sechnaill and offer his services, and the information he held concerning Cormac Ua Ruairc's plans and his current incursion into Brega.

And now, it seemed, Máel Sechnaill's daughter was at his feet and begging assistance.

"My name is Magnus Magnusson, I am a friend of your father's," he said, hoping she understood the Danish tongue. But apparently she did not, because her eyes grew wide at the sound of his words. She took a step back, and then another.

"No, wait!" Magnus shouted, but it was pointless as she clearly did not understand. The girl turned and fled, back in the direction she had come from.

"Oh, Thor take this bitch!" Magnus shouted in exasperation. He dug his heels into his horse's side and charged after her. She was running hard, trying to reach the wooded place in which she had been hiding. Magnus got his horse in front of her and she stopped, turned, ran in another direction.

Magnus worked the horse to cut off her escape, but he knew he could not catch her that way. He reigned hard to a stop, slipped to the ground as the girl sprinted for the trees. The muscles in his legs protested as he ran after her, the stiffness of mile after mile in the saddle made him hobble like an old man. The girl was nearly at the trees by the time he got a hand on her shoulder and pushed her to the ground, stumbling and falling on top of her as he did.

He fell with a grunt, half on the grass and half on the girl, and even as he was sorting himself out she slammed her elbow into the side of his head with such force that it snapped his head around and blurred his vision. He felt her foot drive into his stomach and he gasped in pain.

"You bitch!" he shouted. She kicked him again, squirmed out of his grasp. He head was still spinning but he managed to grab her ankle and pull her down just as she was struggling to her feet.

She twisted around and raked his face with her fingernails and Magnus felt the five searing lacerations across his cheek. She wound up to slash him again, but this time he caught her wrist and jerked her arm toward him, pulling her over so she was face down on the grass. She was kicking and screaming Gaelic curses, but he had her now. He threw a leg over her back, straddling her as she twisted and tried to get her hands on him.

It was like riding a bear - he was safe as long as he did not get off. He remained on top of her for a moment as the pain from his various wounds subsided and his head cleared. Then he took the belt from his waist and lashed her wrists together. It was no easy feat, but Magnus had spent his boyhood fishing off the coast of his native Denmark and was well used to subduing a thrashing and squirming catch.

He stood at last and pulled the girl to her feet. "I am trying to help you, you stupid girl," he said, spitting the words, though he had no hope that she would understand him. From the fury in her eyes and the vicious sound of the words spitting from her mouth it was clear she did not think she was being helped.

No matter. If she was the daughter of Máel Sechnaill she was worth everything to Magnus, either as a way of winning Máel's gratitude by returning her, or by holding her as a hostage for money and safe conduct. He pulled at the bitter end of the belt. The girl struggled mightily - it reminded Magnus of trying to get a goat to go where it does not want to go - but he managed at last to pull her over to his horse.

Magnus gave a hard pull and the girl fell to the ground. He wanted to put her up on the horse, have her ride in front of him, but he could think of no way to get her up there without getting his head kicked in. He could beat her into submission, sure, but that would not earn him Máel Sechnaill's gratitude.

"Ah, damn you!" he said out loud. He pulled a length of walrus skin rope from his saddlebag, tied a loop in the end and looped it around the girl's neck. He tied the other end around his waist and climbed up in his saddle.

"For the sake of your neck, I suggest you follow," he said, his voice calm as his equilibrium returned. He nudged his horse into a walk. The girl, her face a mask of unadulterated fury, struggled to her feet and followed behind. She had no choice if she did not care to be strangled.

They headed off across the field, Magnus chaffing at the slow pace, since he could move no faster than the girl could walk, and she was doing nothing to help quicken the pace. He felt very exposed, out in the open, tied to the girl in that way.

Hostage... he thought. He could not ride up to Máel Sechnaill mac Ruanaid dragging his daughter by the neck. He would not be welcomed as a hero that way.

So he would have to find a place to stash her, go and find Máel Sechnaill, hope there was someone at Tara who could speak Danish. He cursed to himself.

He had thought, on finding the girl, that his ill fortune was turning around, but now it seemed it was getting worse. He was not sure what to do with her now. And he couldn't let her go either, let her go to her father and tell tales of what he had done, not if he wanted an alliance with Máel Sechnaill, which he did. Without Máel Sechnaill he would be alone in Ireland and as good as dead.

I suppose I could always kill her, he mused. *Hide her body, she would play no part in this...*

The more he thought on it, the more it seemed that might be the only way off this bear. He had thought the girl a gift from Odin, but now he wondered if Loki, that cunning trickster, had not arranged this. This was how the gods played with men, handing them a thing that looked like good fortune, then turning it all around.

Perhaps kill her, bring her body to Máel Sechnaill, tell him I tried to save her from bandits...

He could not decide, and the cuts on his face from the girl's nails were starting to hurt. He stopped and slid off the horse and tied the rope that was around the girl's neck to the horse's reins. He took a skin of wine from where it hung on his saddle and with the corner of his tunic dabbed at the cuts on his face. The girl glared at him.

"This is thanks to you," he said. The girl spit out some words that did not sound like an apology.

Magnus drank some of the wine, then fished out some of the dried meat he had taken from a traveler he met on the road. He squatted on his heels and ate. He held up a piece to the girl, an offering, and she spit at him.

Magnus stood and stretched and would have loved to lie down but he did not dare as long as he had this Irish wildcat on her long leash.

He walked some distance away and sat and pondered his circumstance, how to parlay this girl into the best advantage. After some time he stood again. *Continue to Tara, see how things lay,* he decided. He could come up with no better plan than that.

He walked back to where his horse stood nibbling at the green, wet grass and the girl sat slumped on the ground. "Time for us to be on our way, my beauty," Magnus said and the girl spat out some Irish curse. And then Magnus saw something move, far off, some motion across the field they had just traversed. He stood quite still and looked.

It was a man. He was running toward them. He was still some ways off, but Magnus could see he had yellow hair and was carrying a staff, perhaps a spear.

The girl turned and looked in the direction that Magnus was looking. If she knew who it was, she made no indication.

Now what? Magnus thought. Whoever it was, he was coming for them. *Is it her lover? One of her father's men?*

He could not get away from this fellow at the pace he was moving, all but dragging the girl on the leash.

Magnus sighed. *Very well, I'll kill this fool,* he thought, irritated at yet another delay.

He unsheathed his sword and worked the kinks out of his arms. The way the idiot was rushing headlong at him suggested that it would not be a long fight, anyway. He swung his shield off his shoulder and worked his hand through the straps and took hold of the handgrip behind the boss.

No more than a boy... Magnus thought as he watched the attacker come on. He seemed to be dressed in the Norse fashion, which made the whole thing stranger still.

The fellow was perhaps three perches away when Magnus braced for the attack. He was young and he did look to be a Viking and Magnus knew what would happen next. The fool, in his enthusiasm, would charge with the spear. Magnus would turn the point aside with his shield and extend his sword and the fool would run right on to it. He had done it a dozen times, fighting these untrained peasants.

Ten paces away and the young idiot was still charging. Magnus smiled, just a bit, at the predictability of the whole thing. He held his shield chest high, braced, and the young fool did something that Magnus never saw coming.

He stopped, so sudden you would have thought he could never keep his balance, and instead of leading with the spear point he flipped the weapon around like a quarterstaff and brought the butt end up from below, below Magnus's shield and right between his legs.

Magnus shouted in surprise. He swept down with his sword, deflecting the spear end before it did serious damage to his genitals. But now his defense was off and the boy pulled the butt end of the spear back and swung it around like a club and would have smashed in the side of Magnus's face if Magnus had not brought his shield up at the last instant.

Magnus staggered back to regroup, get fighting room, with a whole new appreciation for his adversary. He readjusted the grip on his shield and circled to the right, eyes on the young man as he followed him with the tip of his spear.

I have seen this one before... Magnus thought. *In Dubh-linn?* But there was no man in Dubh-linn who would not recognize Magnus Magnusson. *Where, then?*

The young man attacked again, jabbing with the spear and swinging it like a quarterstaff as Magnus deflected the thrusts. *He is good, but he is young...* Magnus thought. As long as he did not underestimate the boy, he would beat him. Most likely.

"You're no Irishman, boy," Magnus said as they both took a step back, assessing. "No Irishman fights with your skill. Are you a Dane?"

"I am from Vik, in Norway!" the boy said defiantly.

"Vik! I am from Trondheim myself, but I have fallen in with these cursed Danes!" It occurred to Magnus that he could use a second, now that Kjartan Swiftsword had doubtless been killed. Maybe the boy would be swayed.

The young Norwegian attacked again, a furious barrage of dagger point and blunt end that Magnus was just able to fend off, and it gave Magnus the idea this boy did not want to deal.

Norwegian? Magnus was breathing hard, but so was the boy. And then he remembered.

The idiot Norwegians from the mead hall! And it suddenly occurred to Magnus that the boy could not be alone, the others must be near by. He glanced over at the distant trees, from where the boy had come, gasped at the sight of fifty or so men racing across the field, and his inattention was rewarded by a hard blow to the side of his head.

Magnus staggered again, and again he caught the second blow with his shield. But this time he stepped into the boy, shoving him with the shield, trying to get him off balance and far enough away to bring the sword to bear.

The boy stumbled back and Magnus thrust. The boy twisted out of the way and seized Magnus's wrist and held it tight.

Magnus tried to force the sword up, up, to where he could put the point through the boy's throat, and the boy pushed back with surprising strength. And then the boy looked down and his eyes went wide and he spoke, just one word, "Iron-tooth!"

And then it was the boy's turn to pay for his inattention. Magnus jabbed with the boss of his shield and hit the boy hard in the jaw. He lost his grip and staggered back and Magnus slashed with his sword, opening up the boy's tunic right across his chest and behind it a line of white flesh erupting red with blood. The boy fell back, swinging with his spear as he went down. Magnus stepped up, ready to knock the spear aside and finish the boy before his fellows could overtake them.

And then, behind him, his horse made a snorting sound, a clomping of hooves in the soft grass. Magnus spun around. The girl had pulled herself half on the horse, draped over the saddle, her hands still tied. She was kicking the animal, urging it forward. Far across the open ground to the west, Magnus could hear dogs, and they were close.

Chapter Thirty-Six

Myself I know
that in my son
grew the makings
of a worthy man.
Egil's Saga

Magnus shouted in rage. He took one last swipe at the youth on the ground, but it was more out of frustration than in any hope of killing him. The boy, bleeding but still in command of himself, turned the sword aside with the spear shaft and thrust the weapon at Magnus, but Magnus was done with him and had already turned and run off, his sword and shield still in hand.

Magnus had bigger problems now.

"Get back here, you miserable bitch!" he shouted as he ran after the horse, which was gaining speed with each kick the girl delivered to its flanks. The Norwegians were coming across the field to the east and someone else - he had to guess it was Máel Sechnaill's men, coming from the west and if he did not catch the horse and ride hard, then one or the other of them would spill his guts on the grass.

"Stop!" he shouted again, just because he was too angry not to shout. The horse was opening up a lead but the rope which was tied from the girl's neck to the reins was dragging behind, making a swath through the wet grass, and Magnus set his eyes on that.

He was breathing hard, and the strength was leaving his legs when he heard the renewed vigor of the barking dogs and he knew they had broken out in the open ground and that spurred him one. A burst of speed and he leapt for the rope, straight out as if he was diving into the water. In midair it occurred to him that if the end tied to the girls came tight, and not the end made fast to the reins, then it would likely break her neck. But there was nothing for it. He needed the horse more than he needed the girl.

He hit the ground with a thud that nearly took his breath. He felt the rope under him, quickly snaking away, and he dropped his sword and clawed frantically for it. His fingers wrapped around the cordage and he held on, as tight as he had ever held any lifeline in a storm at sea.

The horse hit the end of the rope and the reins came tight, twisting the horse around and jerking it from it's feet. With a shout the girl flew from the saddle, hitting the ground hard, unable to break her fall with her hands.

The three of them, Magnus, the girl and the horse struggled to their feet, but Magnus was up first. He jammed his sword in his sheath as he ran, slung his shield over his back. The girl was standing when Magnus snatched her around the waist and tossed her over his shoulder, so quick her shout of protest came out as no more than a grunt.

He could see the dogs now, charging across the field, and behind them, men on horses, wearing bright tunics. King's men. Irish warriors.

Magnus grabbed the horse's reins. He tossed the girl over the horse's neck, her legs kicking hard, trying to make contact with him, but he kept clear. He got a foot in a stirrup, swung up onto the horse. The men and dogs were still a quarter of a mile away - he still had a chance. He kicked the horse hard in the flanks, reined him around. The Irish were coming from the west, the Norwegians from the east. Magnus raced off, due north.

It was easy enough for Thorgrim to follow Harald's trail. Even if he had not made it obvious, leaving torn bits of cloth on branches along the way, Thorgrim Night-wolf and his men would have been able to follow the broken twigs, the wet, flattened grass as easily as a beaten path.

They were armed with everything they had, which was still meager by the Vikings' standards. They all joined the hunt, all forty-two men, all that was left of the original crew. There were not enough men now to guard the longship and hunt for Harald. They would have to band together if they had any hope at all.

Thorgrim heard the dogs first, far off but getting closer. "Hold up," he said, held his hand in the air. He strained his ears against the rustling of trees, the birds in the brush. There were many dogs, and that meant a big hunting party. They might have been driving game, but he doubted it.

"Come along," he said, hurrying forward, his pace much faster now and soon he was running over the trampled grass.

They came to a place where a struggle had taken place, the grass flattened and the turf chewed up, but there was no blood anywhere. *Did Harald fight here?* Thorgrim wondered. If so, he would have expected to find either Harald or his opponent lying dead. Or at least some blood.

They raced on, and it seemed that they and the dogs were converging on the same spot. They pushed through a patch of wood and now a new sound came to Thorgrim's ear. A fight. He could hear the clash of weapons - not iron on iron, but weapons, still - the grunt and thump of combat.

They broke out of the woods. A quarter mile off, in the middle of the wide open ground, two men were fighting. One was Harald. Thorgrim was certain of it.

"Oh, by the gods!" Thorgrim shouted. His son, locked in a fight, within his view, beyond his reach. "Come on!" He broke into a run, forcing his legs on, his no longer young legs, he could feel every inch of ground he covered, but he was frantic to get to his boy. Weeks of worry, and now he had found Harald and Harald might be cut down before could reach him.

The dogs sounded louder, but Thorgrim could not take his eyes from the fight. He saw Harald stumble back, his arms flung out, the one he was fighting making a broad sweep with his sword.

"No!" Thorgrim shouted. Harald was down, lost in the grass, dead for all Thorgrim knew. And the other one had turned away and was chasing after a horse that already had another rider mounted on it. The horse stumbled, but then it was up again, and the two were mounted and riding off.

Harald was not dead. Thorgrim knew it, deep inside he was certain of it, and as he ran, his eyes locked on the place where Harald had fallen, he saw his son rise, gripping his chest, saw him stumble towards them, one foot planted laboriously after another.

And behind Harald, Thorgrim saw the dogs and the riders.

There were thirty men on horseback at least and they were riding hard. They wore tunics and helmets that shone dull in the overcast.

Thorgrim saw Harald stop and look over his shoulder. He could taste Harald's panic in his own throat as his son turned back and redoubled his effort to flee. He knew, as Harald did, that it was too late. The Vikings on foot would not reach him before the Irishmen on horseback.

"Oh, no!" Thorgrim shouted, a cry of despair, but his pace did not slow, not at all, and he charged with the full intention of throwing himself at the mounted men and dying in defense of his boy.

The riders were no more than a dozen perches behind Harald but Harald did not slow his limping, wounded gate. Thorgrim reached for the sword in his sheath. He felt strong hands on his shoulders, right and left, and the hands held tight and forced him to slow. He thrashed his shoulders trying to break the grip.

"Let me go, you whores' sons!" he shouted. Snorri Half-troll was on his right side and Skeggi Kalfsson on his left. Thorgerd Brak was holding him as well.

"Damn you, let me go!" Thorgrim shouted, a pleading note in his voice. The riders had covered the distance to Harald and Thorgrim braced himself for the sight of his son run through with a spear or hacked down with a sword. But instead the riders circled him, blocking the boy from Thorgrim's sight, trapping him like a fox at the end of a good hunt.

"Bastards!" Thorgrim shouted, the word encompassing everyone, everyone, but his beloved son.

Ornolf, who had been trailing far behind, came huffing up. "Thorgrim, stop this!" he ordered between heaving for breath.

"Let me go, Ornolf, you bastard, they'll kill my son!"

"They'll kill him anyway, and you too if you charge blind at them!" Ornolf shouted, then bent over and gasped for air.

"Let them have me, I'll set Harald free!" Thorgrim shouted and thrashed and twisted with greater effort. He managed to shake Skeggi Kalfsson loose and punch him in the jaw, but left-handed. He did little damage and another jumped in to take Skeggi's place.

"You coward, Ornolf, you black-hearted coward!" Thorgrim wailed. Ornolf straightened. He met Thorgrim's eyes and the two men stared at one another, as if they were the only men on the field. "I will forgive that, Thorgrim Night Wolf, because I know you are sick with fear for your son, as I am for my grandson. We cannot save Harald if we are dead. We must live. We must be smart." He paused, sucking air into his lungs, then added, "If they did not kill him when they came on him, there is a reason, and we must find it out."

A quarter mile away, they could see Harald, hands bound behind his back, hoisted up onto a horse. The rest of the mounts pranced nervously, the dogs raced and yapped and barked. And then the entire war party wheeled around, turning backs to the Norsemen, and rode off, unhurried, the way they had come.

Thorgrim stopped struggling and the men let him go. He watched Harald as his son was led away. And then Harald turned, twisted in the saddle, looking back at his fellows who had not been quick enough to save him. It was like a dagger in Thorgrim's heart, only worse, because a real dagger was quick, but this pain went on and on.

Cormac Ua Ruairc and Niall Cuarán were sitting on either side of a hearth before a blazing fire, eating chicken and tossing the bones into the flames. Off in the dark end of the house, some of the more prominent men of the small army were gaming or sharpening weapons or sleeping. The rest, nearly all of Cormac's men, were spread out in the yard or the outbuildings of the small ringfort they had taken as temporary dwelling.

Those not at the ringfort were riding over the countryside. They were looking for information. Where the longship had sailed to. What Máel Sechnaill was about. What monasteries might be worth sacking before they withdrew back to the safety of Leinster. Cormac was still desperate to wear the Crown of the Three Kingdoms, but if the fin gall had carried it off to Norway, he would have to content himself with hurting Máel Sechnaill as best as he could before leaving Brega and considering his next step.

"We're a bit thin here, you know," Niall said, pulling the leg from another chicken and examining it in the dim light. "If Máel Sechnaill were to discover us, and fall on us, we'd be quite done, with our dubh-gall friends butchered and a dozen of our men scattered about the country."

Cormac made a grunting noise. Niall, he felt, was often a bit backwards in his courage, and he did not care for it. He would prefer a second who would bolster his own sometimes wavering resolve, not add to his uncertainty.

"Máel Sechnaill is just a man, and he does not command some grand army, not even with the fyrd called out, which it is not. Don't be such a damned...don't worry so much."

Niall looked up sharp at Cormac. They had been two days at the ringfort while they waited for some word from the people sent out around the countryside. Tempers were getting short. There was a sense among the men that their luck was running low.

Whatever retort Niall may have come up with was cut short by a pounding on the door that made both men turn quick and look. Cormac's men were on their feet, swords drawn.

A voice came muffled through the oak and iron-bound door. "Lord Cormac! It is Fintan, come with news!"

One of the men by the door lifted the bar and swung the door open and Fintan, wet and mud-splattered, came into the room and bowed to Cormac. "Lord Cormac I rode north along the banks of the River Boyne. There I met with some sheep herders who told me a longship had passed by, bound up-river."

"Indeed. Ireland is filthy with the damned Norse. What makes you think it is the longship we are seeking?"

"I can't be certain, that's true. But the sheep herder said there were no more than a dozen shields in the longship's shield rack, which was true of the one we sought. Some of the shields were bright painted, such as those the dubh gall carried, and some leather, such as ours. And the longship carried its dragon head mounted, and not stowed away, as the Norse generally do when they approach the land."

Cormac nodded. It could be another longship, but he doubted it. This description matched too closely the one they were chasing. He began to feel a surge of optimism. For three years he had thought about little other than getting his hands on the Crown of the Three Kingdoms. He had come so close, and then had the dream snatched away. But here it was again, dangling like a carrot on a stick.

Why would the fin gall be on the River Boyne? Cormac wondered. Perhaps they were intending to plunder inland. Perhaps they were going to fall on Tara, which was best reached by passage up the Boyne.

Cormac sat upright. *Tara!* Perhaps the fin gall were in league with Máel Sechnaill. There were plenty of Irish kings who had held their noses and made alliances with the filthy Norse intruders for their own gain. He had. Why not Máel Sechnaill?

The more Cormac thought on it, the more certain he became, and the more desperate he felt to stop them.

"Get the men ready to move," Cormac snapped at Niall Cuarán. "Fintan will lead us to where the longship is. We will not stop until we have taken them, or have been cut down trying."

Chapter Thirty-Seven

Repay laughter
with laughter again
but betrayal with treachery
Hávamál

The Red Dragons backed off, warily, watching the riders as they raced off west with Harald prisoner. They retreated to the line of trees, which would protect their backs in case the horsemen turned and bore down on them. Overhead, the sky grew blacker and far off the thunder began to peal. The Norsemen looked warily at the thick clouds, wondering on whom the gods would unleash.

Thorgrim Night-Wolf paced, twenty feet in front of the rest. Back and forth. Every once in a while he would look out across the field to see if anything was happening. He hoped desperately that the Irish would attack. He did not think he could rally the men for an attack on them.

Back and forth, hand gripping and ungripping the hilt of the unfamiliar sword. The men did not speak to him. They did not dare, and that was fine. There was nothing to say in any event.

It was Egil Lamb who broke the silence. He had managed to climb one of the scrawny trees and was peeking out through the prickly foliage. "Riders coming!" he called.

Men who had begun to relax, just a bit, scrambled to their feet, weapons ready. "Just three!" Egil called out a moment later.

They could see them soon enough, three mounted men riding across the open country. There were no others, no riders sweeping in for a flank attack. At least not that the Norsemen could see.

It took twenty minutes for the riders to cover the ground. Half way to where the Norsemen were formed up they stopped and held something aloft, then continued on, the object still held high.

"It's a shield, they are carrying a shield on a spear," Egil called from his perch. An imitation of the Viking custom of running a shield up to the top of the mast to indicate that a ship coming from sea had peaceful intentions.

"Now we will see how things lie," Ornolf said. He, of all the men, had dared to come and stand beside Thorgrim. He no longer trusted Thorgrim's judgment, Thorgrim knew it. He was assuming the command that was his to take. That was fine. Thorgrim was worried only about Harald now.

The riders approached, slowing as they came within a long spear throw of the Vikings, and then they stopped.

"We have come to talk," one of them called out. He spoke good Norse with a thick Celtic accent.

"Come and talk," Ornolf called. "We won't harm you, if your word is good."

The horsemen walked their mounts forward until they were a perch away from the Norsemen, no more. "My name is Flann mac Conaing, and I am the chief council of Máel Sechnaill mac Ruanaid, who is high king of Tara and the land of Brega."

Ornolf stepped forward. "I am Ornolf Hrafnsson, jarl in the territory of Vik, and these are my men."

"Ornolf Hrafnsson, you are the one I have come to speak with," said Flann. "And one called Thorgrim."

Thorgrim stepped forward, stood beside Ornolf, fought the temptation to cut them all down, all three Irishmen, raised shield or no.

"I am Thorgrim."

Flann nodded. "We have a hostage, by the name of Harald Thorgrimsson. He is one of your men?"

Thorgrim and Ornolf remained silent. After a moment Flann gave a nervous cough.

"In any event, I have it on good authority that he is your son, Thorgrim, as his name would suggest, and grandson to Ornolf. And that being so, I imagine you want him back. Alive."

"You have other men, too," Ornolf said. "Stolen from Dubh-linn. Olvir Yellowbeard and Giant-Bjorn. What of them?"

Flann thought about that before answering. "They were wounded when they arrived at Tara. They did not survive their wounds."

Thorgrim pressed his lips together, tight. *Murdering bastards...* he thought. His hand reached for the hammer and cross around his neck. *Odin, all-father...Christ...protect Harald from these bastards...*

"You have something we want," Flann continued, "and it is of little use to you in any event. The crown. The Crown of the Three Kingdoms."

"What makes you think we have this crown?" Ornolf asked.

"Because it has all been arranged, far beyond what you can understand. Why else would you come up the River Boyne, with so few arms and a ship so poorly fit out?"

"Very well, the crown for the boy," Thorgrim said. He was finished with fancy talk. "How shall it be done?"

"At first light on the morrow," Flann said. "In the middle of that open ground." He pointed to the rolling country over which he had just ridden. "Where we took your boy this morning. I will ride out alone with Harald, you, Thorgrim, will come alone with Morrigan and the crown. We will exchange there and go our ways in peace."

Thorgrim frowned. This Flann mac Conaing knew that Morrigan was with them. Flann was not lying about the intricate arrangements. Thorgrim did not trust him. There was no one in all of Ireland he trusted now, including Ornolf the Restless, his father in law. There was no one he trusted, save for Harald.

"Very well, it is agreed," Ornolf said.

"Very well," Flann said. "On the morrow, at first light." He wheeled his horse and the three riders headed back the way they had come, moving at an unhurried pace, as if they had no fear at all. The Vikings watched them go.

"Good," Ornolf said at last. "Tomorrow we get our boy and say good bye to this cursed land."

Overhead the thunder cracked again, much louder. The first drops of rain began to fall. Thorgrim had a very bad feeling.

We bring them the crown and Morrigan, we get Harald. They cannot betray us, if it is just this Flann and me on open ground.

And then another thought came to him. He looked around. "Where is Morrigan?" he asked.

Crouched in the brush, Morrigan waited and listened. She could hear the sound of heavy drops hitting the leaves, could see the splat of the rain on her cloak as the storm moved in overhead. It would make for a miserable night, but a safe one. No one could track her in a downpour, with night covering the wood.

She had been sitting, quite still, for half an hour by her estimate. No noise of pursuit, no one crashing through the woods after her. With all of the fin gall tracking Harald, she imagined they were not thinking of her. By the time it occurred to them to look, it would be too late.

She stood and grimaced as cramped muscles stretched. In her hand she held her basket of medicines and food. It was heavier now with the weight of the Crown of the Three Kingdoms. Somehow, Harald had freed himself. Thorgrim did not need the crown now.

She moved off through the woods. Night would come early with the storm building in the west. Soon she would not be able to see and then she would have to find a place to curl up, some place that offered a modicum of protection, but until then she wanted to get as much distance as she could between herself and the longship.

She was walking west, generally following the River Boyne. Sometimes she was in trees and sometimes she was in open country, but it was all her land, her Brega, and she felt safe there.

It was starting to get fully dark when she first smelled the smoke. She paused and sniffed and looked around. The wind was out of the west, coming on the front of the rain. Somewhere ahead of her there was a fire burning. She wondered if there was a cottage ahead, and if so, did she dare approach. The thought of a warm house on such a night was tempting, but she was not sure she could risk it.

Let me see what this is, Morrigan thought and she headed off in the direction of the smoke, moving slowly and stopping often to listen and to look. She did not want to be seen unless she chose to be seen.

To the northwest, closer to the river, Morrigan could see a stand of trees, the occasional snatch of smoke whipping out from the wood. *Not a cottage, then, some poachers or traveling merchants or some such,* she thought. Someone seeking some protection for the storm among the trees. She did not want to cross the open ground while there was still light in the sky. She found a place where the grass was tall enough to hide her, and she crawled into the middle and waited.

Twenty minutes later the rain was falling in earnest and the thunder like the handclap of an angry God rolled over the countryside. The daylight was all but gone. Morrigan could make out dark shapes and darker shapes, and no more. She stood and picked up her basket and headed toward the stand of trees and the promising smoke rising from there.

Morrigan reached the trees and began to slip through them, and soon she could catch glimpses of a fire burning in a small clearing in the wood. She moved cautiously, easing down with every step so as not to snap a twig or trip on some obstacle, but with the rain and the thunder she doubted she would be heard if she was playing a war drum.

Near the edge of the clearing she stopped and peeked through the tangled bracken. There was a horse tethered to a tree. A blanket had been strung between trees to form a rude shelter, and under that a small fire sputtered and crackled and blazed.

Morrigan looked longingly at the fire, as longingly as she had ever looked at one of the noblemen's feasts at Tara while she herself and all those of her class had near starved in the late spring famines. She wanted to sit under that blanket, warm her hands over that fire.

Her eyes moved to the man sitting beside it and she tried to make him out, to see what sort of a man he appeared to be. If he had a horse, then he was a man of means, but that certainly did not mean he would not harm her. She knew better than that.

There was something familiar about him, she was sure of it, though in the dim light she could not make out the features of his face. *One of the rí túaithe who frequented Tara? Perhaps.*

The rain was running down her face and she wiped it away. The fire in the clearing began to sputter and the man added more twigs. He leaned toward the flames and blew on the coals, and in that instant the fire flared and illuminated his face as if a lantern had been unshuttered in front of him.

Magnus Magnusson! Morrigan gasped, despite herself, and Magnus looked up sharp, looked right at her. Morrigan tried to make herself more compact, tried to shrink away. Magnus stared at the edge of the wood, but Morrigan was well hidden and Magnus had just been staring into the fire and there was no chance he would see her. Finally he looked away. He said something out loud, as if he was talking to another person, but Morrigan could see only him.

Magnus Magnusson... What on earth was he doing there? The rain and the cold were suddenly forgotten as Morrigan watched this man, this vile man, who did not know she was there.

Vengeance is mine, sayeth the Lord... Morrigan considered that old injunction. Revenge was the province of God, not man.

And sometimes I am called upon to be God's handmaiden, she thought.

Chapter Thirty-Eight

They will surely feel
my weapons bite their armor
if rage comes upon me now.
Gisli Sursson's Saga

The darkness and the fury fell on Thorgrim like the ever-strengthening rain, covered him completely, seeped into every part of him, until he was swimming in his anger, spitting his hatred.

He sat alone, cross-legged in the grass, away from the others. He stared off into the darkness, off to where Harald was, his boy, out there somewhere, with strangers doing what they wished with him.

His mind was not clear, he could not think, the fury that he often felt as the sun went down now ten times, twenty times greater than ever before.

Morrigan was gone. Thorgrim had assumed she was with them, following along as they tracked Harald. She had always come with them before, during the attack on the baggage train, digging up the crown, he had never been able to leave her behind. But this time, when they looked, she was not there.

A band of men had gone back to the longship in search of her, but she was not there, either. Her basket was gone, the Crown of the Three Kingdoms was gone, too. There was no sign of her, no indication that she had been attacked, taken by force. She was just gone.

Ornolf broke the news to Thorgrim. No one else dared. Thorgrim walked away and sat in the grass. He did not speak. His mind raced. In the

223

morning he would meet Flan. Flan would have Harald. He would have nothing.

He could trick Flan. Carry something wrapped in canvas, tell Flann it was the crown. Tell him Morrigan had run off, or they were keeping her hostage. He did not have to fool Flann long, just long enough to grab Harald before Flan slit his throat.

He did not think he would get the chance. The Irishman was not fool enough to let that happen. He would stand fifty paces away and make Thorgrim show him the crown before he set Harald free. When Flann saw that Thorgrim was pulling a trick, he would kill Harald then and there. Thorgrim would kill Flann in turn, but that would do Harald no good.

From there, Thorgrim's thoughts devolved into dark and twisted things, following no path, just a senseless fury as he stared out into the dark and felt the rain running down his face.

Behind him, by the trees, the men managed to build a fire but Thorgrim would have none of it. He could sense men out in the dark, men on either side, but not close, and he imagined that Ornolf had ordered them there to keep an eye on him, see that he did not do anything stupid.

The rain grew harder, until it was coming down in sheets, lashing the ground. The thunder broke overhead, so loud it hurt the ears. The lighting flash illuminated the open field and those men crouched a few perches away, miserable, watching Thorgrim as Thorgrim watched the night.

Despite the rain and the thunder and the red-hot fury, Thorgrim realized he must have fallen asleep, because he saw himself running through the woods, running alone, moving fast and silent, his eyes cutting through the darkness. He could not feel the rain anymore. The fury was gone now, completely gone, and in its place a calm sense of purpose, an unwavering resolve to do what he had to do. The taste of blood was in his mouth.

He moved across open country, tireless, a hunter on the prowl, senses wolf-sharp. There was a fire some ways off, a small fire in a thicket and he looked there but it was not what he was looking for so he moved on. The ground flew under his feet, he raced over the rolling countryside, the land over which they had taken Harald, his Harald. It was all strange, dream-like, a moving sleep.

And then some time later he stopped and he panted for breath as he looked out from the bracken. The Irish camp. A big tent, round with a pointed roof, where this Máel Sechnaill slept in comfort. A hundred men, some huddled around fires, some standing sentry. He had passed pickets on his way into the camp, slipped easily around them in the dark and rain, paused as lightning lit the watching men up like yellow statues. They did not see him.

Thorgrim could smell dogs and horses but the wind was with him and the animals could not smell him. No living thing was going to hear him on such a night, not moving as silent as he was.

Harald was near. Thorgrim could sense it. His son's closeness seemed to tremble in his mind, made the hair stand up on the back of his neck. But he did not move. He only watched. A hunter was patient. A hunter observed, and a hunter moved only when the moment was right.

Morrigan was watching as well. Fascinated, wondering how it could have happened that Magnus Magnusson was here, under her eye, and he did not even know it. She watched him fish some small bit of bread from his saddlebag. She heard him offer some to someone lost in the shadows on the other side of the fire, but that person made no reply. Morrigan could see no one. She wondered if there really was someone there, or if Magnus had gone insane.

The rain was falling hard now, making a loud noise in the trees and the thunder cracked deafening overhead. In the flashes of lighting Morrigan could see Magnus looking up at the sky, or out at the trees. She could see the palpable fear in his face.

You had better be afraid, you heathen dubh-gall pig... Morrigan thought. She knew these Norsemen were terrified of trolls and spirits and all the things they thought were lurking in the night. She smiled. The only real threat to Magnus's life was one he did not even know was there.

After a while Magnus added more wood to his fire, building it up to a brighter blaze. He lay down beside the fire, pulling a wet blanket over him. With the blanket stretched between the trees as a roof, he had a modicum of shelter as he closed his eyes. Morrigan wondered about the other person, and why he did not warrant any shelter. A slave, perhaps. She knew Magnus Magnusson did not concern himself with a slave's comfort.

Long after Magnus closed his eyes, Morrigan continued to wait and to watch. The trees above kept the rain off her, mostly. The fire illuminated Magnus's face enough that she could watch every twitch, every grimace of his fitful sleep.

The hours passed slowly, and the fire by Magnus's face began to grow dim, and Morrigan was ready to move. She shuffled back into the brush a few feet, set her basket in front of her. She lifted out the canvas covered crown and set it aside, then carefully removed the contents of the basket. When she came to the false bottom she opened it up and reached her hand in to the very bottom of the basket.

There was not much in there now, and her fingers fell on the small glass bottle tucked in the corner. She had filled it more than a year before, wondering in what circumstance she might ever use it, and on whom. She had long had an idea that she might use it on herself.

She pulled the little bottle from the basket, held it as she replaced the other things, this time putting the crown in first and piling the rest on top of it. She took one last look around, was ready to move, when she heard something, out in the dark.

She stopped and listened. There was something moving in the trees, some animal. She could not see it, but she could hear it, faintly, and even more than that she had a sense of its presence, as if its spirit radiated out as it moved. Magnus's horse sensed it too. He made a snorting sound, shifted from foot to foot and tugged a bit on his halter. Morrigan was afraid the animal would wake Magnus, but its sounds of vague alarm did not rise much above the drumming of the rain.

Whatever it was, Morrigan could feel it moving past. It was the strangest sensation, like nothing Morrigan had ever experienced before. She waited and listened, crossed herself and mouthed the words to a prayer, but she was not as afraid as she knew she should be. And then whatever it was was gone, off into the dark, a night-creature swallowed up by its element.

Morrigan did not move for some time after, until she was certain that whatever had come through the woods had not disturbed Magnus and the other. When she was certain, she stood slowly and stepped with great care through the bracken and into the small clearing in which Magnus lay sleeping.

She moved to the left, away from Magnus, circling around. The horse shifted nervously as she approached, but she spoke to it, soft, soothing words, and it calmed the animal. Morrigan continued to circle the little camp until at last in the dim light of the fire she could see the other person, lying like a dead thing, huddled near the trunk of a tree.

Morrigan moved closer, easing her weight down with each step. The person was lying on his side, hands behind his back in a very odd position. Two more steps and Morrigan realized that the person's hands were tied, bound behind their back and the rope tied to the tree under which they slept.

This is a fortunate day for you, my friend, Morrigan thought. She took a step closer, curious as to who this poor soul was. She kept an eye on Magnus's sleeping back as she moved, but he slept on, undisturbed.

Morrigan was only a few feet away from the prisoner when she realized it was a woman, her pale skin just visible in the reflected light of the fire. Some Irish girl captured and bound for the slow death of slavery, Morrigan imagined. She took another step, crouched down by the motionless figure, and nearly shouted out loud with surprise.

Brigit? Brigit nic Máel Sechnaill? Princess Brigit?

How in the world had she come to this place? Morrigan crossed herself. If she had any doubts about her intentions, they were gone now. Here, as clear as water, was the hand of God guiding her.

Morrigan stood quickly, moving now with a renewed determination.

She circled back around the clearing. She set her basket down and moved with cautious steps toward the sleeping Norseman, her soft leather shoes silent on the leaf-strewn ground. Five steps and she knelt down next to Magnus, so close she could smell his breath and hear his soft breathing.

Morrigan shifted the bottle from her left hand to her right. She held it up to the fire and watched the dark liquid swirl around inside. She pulled the stopper out and said a quick prayer. With her left hand she grabbed Magnus's nose and squeezed it hard. His eyes and his mouth flew open and Morrigan jammed the bottle, neck down, into his mouth.

Magnus's arms began to flail as he grabbed at his throat and Morrigan leapt out of the way. Choking, gagging, Magnus pulled the bottle from his mouth and leapt to his feet, spitting hard. His sword was in his hand, fury was in his eyes. Fury, confusion, fear.

He took a step toward Morrigan and Morrigan stepped away. "You..." Magnus said. He recognized her, but it was not clear if he knew who she was. He began to swing his sword, backhand, ready to deliver a slashing blow, and then his eyes went wide and he made a little choking sound and then he was down on his knees, his sword on the ground, his hands at his throat.

Magnus's breathing took on a quick, gasping, panicked quality. He looked up at Morrigan with a pleading look.

"Tincture of monkshood," Morrigan said softly.

Even in the dim light of the fire, Morrigan could see how red Magnus's face had become. He clawed at his throat and fell on his side, legs kicking at the air.

Morrigan took a step closer. She had heard of what monkshood could do, but now in actual practice the tincture seemed much more effective than she had thought it would be. Of course it was hard to know just how much he had swallowed.

Magnus's eyes were bulging and a strangling noise was coming from his throat. His arms and legs jerked uncontrollably, as if he was being attacked by a swarm of bees. His back arched and fell, arched and fell.

The spasms grew worse. Magnus's heels pounded on the soft ground, his hands clawed up clumps of dirt and leaves.

Then suddenly he stopped, froze, lay tense and motionless. His wide eyes looked into Morrigan's and she could see the terror there, the absolute terror.

"Off to hell with you, you heathen pig," Morrigan said, and, as if following her command, Magnus exhaled, loud breath, and his body went entirely limp.

Morrigan took a step closer. Magnus's eyes were closed. He did not seem to be breathing. Then his body gave one last jerk that made Morrigan jump and gasp. It was, she guessed, his soul's last desperate effort to cling to the corporal, to save itself from the eternal fires.

For a minute or so Morrigan just looked at him, the color draining from his face as if the rain was washing it away. Then she stepped around the fire and the blanket shelter, over to where the princess Brigit was watching, her eyes wide with shock.

Morrigan crouched down in front of her. Brigit's eyes stayed on hers like a bird hypnotized by a snake.

"Do you know who I am?" Morrigan asked.

Brigit nodded. "Morrigan nic Conaing. Flan's sister."

"That's right. Now I can let you go, Brigit, or I can kill you here and now. No one will know."

"Kill me?" The words came out as barely a whisper. Apparently it had not occurred to Brigit that Morrigan would consider that an option. "Why kill me? You'd damn your soul to hell for eternity!"

"That would be for God to decide, not you."

"Please, please, don't kill me. Whatever is in my power to promise, I promise to you."

"Very well. There are two things. The first is that you will never mention seeing me here, and what has happened. Ever."

Brigit nodded vigorously. "On my hope of heaven, I swear it."

"Good. The second is that you deliver a message to my brother. And it, too, must be a secret held to your heart forever. Do you swear it?"

"I do."

"Good." Brigit would not betray her, Morrigan knew it. She thought for a minute, tried to compose a message simple enough that Brigit would remember it, sufficient for Flann to understand. Just a few words. When she had, she told Brigit. Brigit squinted at her, a confused look on her face. Morrigan said it again and made Brigit repeat it. Then Morrigan took the knife she kept in her belt and cut the bonds free from Brigit's hands.

Brigit sighed with relief, rubbing her chaffed and bleeding wrists.

"Come here," Morrigan said and she led Brigit under the blanket, by the fire, where they found just the tiniest degree of comfort. Brigit took a poultice from her basket and bound it around Brigit's wrists. Brigit smiled with relief.

"Now, you must go," Morrigan said. "The River Boyne is in that direction, not far. Take the dubh-gall's horse and follow it north. Can you find Tara?"

"I think so. But my father's men are out looking for me. I should think I will find them soon, along the river."

"Good," Morrigan said. *Good you have told me this,* she thought. It had not occured to her that Máel Sechnaill would be roaming the countryside, but of course he would, his daughter captured by the dubh-gall. "Go, and remember our bargain."

"I remember. Bless you, Morrigan," Brigit said. She stood and with practiced ease set the blanket and saddle on the dubh-gall's horse. It was only a few minutes before she led the animal out of the clearing and disappeared in the dark.

This is going better than I had hoped, Morrigan thought. The hand of God was truly at work. She stood and looked down at the dead Norseman and in death hated him even more. Her eyes fell on his sword, lying where he had dropped it, just before he would have cut her down. The silver inlay, wet with the rain, glinted in the firelight. Overhead a flash of lightning lit up the clearing and the thunder crashed not a second later.

Morrigan bent over and picked up the sword. "Iron-tooth," she said. Suddenly the night became much more complicated.

Chapter Thirty-Nine

Thorgrim moved through the shadows along the edge of the camp, ducking behind clumps of brush, tents, carts. A big fire was burning in the center of the camp and the Irish soldiers stood around it, their eyes blind to the dark as they stared into the bright flames. Thorgrim could smell the burning wood and roasting meat. He could smell men and blood.

But the Irish were not foolish and they were not lax. There were guards around the perimeter, men not staring into the flames, but looking out into the night, their eyes trying to pierce the dark and the driving rain, but they would not see as well as Thorgrim Night-Wolf.

Around the back of a donkey cart, Thorgrim, crouched low, stepped silently, saw a guard ten paces away, shoulders hunched against the rain. He carried a shield over his shoulder, a spear in his hand, which he leaned on as he looked out over the countryside. Thorgrim stalked, one step, two steps, so low to the ground he could not be seen. So close to the guard he could smell him. On powerful legs he leapt and hit the guard and brought him down. The man died quick and silent, wide-eyed, blood running like the rainwater, his throat torn clean out.

Thorgrim moved on, and his heart had no more pity for the man than the wolf has for the hind brought down on the hunt.

He circled the camp, halfway around, searching for the boy. There were more men at the far end of the camp, far from the warming fire. A half-dozen perhaps, and some seemed alert and some bored and they all seemed miserable in the cold rain that was soaking them.

Thorgrim retreated into the dark, circled wide, approached the men from beyond the perimeter. Harald was much closer now, his nearness reverberated in Thorgrim's head, the nearness of kin.

There was a guard directly in Thorgrim's path. The Night Wolf moved on silent feet toward the man. He was three feet away and the guard still had not seen him when lighting flashed and lit the scene like day, just an instant, and Thorgrim saw, frozen on the guard's face, a look of shocked horror. The guard made the first note of a scream and Thorgrim killed him before another sound came from his throat.

"Father?"

It was Harald's voice, soft and weak, come from the dark. It snapped Thorgrim from his dream-state like a bucket of seawater. He crouched lower and pulled the big knife from his sheath, his mind racing now, when before he was driven by instinct alone.

Harald...

Then, as if an answer, from the dark, came a call, "Tomrair?"

Thorgrim retreated a few steps. The dead man was like a mound of earth in the dark.

"Tomrair?" The voice was closer. *Was this the dead man's name?*

"Tomrair!" the man shouted again, and then something in Irish which Thorgrim did not understand, and then the speaker appeared out of the dark and saw Tomrair, stretched out on the ground. He knelt quick, rolled him over, and Thorgrim sprang from the dark, leading with the big knife, right for the man's throat.

The man screamed in surprise, twisted and Thorgrim's knife missed its mark. The man shouted. Thorgrim recognized the tone of outrage and terror. He swung wildly at Thorgrim with his fist but he could not really see what he was swinging at and Thorgrim buried the knife in the man's side, right under his arm.

The man fell writhing and Thorgrim let the knife go with him. The damage was done, the alarm sounded. Men were shouting, feet making wet sucking noises as soldiers raced toward the sound of the fight.

There were two spears on the ground and Thorgrim snatched them up and leapt away. A figure loomed out of the dark, stood over Thorgrim's still thrashing victim and Thorgrim hurled a spear at his chest. He heard a thumping sound, a gasp as the man tumbled back with the impact and Thorgrim raced off into the dark.

He moved further around the perimeter of the camp, hunched over, while chaos broke out behind him and spread like fire. *Good, good...* he thought. Dark, rain, chaos, they were all powerful allies. He had only to find

Harald.

There was a tree fifty paces off, Thorgrim could just make out its looming shape against the night sky. A small, flickering fire beneath it lit up some sort of shelter held up by poles. There were men there, five or six, and they looked for all the world to be guarding a prisoner.

Thorgrim stopped to get his breath back. He had only one chance to make a surprise attack, and if Harald was not there, under that shelter, then the opportunity was lost. The shouting was growing louder, more men were running. He did not have long to think on this.

He started jogging toward the tree and then running. He could feel the mud sucking at his shoes and the rain cool on his face and his eyes were locked on the half-dozen uncertain-looking men in front of him. He felt the edge of reason leaving him, the berserker rage start to build. It came out as a scream that started low and built with every pounding footfall.

The men at the tree raised spears, unslung shields, peered into the dark but they could not see from where this unearthly sound was coming. Twenty paces away, then ten, and Thorgrim leveled his spear and ran on, ran right for the closest man. And that man did not see Thorgrim at all until a second before Thorgrim's spear tip ducked under his shield and embedded itself in the man's stomach.

Thorgrim let the spear go. His sword flew from its sheath and he cut down the next man, then twisted around to look under the shelter. There was Harald, eyes wide with surprise, hand pressed to his torn tunic, leaning against the tree.

"Come on, boy!" Thorgrim shouted, met a leveled spear thrust at him, knocked it aside, kicked the spearman hard. The spearman's fellow was practically climbing over him to get at Thorgrim, and as they fumbled with one another Thorgrim cut them both down as if he was chopping wood.

Another was coming at Thorgrim, wielding a sword which Thorgrim met with his own, the iron ringing loud. Someone was shouting, shouting for all he was worth, and Thorgrim had to guess he was calling for help. Thorgrim wanted very much to make him stop. But he had to get past the man with the sword, and that was proving difficult.

Thorgrim knocked the man's blade aside and lunged but the man twisted clear, hacked down on Thorgrim's sword, all but ripping it from Thorgrim's grip. The man's elbow caught Thorgrim in the jaw and knocked him staggering back. Swords ready, they faced one another.

The man behind was still shouting for help, then suddenly, as quick as he had started, he stopped, his words cut off in mid-sentence.

Thorgrim looked. Harald had found a spear and had driven it right into the man's back. The man with the sword looked as well, turned his attention for a fraction of a second from Thorgrim's sword, and in that instant Thorgrim lunged and drove the point home.

"Come along! Can you run?" Thorgrim shouted.

"Yes, father!" Harald said, but his voice was weak. *Yes, father...* It was practically the only thing Thorgrim had ever heard from Harald, Harald the Willing, Harald the Eager. *Yes, father...* A boy worth saving.

Thorgrim backed away from the tree, sword held ready for the next attack, but the guards there were dead and the rest had not yet discovered where the real fighting was. Not for long. Thorgrim looked at Harald. "Let's hurry, son," he said and Harald nodded. Thorgrim turned to run and Harald ran after him.

They ran into the dark in a straight line away from the camp, but that direction also took them farther away from Ornolf and the others. They would have to circle back around the Irish to get back to their fellows, and that would not be an easy thing.

Once they were well away from the camp, lost in the dark, Thorgrim turned to lead the way back toward where Ornolf's men were hunkered down. He could not really recall how far off that was. A mile or five, he could not remember how far he had come.

He turned to look for Harald but Harald was not there. He looked back. Harald had dropped behind and was stumbling to catch up. Thorgrim met him half way. "Are you hurt?" he asked.

Harald shook his head. "Nothing," he said, but the word came out more like a gasp. He was holding his tunic closed with his left hand.

"Let me see." Thorgrim pulled the rent edges of the tunic apart. He could see a dark line on the white flesh, seeping blood that was washed away in the rain. It was far from nothing. But if Harald died he would die a warrior's death, and that was what mattered, because then, if the gods were generous, father and son would feast together in Valhalla.

The shouting was louder now, and added to that the sound of dogs, barking and howling. Harald looked up sharp. He hated dogs, Thorgrim knew that. "Don't worry, they will not track us in this rain," Thorgrim said, but he was not so sure that was true. "Still, we must move."

He put his arm around Harald, holding his weight, and Harald draped his arm over Thorgrim's shoulders. The boy was heavy, heavy as a grown man, and together they limped off, toward the far trees where the Norsemen were hunkered down.

They were moving around the perimeter of the Irish war camp. Thorgrim could see the big fire now in the center of the camp and the figures of men racing in every direction, orders shouting in the Gaelic tongue, dogs barking.

Off to the west he could see men mounting up, mounted troops who would sweep along the flanks of the army. Something was buzzing in Thorgrim's head, something was not right, and then he realized. *I can see!*

He looked to the east. The darkness there had softened a bit, the black sky yielding just a bit to gray. Dawn came early at that time of year, and now like an assassin it was sneaking up on them.

"Now, Harald, we really must hurry," Thorgrim whispered and he picked up his pace and Harald, dutifully, moved his legs faster, but his breathing was more labored.

Thorgrim wiped the rain water from his face and his eyes and looked around. It seemed the Irish soldiers were spreading out across the countryside. He could see movement in the dark, and figures just visible in the gathering light. Soon there would be no clear way back to the others.

They hurried on, foot after agonizing foot, with the sound of the dogs getting louder and Harald getting weaker with every step. They came to a place where the grass grew waist high. Thorgrim stopped. He could hear the dogs hard on their heels.

"Sit here," he said to Harald, easing him down into the grass. He pulled his sword and braced himself, looking right and left. He could hear the dogs' feet, hear their bodies parting the grass as they ran, the chilling sound of animals on the hunt growing louder.

The first dog seemed to come from nowhere, hurtling though the air, hitting Thorgrim in the chest, burying it's teeth in his arm and making him stagger.

"Ahhh!" Thorgrim shouted, hit the dog's head hard with the pommel of his sword, hit it again and again. Another dog was on him now, teeth ripping into his leg. He could feel the blood running and it made the dog wild, growling and trashing its head.

Thorgrim hit the dog on his arm again and again and finally it let go and he slashed at the dog at his leg. He felt the sword bite, heard the dog whimper as it released his leg. Another dog came out of the dark and Thorgrim hit it with the flat of his sword, knocking it aside. It backed off, beyond reach of the sword, crouched low and growled.

Thorgrim was standing over Harald now, turning this way and that, looking for the next attack, man or beast. He could hear the sound of horses riding hard, sweeping out from the camp. In the dim light he could see the mounted soldiers as they followed the baying dogs. They were still some ways away but closing with them, and the dogs were on their trail, despite the driving rain.

Harald pulled himself to his feet. "I have no weapon," he said. Thorgrim pulled the small knife from his belt and handed it to Harald. It was not right that a warrior should die with no weapon in his hand. The Valkyries would not look favorably on that.

"I fear you've sacrificed your life to try and save mine, father," Harald said.

Thorgrim smiled, a broad and genuine smile. He put his arm around Harald's shoulders. "Tonight we feast at Valhalla, man and boy, and there is no more we could ask from this life." The riders were coming toward them now, pushing their mounts fast, and Thorgrim felt a sense of peace more profound than he had ever known.

He lifted his sword and prepared to meet the first attack when out of the dark, louder than the dogs, louder than the riders and the driving rain, he heard a sound that made the hair stand up on the back of his neck, a sound that sent him whirling back in time to his days a-viking when he was not much older than Harald was now. It was the wild, half-mad battle cry of Ornolf the Restless.

Chapter Forty

Not all men
are matched in wisdom
the imperfect are easy to find.
Hávamál

Ornolf had been sleeping, restlessly, his bear-skin pulled
entirely over him. It was a noble bear-skin, twenty years old,
the hide of the largest bear ever seen in the vicinity of Vik,
but it was just barely enough to cover all of Ornolf's corpulence.

The rain made a drumming sound on the hide and it might have been
soothing if Ornolf was not so wet, cold, miserable and sober. With no drink
in his stomach he had to sooth himself to sleep with cursing Ireland and the
Irish and thinking on what it would be like to sack a more civilized place.

He finally managed to get to sleep when he felt a hand shaking him.
He came awake slowly. "Ah, may Thor pluck your eyeballs out, you son of
a whore!" he shouted at whoever was waking him, once he was awake
enough to understand what was happening. "What is it?"

He tossed the bearskin off and glared at Egil Lamb, who had been
shaking him but now pulled his hand away as if from a vicious dog he had
tried to pat. "It's...Thorgrim...," Egil stammered.

"What of him?"

"He's...gone..."

"Gone?" Ornolf sat upright. "Oh, you blind, poxed, feeble-minded
idiot! Where did he go?"

"I don't know. I swear it. I was watching him, never took my eyes

236

away. He was there. There was a flash of lighting, and he was there, and then a thunderclap. Then another flash and he was gone."

Ornolf looked out toward the dark place where Thorgrim had been keeping his vigil. He wondered if Thorgrim had shape-shifted. He wanted to ask Egil Lamb if he had seen any such thing, but guessed Egil would have mentioned it if he had.

Muttering curses on the heads of everyone he could think of, Ornolf the Restless struggled to his feet. Egil handed him his helmet and as Ornolf settled the iron cone on his head Egil draped his cloak over his shoulders.

"You are very thoughtful Egil Lamb, but it does not excuse your poor job of watching Thorgrim," Ornolf said, though in truth he did not blame Egil. If Thorgrim wanted to leave without being seen, he would, and no human eye would catch him.

Ornolf stepped around the fire, walked out into the open ground that stretched away to where the Irish soldiers had made their camp, a mile and a half or so to the west. There was nothing to see in the dark and the driving rain, but Ornolf stared off in that direction and thought his thoughts.

He has gone for Harald... Ornolf sighed a great sigh of self-pity. Things were much easier when Thorgrim took care of everything, leaving Ornolf to just pay for things, and to eat and drink and fornicate. Thorgrim had kept his mind together wonderfully after Harald was taken. The little Irish doxy had helped, no doubt. But now she was gone, Harald was gone, and the crown was gone. It was more than Thorgrim could bear, and now he was gone, too, leaving Ornolf to take command.

Ornolf thought of his grandson, off there in the dark, held at spear-point by the rutting Irish and it made his blood hot for revenge. That fighting spirit he had known in his youth had not been entirely smothered by an excess of food and drink and he felt it rising now. Time for action.

"Egil Lamb, get the men up and to arms. Only women and slaves lay around like this, waiting to get buggered."

Ten minutes later they moved out, stepping out across the dark, wet ground, grim and determined, clutching the odd assortment of weapons they had picked up since their escape from Dubh-linn. They walked through the rain, stumbling and cursing, but glad for the impenetrable dark that would hide their approach, the rain that would cover their footfalls and their smell. The lightning cracked around them, illuminating the open ground for a fraction of a second, followed by the thunder that made the earth tremble beneath their feet.

It was slow going in the dark, and they pushed on for close to an hour before a flash of lightning revealed the Irish camp not more than a few hundred paces ahead. The Norsemen dropped to the ground, reflexively, as if on command, and lay still, listening, straining to hear if their presence was creating some alarm.

They could hear nothing beyond the drumming rain. Minutes passed. Another flash of lighting revealed the Irish camp undisturbed.

"Come along," Ornolf growled. He stood in a half crouch and raced forward, keeping as low to the ground as his midriff would allow. He covered a hundred paces and then dropped again and behind him the rest did the same. A stealthy approach. They were vastly outnumbered, and worse, the Irish were better armed, a situation the Vikings did not generally encounter.

It's brains that are called for here, Ornolf thought. He turned to Sigurd Sow, crouched beside him. "We need a diversion of some sort," he said. Sigurd Sow nodded. From somewhere up ahead, a man shouted, and then another one. Dogs began barking. Someone shouted orders in Gaelic. The Vikings cocked their ears as the sound of chaos mounted.

"Sounds like Thorgrim Night-Wolf has created a diversion for us," Sigurd said.

The Vikings rose to their feet. The lighting flash revealed a camp like an overturned anthill, men running in every direction. The clamor was building, men, dogs and horses.

"First light soon," Snorri Half-troll said. To the east there was a hint of gray in the black.

"Let's move," Ornolf said. "Form up in a swine array, we'll hit them where ever seems best. Step aside, Snorri Half-troll, I'll take the lead."

Ornolf stepped in front of his men who were forming up in a wedge-shaped swine array, ideal for punching through a shieldwall if the Irish were able to arrange such a thing in time.

"Here we go," Ornolf said and he headed off toward the Irish camp, moving at a quick walk. In the younger days he would have run, running made for a more powerful attack, but he did not wish to collapse from exhaustion the moment he arrived in front of the enemy. He knew the men behind him were chaffing at the slow pace, but he did not care.

Ornolf felt his muscles warm as he walked, swinging his sword and beating it on his shield. He felt the excitement grow, like a burning coal inside that spreads a flame to everything it touches. It was like the excitement that proceeds taking a woman to bed, that delicious anticipation. This, he remembered, was why he so loved to go a-viking.

The Irish camp was in chaos. Ornolf smiled. No one man alone, save Thorgrim Night-Wolf, could cause such panic, he thought.

They were perhaps a hundred paces from the Irish camp when they were finally seen. Ornolf could not understand the words flying around but he could see the men in the light of the fire pointing in their direction, he could see men hustling together, forming a shieldwall, the round shields overlapping each other in a defensive line, and Ornolf's heart sang. There was nothing like charging a shieldwall to give him back his youth. And with their supply of drink exhausted, and little chance of getting more, the thought of reaching the divine mead hall of Valhalla soon was not at all unpleasant.

He picked up his pace to a brisk walk and there was a palpable sense of relief from the men behind him. His old legs, which had begun to falter, found a new strength. He felt the energy coursing through him, he felt young and a hundred pounds lighter. He broke into a jog, shield in his left hand, sword held in front of him like the prow of a ship.

Ornolf had not shouted his battle cry in a long time, not in all the raiding in the past years. He never seemed to have the energy. It was a sound from his youth, an era gone, but he felt it building now, rather like a great belch, building in his gut, crying for release.

They were twenty paces from the shieldwall and running when Ornolf let his war cry go. He opened his mouth and let the full-throated shout come up from below, that wild, exuberant, animal sound of years past. He shouted and let the madness come out and behind him the forty-odd Vikings under his command did the same.

A spear came sailing through the rain and hit Ornolf's shield with a thump. It stuck in the shield and dragged along for a few paces before it fell off. Another flew past Ornolf's head and he heard it strike someone behind him but he did not slow a bit.

And then Ornolf hit the shieldwall. He slammed into it shield-first, with all the force of a three hundred pound man running as fast as he can.

The Irishmen, braced though they were for the impact, never had a chance of standing up to that. The two men that Ornolf hit crumpled like paper and Ornolf ground them into the mud as he stomped over them. He turned left and slashed at the next man in the shieldwall and behind him the Vikings poured through the hole Ornolf had smashed in the Irish defense.

It was an awkward situation for the Irishmen. Arrayed in a line, shields overlapped to stop a frontal attack, they now had to disengage and turn to meet an attack from behind, and they died as they tried to do it.

The Vikings, screaming their pagan screams, bloodlust up, driven by the hope of a warrior's death, poured down the line, meeting spears with swords, swords with battle axes. The Irish were bowled over by the ferocity of the attack and they started to back away, step by step, waving on the point of breaking.

Ornolf was roaring and swinging his sword in great arcs. An Irishman appeared in front of him, sword raised to deliver a deathblow, and Ornolf drove his shield into the man's face, sent him staggering, cut him down with a stroke of his sword. He could hear the Valkyrie singing in his ears as his sword ripped though cloth and mail and flesh and the shielded defenders stumbled over themselves to flee before him.

"Don't run away! Don't run away!" Ornolf shouted as his sword sung through the air. He knew he was pushing his luck and his endurance. He didn't think he had the energy to chase Irishmen all over the countryside.

It did not seem that the Irish were paying attention to Ornolf's wishes. They were starting to peel off, to throw weapons aside and race away, one by one, and Ornolf had seen enough battles to know that that spirit would spread quick and soon they would all be running.

Snorri Half-troll was at his side. He had picked up an Irish shield and he had a wild look in his eyes. "Once these bastards run, we'll have to find Thorgrim!" he shouted.

Of course, Thorgrim... Ornolf thought. In all the pleasure of the fight, he had forgotten why they were there.

And then over the ringing of iron weapons on iron weapons came the drum of horses' hooves and a mounted rider appeared out of the rain, shouting in Irish and waving his sword, and the men on the edge of panic seemed to find new courage.

Damn his eyes... Ornolf thought. Now he wanted the Irish to run, now that he remembered Thorgrim.

"Kill that swine!" Ornolf shouted and pointed with his sword at the mounted man. The man on the horse looked down at him.

"Ornolf Hrafnsson, you gave your word of honor! I'll kill you, you treacherous bastard!"

"Flann mac Conaing, come and get me!" Ornolf roared. Flann dug the spurs in his horse's flanks, charged through the men, Irish and Norse, sword raised, and Ornolf braced to meet him.

Flann slashed at Ornolf as he thundered past and Ornolf caught the blade with his shield and thrust his sword at Flann but found only air. Flann reined in hard, spun the horse around. He charged again, sword raised. There was an Irishman beside Ornolf, back to him, fighting with Skeggi Kalfsson. Ornolf grabbed the Irishman by the collar and spun him around and Flann, unable to check his swing, cut the man down.

Flann rode past again, his face contorted with fury. The battlefield was lit with the gray light of a stormy dawn, and Ornolf realized his Norsemen were being quickly overrun. There were Irish coming from every part of the field, called by the sound of the fight.

"Skeggi Kalfsson, we might think about retreating," Ornolf shouted but Skeggi could do no more than nod as he was fighting two men at the same time.

Flann kicked his mount hard, his eyes fixed on Ornolf. The horse was starting forward again when the morning was ripped by a wild animal cry from beyond the fighting, a wolf howl, but more than that, more frightening than that. Ornolf smiled. Flann jerked his head toward the sound. Thorgrim Night-Wolf came pounding out of the dark.

It was still too dark to make out much, indeed if Ornolf had not recognized the sound of Thorgrim's battle cry he might not have know it was him at all. Thorgrim carried no arms that Ornolf could see, save his sword. He was running as hard as he could.

Between Flann and Thorgrim there was a soldier with spear held ready, held low, as if he was going to impale Thorgrim like a charging boar, but he never had the chance. Thorgrim swept the spear aside with his sword, never breaking stride, and leapt into the air, set a foot on the soldier's chest and launched himself at Flann. He hit Flann square and the two of them went over the far side of the horse and landed in a heap in the wet grass.

Thorgrim was up in a flash and he slashed at Flann, still on the ground, but Flann was no poorly trained foot soldier. He had his sword up and he met Thorgrim's attack, turning the blade aside and slashing at Thorgrim, making him jump back and allowing Flann to scramble to his feet as well.

Thorgrim attacked again, a wild flurry of thrusts and sweeps that Flann turned aside. Ornolf would have loved to sit and watch the fight - wonderful sword work on both sides - but he had fighting of his own to do. Svein the Short was getting the worst of his encounter with a clutch of Irishmen and Ornolf waded over, cut one down from behind before the fellow even knew he was there. Ornolf let Svein deal with the others as he charged into the maelstrom, hacking his way through the line.

He saw Harald beyond the knot of struggling men in front of him and his heart leapt with joy and with fear that Harald might be killed where he stood. His grandson did not look so well. He was staggering along, his hand clamped on his chest, unarmed, seemingly oblivious to the fighting going on around him.

"Harald!" Ornolf roared. He ran forward, crashed into the fighting men in front of him, sent them all sprawling, Vikings and Irish alike. He had no thought now but to get to his grandson.

He was not alone. Out of the fight, spear held low, an Irishman saw Harald too and charged at him, screaming a wild scream. Harald jerked his head up, took a step back. Ornolf saw he had a small knife in his hand, useless against the spear.

"Oh, you bastard!" Ornolf shouted and he ran like a bull, charged for the man who would strike his grandson down. They were converging on the spot where Harald stood and Ornolf could see he would not make it, that the wicked tip would pierce Harald's breast before he could get there.

Ornolf saw the spear point reaching out for his grandson as his grandson fell to the ground, collapsed right there, and the man with the spear could not react fast enough. His feet hit Harald's prone body and he fell forward and then Ornolf was over him and with one swipe of his sword took the man's head clean off.

"Harald!" Ornolf shouted. He did not know what had happened, if the Irishman had struck his grandson down. But Harald was smiling, a weak effort, but genuine, and Ornolf realized the boy had not fallen by accident or injury.

"Smart lad, smart lad!" Ornolf held out his hand and helped Harald to his feet. "Come along," he said and he realized that Harald could not stand straight, but rather was hunched over, hand clutching his chest.

"Let's see here…" Ornolf pulled the rent tunic aside, saw the vicious wound across Harald's chest. "Oh, these bastards, I'll have their guts!"

"Grandfather, we have to get out of here!" Harald said, loud as he could. "Our men are being overrun, we must fall back!"

"What?" Ornolf looked around, as if seeing the fight for the first time. The Norsemen were on a small rise, a bit of a hill, fighting in a cluster, almost back to back. Thorgrim and Flann were still slashing at one another, but slower now, their arms tiring with the effort. The Irish were coming from every quarter of the field and soon they would have the Vikings enveloped.

"Red Dragons, make a shieldwall, make a shieldwall! Come on, now, let us fall back!" Ornolf shouted, his great voice booming through the fight. His men were fighting side by side and they overlapped their shields, forming up as best they could in the face of the determined Irish assault, backing away step by step. Ornolf looked back over the vast open land they had to cross before they had anything like cover, before they could flee to the relative safety of their ship.

"Ah, Odin, All-Father, we'll lift our horns together on this day, I'll warrant!" Ornolf shouted to the sky, then giving Harald a supporting arm they limped off toward the shieldwall, fighting their way toward their shipmates and the Vikings' last stand.

Flann's horse had got between Flann and Thorgrim, and Thorgrim was darting to either side, using the horse as a shield, trying to get a sword into Flann as Flann did the same. No one seemed to be paying attention to the two men, so Ornolf deposited Harald at the shield wall, snatched up a shield off the ground and gave it to him, then lumbered off after Thorgrim.

Why must it always fall to me to look after these two? he wondered as he hit the horse hard with the flat of his sword, making the animal bolt, and then taking a wild swipe at Flann.

"Come along, Thorgrim! I have Harald and now we must step away from here!" Ornolf shouted, and shoulder to shoulder the two men backed off, stepped back in the face of Flann's sword and the men who came at them with sword and spear.

Thorgrim had a great bleeding gash on his shoulder and his face was smeared with blood from a laceration, bleeding so fast the rain could not wash it away. He had managed to pick up a shield, and used it to ward off the iron wielded by the close-packed Irish.

Ornolf parried a spear thrust but the attacker was quick, swung the point around, managed to get it under the sleeve of Ornolf's mail shirt and rip a great gash in his arm before Thorgrim struck him down.

"Not long now, eh, Thorgrim?" Ornolf shouted, his heart and his sword singing.

They backed into the shield wall and the men there made an opening for them and they took their place and locked shields with the others. The left and right sides of the shieldwall were bending back, fighting off any attempt by the Irish to get around behind. Soon the ends would meet and the Vikings would be formed up in a square, good for countering mounted soldiers, not very good for escaping.

"Not long!" Thorgrim agreed, reaching out beyond the shieldwall to lunge at one of the Irish. "Here come more of them, see?"

He jerked his head back toward the open ground over which Ornolf had led his men, back in the direction of the river and the longship. There were more men-at-arms coming across the field, a hundred at least, some mounted, some on foot.

Ornolf took a long look, but in the dim, gray light, and with his aging eyes, he could not make out who they might be. But if they were men belonging to this Máel Sechnaill, it made no sense that they should have gone half a mile across the open ground before turning to attack.

"Now who from the depths of Hel is this?" Ornolf wondered out loud.

Chapter Forty-One

*Ireland is almost the best
of all countries one knows about.*
Konungs Skuggsjá

Flann mac Conaing pushed himself forward, his sword held ready, but his opponent was gone, taking his place in the Viking shieldwall. Thorgrim. Flan had been in more desperate fights than he could recall, but it had never even occurred to him, not since the age of nineteen, that an opponent might best him. Until that morning.

But Thorgrim had broken off the fight on Ornolf's urging, hoping, apparently, to retreat back to their ship and make their escape. But that would not happen. They were outnumbered three to one, and Flann could see many of the fin gall dead on the ground, run through with spears or hacked down with swords.

The Norsemen had formed a shieldwall and they were defending a small knoll against the onslaught of the Irishmen. They were putting up a desperate and skilled defense, but they would be overwhelmed, and soon.

Flann wondered where Máel Sechnaill was, why the king had not come out to the fight. He looked around, suddenly afraid that Máel would appear, staring down from his horse, wondering why Flann was not joining the attack. Flann had lost much favor with the king in the past weeks, with their plan to retrieve the Crown of the Three Kingdoms falling apart and the boy Harald stealing Brigit. Flann feared for his position at Tara. Indeed, if things did not much improve immediately, he feared for his life.

His horse, a well-trained beast, had not gone far and Flann grabbed up the reins and pulled himself up into the saddle. From that perch he could see the Irishmen racing from the camp to fling themselves at the Vikings. Ornolf and his crew were almost lost from sight behind the wall of struggling men trying to get at them. It would not be long now.

And then his eye caught movement further away on the open ground, half a mile or so. It was full daylight now, but dark and gray, with the rain still coming in fits, and it was hard to see, and Flann's eyes had never been the sharpest. But it looked for all the world like men, a line of men, advancing.

"Donnel!" Flann turned to the former sheep herder who stood behind and to one side of the horse, spear and shield in hand. "Come here!"

Donnel hurried over. "What do you see, far down the field there?"

Donnel looked in the direction Flann was pointing, past the struggling mass of fighting men. His eyes were young and particularly keen.

"It's men, my lord," he said with confidence. "Some on foot, some on horseback. Must be near one hundred and more!"

Flann frowned and looked down the field. *A hundred and more men...?* An army, and it could not be any of Máel Sechnaill's command, or he would know of it.

"What the devil is this?" Flann demanded out loud, and Donnel, thinking it was a genuine question said, "I'm sure I don't know, my lord, but I reckon it's an army of men!"

Flann scowled at the young man. He wanted to see all the fin gall dead before he sought out Máel Sechnaill, he did not want to speak to his king without some good word to report, but he could not let this go. He wheeled his horse around and pounded off for the big round tent near the center of the camp, scattering men-at-arms before him as he rode.

The pages were strapping on Máel Sechnaill's armor as Flann rode up, reining to a stop in a spray of mud and water. Máel Sechnaill looked up at him, annoyed and dismissive at the same time, a neat trick.

"I pray you have come to tell me these heathen swine are dead," Máel said. "I thought it would not need my attention. Thought they were easy enough for you to deal with. But as I hear the fighting still going on, I imagine now I had best come and take charge myself."

"You'll do well to arm yourself, my lord," Flann said. He did not dismount because he knew it irritated Máel Sechnaill to look up at any man on a horse, and he found himself suddenly more interested in tweaking Máel than in looking to his own safety. "There is an army moving across the field toward us, more than a hundred armed men, some mounted."

Máel Sechnaill frowned and looked toward the distant field, though from that place he could not see the newcomers. "Who the devil are they?" he demanded.

"I don't know, my lord. But the fact that neither of us knows who they are tells me they are not your men. And if they are not your men, then they must be enemies to be fought."

The page finished buckling Máel Sechnaill's breastplate. Máel turned to another page and ripped the helmet from his hand, waved his arm for his horse. When the animal was led up, Máel Sechnaill swung himself into the saddle. Now, eye to eye with Flann, he spoke at last.

"You have made a damnable hash of everything you have set your hand to, this past fortnight. Now my daughter is stolen, out there somewhere, and we are attacked by two enemies at once, and you do not even know who they are. By God, if you don't manage to do something right I will see you drawn and quartered, depend upon it!"

He looked toward the open ground to the east and now he could see the men spread out and making their way toward the Irish camp. "They're not Norsemen, they don't attack like Norsemen," he said. "Niall Caille from Leinster, perhaps, but if so, then he must have more men somewhere ready to fall on us, because he is not such a fool as to attack with so few.

"In any event, we'll break off from your pathetic attempt to kill a few mangy Norsemen, which you seem to be failing at in any event, and prepare to meet this new threat. I will see to the center of the line, since you clearly are not competent to do so, and you see to the left flank. I want mounted troops there to sweep in once these bastards get close enough. Now, go!"

With that Máel Sechnaill put spurs to his horse and charged off for the place where the Vikings and the Irish were still locked in battle, leaving Flann, smarting and humiliated, sitting his horse in the light rain.

Oh, you are a fine one, Máel Sechnaill, who would be dead a dozen times over were it not for me... he thought as he rode slowly off to the left, to gather up the mounted troops and prepare for a flank attack on this new enemy's line.

"You there, you there, form up here!" he shouted to the mounted rí túaithe as he rode past. The men fell into line behind him and he led them off to the left side of the field where he could sweep around Máel Sechnaill's shieldwall and roll up the enemy's flank, if they had the chance.

"Brian Finnliath, round up all the mounted troops, I want them here with us!" The master of the guards nodded and rode off and Flann turned his attention to making certain the horse troops were ready for their work.

"My lord!"

One of the mounted soldiers, one of the rí túaithe of a minor holding south of Tara, was pointing toward the tree line off to the north, close by the River Boyne. It took Flann a moment before he saw what the fellow was pointing at, a rider coming toward them, a lone rider, but Flann could make out no more detail than that.

"Looks to be a woman, my lord," the rí túaithe added.

Flann squinted but still could make out nothing, but a thought was forming in his head and it demanded attention. "All of you, remain here," he ordered, "and I'll see what is acting here." With that he rode off, spurring his horse to a canter, closing with the figure on the horse. He saw the person dismount and come running toward him. The closer he got the more he could see, and soon even he was certain that it was a woman, and by her gait and her shape he was soon convinced of what woman it was.

Twenty paces away he reined the horse to a stop and leapt from the saddle. "Princess Brigit!" he shouted, and Brigit, stumbling, weeping, now smiling with relief, fell to the ground. Flann raced over to her, held her in his arms and she pressed her face into his tunic and cried, sobbed uncontrollably.

"There, there," Flann said, thinking that was the sort of thing to say. He was a soldier and not good at such things as this. "You're safe now..."

He could hear a change in the pitch of battle. He guessed Máel Sechnaill was realigning the men, drawing them off from the Vikings and forming a shieldwall. He had to get his flank attack organized. There was no time to spend comforting a weeping girl.

"Brigit, my dear, I must go. Let us share my mount and I will ride you to safety."

Brigit looked up at him. Her eyes were red, her face was streaked, her hair tangled. Flann had never seen her looking so bad. "Flann mac Conaing," she said, and her voice cracked. "First, I have a message for you. For you alone."

Brigit stammered as she told him the words. Words from Morrigan. Flann frowned.

"Say that again, I beg you," Flann said. Brigit said the words again, slowly. Flann realized then they were Norse, the message was in the language of the fin gall so that only he and Morrigan, of all the Irish, would understand.

Flann nodded as the meaning became clear. "Very good, Brigit, my dear. Let us mount and ride to safety."

Flann helped Brigit up onto his horse - he did not think she had the strength to sit the horse she had been riding - then climbed up behind her and rode off. He deposited her at Máel Sechnaill's tent, then rode back to the mounted troops he was organizing. They were the rí túaithe, the minor lords without whom Máel Sechnaill would be powerless. That was what made the Crown of the Three Kingdoms so powerful - it would assure the allegiance of the rí túaithe. The strength of the king depended on the support of these men.

And they liked Flann and trusted him.

"Listen you men!" he shouted as he tried to control his restless mount. "You know our orders?"

The rí túaithe responded with shouts, raised swords and shields. They knew their orders.

"Now, listen," Flann said, in a lower voice. "Our king, Máel Sechnaill, rides into battle today! There is always danger in battle, and our king has no heir! Have you men, who wield such power in Brega, put thought to who should assume the crown if, and pray God it should never happen, Máel Sechnaill should fall in battle?"

Chapter Forty-Two

I, battle-oak, have brought
death's end to many a man,
making my sword's mouth speak.
                    Gisli Sursson's Saga

This is a fine place to die, a good place, Thorgrim thought as he worked his sword over his shield. He felt a spear tip catch in his hair as it thrust past. He tried to cut the man who wielded it but he could not reach.

The Vikings' shieldwall had bent around until the right and left flanks met. The Vikings were formed up in a square now on top of the small rise, surrounded by the Irish men-at-arms, like a great bear baited around by dogs.

Harald is here, and Ornolf, and we will die together. Freya will lead the Valkyrie over the Bifrost bridge and they will take us all to Asgard where we will feast in Valhalla...

It was a pleasant thought, and hungry as he was, the idea of feasting at Valhalla, where he always imagined the food was excellent and plentiful, was very inviting indeed.

If only they were on their native soil, and not soggy, miserable Ireland, damned by the gods, then all would be fine.

Now someone was shouting something, shouting in Irish, shouting to be heard above the fighting. Over the tops of the warriors' heads Thorgrim could see a man on horseback. He wore a bright, shining helmet trimmed in gold, and a cape trimmed in fur over a mail shirt. His sword gleamed dull in the morning light. Thorgrim wondered if this was that Máel Sechnaill he had heard of, the one Morrigan called the king of Brega.

He was shouting orders and one by one the men were obeying, backing away from the Viking shieldwall, stepping back and forming a shieldwall of their own.

"Now what are these poxed whores' sons about?" Ornolf shouted in Thorgrim's direction. Thorgrim lowered his sword. There was no one left to fight. The Vikings had been abandoned on their little rise, left in their defensive square with no one to defend themselves against.

Thorgrim turned and looked across the open ground. The line of advancing men was much closer now, a quarter mile or so. They were coming on in a battle array, with foot soldiers in front and mounted warriors behind, banners flying at the end of lances, tunics making bright spots on the gray-green field.

"These Irish are more worried about these fellows than they are about us," Thorgrim said, pointing with his sword at the advancing army.

"There's a lot of them," Ornolf agreed. "I reckon we had best worry about them, too."

The Vikings backed away from Máel Sechnaill's men, wary of an attack from that quarter, but it was soon clear that the Irish had forgotten about them. Thorgrim looked for a way out. He did not want his men caught between these two armies, crushed like a bug between two hands, but there was no exit from the field.

"Let us form a shieldwall, here!" he pointed to a spot of land halfway between the armies and led the men at a trot to that place. They stood, shoulder to shoulder, shields overlapping. They were pathetically few, perhaps thirty in number, the rest were dead on the field behind them.

We will have friends to welcome us to Valhalla, Thorgrim thought. He had no doubt that his brave men had been picked by the Choosers of the Slain.

"Stand fast!" Thorgrim shouted down the line. The men were braced for the assault, their shieldwall as solid as it was going to get. Thorgrim guessed they might stand up to the attack for ten minutes perhaps, before they were all cut down.

It's still a fine place to die, he thought.

Cormac Ua Ruairc, sitting on top of his horse, looked along his line of fighting men and then across the field at those of Máel Sechnaill and he tried to fight his rising sense of panic.

He thought of Niall Cuarán's body, lying dead on the field a half a mile back. Cormac had killed Niall himself, struck him down with his sword. Niall Cuarán had argued, vehemently, against this attack, until at last it was clear to Cormac that Niall Cuarán was no more than a coward. Cowards could not be suffered to live.

Worse, Cormac found that Niall Cuarán's doubts shook his own resolve to do the bold thing, and he could not have that. Killing Niall Cuarán with a single stroke of his sword did more to bolster Cormac than anything else could have done.

He had pushed his men hard, once Fintan had brought word of the longship on the River Boyne. They had pressed north to the river and then west along its banks. They had marched through the rain and through all the long daylight hours. They had slept fitfully and uncomfortably the night before, woke to the sound of fighting far off. Mounted scouts had brought word back. Máel Sechnaill's army was out and they were fighting. It was the perfect chance for Cormac Ua Ruairc to fall on him and take him, Crown of the Three Kingdoms or no.

Now they were bringing the attack to Máel Sechnaill, not twenty miles from Tara. Cormac swallowed and tried to take a disinterested look at his enemy. Máel Sechnaill had more men, to be sure, but not so many mounted, as far as he could see, and mounted troops could swing a battle one way or another. What's more, Máel Sechnaill's army had been fighting, they were tired and hurt, and Cormac's men were fresh.

I can beat this bastard, yes I can, Cormac thought. *I'll have his bitch daughter in my bed tonight.* Brigit had always rebuffed him, out of some misbegotten loyalty to his brother Donnchad, but there would be none of that tonight.

I will have her or my men will, he thought.

There was movement in the line ahead, some group of Máel Sechnaill's army breaking off and moving to the front. A small band, thirty men or so, forming up a shieldwall a hundred perches in front of the rest.

What the devil... Cormac frowned and tried to guess what Máel was up to. He swiveled in his saddle and shouted out to the rí túaithe who were leading their parts of the battle array.

"They've sent men ahead!" he shouted and pointed with his sword. "They want to tangle us up with that small band and fall on our flanks! Ignore that small shieldwall! Go right around it and right for the main battle line!"

The rí túaithe on his right and left raised their swords in acknowledgment. The foot soldiers in front began to pick up their pace, a fast walk and then a jog. Cormac could see the men in the advanced shieldwall brace for the impact of the charging troops. Four perches away and Cormac's troops broke right and left, sweeping to either side of the small band of men, running right past them.

Cormac and the rí túaithe were right behind the running men, their horses cantering to keep up. Cormac had a glimpse of surprised faces behind shields as he raced past, leaving that small band behind as they concentrated on the chief target, Máel Sechnaill's shieldwall.

That trick didn't fool me, Máel Sechnaill, Cormac thought. If that was the best that the King of Tara could do, then he did not deserve his kingdom.

Cormac's men were yelling as they crossed the last one hundred paces and crashed into Máel Sechnaill's men. The shieldwall bowed in places, weapons waved and slashed above round shields, men screamed as they died.

Cormac rode his horse back and forth, waving his sword, shouting encouragement to his fighting men. It was going well. Not great – they had yet to break the shieldwall - but well, and if his men could sustain the attack then there was a good chance that they would win the day.

The rí túaithe on horseback were charging in where they could, reaching over the heads of men to deliver death blows to the enemy. That was good. Horses could win the day.

He heard shouting from the right, beyond the line of battle. He whirled his horse around, moved back to a place where he could see.

They were coming from the north, sweeping around the right flank. Horsemen. Thirty or forty mounted troops with long lances, swords and shining helmets. Held in reserve, waiting for the moment to ride out and make a flank attack and roll right up the line of Cormac's men.

"Oh, God!" Cormac wailed. He felt his stomach sink. Máel Sechnaill had tricked him, led him into a trap. He was a dead man, and he knew it. Him and every man he had led north into Brega.

Chapter Forty-Three

*We'll return to where
our countrymen await us,
head our sand-heaven's horse
to scout the ship's wide plains.*
Eirik the Red's Saga

Thorgrim was more than a little surprised to see the attacking army break around the Vikings' shieldwall and charge on past as if they were no more threatening than a boulder jutting out from the earth.

Bewildered, the Norsemen spun around and watched the backs of the men-at-arms and the horses' hindquarters as they raced past.

"Well, Thor take them all!" Ornolf shouted. "They think they can just ignore Ornolf the Restless!" Sword raised he started after them, but Thorgrim called him back. He had not seen Ornolf's blood so hot for battle in many years.

"Ornolf, let us leave the Irish to fight the Irish and we'll go about our own business. We've lost enough men already, and the day is no more than an hour old."

Ornolf looked at the Irish, looked at the Red Dragons, then spit on the ground. "You are right, Thorgrim Night-Wolf." He slid his sword into its scabbard and suddenly he looked very tired. "Let us go back to our ship."

Every man of Ornolf's crew was wounded in some fashion, but most were able to make their own way, and others with the help of their shipmates. Thorgerd Brak and Svein the Short lashed a tunic between two spears, fashioning a litter on which to carry Harald. Gizur Thorisson was wounded in the arm, an ugly wound, but his shipmates bound it up and he said he would be all right.

They headed off across the field, oblivious to the fighting going on at their backs. They had seen fighting enough that morning that they were not particularly curious. They turned around once at the sound of charging horses, afraid that they would be run down. But it was only mounted troops attacking the flank of the new arrivals. The Norsemen watched for a few minutes as the riders cut down their enemy, scattering them and killing them as the ran. Whoever it was who had charged across the field and attacked the army of Máel Sechnaill, it was an ill-advised thing to do, and now they were paying for their foolishness.

The Norsemen watched the butchery in silence, and then, with never a word, they turned back and continued on.

They reached the trees and the black patch where their campfire had burned itself out. They retraced the path they had taken the day before in search of Harald. They hacked their way through the woods and came to the banks of the River Boyne. The Irish fishing boat and the *Red Dragon* were still tied to the bank, lovely and unharmed.

It was with a great sense of relief that the Norsemen tumbled over the sides of the ship, a relief such as one feels coming through the door of his home after a long journey. They were still many leagues from Norway, ill-provisioned, weakly-armed with only a makeshift sail to drive their ship. But they were aboard a longship. They were afloat. And that, to any Viking, bred to ships and the sea, was a great relief. The ancient sea gods Ægir and Ran might be dangerous and unpredictable, but when it came to treachery they had nothing on men ashore.

Thorgrim's eyes ran the length of the ship, fore and aft, inspecting the vessel, a thing he did unconsciously, a habit developed after years at sea. His gaze settled on something aft, opposite the steering board, something he could not identify, standing in the place he normally stood when not at the tiller. The place where he and Morrigan had made their bed.

He made his way aft. As he came closer he could see it was a sword. He felt his pulse racing. He stepped quicker, hopped up to the afterdeck.

It was a sword. It was Iron-tooth. Stuck point-down into the deck.

"How in the world did you find your way home?" he asked the sword, kneeling in front of it, slightly afraid to lay hands on the charmed weapon. There was something hanging from the hilt. He leaned closer. A bit of linen thread, and hanging from the thread, a tiny silver cross.

Thorgrim reached out and held the little cross between his thick thumb and forefinger, rubbed its smooth surface. He wondered if it was some sorcery of Morrigan's, some Christ-magic. He glanced over his shoulder and when he saw no one was watching he made the sign of the cross the way he had seen Morrigan do it, hoping that charm would bring him luck. Any magic that could make his beloved Iron-tooth reappear had to be powerful indeed.

Thorgrim took the tiny cross off the hilt and threaded it through the thong that held his other cross and his hammer of Thor. He pulled the sword he carried from its scabbard and tossed it aside, then plucked Iron-tooth from the deck. He took a moment to enjoy the balance and weight of the weapon, the beauty of the inlay and the etched designs on the pommel and hilt, then he slid the sword into its rightful place at his side. He felt whole again, and strong.

"Come along, you men!" he called to the exhausted, half-dead men slumped in various places around the deck. "Let us break out the oars and leave this place, forsaken by the gods, behind."

They did not move with their usual vigor, but they moved, getting the oars over the side, sitting themselves on their sea chests to row. Harald took his place and insisted on rowing until Thorgrim had actually to raise his voice to the boy and order him to lie down.

They cast off from the bank, and with the Irish leather boat in tow made their way down river. They were less than half in number from their original company, which meant less than half the oars propelling the *Red Dragon*. But the current was with them now, and the riverbanks swept quickly by. The rain stopped and even the heavy mist cleared away so that the day was dry under a gray overcast. And then, greatest gift of all, a breeze sprang up from the southwest, enough of a breeze and with enough westing in it that they were able to set their pathetic sail and stow their oars away and let wind and current carry them effortlessly to the sea.

At midday they anchored in the stream and Thorgrim and half a dozen of the less wounded men used Harald's leather boat to go ashore. There a sheep herder gave them four sheep in exchange for their not killing him. They butchered the sheep on the riverbank and cooked them and ferried the meat out to the safety of the longship. They weighed anchor, set sail, and ate their fill as the river carried them east.

Night came on while they were still on the river, so they anchored again and set an anchor watch and slept. Thorgrim put his furs on the deck beside Harald and for a while he watched his son sleep. His face was peaceful. There was no fever this time, and his breathing was soft and steady. Finally, Thorgrim closed his eyes and slept, deep and peaceful, and he was not visited by wolves in his dreams.

The next morning brought clearing weather, blue skies and a fresh breeze that dried the Norsemen out completely and lifted their spirits higher than they had been since they first raised Ireland out of the sea. They weighed anchor again and set the sail and then there was little to do but haul on the braces every once in a while and watch the green riverbanks slip by and laugh at the sheep herders and cow herders who frantically drove their flocks away from the river when the longship hove into sight.

It was past noon when they finally saw the wide river mouth spread its arms in welcome to the open ocean. The small, limping, wounded band of men crowded around the bow and stared out to sea, stared longingly at the wide blue glinting ocean, the ship's wide plains that would carry them back to Norway, poor, perhaps, but alive.

Thorgrim, standing at the tiller, looked out across the ocean and felt, as the others did, a sense of relief. Of escape. The sea was their land, as surely as was Vik in Norway.

It is better to live
than lie dead.
A dead man gathers no goods...

Thorgrim thought of the ancient words of advice, wisdom handed down from Odin himself.

I saw a warm fire
at a wealthy man's house
himself dead at the door.

Not that he or Ornolf would end this voyage poor. They would be less wealthy, for all their expense and nothing to show for it, but they would still be wealthy. And alive.

The mouth of the River Boyne grew wider, the shoreline tapered away to sandy beach as river melded into sea. The *Red Dragon* stood on, leaving the shore behind, the ocean opening up on either side as the last spits of land fell astern. Thorgrim could feel the ship move on the swells, the fine, alive feeling of a ship at sea.

And that was when Egil Lamb saw the other ship. It was to the north of them and a bit more than a mile and a half off, driving south under a red and white striped sail, hauled fore and aft and tacked down tight. A longship. A line of bright color indicated where shields were set in the shield rack along her gunnel.

The gods toy with us, they do not stop, Thorgrim thought. *They give us a taste of good fortune, and then they snatch it away.*

Chapter Forty-Four

We feared
no fellow on earth;
we were fit, we fought
in the battle-fleet
Saga of Arrow-Odd

If Thorgrim Night Wolf was cursing the gods as fickle, Asbjorn the Fat was blessing them for their kindness.

Orm had put to sea the very day Asbjorn arrived back at Dubh-linn with word of the crown and Magnus's treachery. He manned his longship *Swift Eagle* with one hundred well-armed warriors. They stood out from Dubh-linn harbor and worked their way slowly north along the coast, searching for the battered *Red Dragon*.

They had seen nothing. They sailed north past the mouth of the River Boyne and with each mile under their keel, Orm become more snappish and curt and made his displeasure more clear.

Orm was afraid, and Asbjorn knew it. He was afraid of the Irish uniting against him, and that made him desperate to get his hands on the Crown of the Three Kingdoms. He was afraid of a Norwegian fleet under Olaf the White falling on Dubh-linn, and that made him desperate to get back to the longphort and see to its defense. He was afraid of treachery at every step, and that kept him from delegating any of the jobs that needed doing.

By the time they were a day north of the River Boyne, Orm's patience had run out. He ordered the *Swift Eagle* turned around, her course south for

Dubh-Linn.

"No longship. No crown. No Magnus," was all he said to Asbjorn as the ship settled on her new course.

"The crown is a valuable prize," Asbjorn offered. "Perhaps the Norwegians have taken it and sailed for home. In that case it can be no threat to you."

"Perhaps," Orm said and said no more.

Now it was Asbjorn's turn to be afraid. Orm would blame him for this. As unreasonable as that might be, Orm would blame him because he was the only one left to blame.

And so Asbjorn's spirits were lifted high when the man clinging to the mast, feet on the mastheaded yard, sang out that there was a longship putting out from the River Boyne.

"It may be Ornolf," Orm said testily, "and it may not." Orm was in no mood for optimism.

"This is true, Lord Orm," Asbjorn agreed. But longships were not so common on that coast that it was likely to be another.

Twenty minutes later, as they ran down on the distant ship, *Swift Eagle*'s bow lifting and slamming down in a welter of spray, Orm said, "I thought you said Ornolf had no sail. That ship has a sail."

"True." Asbjorn had been considering that. "But see what an ugly and misshapen thing it is. I am guessing that Ornolf has fashioned a sail from something. Perhaps the tents he plundered from Cormac."

Orm did not reply. After a while he said, as if speaking to himself, "If they are coming down the River Boyne, they are most likely coming from Tara, which means they have delivered the crown to Máel Sechnaill. So we will have vengeance, and nothing more."

Whoever was in command of the distant longship, Ornolf or Thorgrim or someone they did not know, they were not eager to cross wakes with *Swift Eagle*. No sooner had they cleared the headland south of the River Boyne than they hauled their wind and stood off, sailing as directly away from the Danes as they could. That gave Asbjorn hope.

The *Swift Eagle* fell into their wake and took up the chase, and it was quickly apparent that it would not be a long chase at all. The ship ahead, with its undersize and poorly constructed sail, was no match for Orm's ship, wonderfully built, perfectly maintained, her bottom newly cleaned. With every mile of southing they made, they came up on their quarry, hand over hand.

Soon they could make out individual men on board the ship. And not so many. Not half the complement of Orm's longship.

Like *Swift Eagle*, this other had shields mounted on the shield rack along her side. Unlike Swift Eagle, which sported an unbroken line of shields from bow to stern, starboard and larboard, this other ship had only a clutch of shields amidship. Not even enough for every man aboard, or so it appeared.

"Whoever this is, I don't think it will be much of a fight," Asbjorn said but Orm only grunted and kept his eyes forward.

It did not matter. Asbjorn was certain now that this was Ornolf's ship. He had inspected her closely enough in Dubh-linn to recognize the sweep of her sheer, the arc of her bow and sternposts, the height of her mast.

You'll pay now for your treachery, Ornolf Hrafnsson, Asbjorn thought. He was mightily relieved to know that now Orm would have someone besides himself on whom to take out his anger.

The Red Dragons grew more morose with each passing minute as the longship in their wake closed with them, slowly and inevitably. It was like a storm moving up over the horizon. You can dread it, you can prepare for it as best you can, but you cannot avoid its fury.

"Odin All-Father and Thor the Thunderer, you think you can toy with Ornolf the Restless this way?" Ornolf bellowed at the sky. "Well, I shall be in Valhalla soon, and then we shall have a reckoning!"

Thorgrim shook his head. He didn't think the old man could be so crazed, not stone sober as he was. Ornolf assumed he would be welcome in Valhalla, but Thorgrim wondered what such threats did for his chances.

"Ornolf, shut your great blustering mouth!" Snorri Half-troll shouted, voicing what the others were clearly thinking as they turned their scowling faces from the longship astern to Ornolf and back again. It was a sign of how desperate the men were that Snorri would dare say such a thing.

"What? You give orders to me, you dog?" Ornolf blustered, drawing his sword, as Snorri Half-troll drew his.

"Enough!" Thorgrim roared. "There'll be fighting a'plenty here, and soon, I'll warrant," he said, and the others seemed to see the truth of that. It was as if the entire longship took a deep breath. Ornolf and Snorri sheathed their swords.

They were sailing almost due south, paralleling the Irish coast, their long yard hauled all but fore and aft. Astern of them, the other ship was doing the same. Generally when the Vikings went into battle they would strike their yards and often lower their masts as well. But that would not happen now, because the Red Dragons were vastly outnumbered and would not offer battle if they did not have to.

Thorgrim wondered if the Danes, with their well-crafted sail and weatherly ship, would try to sail higher on the wind, come up to windward of the Red *Dragon* and blanket her sail.

No. He could see they were not. In fact, they were sailing a lower course, which would bring them down wind of the *Red Dragon*, but would also make them sail faster. Thorgrim could make out individual shields now on the starboard side. There had to be fifty at least. This fellow was not much worried about tactics, not with such an advantage.

They plowed on south for another twenty minutes before Thorgrim decided it was time to ready for the fight. He called the order, and with grim and set faces the men donned what helmets and mail they had, took up their shields and swords and spears.

Harald armed himself and took his place amidships. Thorgrim did not protest. It was only right that the boy should die a warrior's death. But Thorgrim could not muster any of the joy he had felt while fighting the Irish. Perhaps once the swords rang out against one another he would feel it, but not now. They had been so close.

Ornolf came aft to take his rightful place by the tiller. "So who do you think this whore's son is, anyhow?" he asked. "Some treacherous Dane gone a-viking?"

"No. I think it is Orm. Orm of Dubh-linn."

"Really?" Ornolf frowned. "Why do you think so?"

Thorgrim shrugged. "I don't know. Just that those Danes were damned eager to get the crown, and it makes sense to me they would not stop. I would expect them to send a longship to look for us."

"No doubt you are right, Thorgrim Night Wolf," Ornolf said. For a moment they were silent, staring at the ship that was growing perceptibly nearer. "Ah, these bastards!" Ornolf shouted in frustration. "Twice our numbers and all the weapons they could want!"

"We had to die sometime, Ornolf."

"I don't mind the dying, but I hate the thought of being cast into the sea. A man of my status needs a real funeral. Weapons, animals, carts. Slave girl at my side. All set on this longship and consigned to the flames. That is how a man such as me should be borne off to Asgard!"

"If you wish to be burned up with the *Red Dragon* we had better do it now. But I don't think the others will care for that plan."

"Hah!" Ornolf snorted. "They should be honored to burn up with Ornolf the Restless!"

Thorgrim smiled. And then he had an idea.

Chapter Forty-Five

Let us go our ways silently;
Though the cove-stallion's ride
be fallen, trouble is astir.

Gisli Sursson's Saga

It was not above twenty minutes before the longship with the red and white sail was so close that the Red Dragons could hear the slap of water under her bow, the creak of her rigging over the sound of their own. Her bow was up with the *Red Dragon*'s stern and no more than five perches down wind. The Danes along her gunnels were keeping up a steady rain of arrows, but the Red Dragons, hunkered down behind the shields in the shield rack, were in little danger from that quarter.

Thorgrim could clearly make out Orm, standing on the after deck, Asbjorn the Fat standing beside him. He wondered if Orm would call for their surrender. He doubted it. He doubted Orm would waste his breath. Orm would understand that the Norwegians would much prefer to die fighting than become the slaves of Danes.

Orm, in truth, would most likely prefer that as well.

"Stand ready!" Thorgrim shouted to the men behind the shields. "Listen for my orders!" Just forward of where he stood and down below the ship's side, Egil Lamb was coaxing a fire in soft tinder.

Ornolf, who had walked the length of the deck, flinging curses at the Danes and bolstering the men for the fight, now came aft, an extra shield in his hand. "You might want this," he said, and by way of emphasis an arrow struck with a thud and embedded itself in the curved sternpost four feet from Thorgrim's head.

"Thank you." Thorgrim held the shield with his left hand, the tiller with his right. The two ships were still moving through the water as fast as they possibly could, but the Danes were starting to edge up to windward a bit, getting in place to draw alongside, lash the ships together and pour over the *Red Dragon*'s gunnels.

"Hurry that along, Egil Lamb," Thorgrim called and Egil shot him an ugly look as he blew on the tinder.

"Unship your shields!" Thorgrim called forward and along the gunnel the men lifted the shields from the shield rack and slipped them over their arms, still holding them up to form a protective wall against the arrows and now spears that were raining down on them.

"Are these bastards going to run out of arrows or aren't they?" Ornolf wondered out loud.

Arrows, spears, swords, men, they have all they need, Thorgrim thought. He felt a solid blow to his shield. He looked over the rim. An arrow was embedded deep in the wood.

"All right, here they come!" Thorgrim shouted. The Danes' ship was all but even with the *Red Dragon* and turning up to come alongside. Fore and aft Thorgrim could see Danish warriors swinging grappling hooks on stout lines to bind the two ships together. Those men would have been easy targets for archers, but the *Red Dragon* had no archers, no bows or arrows.

The distance between the ships dropped quickly as the Dane swung in toward the *Red Dragon*. The men on board the Danish ship had shields on arms now, helmets in place and swords and spears held in their hands. *By Thor, there are a lot of them,* Thorgrim thought. *Easily a hundred, and hardened fighters by the look of them.* This had all the makings of a slaughter.

Fifteen feet between the ships, then ten. The flight of arrows stopped as all the men on the Danish ship made ready to board. Five feet and the grappling hooks flew, a dozen lines arching through the air and hooking over the *Red Dragon*'s gunnels and the Danes hauled hard on the lines, drawing the ships into their awful embrace. The Red Dragons made no move to cut the lines. They did not move at all.

Both ships were still making considerable speed through the water when they slammed together, gunnel to gunnel, with a cracking and snapping sound as the shield racks were crushed under the impact and the fabric of the ships took up the shock.

Then the morning was split by a great roar of voices, a wild shout as Danes and Norwegians both launched themselves into battle, crying their battle cries, smashing shield into shield as the Danes tried to pour over the rail and the Norwegians tried to stop them.

Thorgrim let go of the tiller - it was useless now in any event - and raced forward, drawing Iron-tooth as he ran.

One of the Danes had managed to get around the Norwegian shields and landed on deck right in Thorgrim's face. Iron-tooth sang in Thorgrim's hand, whistled through the air. The Dane raised his spear shaft to block the stroke and Iron-tooth clove the wooden shaft in two like it was a dried and rotten twig. The Dane swung his shield at Thorgrim and Thorgrim danced back, clear of the blow, and ended the fight then as Iron-tooth found his mark on the Dane's chest.

Thorgrim felt the red madness creeping around the edges of his vision and Iron-tooth seemed to move of his own will. He slashed out at the crowd of Danes who were pushing over the rail, pushing the Norwegians back, as irresistible as the tide. It was shieldwall to shieldwall but the Danes with their great numbers were onto the *Red Dragon*'s deck now, and more were coming, and they were surrounding the struggling men of Vik.

Snorri Half-troll, his great ugly face split in a grin, was hacking for all he was worth at the two men in front of him, but he did not see the man to his side, did not even know he was there until the man drove the vicious point of his spear right into Snorri's side. Snorri went down with a great shout and one last lash at his enemy and Thorgrim cut the spearman down, too late to do Snorri any good.

The Norwegians had been pushed back to the midships line and they were falling fast. Thorgrim watched helpless as Gizur Thorisson's arm, the one that they had bound the day before, was cut clean off and then Gizur was chopped down as he screamed in pain.

Thorgrim was howling and shouting as loud as any, louder. He plunged in where Ornolf was bound around by fighting men and Iron-tooth cleared a path for the jarl.

"Thorgrim! Isn't it time?" Ornolf yelled and his words brought Thorgrim back from the thoughtless fighting madness that was consuming him, back to the reality of the ship, the men, their only hope.

He backed away, Iron-tooth lashing out at the Danes who challenged him, until he was aft and away from the fight. He looked up. The makeshift sail was still straining at the sheets and buntlines, still hauled fore and aft and driving the *Red Dragon* along. Egil Lamb was dancing from foot to foot. He held a flaming torch in his hand.

"Now, Egil Lamb!" Thorgrim shouted. Egil swung around and touched the torch to the edge of the sail. It burst into flames and Egil ran forward, setting the sail on fire all along it's length. It caught fast, the dry cloth curling, charring, blazing as the fire worked its way up.

Thorgrim turned to the men on the braces. "Now, now!" he shouted and Harald on the leeward brace let the line fly and the three men on the weather brace hauled away. The blazing yard and sail swung athwart ships, turning over the fighting men's heads, swinging out over the Danish ship.

Someone among the Danes saw what was happening. Thorgrim heard a warning shouted over the brawl, but it was too late. The *Red Dragon*'s sail, fully involved, and the yard which was now burning as well, fetched up against the mast and sail of the Danish ship. There was a moment's hesitation and then the Danish rig caught fire too, the grand red and white striped sail collapsing as it burned through, the tarred ropes lighting up, orange and yellow lines against the blue sky.

"May Thor strike you dead!" Thorgrim heard someone roar and looking up he saw Orm Ulfsson looking right at him, pointing with his blood-stained sword.

"He'll take us both!" Thorgrim shouted back. The Red Dragons were backing away quicker now, letting the Danes push them to the weather side of the ship. Overhead the rigging and sails and spars of both ships were burning well and bits of flaming cloth and rope were dropping onto the deck below.

Now! Thorgrim drove his shield into the Dane standing in front of him, knocked him to the deck, leapt aside as the man flailed at his legs with his battle-ax. Thorgrim brought Iron-tooth back, swung him around in an arc and severed the halyard with a stroke.

The *Red Dragon*'s flaming yard came crashing down, falling across the longship's deck and the Dane's deck, cracking in two with the impact and scattering flaming debris in every direction. Danes fell screaming under the weight of the falling spar, but the Norwegians stood clear because they were ready for Thorgrim to do just that thing.

It was the signal. One by one Ornolf's men backed away, stepped back toward the ship's starboard quarter, fighting the Danes in their front as they did. Even now a nearly unbroken wall of flame stood where the yard had fallen across the ships.

Egil Lamb bent over and grabbed up Sigurd Sow by the arms, Sigurd bleeding fast from a sword blow that had opened up his shoulder. He pulled Sigurd out of the way and took an arrow in the side for his efforts, but he did not seem to notice. He hefted Sigurd Sow half to his feet and tumbled him over the side of the *Red Dragon*, down into the Irish leather boat that was tied alongside.

"Go, go!" Ornolf roared to the men as he himself laughed and swung his sword and took blow after blow against his battered shield.

One by one those men who were whole enough dragged their wounded brethren to the gunnel and deposited them over the side, then leapt over themselves. Happily, only a fraction of the Danes still living were still in the fight. Most had turned their attention to the flames, throwing burning material over the side, beating at flames with their swords.

Useless, Thorgrim thought. The ships were well ablaze now, their tar-coated sides engulfed. Even from where he stood, well aft, Thorgrim could feel the great heat of the fire. He had seen enough funerals to recognize when a ship was alight and would not be put out.

Someone was shouting orders to the Danes, high pitched and near hysterical. "Put the fire out! Put the fire out, you idiots! Let the Norwegians go, don't worry about them, get the fire out!"

It was Asbjorn the Fat, standing on the deck of the Danish longship and waving his arms. His eyes were wide, his panic unadulterated, screaming deprecations at the men. He was in mid-scream when Orm leapt from the *Red Dragon* back aboard his own ship and severed Asbjorn's head from his neck with a single stroke of his sword. Asbjorn's rotund body stood upright for a second more, an almost comical sight, before it fell slowly forward in the manner of a tree chopped down at the base.

Asbjorn's only concern might have been the fire, but Orm seemed not even to notice the flames. He leapt back aboard the *Red Dragon*, sword and shield in hand. He had lost his helmet somewhere in the fighting, and his hair was wild, his face smudged with soot, his eyes fixed on his enemy.

"Go on! Go on!" Ornolf shouted at the men. Thorgrim looked around. Most of the Red Dragons were in the Irish boat now, as far as he could see.

"Go, Ornolf, and I will follow!" Thorgrim shouted. Ornolf with a grunt hefted himself over the side. Thorgrim looked around the deck, saw none of his men. He looked down into the boat. He did not see Harald. He looked around again. Still no Harald.

"Where is Harald?" Thorgrim shouted down into the boat. This time he saw him, sitting on the bottom of the boat, half hidden by Sigurd Sow. Their eyes met, Harald's eyes grew wide. "Father!" he shouted.

Thorgrim spun around and raised his shield because he knew from that one word what was coming. Orm's sword crashed down on the shield, tore a great piece from the edge and Thorgrim felt the blow reverberate along his whole arm. He staggered, managed to lunge with Iron-tooth but Orm easily deflected the blow.

Thorgrim took a step back to gain fighting room. Both ships were fully involved now, with black smoke rolling up and away in the wind. Orm stood framed against the bright fire, the struggling men behind him, trying to save their ship and themselves.

Orm lunged, a tricky twist of the sword and Thorgrim just managed to knock the blade aside. Orm hit Thorgrim's shield with his own, knocking Thorgrim back, but Thorgrim managed to get his sword past Orm's shield. Iron-tooth ripped through the Orm's tunic and scraped along the mail shirt beneath.

Orm knocked the sword away. He swung his own sword up and around and down at Thorgrim with great power. Thorgrim met the sword with his shield and the shield shattered under the blow, ripped apart, so that Thorgrim was left holding no more than the boss and a few bits of wood clinging to it.

Damn Irish shields... Thorgrim thought as he lunged again, hit again, but could do Orm no injury through his mail.

"Come along, Thorgrim!" Ornolf shouted from the boat, as if Thorgrim was wasting time, amusing himself. Orm attacked in a flurry of sword and shield and there was nothing that Thorgrim could do but back away under the onslaught, back away from the place where the boat was tied to the longship's side.

This is not good... Thorgrim thought. Iron-tooth against Orm's sword, shield and mail. Maybe if Orm was not skilled at combat Thorgrim could prevail, but Orm was a good fighter, a very good fighter.

Odin All-father was like a great cat, and he, Thorgrim, a mouse to be toyed with endlessly before death.

The longship gave a lurch underfoot and Thorgrim and Orm stumbled. The planks had burned through to the waterline, the sea was rushing in. Over the shouting and cracking of flames they could hear the hiss of seawater meeting burning wood. Thorgrim could hear his fellows shouting for him.

"You've killed me, Thorgrim Night Wolf," Orm said, pointing with his sword at Thorgrim's chest. "But I will kill you. We go out together."

Thorgrim took a step back, steadying himself as the longship shifted again. He adjusted his grip on Iron-tooth.

"Together," he said. With a practiced motion he slid Iron-tooth back into the scabbard. He stood before Orm, weapon sheathed, hands spread in welcome.

Orm smiled. He took a step forward. He raised his sword high and brought it whipping down at Thorgrim's head. Thorgrim leapt aside and the sword came slashing down and met only air. Thorgrim had a fleeting look at Orm's startled face as he leapt at Orm, grabbed him around the waist, and shoved him back, back over the gunnel, over the *Red Dragon*'s side.

Thorgrim had a fraction of a second of falling, just long enough to be aware of it, his arms and Orm's arms tangled, and then they hit the water together, the cold sea wrapping around him, the salt water filling his mouth, stinging his eyes.

Orm had a death grip around Thorgrim's neck. Thorgrim kicked hard but he could not get to the surface. He felt Orm's legs kicking as well. He could see the bright surface moving away overhead.

He grabbed at Orm's arms and pulled and felt Orm holding tighter still. He kicked and jerked and tried to break Orm's hold as they sunk down, deeper and deeper. His lungs burned and he fought to not open his mouth and gasp for air.

It was getting dark. Thorgrim grabbed Orm's face and pushed, managed to get some space between himself and Orm. He brought his knee up. Orm tried to push it way and in doing so broke his hold of Thorgrim's neck. Thorgrim pushed with his knee, pushed with his arms, felt Orm's grip slipping, slipping. In the dark water he could just see Orm's white face, his mouth open in a silent shout.

He kicked Orm free and thrashed for the surface. Below him the figure of Orm Ulfsson grew dim as it sank away.

Thorgrim broke the surface and gasped and gasped, sucking air into his aching lungs, air and smoke from the burning ships, the Danes' funeral pyre. The black hull of the *Red Dragon* loomed over him, and above it, bright flames reached up for the sky.

He swiveled around. Harald's Irish leather boat was pulling for him, and a second later it stopped alongside and strong arms reached out and pulled him from the sea.

For the first time since being stripped of his weapons at Dubh-linn, probably for the first time ever, Thorgrim was profoundly glad that his enemy was wearing mail, and he was not.

Epilogue

There were twenty-seven of the Red Dragons crowded into the leather boat. That was all who had lived through the trials of the gods since they first raised the green shores of Ireland. And it was just as well, since even one more man would surely have put the boat's gunnels underwater.

They manned the oars and rowed as hard as they could away from the burning ships. They feared the leather boat might catch fire, or desperate swimmers could reach it and upset it as they tried to climb aboard. But mostly they could not stand to hear the shrieks of men dying in flames. Veterans of many battles, men inured to the cries of the wounded, they could not listen to that horrible sound.

Not that all of the Danes died in the fire. Far from. Some managed to cling to bits of wreckage and kick their way for shore. Others chose to follow Orm down into the kingdom of Ægir and Ran, leaping into the sea, no doubt clutching gold coins to pay Ran for the trip to Valhalla.

This the men of the *Red Dragon* watched as they pulled away from the burning ships. They watched as the two proud longships sank deeper and deeper into the water, until at last only their twin dragonheads and the flaming remnants of their masts showed above the surface and then in an instant they were gone too, and nothing remained of the ship in the surface world save for the oars and casks and sundry charred debris still floating.

These things would wash ashore and spend the rest of their days as part of some fisherman's lean-to, or augment the home of a sheep herder's wife.

Once the longships were gone, the men at the oars continued their easy stroke, pulling south along the coast, the boat plowing silent through the sea. No one spoke. No one seemed to have a notion of where they were bound. They just rowed.

The sun was well on its way to the western horizon before someone broke the silence. It was Svein the Short, who had been pulling an oar for hours, and he said, "So tell me, Ornolf, are we just going to row to the place where the sea pours off the edge of the earth, or do you have some other destination in mind?"

Thorgrim answered for Ornolf. "There is a settlement of Norsemen at a place called Wexford, south of Dubh-linn. We'll make for there."

"We'll not get far without food or water. A sail would be of use," Egil Lamb said.

"There is a monastery, at a place called Baldoyle. Not far from here. Tomorrow we will reach it and see if we can get what we need there."

"Baldoyle? Isn't that the one we saw sacked, coming north?" Ornolf asked.

"Yes."

"Now what is the point of sacking a monastery that was just sacked?"

"They will not be able to put up much of a fight, which is good, because neither can we," Thorgrim said. "Besides, we are not looking for riches, just food and water."

"Humph," Ornolf said and then fell silent.

They decided to remain at sea for the night, because they did not know if the Irish army that had been following them on shore was still there. Happily, the clear, moonless sky gave them a view of the stars by which they could keep on course as they continued to row south, the open boat rising and falling in the long ocean rollers.

It was in the early morning hours, with dawn still some time off, when they first began to suspect they were not alone. Thorgrim heard it first, a sound that did not come from the leather boat, but not an ocean sound either. A thumping sound, like wood on wood.

He sat more upright and turned his ear to the dark. There was a splash. "Did you hear that?" he whispered to the others.

"What?" Ornolf asked, but no one answered. Every ear was turned outboard.

"Listen," Thorgrim hissed a moment later. It sounded like voices, murmuring, too low to make out the words. There was a creaking sound.

"It is Ægir. Or his daughters, deciding our fate!" Svein said, with a less than successful attempt to hide his panic.

"Perhaps," Thorgrim said. "Or perhaps not. Let us muffle our oars."

Eager hands pulled off tunics and wrapped them around the looms of the oars so they would not creak in the tholes. Slowly the men bent to the oars and began the slow pull to the south.

Thorgrim peered into the dark but he could see nothing. The forward motion of the leather boat was imperceptible. It seemed they were going up and down, up and down, and no more than that.

And then Thorgrim could see, or thought he could see, a dark shape just ahead, a darker place in the night.

"Hold your oars," he whispered and the men stopped pulling and waited. Thorgrim could feel the tension in the boat.

He stared forward. "Egil, you are sharp-eyed. What do you see ahead?"

Egil Lamb turned and looked forward. After a moment he said, "It's a ship."

It was a ship. Thorgrim was certain. The more he looked, the more the long, low shape resolved out of the night. A ship lying a-hull, not moving.

"We must go the other way," Thorgrim whispered, "because we have to assume this is no friend. Starboard, pull, larboard, backwater."

The leather boat spun around on her keel and began to slowly, silently, crawl in the other direction. Soon the dark shape was lost to Thorgrim's eyes.

"Thorgrim!" Egil whispered. "There is another!"

Ahead, another dark shape, much like the first, as if that ship had by magic shifted its place to remain in front of the leather boat.

Thorgrim turned the leather boat east and the men pulled away from the shore, but it was not long before they found another dark ship under their bow. They turned south again, hoping to skirt astern of the first, but again the ship was there.

"This smells of Loki's trickery," Thorgerd Brak whispered. The panic was settling in.

"Unship oars," Thorgrim ordered. There was no point in rowing all over the ocean when it seemed there was always a longship in front of them. Better to wait for dawn and see what was up. "Get some sleep," Thorgrim ordered, and to lead the way he settled himself down as best he could, closed his eyes, and remained in that position, wide awake, for the next two hours.

It seemed he had finally managed to doze when someone shook him from his slumber. He opened his eyes and sat up. The sky to the east was growing light, just a hint of gray. He rubbed his eyes. The day would come quick.

"Is everyone awake?" he asked and he heard murmured replies fore and aft.

"See to your weapons," he said. He had no idea what the light would reveal, whether something of this world or another.

And then not twenty feet ahead of the boat they heard a voice call out, calling for men to wake up. Thorgrim jumped in surprise and he heard others gasp and curse. From across the water came the sound of men rustling out of beds, groans and words flying around. And then the dawn light revealed the ship, as if it was materializing out of the ocean mists. A longship, a dragon ship, a hundred and fifty feet long. Its wicked serpent head at the bow towered high over the sea, its yard, almost as long as the *Red Dragon*'s hull, was swung fore and aft with sail stowed.

"By the gods..." Sigurd Sow whispered.

"Look there!" Egil Lamb said. The men looked astern. They looked to larboard and starboard. The ocean was filled with ships, longships in every direction. They had rowed themselves right into the middle of a fleet.

It was then that someone aboard the dragon ship noticed the overloaded boat two perches away.

"You there!" the man shouted. "Get over here!"

The men looked aft to Thorgrim. Thorgrim looked at Ornolf. Ornolf shrugged. "Don't see as we have much choice," he said.

The men shipped their oars and with just a few strokes came up alongside the massive vessel. A big man with a fur cloak and a shining helmet leaned on the rail and looked down at them. "Who are you?" the man demanded.

Ornolf answered with a tone every bit as haughty. "I am Ornolf Hrafnsson, jarl of East Agder in Vik!" he shouted. "And who are you to presume to order me about?"

It was absurd, Ornolf in his little boat acting so grand to the man on the rail of a dragon ship, but before the man could reply, another voice came ringing down the deck.

"Ornolf? Ornolf the Restless, you great buggerer!" An older man appeared over the rail, long white hair bound in a queue, his beard white as well.

"Olaf?" Ornolf shouted. "Olaf the White? Is that you, you great whore's son?" Ornolf laughed out loud and Olaf the White did as well.

"What are you doing here, Olaf, with your great fleet?" Ornolf asked.

"Why, we have heard in Norway that those whore's sons Danes have taken Dubh-linn, and we have come to take it back."

"That's well done, Olaf," Ornolf agreed.

"Will you and your men join us, or are you having such fun rowing about that you don't wish to stop?"

"What say you, men?" Ornolf asked. "Shall we go to Dubh-linn again? I reckon the welcome will be a better one this time. Do you agree?"

They did agree. And after a short fight against the surprised, leaderless, and greatly outnumbered Danes, Ornolf and his men found the longphort decidedly more hospitable than they had the first time around.

The funereal feast for Máel Sechnaill mac Ruanaid took place three days after the battle in which the fallen hero's army defeated that of Cormac Ua Ruairc.

Brigit, as princess, took her place at the head table, next to Flann mac Conaing, who had somehow, and by mutual consent of the rí túaithe, assumed the protectorate of the kingdom, Máel Sechnaill having no male heirs.

One of the rí túaithe was standing, silver chalice raised. "Our noble king of Tara, who defeated the dubh-gall host and the traitorous army of Cormac Ua Ruairc one after another on the same field on the same morning! A feat never seen before, never to be equaled!"

The others cheered. Flann beamed, but solemnly, as the occasion required, and raised his cup. Brigit rolled her eyes. She was not sure if the man was referring to her father or Flann mac Conaing, and she guessed the ambiguity was purposeful. Already the rí túaithe were playing up to Flann the way they had to her father.

Damned sycophants, she thought. Her food sat untouched before her. Her appetite was gone, had been since she witnessed Flann's disposal of Cormac ua Ruairc. Máel Sechnaill's death on the battlefield had not spared Cormac a disemboweling, the last of the Ua Ruairc line going out just as the penultimate had. Brigit had to admit she felt considerably less sympathy for her former brother-in-law, who had tried hard to cuckold his brother, than she had for her former husband, Donnchad.

Cormac had also shown considerably less bravery in the end than had Donnchad. Unlike Donnchad, who had gone grim-faced and silent to his death, Cormac had wailed and cried and pleaded for life, a pathetic sight that had accomplished nothing beyond wasting his final chance to be remembered as a man of courage.

The rest of Cormac's army had been butchered, mostly, and those who were not were now the chattel slaves of Flann and the other rí túaithe, and soon they would wish they had met a quick end on the battlefield.

Flann was talking now, but Brigit did not listen. She glanced over at Morrigan, sitting at the far end of the table. There was something very odd about it all. Máel Sechnaill had come unscathed through so many battles, only to be cut down in what was really a minor fight. No one had seen him fall, they just found him dead, run though the throat.

Brigit thought back on the words Morrigan had made her learn. No words in any language she knew, she wondered if perhaps they were some magic incantation, a spell to bring about her father's death. Certainly Flann and Morrigan had gained the most from the king's passing.

What do you know of this, Morrigan? She wondered. She jerked her glance away before Morrigan caught her eye. Brigit had to be careful, and she knew it. Flann had declared himself protector until the succession was worked out, but protectors had a way of turning themselves into kings. Any real threat to his power would come from her, or her children, and Flann and Morrigan would be watching.

Brigit looked out over the rí túaithe seated at the long tables, moved her eyes from man to man as they ate and drank like swine at the troth. They were mostly drunk already. She sighed.

She would have to marry one of them. She would have to do it soon. Conlaed uí Chennselaigh was blond-haired and blue-eyed and he was not the worst of them, so he would probably do.

Brigit was still fresh from the horror of her kidnapping and the sight of her brother-in-law dying his horrible death, and that was excuse enough for the nausea and puking every morning. Her chambermaids seemed to believe her ordeal was the cause of her sickness, but they would not for long, and then the rumors would start.

Brigit needed a husband. The heir to the throne of Tara needed a legitimate father, one who would look like a legitimate father, with the same blond hair and blue eyes as the baby. Particularly now that Flann was sure to try and keep the throne for himself.

No one, no one but Brigit nic Máel Sechnaill, would ever know that it was fin-gall blood that ran through that heir's Irish veins.

Morrigan thought she saw Brigit looking at her, but the princess turned away before their eyes met.

What are you thinking, my dear? Morrigan wondered. No doubt she was trying to figure out how Flann had so quickly consolidated power.

Certainly it would seem quick to her. She did not witness the years during which Flann mac Conaing had won the trust and love of the rí túaithe, the fear and mistrust of Máel he had planted in their hearts and made to grow to fruition with his tender ministrations. A few of the precious jewels plucked from the crown, some gold shaved from its base had won over the rest. Brigit herself had carried Morrigan's word to Flann that the moment had come for them to act. *Let Tara fall and Flann rise in his place.* The daughter had given word to Flann that he should strike her father down.

Máel Sechnaill mac Ruanaid was an evil man. That was all there was to say about him. Rather than make war on the pagan Norseman he would fight his fellow Irish, sack monasteries, Christian churches, just because they were in the kingdom of another king, whom Máel Sechnaill mac Ruanaid deemed enemy.

No more. Brega was ruled by a just man now.

Morrigan thought about Brigit. Flann's men, Patrick and Donnel, were carrying on with Brigit's chambermaids, and through them Morrigan heard all about the princess's morning sickness. The foolish girls attributed it to the suffering Brigit had endured, but Morrigan knew better. She looked out over the rí túaithe, wondering which of them was the father.

Then another thought struck her. *Harald?* It did not seem possible. Then again, Harald was a strong and handsome young man. He had stolen her away. Even if she had not given herself willingly he might have taken her by force.

Could it be? Morrigan looked over at Brigit with renewed interest.

In the end, of course, it did not matter. In nine months there could be an heir to the throne of Tara, if Brigit gave birth to a boy. Nine months for Flann to establish himself in his protectorate, so that his rule would go on while the heir was still a child.

And then, when Flann's rule over Brega was established, firmly established, then out would come the Crown of the Three Kingdoms. Then, Flann mac Conaing, king of Brega, would be king of Leinster, and of Mide as well.

Then Flann would be too powerful even for the grandson of Máel Sechnaill mac Ruanaid to challenge him, and things in Ireland would be different. Then they would make war on the right people.

Flann mac Conaing would not be stopped, not if Morrigan had any say in the matter. And she did.

Historical Note

That part of the Irish coast where the city of Dublin now sits has seen human occupation for thousands of years. Prehistoric communities kept dogs, sheep and pigs, built great middens and crafted pottery and jewelry. But there was never anything that might be called a town until the Vikings came.

The first Norse settlement appeared in the summer of 837, when a fleet of sixty-five ships, manned by Norwegian warriors by way of Scotland and Orkney arrived at the mouth of the Liffey. They found there two small settlements, which possibly contained churches and monasteries, Ireland being by then solidly Christian. One settlement was called Ath Cliath. The other, named after the pond formed where the Poodle River met the Liffey, was called Black Pool, or, in Gaelic, Dubh-Linn.

The sixty-year history of the original Norse longphort, or ship fort, was as violent and contentious as any in Viking or Irish history.

Soon after the Norwegians settled Dubh-linn, they were driven out by a force of Danish Vikings, who recognized the importance of the longphort. Then, in 852 another Norwegian fleet under Olaf the White arrived to reclaim the town for Norway. That original settlement remained in Norwegian hands. Interestingly, of all the victims of Viking depredations, the Irish are the only ones who differentiated between Norwegians, whom they called fin gall, or "white strangers" and the Danes, whom they called dubh gall, or "black strangers."

Considerable archeological evidence of Viking settlement has been unearthed in the center of modern Dublin, but all of it dates to the beginning of the tenth century, leading historians to surmise that there were in fact two different Viking settlements in the area. The original longphort appears to have been located farther up the Liffey from where the heart of Dublin is now located. In 902, the Norsemen in that settlement were driven out of Dublin by an Irish army, only to return seventeen years later. This second settlement, which lasted around two hundred years, is apparently the one upon which modern Dublin is built.

The Vikings came first to the coast of Ireland to raid, and they were devastating in that endeavor. But one aspect of Viking culture that would differentiate them from later sea raiders is that after raiding, the Norse came to stay.

There were a number of factors that led to the Vikings' territorial aspirations, including a dearth of farmland in Scandinavia and political upheavals there. Whatever the reason, the Irish (as well as the English, who were also suffering Viking incursion) were horrified at the thought of the Norse moving in. As the Native Americans would do with the European colonists 800 years later, the Irish endured the first Norsemen on their shores, and only when it was too late did they realize those settlements were just the beginning.

Along with insinuating themselves into the Irish landscape, the Vikings inserted themselves into the volatile Irish political scene. Many modern Irishmen claim to be descendants of kings, and that claim is not too unlikely when one considers how many kings Ireland enjoyed. With a complicated structure of over-kings and subordinate kings, the country had generally around 150 kings at any given time between the fifth and twelfth centuries.

Of these, most were no more than minor lords, while others ruled larger kingdoms such as the historic kingdom of Brega and Leinster. But during the period of Viking invasion, there was no one single ruler of Ireland, and no unified government capable of organizing a real resistance to the Norse incursion. With Irish kings constantly at war with one another, the Vikings represented powerful military allies. One Irish king after another, deciding that the Vikings were not so abhorrent as whomever of their countrymen they were fighting, made treaties of mutual aide with the Norsemen.

As the Vikings joined in the fighting in Ireland, expanded their settlements and increased their population, they became more and more entrenched. Vikings married Irish women and set up legitimate trade with the Irish, importing many of their skills from Scandinavia. It would be more than two hundred years after the founding of Dubh-Linn before the Irish king Brian Bóru united the country sufficiently to drive the Vikings out for good. But by that time the Norse influence, from crafts to language to blood, was so well established that it would never be eradicated from the Island, and, indeed, still exists today.

Most of the place names that appear in this book will be familiar to anyone who is acquainted with modern-day Ireland, as the names have not changed. One name which might not be familier is Brega. In medieval Ireland, the territory of Brega (which means "the heights") constituted the modern county Meath along with some portions of Louth and north Dublin.

The Crown of the Three Kingdoms is fictitious. But if such a thing had existed, there certainly would have been as much intrigue and violence surrounding it as is portrayed in the book. It is how things were done in medieval Ireland.

Glossary

Asgard - the dwelling place of the Norse gods and goddesses, essentially the Norse heaven.

berserkir - a Viking warrior able to work himself up into a frenzy of blood-lust before a battle. The berserkirs, near psychopathic killers in battle, were the fiercest of the Viking soldiers. The word berserkir comes from the Norse for "bear shirt" and is the origin of the modern English "berserk".

Bifrost bridge - In Norse mythology, the bridge that spanned the skies to the entrance of Asgard.

boss - the round, iron centerpiece of a wooden shield. The boss formed an iron cup protruding from the front of the shield, providing a hollow in the back across which ran the handgrip.

brace - line used for hauling a yard side to side on a horizontal plane. Used to adjust the angle of the sail to the wind.

bride-price - money paid by the family of the groom to the family of the bride.

byrdingr - A smaller ocean-going cargo vessel used by the Norsemen for trade and transportation. Generally about 40 feet in length, the byrdingr was a smaller version of the better-known knarr.

curragh - a boat, unique to Ireland, made of a wood frame covered in hide. They ranged in size, the largest propelled by sail and capable of carrying several tons. The most common sea-going craft of medieval Ireland.

Danegeld - money paid by English royalty to Viking raiders in exchange for the Vikings' leaving an area unmolested. Danegeld means literally "Danish money" and comes from the English habit of calling all Vikings "Danes" regardless of where they came from.

dragon ship - the largest of the Viking warships, upwards of 160 feet long and able to carry as many as 300 men. Dragon ships were the flagships of the fleet, the ships of kings.

278

dubh gall - Gaelic term for Vikings of Danish descent. It means Black Strangers, a reference to the mail armor they wore, made dark by the oil used to preserve it. See fin gall.

earldorman - one of the highest ranks of nobleman in pre-Conquest England.

fin gall - Gaelic term for Vikings of Norwegian descent. It means White Strangers. See dubh gall.

Freya - Norse goddess of beauty and love, she was also associated with warriors, as many of the Norse gods were. Freya often led the Valkyrie to the battlefield.

fyrd - In pre-Conquest England, the military host of the whole country, the army of one of the four kingdoms that made up England.

halyard - a line by which a sail or a yard is raised.

Hel - the underworld in Norse mythology, the Norse hell.

hird - an elite corps of Viking warriors hired and maintained by a king or powerful jarl. Unlike most Viking warrior groups, which would assemble and disperse at will, the hird was retained as a semi-permanent force which formed the core of a Viking army.

hirdsman - a warrior who is a member of the hird.

housecarl - member of the elite bodyguard of a Danish or English king or nobleman, not unlike the Norse hird. The term dates from the latter part of the Old English period.

jarl - title given to a man of high rank. A jarl might be an independent ruler or subordinate to a king. Jarl is the origin of the English word earl.

knarr - a Norse merchant vessel. Smaller, wider and more sturdy than the longship, knarrs were the workhorse of Norse trade, carrying cargo and settlers wherever the Norsemen traveled.

levies - conscripted soldiers of 9th century warfare.

Loki - Norse god of fire and free spirits. Loki was mischievous and his tricks caused great trouble for the gods, for which he was punished.

longphort - literally, a ship fortress. A small, fortified port to protect shipping and serve as a center of commerce and a launching off point for raiding.

Northumbria - the northernmost of the four kingdoms that comprised England in the mid-ninth century. To the south and east of Northumbria was East Anglia, to the west, Mercia, and south of the Thames River was the kingdom of Wessex.

Odin - foremost of the Norse gods. Odin was the god of wisdom and war, protector of both chieftains and poets.

perch - a unit of measure equal to 16½ feet. The same as a rod.

port reeve - see reeve

Ragnarok - the mythical final battle when most humans and gods would be killed by the forces of evil and the earth destroyed, only to rise again, purified.

ringfort - common Irish homestead, consisting of houses protected by circular earthwork and palisade walls.

reeve - tax collector and general manager of a district, answerable to the nobleman, bishop or king in overall authority. The port reeve was responsible for duties on merchant ships arriving in port. The shire reeve of the tenth-century became the modern English sheriff.

shieldwall - a defensive wall formed by soldiers standing in line with shields overlapping.

skald - a Viking-era poet, generally one attached to a royal court. The skalds wrote a very stylized type of verse particular to the medieval Scandinavians. Poetry was an important part of Viking culture and the ability to write it a highly regarded skill.

sling - the center portion of the yard.

swine array - a viking battle formation consisting of a wedge-shaped arrangement of men used to attack a shield wall or other defensive position.

thing - a communal assembly

Thor - Norse god of storms and wind, but also the protector of humans and the other gods. Thor's chosen weapon was a hammer. Hammer amulets were popular with Norsemen in the same way that crosses are popular with Christians.

thrall - Norse term for a slave. Origin of the English word "enthrall".

thwart - a rower's seat in a boat. From the old Norse term meaning "across".

Valhalla - a great hall in Asgard where slain warriors would go to feast, drink and fight until the coming of Ragnarok.

Valkyries - female spirits of Norse mythology who gathered the spirits of the dead from the battlefield and escorted them to Valhalla. They were the Choosers of the Slain, and though later romantically portrayed as Odin's warrior handmaidens, they were originally viewed more demonically, as spirits who devoured the corpses of the dead.

Vik - An area of Norway south of modern-day Oslo. The name is possibly the origin of the term Viking.

wattle and daub - common medieval technique for building walls. Small sticks were woven through larger uprights to form the wattle, and the structure was plastered with mud or plaster, the daub.

wicing - old Anglo-Saxon term for a sea raider, later used exclusively to refer to Scandinavian raiders. Another possible origin for the word Viking.

yard - a long, tapered timber from which a sail was suspended. When a Viking ship was not under sail, the yard was turned lengthwise and lowered to near the deck with the sail lashed to it.

Made in the USA
San Bernardino, CA
08 July 2014